A CAGE OF CRIMSON

A

CAGE

OF

CRIMSON

USA TODAY BESTSELLING AUTHOR

K.F. BREENE

ALSO BY K.F. BREENE

Demigods of San Francisco

Sin & Chocolate

Sin & Magic

Sin & Salvation

Sin & Spirit

Sin & Lightning

Sin & Surrender

Leveling Up

Magical Midlife Madness

Magical Midlife Dating

Magical Midlife Invasion

Magical Midlife Love

Magical Midlife Meeting

Magical Midlife Challenge

Magical Midlife Alliance

Magical Midlife Flowers

Magical Midlife Battle

Magical Midlife Awakening

Finding Paradise

Fate of Perfection

Fate of Devotion

Deliciously Dark Fairytales

A Ruin of Roses

A Throne of Ruin

A Kingdom of Ruin

A Queen of Ruin

A Cage of Crimson

A Cage of Kingdoms

Demon Days,
Vampire Nights

Born in Fire

Raised in Fire

Fused in Fire

Natural Witch

Natural Mage

Natural Dual-Mage

Warrior Fae Trapped

Warrior Fae Princess

Revealed in Fire

Mentored in Fire

Battle with Fire

Don't tell my family that this series exists.
They might be concerned with how dirty I like my
fairytales...

IMPORTANT TRIGGER NOTICE

This book contains dark themes and situations, with mentions of a troubling past. Please take note of items that may be triggering, such as:

Abduction
Bullying
Death
Death by fire
Drug production/use
Emotional abuse
Graphic on-screen sex
Graphic violence
Guard/Prisoner hate fucking
Homelessness

Hallucinations
Kidnapping
Knotting
Mental abuse
Possessive MMC
Poisoning
Profanity
Public nudity
Sexual harassment
Starvation
Torture

As well as kinks like dirty talk, exhibitionism, voyeurism, dominance games, praise and primal play.

Please enter with caution. Your mental health is important.

Of all the women in the world....

why her?

AURELIA

"*Once upon a time, in a land far away...*"

Fairy tales. What bullshit.

I'd heard it all in my youth. Handsome princes and thrones made of gold. Dresses and balls and animals that talked.

Sure, why not.

And yeah, maybe I'd believed it as a kid. I'd sit with my mom, reading until the small hours of the morning even though I should've been in bed hours before, lulled by her soft tone, held tightly in her arms. I'd dream of one day flying like the dragons. Of leading a hunt with the wolves. She'd said I could be anything, live anywhere. It wouldn't matter where I started because my prince would find me. He'd save me. He and I would eventually lead the kingdom wearing gemmed crowns and creating a safe space for everyone to co-exist, even those who couldn't quite feel the magic they were supposed to be blessed with.

Turned out, there were no princes for the magically

inept. No friends, either. Most of the time, especially in my youth, there was not even kindness. We were the outcasts. The unwanted. If I wanted to be saved, I'd have to do it myself. There was a freedom in that which I valued, an empowerment to claim my future. Though I will admit . . . it would've been nice for a prince to sweep me off my feet.

I inhaled the slightly stale air of the work shed where I spent the majority of my time. Two windows let in the light and a few desks acted as work stations, positioned around the single room space. My fingers moved quickly from years of experience, twisting a particular vine around the Nimfire leaf. After this batch was done, I'd take to my rigged-up contraptions to add pressure and heat, turning the contents into a powerful hallucinogen.

A drug, in other words. The fun kind. The kind that was against the law and would get us all brought in by the royal guards and put to death if anyone should find out we created it.

My life was anything but a fairy tale.

I yanked the vine into a knot. A thorn sliced my calloused finger and little spots of crimson welled up along the cut. The sting of it barely registered.

Another knot, and I dropped that piece into a basin of warm water before picking up another vine.

"You about done?" Razorfang asked. His name was one he'd chosen for himself after taking too much of the particular product I was making. A scratch ran down his cheek and frown lines etched into his ruddy face. The grizzled older man had a slight hunch from many years of tending the village gardens, a necessary element to our operations.

He stopped a few paces away from my workstation, a rickety little desk tucked into a corner with a slight lean to the right. He never dared get too close, which was fine by me. He didn't bathe as much as he really needed to.

I leaned back a little and reached for my tea perched on the edge of my desk. "Yeah. A dozen more or so. Why? Is it date-night with your mate?"

He swayed toward me a little, his eyes a little too wide, a touch manic.

"What's that supposed to mean?" he demanded, his tone accusatory. "You plottin' on me, girl? Tryin' to get me out of here so that you can rig up a trap on my desk?" He stuck out a hammy finger, stained purple. "I know what you're up to. No dud is going to catch me unawares. I've got eyes in the back of my head." He half-turned to point. "I know all your tricks. Don't think for one"—he squeezed his eyes shut with the force of the next word— "*moment* you can catch me with my hands tied!"

I let loose an annoyed breath, re-focusing on my task. Clearly, he'd sampled the product again. He was unreasonable when he was like this, paranoid I'd try to harm or kill him. It wasn't him who needed eyes in the back of his head, though; it was me. I'd gotten very good at sensing when he was sneaking up on me with a knife or some other sharp object, trying to do the village a "favor" by getting rid of the dud, a slur for a shifter without magic.

"I'm not the one you should be worried about," I

warned. "Granny is in town. You can't be sampling the product when she's here. You know that."

"Let me worry about her. I know what I'm about. You just mind your manners, filthy dud."

I shook my head as he stared down at me. After a few moments of getting no response, he finally shuffled away.

As a rule, I didn't create chemically addictive products. My life afforded me very few moral principles, so I stood by those I had carved out. The product could be habit-forming, though, if a person wasn't careful. Raz wasn't careful, not in the slightest. He hated his job, he hated his dependency on Granny, our benefactor, and most of all, he hated working with what he correctly suspected was a violent dud.

I didn't know why he was so concerned. Without access to my animal, I didn't have a shifter's enhanced strength and speed. I couldn't heal quickly. He had the advantage over me in every way. I'd gotten quick with a lot of practice, but that's about all I had going for me. Well, practice, and honing my sixth sense regarding danger so I could anticipate when he would strike. The guy was delusional in all ways but one: the village definitely wanted the filthy dud gone. They'd all, at one time or another, made that quite clear.

Thank the gods for Granny's protection. She wasn't blood—everyone called her that—but she *was* my fairy godmother. She'd taken me in as a kid when I was on the brink of starvation, chased by dud-hating hordes, having no coin and nowhere to go. She gave me a home, found me this job, created connections with sketchy shadow markets and forced this village to (mostly) leave me be. She was my guardian angel. My divine intervention. I owed her everything.

I dropped the vine-wrapped leaf into the water before stopping for a quick sip of my lukewarm tea. Cup returned, I proceeded to wrap the next vine. Then the next. My mind drifted, conjuring up images that I might try to draw in charcoal. Before I knew it, I stared down at an empty desk with two more slices in my thumb.

I pulled a little jar from the top of my station, by the wall. The few petals within started its slow, mournful throb, glowing a pale, pastel pink. Or maybe 'mournful' was just my reaction to having picked the whole flower, thus condemning it to death. I should've taken a few petals and memorized the location so I could go back and pick more another time. The flowers were supposed to bloom all through spring and summer.

After unscrewing the jar, I delicately removed one of the petals and paused, holding it in my palm and watching the pretty glow intensify.

"That the Moonfire Lily?" Raz once again approached. He forgot to maintain his distance this time, his head cocked as he stared at the flower.

"Yeah. Pretty, isn't it?"

He grunted, not tearing his eyes away.

I placed the flower onto a sturdy dish and headed to the hearth with its dainty flame.

"What are you going to—" Raz cut off with a violent scream.

I jolted, nearly dropping the dish.

"What?!" I looked around in confusion, seeing the

simple and well-organized interior of our work shed, save the chaos of his desk. "What's the matter?"

"No! No, no, no, no!" He rushed toward me. I barely moved the dish in time to avoid his strike, cupping my hand over the petal so that it didn't flutter to the ground. "You'll kill the glow! You can't kill the glow, it'll destroy the world!"

He screamed again and spun in a circle, his face contorted in anguish and his pupils blown wide. Terror lined every inch of his body as he contemplated the fate of the flower.

"Great heavens, bub, you took too much." I set the dish down on the nearest table. What a pain. When he got like this, he slowed everything down.

I held up my hands to show him they were now empty. By rule—another of my few principles—I didn't make the product too extreme. To get to this level, he'd had to take two or more doses. He was starting to get out of hand.

"Okay, buddy." I eased toward him slowly. If he wasn't talked down, I'd have to lock him up. Otherwise, he'd probably turn violent and I wasn't in the mood. "I apologize. I don't want to kill the glow. I realize now that it would indeed end the world, yes. I've put it down, see?"

He leaned to the right, his head tilted, his eyes definitely manic.

"Let's just take a breath and think about the emberflies . . ."

He leaned the other way, almost looking at me sideways. Great gods, the product had really gotten on top of him. His journey on this product had taken a sharp left turn and landed him into a field of nightmares. I might not be able to bring him out.

"Let's drift like the emberflies—"

He balled up his fists and shook them at the heavens, leaning back as he did so. "Who cares about the fucking emberflies! You're trying to kill the glow!" he shouted, spittle flying. He tilted forward, stumbled, and barreled my way. One big fist swung out as he fell.

I dodged easily. His momentum carried him forward, his legs left behind. He hit the back wall head-first and then fell to the ground. A moment later he scrambled up, howling like some enraged beast.

No, I would not be able to talk him around. Damn it.

"Good point," I agreed in a soothing tone, moving fast toward the entrance. "The glow is the most important thing. Let's focus on that glow. It's outside. There's more of the glow outside. Let's go look at it, okay? I won't touch it. We'll just—"

"I know your dirty tricks, you pig-faced monkey man!" He levelled a finger at me. His red face was screwed up in rage. "Your bag is out there, isn't it? *Isn't it*? You have your weapons stored just outside."

My "weapons" consisted of everyday items, some so dangerous as a nail file. If he got in this state when the pack was inside, he'd empty it on the floor and hold up each item in turn, asking how I planned to kill him with it.

I'd just started leaving the thing outside, because yes, I could probably lodge a nail file in his eye or maybe even reach his kidney, but would I? No. I was only violent if I had no other options—principle number three.

"I don't have a pack." I kept my hands high. "See? No pack. I just want to say hi to the moon man. Want to say hi to the moon man with me?"

"I don't trust you for one second. You're trying to kill me like all the others. Oh yes, by the gods' hammer stone, they've tried. They'll never take me alive!"

Fantastic, I thought sarcastically. He'd turned nonsensical. This was when he got the most violent.

Plan B.

"Here's the glow, here it is," I said, moving toward the supply closet at the back. "It's right here."

He paused in his tirade, his head tilted to the side again, a little drool dribbling out of his mouth.

"Here, here's the glow." I motioned him over. "Right here." I lifted the lid on a wicker basket where the rest of the petals had been stored. Their glow was in its zenith, pale in the room but enough to grab his attention.

"Yes," he whispered, seeing them and homing in. Louder now. *"Yes!"*

I acted quickly as he neared. I hooked my foot on his right ankle and grabbed his meaty shoulders. He tripped and I guided his fall toward the supply closet where I kept my contraptions, the transformed apothecary mechanisms. Those on the lower shelves could be fixed by other villagers if he broke them. They'd had practice.

The shove I gave him sent him flailing through the opening. He crashed into a shelf, screaming again. I grabbed the door handle and pulled it shut before he could get his bearings and turn. I latched the door from my side, knowing there was a door at the back of the closet that led outside. It wasn't locked. All he'd have to do was find it and free himself.

I doubted he'd figure out how for a few hours. He hadn't in the past.

This was another of my principles: a way out. All products that induced a journey, whether it was good or bad in the moment, had an "off" switch. If a person hunkered down into a small, dark place, the drug's effects on the brain would greatly recede. The drug would go dormant, in a way. The product didn't leave the system, but it gave the brain a way to handle things a little better.

This was great for a person in Raz's situation. Not so great if a person was having a lovely time and was just trying to get cozy. Couldn't be helped.

Discovering that trick had been an accident, but once I realized its usefulness—to me first, and then to others—I baked the "off" switch into any product that might need it. Like this one.

He howled again, beating at the wood.

"Go to sleep," I called through the door. "Settle down now and go to sleep. You can't let Granny see you like this or she'll punish you something awful."

"You filthy dud!" he roared. "You dud-whore, locking me in here. You won't take me alive!"

Sometimes the product made him all kinds of awful. Then again, some people were like this to me stone sober. It was something the magicless just had to get used to, like how the fair of skin dealt with sunburns. It was part of life. There was no sense in letting it get to you.

I took a deep breath, letting the adrenaline from the

sudden episode level out before turning back to the Moonfire Lily. After grabbing a large stick from the hearth and ensuring the end had a flame, I took the dish outside and set it on the ground. The moon glowed weakly above, barely a sliver. Stars speckled the vast night sky. When I got home, I might open a bottle of port and sit out for a while, taking it all in. I loved these tranquil early spring nights; the air was still crisp with winter's chill but held the promise of warmer days to come. Flowers bloomed for the first time since the fall, and it felt like the world was getting a fresh start.

Emberflies hovered and drifted, little glowing insects that looked like fairy dust softly swaying in the air. They weren't spooked by anyone in our village. They only scattered when strangers or danger came around, which was often one and the same.

It would've been better to treat the petal at the full moon, but Granny wouldn't want to wait. She didn't have a lot of patience where the product was concerned. There was an increasing demand, and it was my duty to keep up.

A slight breeze rustled the petal. I held it down for a moment until all was calm again. As I hunched over the dish, I applied the flame.

The petal crackled. Its glow intensified, shimmering like the stars. The color changed from pale pink to vibrant magenta and then to blazing red. The fire on the end of the stick grew, a cue to pull it away. The petal continued to burn for a moment, the middle of it pulsing like an ember in a smoldering fire. Its perfume had changed, now verdant and earthy and wild; all things that teased the senses of a wolf on the hunt, or so

I'd overheard. After a moment the flame and smell died away, leaving the color and continuing the ember-like soft glow.

I picked it up; the petal felt cool against my skin. The fire never seemed to heat it, just change it.

A strange tickle started between my shoulder blades. A slight pressure fanned out, over my shoulders and then crawling down my spine. It felt like someone was watching me.

Wary, I glanced back at the work shed, wondering if Raz had found his way out and was coming for me. No thrashing of limbs, howls, or stomping— all things he'd be doing if he'd escaped—accompanied the feeling, though. Couldn't be him.

With the Moonfire Lily petal tucked into my cupped palms, I looked out at the darkness.

Trees stood sentry beyond the field next to the shed, hiding the creek that gurgled within their depths. An old fence with awkwardly leaning posts and a gate in the middle divided the land for no discernible reason. My various tubs were placed in an organized fashion, some against the shed and others out in the night, against the fence. They were set to catch the moonlight or the sunlight, or both. I'd learned those things had an effect on the end product.

I'd learned young to pay attention to my sixth sense, keeping it fresh in my life here. The feeling of being watched grew, as though a predator were focusing hard.

The night lay quiet. Nothing made a sound. The soft breeze hardly worried my hair.

Still, it felt like someone was out there, a foreign density within the shadows. The emberflies didn't seem troubled, though. They would scatter if a threat was within their midst; I'd seen it happen when Granny brought in a new person for the perimeter patrol.

I tipped my face down. My eyes were no good to me. I couldn't see in the darkness like those with magic could. Continuing to stare would just alert the possible watcher that I'd sensed their presence. They might then get bold and come closer. There were a few people in this village that would, even with Granny in town, and those were the last people I'd want to do so.

I turned for the work shed. As I crossed the threshold, I heard muttering coming from the supply closet. Clearly Raz was still in there, now calming down. Hopefully he hadn't broken much.

I set about picking the burnt flower petal apart. That done, I crushed it with a pestle and mortar. Here again the fragrant aromas drifted up, so pleasant. I wanted this smell for my cottage. Maybe to transform it into a perfume. A candle, even . . .

Yeah, right. Granny would never let me waste my time on something like that. Candles didn't bring in the kind of gold my product did, and if I was in the work shed, I needed to be making sellable products. Those were the rules.

I wondered if I could make candles at home . . .

I poured the crushed petal into a jar to keep it safe, helping the last remnants in with my fingers. Once it was done and lidded, ready for me to work with it tomorrow, I sat back and finished my tea.

"It's got my leg!" Raz screeched. "Help me, it's eating my leg!"

"Fuck's sake," I murmured. "You took way too much.

Way too much." Then louder. "The beast will sleep when you do! Show it how to sleep!"

I rubbed an itchy nose, scenting the Moonfire Lily again. My fingers smelled a little too much like it, actually, like pollen when all the flowers were in bloom.

My sneeze quieted Raz for some reason. Small miracles.

As I finished my tea and set my cup down, I hauled myself up. Raz was in charge of taking the nightly satchel to Granny when she was in town, a trip she made every few months or so. Given he was not fit to exist outside of that closet, let alone interact with his boss and benefactor, that left me. If it didn't mean I'd get to see and chat with Granny, I'd have been severely annoyed.

I tidied everything up before stopping by the unused front workstation. It would've been nice if we could've found someone to occupy this space and help me with the creations, but sadly no one else showed an affinity for the technical aspect of the job. Not even Raz. He was primarily the plant guy. He had a few helpers in the garden and we both had a few runners for supplies, but otherwise the duty to make the product mostly fell to me.

So far, that was fine. I was keeping up, albeit barely. Hopefully orders didn't continue to increase. I was already working every day, often sun up to sundown. Given I didn't have family and no one would suffer my friendship, I didn't mind. It gave me something to do. Besides, I owed Granny everything. I'd reach for the moon if she needed me to. But if orders continued to increase, I knew eventually there just wouldn't be enough time in the day. At that point, I'd need to bring in some help. I'd have no choice.

A fern-green, velvet sack waited on top of the workstation, tied with a pull-string at the top. I pulled it open and filled it with four new products, two of which I'd adjusted from the original version for a better experience. That brought our total to twenty products, including everything from a sleep aid to a relaxant to the fun-time hallucination creation.

Not all of these were explicitly against the laws of the land. The sleep aid, for example, rivaled something the dragon kingdom sold. Mine worked better. The relaxant? The faerie product couldn't hold a candle to it, try as they might. Those really could've sold in the more medicinal markets. The other stuff? Well, those were the reason Granny sold everything through the shadow markets. Guilt by association, I guess.

It was fine. Even the unlawful stuff wasn't expressly dangerous or life-threatening. Not like some of the other items in the shadow markets. None of my product's effects would linger after the drug had worn off . . . except for maybe a questionable life change like Herold becoming "Razorfang." For the nightmare journeys there was the "way out" I'd devised. I'd told Granny to pass that on to everyone who sold the product, and for them to pass it on to anyone who bought it. My conscience was clear. I didn't lose any sleep at night over being a criminal. And if I did? Sleep-aid!

"My life is definitely not a fairy tale," I murmured, picking up the velvet pack.

Under it, a scrap of paper held Raz's handwritten scrawl: "Don't veer off the path."

My brow lowered as I read it again.

My eye started to twitch.

"Very funny, Raz," I said, not caring if I excited the little beasties in his brain again. "Very fucking funny. It was only the one time, by the way." A thud sounded against the wall in the closet. "Just the one time and everyone is a funny guy, huh? No one is going to let me forget it. You get stuffed in a closet, for fuck's sake, and this is the thing everyone remembers?"

"Don't veer off the path!" he shouted, clearly knowing what I was talking about. Manic laughter followed me toward the door.

One time. Seriously, I'd veered off the trail *one time* out of the thousand I'd walked it and it was all anyone talked about. There had been a good reason, too! I'd seen the glow of the Moonfire Lily from the path. They were incredibly hard to spot, often hiding between and under other flora, its glow usually contained unless you were right on top of it. If I hadn't grabbed it then, I might've lost it.

Sure, I accidentally fell over a log, doused my lantern, left it, and made a mad dash for the flower. I admit I might've lost my head a little. It happens.

And okay, yes, after picking the flower and then standing in pitch black as its throb ebbed, I had gotten a little turned around and then couldn't find where I'd left the fallen lantern. I shouldn't have left it behind. That was stupid, I could admit.

But what was I supposed to have done at that point, just stand there all night and hope someone would have come to find me? No. I'd done what any rational person with a terrible sense of direction would do—I'd decided to walk until I found either the village or the perimeter line and our sentries. I had known I'd stumble into one or the other eventually.

It was not my fault that the perimeter patrol thought I was trying to sneak out without an escort. They hadn't given me a chance to explain what had happened; they'd just tossed me over their shoulder and marched me back to Granny.

It had all worked out in the end, though. Even though leaving without permission hadn't been my intention, I'd gracefully accepted the punishment: a hardcore beating by Granny's watchdog, Alexander.

Crisis averted.

Did everyone really need to keep bringing it up? Literally every time I had to take the path to see her in town—every *single* time—it was mentioned. It had been two months! It was past getting old.

Besides, I'd gotten the flower. Given the enhancements I was already making with it and my ideas for new product, it had been a stroke of genius leaving that path, questionable decision-making along the way notwithstanding.

On a little table by the door stood my faerie-made lantern. I grabbed the handle as I exited. Outside, I tapped the top three times quickly, then two slow, followed by rubbing the base. Lights flickered a metallic blue within the shiny metal before burning brighter and brighter until the whole thing glowed indigo with swirling patches of lighter and darker blues. The effect was as beautiful as it was useful, the lantern a prized gift from Granny.

Despite the situation that led me to traipsing this

path so late at night, I felt lighter, content, my heart swelling at the thought of seeing Granny. She wasn't just my benefactor and savior; she looked out for me, provided protection from the outside world, and ensured I had all I needed. She wasn't blood, but I thought of her as family—the only family I had left. I took every opportunity available to meet with her when she visited, chatting and soaking in her proximity.

Her cottage was a fifteen minute walk from the work shed. The indigo glow illuminated the wide tree trunks on either side of the path. The trees now crowded me closely and a hush permeated the area as crickets, night birds, and other creatures stilled or quieted within my vicinity. Ancient trees leaned far over me and strangled what little light the moon shed. Branches entwined along the sides as though in an intricate dance. With each step, the forest floor surrendered below my feet, cushioning my passage as though the path itself remembered me. Not surprising given the number of times I'd walked this route.

With the lantern held aloft, I reached the fork. To go left would take me back to the village, on the outskirts of which was my modest home. I veered right toward Granny's cottage, a solitary dwelling that never got many visitors, as was her choice. I was one of the few. If she had business with someone—a rare occurrence— she went into the village to speak with them directly. Otherwise, she kept the village fed and clothed, ensured their houses were in repair, and saw to everyone's needs. We wanted for nothing. All we had to do was make certain the product was quality and consistently ready for pick-up.

The path narrowed until it was hardly more than the width of a person. The glow of my lantern struggled within the oppressive darkness, the night pushing back at the light.

I trekked on as the emberflies gradually dwindled, slipping between the trunks and then behind without daring to peek back out at me. Their numbers would dwindle even further the closer I got to Granny's. They didn't continue their drifting too far away from the village, it seemed. No one had any idea why.

My soft footfall invaded the pervasive hush as my gaze wandered to the left. It was at about this spot that I'd spied the Moonfire Lily's glow in the trees. Surprising, given how choked with vegetation and foliage the land was. It had somehow been able to glimmer through the reaching ferns and tangled vines and moss. The books said that for every flower you were able to find, there were five nestled close by, waiting for discovery.

That's about all the information about the flower the books contained, except for the effects of using its altered, burned petal in brews, elixirs, and potions. It was an enhancement; that's all the books said. Given the vast quantity of books I'd read about plants and their uses—all acquired from various places by Granny—and the startling lack of information on the Moonfire Lily in comparison, I had a feeling it could do so much more. Figuring out what, though, would require time for experimentation. Time I definitely did not have. Still, the enhancement portion of its powers served me well.

Walking slowly, eyes scanning both sides of the path, I watched for another plant. My focus was so acute that

I almost didn't notice that strange feeling again, like I'd felt at the work shed. Tingles washed over me, as though someone were watching my progress.

My breath halted in my lungs as a warning prickle crawled along my spine. My body froze in fear, steps ceasing. I strained, listening for movement. My knees trembled along with my hand, cold and clammy, holding the lantern up.

The emberflies started to move. A wave washed over the path in front of me, exiting left. Behind, the bugs headed in the same direction, slow at first and then fleeing madly. I'd never seen them move so fast.

Terror gripped my heart. I felt it in every inch of my body. It wasn't just me; they felt it, too.

Danger!

I spun, starting to jog toward Granny's house. If there was danger present, she'd handle it. Worst case, she'd know what to do to escape it. Even though she was getting on in years, she was still an alpha wolf. She had thwarted raids in the past, when other packs had invaded her businesses, intent on grabbing anything or anyone of worth. She had experience with these things. She'd know if there was a breach and she'd probably already be working on defenses-turned-attack strategies. I just had to make it to her cottage and I'd be okay.

The lantern's glow danced wildly on the path, making the shadows lurch and jump. My foot hit a divot and my ankle rolled. I compensated immediately, carrying my weight in that direction and stepping with the other foot to keep my ankle from bending too far. Too late. Tingles replaced what probably should've been pain, my tolerance for pain incredibly high. My foot wasn't accepting much of my weight.

Greatly slowed but not deterred, I limped on. I didn't care about a sprained ankle. It would heal eventually. Granny had procured the best healing ointments and elixirs gold could buy, all the way from the dragon kingdom. Anything short of a severed leg would be fine, and even that would be preferable to what would happen if a raid captured me. I was the any*one* of value they'd be seeking. Granny had taken painstaking efforts to ensure I knew what might happen to me if I was taken. What they'd do to make me cooperate. How they'd treat me when they found out I had no magic.

What I'd be forced to endure if the pack leader was male.

Tears of fear prickled my eyes as I hobble-jogged. That feeling of being watched continued, a constant itch between my shoulder blades. Whatever was there was keeping pace.

I was nearly at the bend, almost there, when the toe on my good leg hit a rock. My momentum kept going, driving me forward. My bad ankle rolled again.

I hit the dirt hard. My lantern clattered against the ground. The light winked out and pitch black washed over me.

"Shit," I swore softly, patting the ground frantically, searching for it. "Shit, shit."

The air thickened with an eerie stillness, interrupted only by my erratic breathing. I felt movement off to the side. *Felt* it, as though a string connected me to a presence in some way. A person.

A predator.

I reached farther, my shaking fingers trailing across the dirt. Wherever the lantern had landed, it was out of reach.

My movements were the only sounds I could hear. I felt it, though, those eyes raking over me. That presence drifting closer. The danger made my heart beat like that of a cornered rabbit.

My primal instincts were fine-tuned to cataloging threats and sensed the presence stopped just beyond the trees. That presence waited, and tingles danced down my spine again. It watched. In indecision? I couldn't tell. I didn't know what it wanted, or what it was doing. It had to be human, though. I felt that about it, a specific sort of danger that animals couldn't duplicate. An intelligent sort of peril. The anticipation of what was about to happen seeped into my bones, making my entire body shudder.

Something else happened, though, too. A strange sort of heat flowered in my chest, like liquid fire dribbling down my middle. Strange currents of scent greeted my nose, too many to really decipher. The thick black of the night lightened minutely, as though pulling back, leaving room for shadows.

And then the presence stepped forward, some sort of decision made.

Adrenaline coursed through me as he neared, because it *was* a he. I had no idea how I knew, but like knowing his presence was there in the first place, I felt it. Felt *him*. His movements created nothing more than a whisper in the night, not a sound accentuating his passage. He stopped in front of me, where I knelt in the dirt at his feet. His height loomed over me while the heat of his body slid along my exposed flesh, cocooning me in his warmth. I swam in it, feeling his over-whelming power, his coiled strength.

Fucking hell, this actually felt amazing. Which meant it couldn't be real. Something had changed. Even though I felt the predator, the danger, I no longer felt threatened by it. I wanted it nearer, actually. I wanted to pull it toward me.

What was happening? Had I somehow accidentally sampled my own product? Because if he'd slipped by Granny's defenses, he'd either grab the product or grab me. He wouldn't wander around this territory so lack-adaisically, with no fear of being discovered.

"Look at me," a deep, gruff voice commanded, and the effect washed over me like a pleasure bath.

His magic wound through me, delicious and exhila-rating, like washing in a cool mountain spring on a warm evening, when everything was freshly in bloom. I closed my eyes within it for a moment, taking my time to savor the feeling before I did look up, sightlessly. Obediently.

Moments passed as he looked down upon me. Stud-ied me.

"Beautiful," he whispered.

His heat settled low now, an ache forming in my core. I almost reached out for reasons I couldn't quite explain. I wanted to feel him. To run my fingers along his skin. Grasp his straining cock.

What in the holy fuck was happening to me? This couldn't be any product I'd created, accidentally ingested or not. I didn't have anything with an effect like this.

Then it occurred to me. The Moonfire Lily! I'd had it on my fingers. I'd been inhaling strong currents of its delicious smell. Maybe I'd ingested it, transferring it to my teacup and sipping it off. Was it causing this strange erotic fever dream? Was I actually on the trail by myself, kneeling in front of nothing, following commands issued by an invisible lover while danger prowled the wood?

Old gods help me, I really fucking hoped so. It was better than the alternative, which was that I was bowing before a predator, desperate to be fucked.

I squinted my eyes shut and lowered my head, willing this all to go away. Willing my mind to eat through the drug and reduce or stop the effects, something I'd learned to do over the years.

"Never bow to me," came that deep, erotic voice full of power and authority.

Fingers touched the bottom of my chin, applying pressure, tilting my head back up. I didn't open my eyes this time, as I still fought the effects of what had to be that Moonfire Lily. Quite the saucy little plant, I had to say. Very bad timing for a journey I was not prepared for, though. I would've rather traveled the path of this drug in the privacy of my cottage, stripped nude and spread wide, imaging this stranger tracing each curve of my body with his sensuous touch. I had a very good imagination when it came to these things.

Pressure filled my chest now, like someone was sitting on it. Heat was all around me, all through me. I practically vibrated with it. My pussy was so wet, wanting to be filled so badly.

"Kneel," the luscious voice commanded.

I was fucking kneeling. That's what it meant when you were on your knees on a path that hopefully no one else would be traveling tonight.

The presence walked around me and I could just barely hear his footsteps. And that smell—was that him? Warm sandalwood with a dark and forbidden smoky undertone. Hints of jasmine. Of sin. It lingered in my senses, manifesting the desire raging through my body. It put the smell of the Moonfire Lily to absolute shame.

"Please go away," I murmured, willing this journey to recede. For the drug to withdraw its effects. I liked it, I couldn't deny that, but now was not the time. I needed to figure out why the emberflies took off. "Go away," I murmured.

I could end the journey of every single drug I'd made for the last five years. Every one, even those that had locked Raz in paralyzing nightmares until I'd shoved him into the supply closet. This one should be no different, regardless of the fact it seemed to be purely the plant without any sort of additive or alteration.

"Stop this. Go away," I said again, more firmly, willing it to be so.

The presence stepped up right behind me. Leaned over me, intimidating, exciting . . . dangerous. His mouth neared the shell of my ear, his breath stirring the sensitive nerves on the back of my neck.

"Do you really want that?" His voice was low and silky, eliciting a delicious concoction of warning and desire. "Or should I stay long enough to give you the satisfaction you crave?"

It somehow felt so much more intense that he wasn't touching me; his words, his scent, his breath caressing me in ways I couldn't seem to fight. I tried valiantly, but he was more intoxicating than any manufactured drug, and possibly just as potent.

Go away.

He straightened, as though hearing the words I couldn't seem to utter.

Fuck off.

He stepped back, giving me space. A chill accosted me, leaving me feeling bereft without his proximity. There he stood patiently, waiting.

I clenched my fists, squeezed my eyes shut, and willed my mouth to give the command.

Unfortunately, my body was calling the shots.

"Fuck me," I whispered.

2

AURELIA

An urgency I'd never experienced before overwhelmed me. On my knees, on the ground, I tried to rub my thighs together to alleviate the mounting pressure of my craving for this man. My body shook from suppressed need, my lack of control in this situation sending adrenaline and arousal spreading over my nerve endings. My peaked breasts, raw and sensitive, rubbed against the thin fabric of my clothing. My jaw clenched as sweat beaded along my forehead.

I needed his touch, desperately. His hard cock pumping inside me. His teeth scraping against my shoulder, ready to bite down.

I internally struggled with the thoughts running through my mind. This wasn't just a light fantasy; it felt devastating. I couldn't seem to step out from underneath this drug. This delicious euphoria consumed me, refusing to let me escape with my usual tricks. If I kept pushing back on it, my journey would take a sharp turn.

I'd end up like Raz, except I'd be out in the open, undoubtedly leaving the path and wandering the forest. I could not allow that to happen. The punishment this time would cripple me.

Was there even any danger? The feeling of being watched earlier had occured when I was working that Moonfire Lily. It had felt the same as a moment ago. Had I imagined the emberflies scattering? Was any of this real?

Thinking logically . . . there was no way a man could've slipped through Granny's incredibly tight security and then decided to leisurely entertain a woman on a dark path, waiting for her consent to do so. That seemed very far-fetched.

Not so far-fetched was succumbing to one of my products, railing against it, wandering the wood, and getting punished to within an inch of my life. I'd been warned when I'd left the path before. I was not in a hurry to do it again, emberflies, predators, and strangers be damned.

Taking a deep breath—and in disbelief I was making this decision—I sank into this feeling. These were the hazards of my trade. I let go of any reservations and gave in to it totally.

Someone's voice echoed in the silence, far away. I couldn't make out the words. Strange desires seeped into me, wild thoughts of the stranger mounting me like some ravaged beast. Oh gods, I wanted him to rut wildly. To dominate me. To claim me. My wetness soaked through my clothes. I didn't even know what he looked like. The darkness shrouded his appearance. He could obviously see me, though. There was something provocative in the realization that he could detail every-thing about me . . . and I didn't even know the color of his eyes.

The stranger's knuckles trailed down my hair, the gentle caress so at odds with the wild, untamed beast I sensed within him. It was only when those same long fingers speared into my tresses, using the loose strands like a leash to gently push me forward, that I moaned. My palms hit the dirt. I may not have been bowing down to him, but I was an offering, bent over in suppli-cation, on hands and knees.

"That's right," he growled, leaning over me from behind, his hand touching down on my ass. It spanned a whole cheek. A vibration ran through my body, the feeling so fucking delicious.

His hand trailed to the other cheek and then to my center. His fingers ran down my cloth-covered core, his middle finger tracing the seam of my trousers. My breathing turned heavy as the tip of his middle finger found the right spot and rubbed.

My eyelids fluttered and I dropped my head, gyrating my hips slowly. Holy fuck, he knew exactly where and how firm to touch, exactly how fast to go. The guy was good with his hands.

This had to be a product of my imagination. No one I'd ever met could seem to get it right, even with instruction.

"More," I groaned, balancing on one hand so that I could hook the thumb of the other in the waistline of my trousers. I peeled the fabric down to my hip.

The stranger's hand paused for a moment, indeci-sive, and then he stepped closer in a rush as though he couldn't help himself. His foot scraped against the ground. He grabbed my trousers with two hands and yanked them down.

The night air washed over my bared skin. His palms slid down my outer thighs. One of his knees hit the dirt behind me. Then the other. Soft lips glanced across my flesh, his kisses gentle, his grip on my legs hard.

His mouth didn't waste time like his hands had. His tongue parted my core, tasting immediately, sending me down to brace my weight on my forearms. His growl of pleasure nearly undid me. He licked up to my asshole and circled, the sensation tickling a little yet strangely pleasureful. He backed off for a moment and I could hear movement behind me, the air disturbed, before feeling his hands grip my hips from below and lifting.

I gasped, walking myself back with my hands as he pulled my hips. My knees hit the dirt again, my shins resting against big shoulders, and I realized I was now straddling his face. He pulled me down like he was starving for me, taking my clit into his mouth and twirling his tongue around it as he sucked in pulses.

"Holy . . . fuck-ing . . . *shit.*" My mouth dropped open in a silent scream.

His fingers rubbed along my wet pussy, his growl deep and low at my obvious arousal, before delving in. They curved exactly right, rubbing firmly. He sucked in perfect synchronicity.

"Holy . . ." My hips jerked of their own accord. "Holy . . ." I had zero control of my body right now. Drug or no drug, I would not have climbed off this ride for my life. *"Holy—"*

I couldn't catch my breath. I couldn't get my bearings. Pleasure coursed through me in a growing swell. I clawed at the ground, overcome. No one had ever been this good. *Ever*. We had clearly entered my wildest dreams.

I was going to find more Moonfire Lily if it killed me.

"Almost . . ." I was right on the edge, tensing up now, riding his face with abandon. If I suffocated him . . . Well, he will have died of noble causes.

His teeth scraped my sensitive flesh and I blasted apart, swearing, yelling, shuddering against him. My mind went completely blank and all I knew was pleasure, taking me to a place I hadn't yet been.

As it settled, I drooped over him, my body tingling. He kept going lightly, his ministrations languid now, his tongue moving slowly. When he was sure I was thoroughly over my climax, he gently lifted me again so he could crawl out from under me. I didn't bother moving, still focused on the pleasant aftershocks making me shiver.

His hand gripped my shoulder and he tugged gently to get me to straighten up before his touch and his body heat disappeared from behind me. My trousers were still secured around my knees, restraining my movement. The cool air kissed my wet core, a sharp reminder that I was bared to the night.

He circled to my front and I let my eyes drift open, finding three things that startled me. One was that the emberflies had returned to drift slowly around us, like our own personal sea of stars. The second was that the blackness had receded just enough that I could make out shapes. There was no more moonlight seeping through the dense canopy than before, no other lights to help; it was that I could just barely see in the darkness. And what I saw was number three.

The stranger stood before me, tall and broad, with wide shoulders and a distinctly V-shaped frame. Bumpy arms and bulging legs indicated well cut muscles, and his strong stance and aura of confidence more than hinted at his power and authority. I half wanted to see more detail, to see the plane of his face and ascertain the look in his eyes. Another part of me, though, found it strangely more arousing with the blank canvas. With the mystery surrounding this man.

He moved, bending a bit, a hand coming slowly toward my face. His thumb and forefinger gripped my chin. He pulled just so, opening my mouth. His hand left my chin and slid along my cheek to the side of my head. He pushed his hips forward until soft flesh butted up against my lips.

My stomach swirled with the uncontrollable need to taste him. To drink him in and swallow him down, to savor the feel of his flesh in my hands. I wanted to make him as mindless and sated as he'd made me.

I licked, finding the little slit and tracing it with my tongue. I braced my hands on his thighs before feeling upwards, tracking the large mass of muscle. I circled his tip with my tongue as one hand found his balls, cupping firmly. He'd clearly stepped onto the path in the nude. I sucked him in, taking him as far as I could and then backing off, gripping his shaft with my free hand and stroking as though my hand were an extension of my mouth.

Liquid danced across my tongue, and though it

must've been precum, it in no way tasted like it. Instead of being tart and mostly horrible, this tasted sweet, like candy with notes of the sticky buns Granny made when she was in a particularly good mood. It was *delicious*.

There could be no more doubt. This was definitely a drug-induced erotic hallucination. And unless there was a particularly horrible come-down, it was going to bring in lots of gold when I figured out exactly what had caused it.

I sucked harder, wanting more of that flavor, taking more of him than I usually would. I massaged his balls as I pulled back. I swirled my tongue around his tip before sucking him in again, feeling his hand fist in my hair. He pulled me away.

My mewl of displeasure was heartfelt for the first time in my life. I usually hated giving head—a chore I did only because I wanted it in return—but this time I had a need to keep going. I wanted his sweet release on my tongue, his knees weakening as a result of my efforts. I wanted to please him.

The strong fingers of his other hand wrapped around the base of my jaw, massaging. He pulled me forward and his cock was back, pushing in deep, hitting the back of my mouth. I just barely kept from gagging as his fingers applied pressure, wanting me to relax just there. To release the tension.

I did as he wished and was rewarded with him pushing in deeper. Receding and then deeper still, down into my throat. Faster now, fucking my face.

This should be highly uncomfortable. Much worse than the pump-suck action I usually employed. But gods help me, I fucking loved it. I wanted more of him. All of him.

His tip dripped and I swallowed greedily, holding onto his thighs as he yanked my hair with each thrust. My eyes watered and I looked up at his face, knowing somehow that he'd get off on it. Not questioning why. Deeper and deeper he went until his balls butted up against my chin.

"Good girl," he growled, so soft.

The rest of my tension drained away, basking in the glow of his praise—which was alarming because usually I got deeply annoyed and often violent if a man talked to me like I was his pet. Like I needed his approval. But this stranger's tone held none of that. We were on the same team, each of us striving to give the other what they needed. Those words now, like this, said like that . . . It was all kinds of hot.

I hollowed my cheeks with suction, loving those little yanks in my hair. I felt his pleasure like it was my own. And then I felt the base of his cock begin to swell. Clearly he was a shifter, a wolf. They were the only magical beings that could form knots, the bases of their dicks enlarging enough to lock them inside of their mates.

My lips butted up against it as he pummeled my mouth and suddenly I needed it inside of me. I craved to be locked with him in a lover's dance, feeling him pulse, answering with my pleasure.

I pushed his legs with my hands and pulled back against the tight grip he had on my hair. He relented his hold immediately; something that must've given him pause. I would've been panicked that the job would go unfinished.

I reached up for him, my hands bumping against his body.

He caught my wrists, beginning to lift me up. I pulled, though, trying to bring him down to my level.

He sank to the ground in front of me, his warm breath dusting my face. I ran my hands across his torso, salivating at the mighty pecs. Up to his shoulders—hulking things, incredibly wide. Around to the back of his neck, pulling him to me.

He leaned in slowly, taking his time. I could feel his gaze on me, roaming my face. Settling on my lips. With him I didn't need detailed sight. I seemed to be connected to him in a strange way, able to anticipate his movements, feel his whereabouts and intentions.

His lips brushed mine, unhurried. Soft, as though we'd been lovers all our adult lives. As though we were reuniting after a long time away, savoring the moment. Deeper now, his lips nibbling, sucking in my bottom lip. I groaned with his taste, drew him closer, nearly crawling up onto him to get closer still.

Our kiss turned urgent. His tongue delved and his hands gripped my butt, lifting me with ease. But my legs were trapped in my trousers. I couldn't wrap them around his hips.

He spun me so I landed with hands and knees positioned on the dirt. He moved in behind me, slow like a predator, readying to take what was his.

Shivers washed across my body, feeling that heat. More warmth leaked through my chest.

A hot, rough hand grabbed my right hip. My breath

sped up. Another hand, at my left hip. His fingers kneaded a little as a knee hit the inside of mine, wanting my legs wider. I complied, the anticipation killing me.

One of his hands disappeared only to have the head of his cock slide up my wet center. His growl sounded possessive as he pressed in, getting him all slick. The blunt tip paused at my opening.

My eyes fluttered closed as my head dropped. It felt like all my nerve endings were sparkling, alive for the first time in my life.

His hand slapped back down on my hip and he thrust.

Lights danced behind my eyes. A searing ache erupted in my core. He was *big*. Larger than I'd ever experienced, stretching me until I whined, panting with the effort of not wiggling away.

He held himself there. "Relax, baby," he whispered, leaning over me, his chest to my back.

I did as he said, trying to give in to that ache. To release my tension.

"That's my girl," he murmured, his voice deep and intoxicating. One hand snaked around my body and his fingers touched down on my clit, massaging. "Get used to me. Relax."

I relaxed further, working on steady breaths.

He started moving, his fingers working, drawing out slowly and pushing back in. The pain receded quickly until all that was left was a slow build of pleasure. I pushed back against his thrusts, feeling that knot against my opening. He lifted my body a little as he leaned, his front still to my back. He thrust faster, hitting me a little deeper. His knot pushed against me, wanting admittance but he held back. His lips pressed against the skin of my shoulder, his teeth just beyond.

I shivered violently, holding my breath. I knew what he was contemplating—to dig his teeth into the place where my neck met my shoulder and apply a special kind of magic. A claiming kind of magic, ruining me for any shifter not strong enough to override his claim with their own.

My body started to shake, knowing I should pull away. I needed to shrug him off. But I couldn't seem to manage it, instead leaning harder, moaning with the onslaught, wanting his mark. Wanting his knot. His seed.

His movements turned frantic to match my own. His finger rubbed against me. His teeth scraped.

An orgasm tore me to pieces, making me scream out my pleasure. He yanked out of me a moment later, his breathing labored, his grunt of release meaning he hadn't come inside of me. The pleasure was so intense I wilted down to the dirt as I continued to spasm with aftershocks.

Rough hands grabbed me and pulled me back, crushing my back to his front. His lips brushed my ear, his voice deep and firm.

"Run. Leave this place. It's not safe for you here. Get out now, tonight. Don't look back. Find your way to another village and disappear. This is the only warning you'll get."

And then he was gone, peeling his body from mine and drifting out into the night like a phantom, leaving me breathless, bare and disoriented.

3

WESTON

*F*uck!
Fuck. Fuck. *Fuck!*
What the fuck did I just do?

"You know what you just did," my wolf said, pushed up near the surface.

I shook my head to block out the words as I hurried away from the path. When I was far enough, I stepped behind a tree, my back scratched by the rough bark. My body still shook with that sweet release. Everything about what just happened was incredibly intoxicating; her smell lingered on my flesh, her touch.

Fuck!

Why now? Why here? Why *her*?

She was the enemy. A monster, making products that tore families apart, whether because of addiction or death or poverty. She was trash. Worse than trash, she was a creature to eradicate. That's exactly why I was here. To take her back to the dragon royalty to face her punishment, which would almost certainly be death. No one could wreak the sort of havoc she had and live to tell the tale. Not from the dragons.

I closed my eyes, breathing deeply.

I'd completely lost my head. My control had fled the very moment I'd caught her scent. My will had frayed the second I saw her beautiful face, looking sightlessly up at me. Long black hair framed her oval visage with high arching brows and exquisite hazel eyes, like a burst of sunshine between dense black lashes. Her lithe little body strained for me, her entire person eager to please. The feel of her skin, of her plump, heart-shaped lips as they wrapped around the head of my cock, weakened my knees.

But why?

"You know why," my wolf sang within me.

"Shut up," I said out loud, pushing off the trunk and walking fast.

I'd put my team in jeopardy. That was inexcusable. I'd walked onto that trail and fucked the enemy in clear view. If I'd been seen, this territory would've known they'd been breached. Their defenses would've gone active and my people would've been scrambling. We were the best at what we did, but being caught unawares would've thrown even us off kilter. I'd been reckless. Stupid. I was a bad excuse for an alpha.

"You acted exactly how an alpha would have," my wolf argued. *"Except you should've knotted her and pumped our seed deep inside of her."*

My legs turned to jelly and I staggered, bending to rest my hands on my knees and dropping my head. I was painfully hard again just thinking about doing that. I'd barely stopped myself earlier, preventing myself from pushing deep into her tight little pussy and locking her to me. I'd wanted to. Oh, heavens how I'd wanted to. It had taken all my will to resist.

I'd lost control. That couldn't be argued. I'd lost control and it could not happen again, regardless of the situation. I had a job to do. A duty I would follow to the end. I owed my allegiance to the dragons. They'd given me a home, a title, a great life, riches, and power. I led a huge faction of that kingdom, and I would not jeopardize their trust in me. I *would not.*

I had to push past this. I had to ignore her effect on me. It couldn't change my feelings about what I was doing. It couldn't make me veer off course.

Gods help me, though, she'd felt so good. Unbelievably good, unlike anyone I'd ever touched. Like a piece of me I hadn't known I'd been missing. An important part of the whole.

"You know why she felt that way," my animal pushed. *"Like air to a suffocating man."*

Yes I fucking did. In this forgotten, out of the way village I'd found something so incredibly rare, so absolutely precious, it was almost a myth. Very few people ever found theirs. Most people only dreamed of it. I'd known it when I'd seen her outside of that work shed; I'd felt her calling to me even from the distance. I'd been sure of it as I beheld her on the path, unable to keep from stepping out to meet her.

That woman was my true mate.

And she was my enemy. My target.

Fuck!

I blew out a long breath, straightening up slowly.

It didn't matter. I was stronger than this. I had

worked my whole life on developing my iron-clad will. She'd taken me by surprise—fine. Now I knew. Now I could prepare. I could get my head in order. She would not derail me.

"And if she runs like you advised?" my animal asked.

Oh. That.

I grimaced and nearly shouted out my frustration.

I definitely shouldn't have told her to run. That had been one slip-up of many. She was the one we were sent here to find, there was no doubt.

I'd just been so thoroughly in the moment that my primal sense had kicked in—my need to protect what was mine. Because she *was* mine. There could be no denying that fact, as shitty as this situation was.

Fuck, why me? Why her? Of all the people in the entire world, why *her*?

Time to do damage control.

In halting steps, I headed for the little cottage far removed from the village and all its people. Granny, they called the owner. Just a lovely, sweet older lady who baked pies and hooked people on drugs. Killed them, sometimes. Ruined them, other times. If it wasn't for Finley, the dragon queen, we would've lost a great many in our kingdom. Others already had. It was inexcusable, what was coming out of this village. Unconscionable. For anyone to be okay with it . . .

My resolve hardened, remembering who we'd lost.

True mates didn't matter; she needed to be taken down. It was my duty to see this through, and I would fulfill my task regardless of the obstacles. Maybe I was being punished for past wrongs, maybe I was being challenged by the Gods, but whatever it was, I would not stray again.

"We'll hunt her down if she runs," I told my wolf. "Just like we hunted her and Granny to this hidden village. She will not escape me."

I rolled my shoulders, taking another moment to collect myself. I'd need to shift and connect with my pack. If the woman got to Granny's cottage and sounded the alarm, we'd need to move in fast.

The only good news was that there didn't seem to be any of Granny's people roaming the internal territory. The perimeter had been well fortified. Granny had a very thorough setup, with an alert sentry line and a well-scheduled patrol. They couldn't be everywhere at once, of course, so Granny had applied faerie spells and potions to the vulnerable areas, blocking admittance. In one space she'd even set up a demon gate requiring a magical key of demon origins to get through. They were the best systems criminal gold could buy.

Too bad for her I had connections to more powerful faeries and demons than she did. There wasn't a door I couldn't get through, and when Granny's people came after us, I'd steal their will and render them immobile. She had no idea the caliber of enemy she'd made, and I wasn't even talking about the dragons.

I'd been blindsided just now, but soon it would be them who'd get a helluva shock. I'd make sure of it.

"We will not engage with that woman again," I told my wolf, restless within me. "She is the enemy. She has done terrible things and she must stand in judgment for her sins, as must we all. Do you understand?"

He did the equivalent of pacing. *"You won't be able to ignore her."*

"We can and we must. Promise me before I give you back control."

He didn't answer for a moment. In the past, he would've outright refused. He would've thought that he knew best. It was just such a judgment that had landed us in a demon dungeon, separated from each other for countless years. He'd been absent for the misery and degradation I'd endured in that place, only knowing the devastation and pain second-hand when we'd reconnected and he'd been privy to my memories. I'd thought I'd die there, the demon magic drugging me to accept the abuse. To like it, most times. But the magic did nothing to stop me from retching when I remembered it all the next day. I'd been powerless. Used for pleasure against my will.

Bile rose in the back of my throat and my hands shook as I fought to shove those memories down, locking them away and harnessing the misery to sharpen my resolve.

It had been a sort of drug to make all that possible—demon-made and administered through magic. It hadn't been my choice, just like the drugs being slipped into people's drinks and food now weren't their choice, nor the ones sold to them under false pretenses. Granny had no boundaries. She had no reservations. The faster she could get people hooked, the better. She didn't care what happened to people along the way.

I'd wasted no time in signing up for this detail. I hated everything these people stood for.

Now, thankfully, my wolf was a bit more cautious.

Or maybe I was just that much harder, having grown brittle in that dungeon. Having lost my humor and sometimes my will to keep going.

Knowing my head space, he relented.

"For now," he said, a good enough compromise. I had no doubt he'd soon see that I was right. This whole place was vile. The things they did were beyond excuse.

I gave up control and my wolf instigated the shift. His four paws touched down onto the ground and he started forward.

We could feel everyone's location through the pack bond as they scouted the area undetected. Granny's cottage wasn't much to look at, just a small dwelling with a curling trail of smoke winding from the chimney. It was nothing like her huge estate near the castle where she made her connections and paid off guards and royals. The village was equally humble, showing none of the extravagance she was known for outside of this rural place. She clearly hadn't distributed the gold these people had helped her accrue.

I worked with my wolf to feed emotions, scents, and various other information through those bonds to the pack while willing them instructions, indicating which direction they needed to go or where they should stop. It was a complex magical system that I naturally excelled at, my alpha magic stronger than any other I'd yet met. It would ensure Granny's people were rendered ineffective when they realized our presence. It meant she would be snared by me the moment she shifted into her wolf form.

It was why it was so important for me to walk in the light. To stay on the side of steadfast morality. I had the power to enslave people to my will. If I veered or wavered, I had the power to be the biggest tyrant any wolf shifter had ever known, something the royals in this kingdom had once hoped to use to their advantage. *Had* used, actually, for too many years, by capturing people and tethering them to the crown.

"I would rather never have met her than to meet her and have to give her away," my wolf whined. *"Especially if we have to deliver her directly into danger."*

"She delivered herself into danger," I said, hardening myself to the idea. I knew well I'd need to do it over and over again. I couldn't let desire win; for this insatiable need for her to win.

"Our duty is to protect her."

"Our duty is to protect our kingdom. She, unfortunately, chose to put our people in danger."

"She is also incredibly rare. They say most people never meet theirs. Ever. And here she is, stashed away for safe keeping, waiting for us to find her. And we did find her, against all odds. Why would it happen if it wasn't meant to be?"

"I don't know," I said honestly, suddenly incredibly tired. *"A cruel joke by the gods? Karma? Take your pick. It seems like this life is bringing us one nightmare after another. Maybe if we can get through this one last trial, we'll finally find some peace."*

He responded with a sardonic laugh and I appreciated him not sharing whatever comment he thought. Even now, I longed to go back to her. To revel in her beauty and free her of her troubles. To learn about her, detail by detail, patiently studying each curve and savoring each breath.

It was crazy to feel this way about a person I'd never met, but even so, I just wanted to hold her. To lose myself in her. To find an equal I couldn't control with my will and didn't have to stay so damn rigid with all the time. My role meant I constantly had to walk a fine line of dominance. I had to constantly prove I was trustworthy, and that I was a *good guy*. That I wasn't asserting my will in an unethical manner, even with sexual partners.

It was exhausting.

Occasionally I just wanted to break free. I wanted to exult in my darkness and fuck like the world was burning around me.

But because of my past, I could not waver in my duty. Not even for something as incredibly rare as finding my true mate.

4

AURELIA

J stared at the blackness for several long moments, still shaking with pleasure, my brain a stupefied, blissed-out mess. A boneless, sated puddle.

What a fucking ride! Ho-ly balls!

I felt the ghosts of his hands on my skin. His fervent kisses. His large, plunging cock . . .

I stood and dusted off my hands and knees before pulling up my trousers, looking back in the direction of the work shed. I wanted to try that flower again. It was important to know what exactly had prompted such an incredible journey, and how easy it was to duplicate. There wasn't time, though. Granny was expecting her delivery and I'd be punished if she didn't get it, despite it not actually being my job.

I crouched down and felt across the dirt for my lantern, finding it at the side of the path. Reviving it, I waited for the indigo light to glow before stooping to pick up Granny's bag and continuing on my way.

Wouldn't it be nice if cocks really did taste like candy.

Huffing out a laugh while shaking my head, I relished in the euphoria from two amazing climaxes. I followed the bend in the path to Granny's house. Once there, I knocked three times, indicating it was me.

Footsteps sounded on creaking floorboards and then the door swung open, revealing an aged woman with sharp brown eyes and curled, gray hair. A flowing dress covered her plump body, the few extra pounds not at all hindering how fast she could move, especially in wolf form.

"Aurelia, what a surprise." Her tone was sharp. "Where's Razorfang?"

"He wasn't feeling well," I said easily. "He asked that I bring this here so that he could go lay down."

Her gaze traveled my face and then swept down my body, coming back up and pausing on my hair for a moment. Her nose flared slightly in distaste.

A rush of anxiety made me wonder what I looked like. I'd envisioned someone clutching it in a fist, yanking it. Hopefully that hadn't been me doing it, projecting my desire onto a phantom hand. Hmm. I'd need to watch someone else take the journey and then recount their experiences to get a better idea of how it worked.

A strange pang of jealousy pinched my gut, thinking of anyone else ending up with my mind creation, touched in the way he'd touched me, kissed with those expressive lips.

"Are you okay?" she finally asked.

I startled, unable to stop myself from reaching up to smooth my hair.

"I'm not really sure actually," I said honestly, my laugh shaky. "I think I've stumbled upon a new drug, created from the glowing flower I found. I seem to have accidentally administered it to myself." I put out my hand. "I'm not totally sure how yet. I hadn't realized I had until I was on my way here. I have a few suspicions but . . ." I shook my head. "I need to think about this some more. I have too many questions."

She stepped back, opening the door for me. "Come in, come in. I've just baked some of those sticky buns you love so much. I was going to bring them to you tomorrow."

My stomach rumbled and then my core tightened, remembering his taste. The feel of his cock sliding across my tongue.

"I'm good for the moment," I said quickly. "I'm tired. You know how I lose my appetite when I get tired."

"Of course, that's why I'd planned to take them to you tomorrow. Yes, of course. Here, please, sit down."

Two rocking chairs sat facing a little hearth, a small table beside each. We lived modestly in this village, with no electricity magically stolen from the parallel human realm, nor running water. We existed as in the old days, tucked away from the rest of the kingdom and safe in obscurity.

She sat in the other rocking chair, offering me a pleasant smile and grasping her hands in her lap. "So, tell me about this new drug that has you looking like a woman freshly and satisfyingly . . . seen to."

My face heated and, given the paleness of my cheeks,

a result of not seeing the sun as often as I'd like, I was sure my embarrassment showed clearly.

"Ahem . . ." I cleared my throat. "It is . . . uh, sexual in nature, this one. Very realistic. Well . . ." I toggled my hand. "It's a dream-world style of realism, where wildest dreams come true, but realistic in the hallucination." I paused for a moment, squinting at the fire in thought. "Actually . . . maybe not visually realistic, now that I think about it. That might be a problem. When my vision was more thoroughly engaged, it didn't enhance the image all that much. Maybe it'll be better in more light. But the feel of it is very realistic, and that's the main thing, I think. That's the thing that'll have people coming back for more."

Her eyes sparkled in that greedy way they did. She clearly sensed that the product I'd inadvertently devised had the potential to be heavily sought-after.

"There are a few products in the trade that enhance the feel of a lover," she said. "I wondered if you would come up with one. I doubted, since you have so few lovers, but this—well, this is a revelation, my dear. The effects of the other products without even needing a lover in the first place? Oh my yes, the lonely hearts will love it. We'll pluck clients right out of the boudoirs' hands. Very well done, my dear. *Very* well done."

I didn't know what a boudoir was—though I certainly had a guess—but I preened at her praise.

Good girl.

That voice stole my focus for a moment. The sentiment dribbled heat through my core. So dirty. So delicious.

I cleared my throat again, looking at the fire. "Yes,

well, don't pat me on the back yet. I still need to figure out exactly what I took and how. Accidents are only fun if I can figure out how they originated."

"Of course. Keep me updated. Now, where do we stand with the rest of your supply? We have an entire trading circle of people clamoring for more. We've extended into all but the demon kingdom at this point. I'm trying to work in there but their new lord— for some reason, he won't accept the title of king—does not want any of our influence, whatever that is supposed to mean. His people are very loyal. Well, they have to be, right? He usurped the old king with the dragons' help and killed all the former king's loyal subjects. Anyway, I can't find an *in* with him. So we'll wait on that. But otherwise, a great many kingdoms are very receptive to us. The vampires are absolutely smitten with our stardust tonic. Can't get enough of it. I've driven up the price."

I frowned at her. "The stardust tonic? I thought that only worked on shifters and goblins as a calming agent."

Granny's gaze turned sharp, her expression hardening to stone. "Did Raz give you the list of products I need?"

I swung my gaze back to the fire. Granny clearly wasn't in the mood for questions. She was probably tired from the day's activities. She tended to lose her patience easily when that was the case. This conversation would have to wait for another day, it seemed. Not that it really mattered. As long as the customers were happy and buying, that was really all that mattered.

"He did, yes," I answered dutifully. "I can do a few

big batches to fulfill that order but I'll be at my limit. If the orders get any larger, I'll need help."

"Is that right?" She steepled her fingers, looking over at me. I could sense her displeasure as I watched the dancing flames. My chest tightened with a thread of worry. I hated when her moods turned sour. It always felt like I was failing her in some way. "Is Raz not satisfactory?"

"He is, it's just . . . the requests for product are getting a lot bigger now and I don't have the—*we* don't have the resources to handle it all."

"I see," she said primly. "And this wouldn't have anything to do with his sudden illness?"

I'd become an expert liar with her, hiding all manner of things so that Raz or I didn't get punished, but I knew I wouldn't be able to work my way out of this one. One lie would lead to many. He was not sticking to the straight and narrow as much these days, and the story would grow too convoluted for me to keep together. In the end, she'd surely catch me up and the explanation would unravel.

"I'm not sure," I said in an even tone.

"I see," she said again. Unbelievably, she didn't push. "And how about the enhancements you wrote to me about? With that plant you found."

I barely kept from sighing in relief. I was comfortable talking about the product, at least.

I went over all my new additions and explained how the Moonfire Lily had enhanced those already in our product line.

"You enhanced all that with just that one little flower?" she asked when I'd finished.

"Yes, and I still have petals left over. It's potent. Incredibly so."

"I gather. You've used it before, though, right? I don't remember it giving this kind of boost."

"I used it early on when I was still learning my craft. Suffice to say, I hadn't been using it in the best possible ways. I still might not be, but I don't have the time or resources to experiment."

She tilted her head at me. "There is no denying you've come a long way. Can I do anything to help you?"

I clasped my hands in my lap. "Remember that journal you were able to . . . procure from the dragon court?" Procure was a much better word than *steal*. "The one written by someone being trained directly by the dragon queen?" She inclined her head. "I'd love something like that. My craft grew exponentially after studying those notes. She's a genius, the dragon queen. She's earned her reputation as one of the best."

"Yes, she has certainly made a name for herself and her kingdom." She pursed her lips, as though annoyed. "I'll see what I can do," she finished tersely.

I knew that tone. Her mood had grown darker. She was definitely tired. Annoying her now risked facing repercussions.

I stood gracefully, hurrying but not being obvious about it.

"Aurelia, before you go." She stood and crossed the room, before bending in the corner. When she straightened, she shook out a bright red cloak made of velvet. "I purchased this for you."

Delight surged through me. I couldn't contain my

smile. Granny's gifts were few and far between, but without any family or friends, they were the only ones I was ever given. Each was as amazing as the next, and this was no exception. The cloak was thick and obviously soft, made of fine material, and nicer than anything I owned. The quality was amazing and the sentiment brought a sheen of tears to my eyes.

"Thank you!" I gushed.

"Now, after hearing about the Moonfire Bloom—"

"Lily," I accidentally interrupted. Her lips pressed together in annoyance. "Sorry. Moonfire Lily. That's what it's called." I shook my head. "It doesn't matter."

She paused for a tense beat and I clasped my hands in front of me with a bowed head.

"Moonfire Lily," she finally repeated, her smile not reaching her eyes. "I think you will need the extra warmth of this cloak if you are to scour the forest in the dead of night looking for more."

My smile burned brighter. Even in a darker sort of mood, she always came through for me. "You mean it? I can leave the paths?"

"You'll be accompanied, of course." She bent her head, her gaze severe. "We wouldn't want you getting lost again."

One fucking time . . .

"But it seems that flower is a boon to your setup," she said. "We'll all benefit if you obtain more. Tell me, why are we not growing it ourselves?"

"I tried with the most recent flower. To replant it, I mean. I think I damaged it too much when I uprooted it, though. I gave the seeds to Raz to plant but I'm not sure if he's had any luck. And honestly, I don't really know how seed harvesting works. I might've done it wrong."

"Hmm, yes." Granny reached around me to drape the cloak on my shoulders. The silk lining on the underside rubbed delicately against my skin and the weight alone told me how much it was worth. Gratitude and love fizzed up through my middle. "Raz is supposed to be the master gardener, is he not? Directing the village on how to garden what you need?"

I paused in drawing the cloak in tighter, my beaming smile freezing. "He is," I drew out, knowing where this was heading. "But before the town locked down into producing the current product, he was a wood worker. He doesn't have the natural inclination for gardening. He's working on it, though. He and I are working on all of this. Together. A team effort."

"But why didn't he step in and help harvest the seeds? That falls under his duties, natural inclination or not."

I searched my brain for a good reason because the actual reasons wouldn't go over well. Truth was, he hated looking in books for answers; he called it cheating. I suspected that was because he didn't read very well. He had to rely on what he could figure out, and his talents weren't in plant investigative analysis. That led to stress, and that ultimately led to sampling way more product than he should—often during the workday, and often at the expense of helping me.

"It's an unfamiliar plant," I said with a confident tone, "unlike many he's used to dealing with. I figured since I had a book that offered some advice, I'd just follow those directions while he was seeing to the garden at large. He probably could've. It was my fault, really. It's okay, I can definitely find more plants, I know I can. Then I'll just pick the petals I need rather than the whole flower. They last for a long time off the plant, for some reason. I can keep going back for more. It'll be better this way. More natural."

She tsked softly. "Trying to take the fall for the malfeasance of others, Aurelia? It's commendable, but beneath you. It holds you back, which in turn holds *me* back. Holds us all back. The wellbeing of the people in this village depends on the quality and quantity of your supply. I cannot keep the children in their expensive boots, or with their many learning devices, or keep roofs over their heads without something to sell at market, now can I?"

"No, ma'am," I said dutifully, my stomach twisting at the mention of the children.

"No. And so you'll need to start taking these people in hand. I can't be here all the time."

Uncomfortable tingles washed over me. I didn't want to step into her job. It made me queasy thinking about upholding the rules and doling out punishments for those who broke them. I'd had a history of bearing the brunt of violence, of watching it destroy everything I knew—I couldn't stomach the idea of inflicting that pain on anyone else, even if it was just temporary.

"Yes, ma'am," I said anyway, hoping it didn't come to that.

She squeezed my upper arm. "Good girl. Now, why don't you run along and get some rest, okay? You've earned it."

"Yes, Granny."

I stepped outside, welcoming the cool breeze, and willed the voice from earlier to wash away her sentiments.

Good girl.

But it didn't come. Instead, my stomach continued to pinch painfully, thinking about what she'd said. Thinking about how this might affect Raz. He wasn't the nicest man to me, but I didn't want any blame for his punishments. I didn't want anything I said to make things worse for him. I certainly didn't want to dole out punishments for anyone else.

Since Granny had saved my life and admitted me here, all I'd wanted was to live in the shadows. I'd wanted a safe, if not peaceful life, a place for quiet reflection and to remember my mom. That was it. To obtain that, I'd ensured I had enough value that I couldn't be cast out. But this?

With slight tremors, I made my way back along the path and through the village to my little cottage.

Many of the people in the village feared Granny. They were scared of her punishments, scared of her watch dog, Alexander. I understood why Granny didn't care—sometimes fear was the only way to motivate people. But she didn't live amongst them. She wasn't even here half the time. My situation was different. These people weren't my friends, many weren't even cordial, but they weren't outright enemies, either. Some even tolerated me these days, occasionally smiling in hello when I got my food rations. If I stepped into her shoes, I'd burn all that away. They'd hate me, one and all, obeying me when I had her watchdogs on hand and possibly disposing of me when I didn't. My life would once again become dangerous and there would be no escape. I didn't want that. Couldn't handle it.

There had to be another way. As long as Granny was getting the goods, she wouldn't press too hard about the details. If the orders got bigger, I'd just need to work harder. Faster, somehow.

My mind turning, I tucked myself into my cottage on the east side of the village and built a fire in the hearth. That done, I settled down onto a chair and watched the flames as I ate.

Run. Leave this place.

I blinked rapidly as his words echoed in my mind. The stranger had sounded urgent. Genuine.

Not the stranger . . . me. I'd conjured up those words.

It's not safe for you here. Get out now, tonight. Don't look back. Find your way to another village and disappear. This is the only warning you'll get.

It was almost like I'd known what Granny would want of me. Like I was warning myself that things were starting to turn in this village. But where could I possibly go? No one wanted a person like me around, a lesson learned through bloodshed in youth. Even if I did want to leave, how would I get out? The territory was fortified. The punishment for leaving without an escort, without permission, was extreme.

My breath came fast, my chest tight.

It suddenly felt like I was living in a cage.

But that was silly. Granny did all this to protect me. To keep her competitors from getting to me and kidnapping or killing me. From destroying the village. These safety systems were in place to safeguard our homes. I knew they were necessary. She'd spent many nights, especially over the last three years, going over why.

I'd need to figure this out. I could handle more workload. I could. I could draw less, write less, and work more. It would be fine. We'd figure this out.

As I watched the flame, though, I couldn't help the little voice in the back of my brain wondering what would happen if I didn't heed the warning.

5

AURELIA

The next afternoon, just outside the work shed, I glanced up to find Xarion sauntering toward me. He swung his long arms with a boyish grin spread across his freckled face. Once close, he leaned against a post in the fence by the work shed. The sun highlighted streaks of blond in his otherwise light brown hair.

"What's up, Red?" He squinted into the sun.

I used my forearm to wipe the sweat away from my face, tempering my annoyance at today's work being interrupted.

He was about the same age as me—twenty-seven—and had been the closest thing to a friend I'd ever had. His dad had taken off when he was a baby, and his mom hadn't been overly interested in his upbringing. From twelve to seventeen, we'd hung out almost every day, at first running through the trees or playing ball in the village square, and then experiencing all our intimate firsts together.

Nothing was forever, though. My life had always been proof of that. When he'd started to hang out with his male friends more often, his interest in me quickly waned. Fraternizing with me subjected him to a life of ridicule. Thankfully, by that age, I was already hardened to the emotional backlash of being cast aside or chased away.

He only occasionally stopped by work now, sharing a little gossip and venting about his life. It was a nice distraction from an often mundane existence. It always had been. After the meeting with Granny last night, today just happened to be bad timing.

I quirked an eyebrow at him. "Red? Have you gone blind? My hair is black, not red." I smashed some Twilight Thistle with a pestle.

"It's not all black."

I rolled my eyes. "Black with streaks of gray, then, okay? Let's all take a moment to notice my premature aging."

"It's white, and it's not premature aging or you wouldn't have had it when you first got here."

Premature aging sounded better than extreme trauma. Truth was, I'd developed one streak at a time, each highlighting some terrible event from my past. Since I'd met Granny, I hadn't developed any new streaks. I'd take rules and punishments over my past any day.

"Sure, white, why not?" I said with a shrug. "Not red, though, like Nadia's. Who everyone calls Red . . ."

"But Nadia didn't get a fancy *red* cloak from Granny and you did."

I squinted up at him. "Who's been talking?"

"Joss, who heard from Alexander."

Alexander, Granny's chief muscle. The guy had a mean streak ten miles wide and he didn't care who he took it out on. He liked the feel of bones breaking under his fists. He'd said as much when he'd broken a couple of my ribs. With a smile.

"Not wise, passing around Alexander's gossip," I said noncommittally, going back to my work.

"So Granny didn't get you a lavish gift?"

"It's just a cloak," I deflected.

"It's a velvet cloak with silk lining and it cost her a fortune. Alexander was there when she bought it. She's gotta keep her prized drug maker warm in the cold."

"Cute," I murmured, emptying the fine powder into a bowl and adding more thistle into my mortar.

His smile slipped a bit. "Does it bother you, what the village does now?"

"How many times are you going to ask me this question?" I worked the thistle.

"I don't know. At least once more, probably." He grinned at me, but his expression faded quickly. "It's just . . . it seems like things are getting more serious."

I paused in my work.

I hadn't been joking; it really wasn't wise to pass on anything Alexander said. He sampled the product, but he was smart about it when he did; he made sure Granny wouldn't know. Sometimes, when he was in the midst of a journey, he talked. Often it was about trivial matters, like the women he bedded on the Outside, or how nice his horse was—something the village wasn't afforded. Sometimes, though, he talked about the business. About Granny's strategies and how things were going. On those occasions, once he'd sobered up, he'd realized he'd made a grave mistake. Granny prized him for his discretion, or so I'd heard. On the Outside, he was her most trusted helper. If she knew he'd loosened his lips when in the village, she'd be furious. To stop that from happening, he silenced those he'd told— almost always with his fists.

I scraped my teeth over my bottom lip. If it wasn't for last night and my misgivings, I would've avoided this whole conversation. As it was . . .

"What'd you hear?" I finally asked.

He licked his lips, glancing behind him. "It's just . . . Well . . ." He hesitated.

"Tell me," I pushed.

He took a deep breath. "Apparently Granny has got the blessing of the king and queen."

I shook my head. "What does that mean? Blessing for what?"

"To sell it, what else? Right out in the open." He grimaced. "Not front and center, mind. Her booths have to be in the way back corner of the royal market in a shaded stall, but everyone knows where she is. She has a guard and everything, and the line is a mile long."

"Wait, wait." I held out my hand, trying to process this information. "No, selling unlawful products in the *royal* market, the main kingdom market, is absurd. That can't be right."

His eyes widened, nodding. "That's what Alexander said."

I frowned at him before going back to my work. "When Alexander is in the middle of a journey, he fabricates."

I had no idea if that was true, but given what Xarion was saying, it must be.

He pushed closer to the gate. "He wasn't even that far along. Jennece was fondling him, how he likes, and he was just underway on the journey. He was letting it all spill out. He said that Granny got in to see the king and queen—she'd made special contacts or something—and for a sack of gold, a *sack*, they'd let her sell in the market. In the corner, I mean. Like way in the far corner."

I stopped working again to level him with a look.

"Xarion, be reasonable. This product is against the law of the land. The law that the king and queen uphold. There is no way they'd let it be sold to common folk in the main market."

"They're not doing it for everyone. None of our competitors are getting this sort of perk."

"Which tells you that this is all false. They wouldn't give us special perks and not the others."

"Yes they would. For enough gold."

"They have their own gold. They're the king and queen, Xarion. They have all the gold in the world. What would they need with the few bits Granny has to offer?" I shook my head, dismissing all of this. "There's just no way. I mean . . ." I stopped again, my mind whirling. "A person exploring our product needs to take some care. It's not lethal, but it is habit forming. They need to know what they are getting into. Stalking the shadows and hunting down the seller means the buyer has to have heard about the product from word of mouth and gotten a caution in the process. There's an element of danger in that, both finding the seller and exploring the product. They'd know the whole experience came with a certain risk. Selling in the main market, where there are children and random people stopping by to have a gawk . . ." I shook my head adamantly. "That just can't be. He's leaving out some details. He must be."

"Well . . . I don't know." Xarion shifted his stance, more confident now. "But he did say that they're packing the product up real nice now."

"They've been doing that for years."

"Even nicer, though."

I rolled my eyes. "A nicer package and a bit of gold isn't going to make the king and queen suddenly decide that our unlawful product is totally fine for common people. That doesn't make sense. He probably just wanted to impress you all and keep Jennece's hands on him. I wouldn't put my faith in what he has to say, and I definitely wouldn't keep passing it along. As far as how I feel about all this, I sleep just fine at night, as always. We're giving people the option of escaping their lives for a while. We're not forcing it on anyone and there are no lasting effects. Meanwhile, the village is no longer poor and the children are safe and getting an education —everyone wins."

He watched me work for a silent moment, thinking that over.

"It's not like we're the only ones doing it, either," he finally said.

"Granny says we have steep competition, but our product has gotten so much better we're now beating out the others."

"Right. And we're not even outlawed anymore."

I sighed heavily. "Sure, fine, yeah. If you want to believe that, great."

His boyish grin worked its way back. "You just don't like him."

"Who, Alexander? No, I don't. That's not why—"

"And it isn't *our* product. It's *your* product, Red."

I gave him a flat stare at the name. "I just make it. I don't grow the ingredients."

"You create it, refine it—"

"Okay, okay." I grappled with a grin and waved him off. "Stop. You're going to give me an ego."

"I heard Alexander was busy this morning," he said. "I heard he paid Razorfang a visit."

I slowed in working the thistle. I'd figured that had been the case when I'd shown up this morning and he hadn't been here. He didn't miss days . . . unless he physically couldn't get out of bed.

"How bad?" I asked softly.

"I don't know the specifics, but Granny wasn't there to supervise, so . . ."

Shit.

I straightened up, squinting into the sun. That wasn't good news. It meant Alexander had been let off his leash. The rules then were simple: don't kill or permanently maim. Everything else goes. Granny must've been *pissed*.

There was nothing for it, though. Raz got out of hand. He must've known this would happen when he chose the product over delivering Granny's pack. He'd been down this road a time or two before—he was willingly playing with fire, and this time he'd gotten burned.

I braced my hands on my lower back and bent back, stretching it out. "Raz needs to lay off the product."

"Yeah, I heard Alexander had to pull him out of your supply room this morning. Razorfang made a big mess of the place. Broke a bunch of stuff."

What in the hell had he taken to render him that out of it? He'd never stayed there the whole night before. He must've mixed products, because even a double dose wouldn't have made him that bad.

I poured the powder into a bowl before crossing to the water pump to wash my hands.

Xarion walked with me, stepping behind the pump to work the handle. "Granny isn't going to be thrilled that you knew Razorfang was sampling and you didn't mention it."

I didn't have to. She'd known.

"Let me handle Granny. You should stay out of it."

"Or maybe you won't get in trouble, since you're the favorite around here."

"If I'm the favorite, it's because I work hard and do more than wander around with my thumb up my ass spreading rumors. Maybe you should try to be useful for a change. You might get a fancy cloak all your own."

He snickered. "Nah, I'm good." He stepped back from the pump. "I don't think I'd like her watching my every move and controlling my every step."

"I don't know why not. That's what your mate does."

"Har, har," he said, dogging my heels as I turned for the creek. "Just think, you could've been my mate." He snapped. "Wait, no, that was the real Red. You, I wouldn't touch again for all the gold in the world."

"Is that why you tried to feel me up at the dance last winter? How're your balls, by the way?"

He crinkled his nose at me in jest. He'd been drunk that time, lamenting about peer pressure and not mating me instead of his woman. Then he'd apparently thought he should try to rekindle old flames. I'd reacted without thinking.

I let myself out of the gate and closed it behind me, keeping him on the other side.

"Wait, you didn't hear the really juicy stuff," he said.

I sighed and stopped, my back still to him. If I didn't listen and get it over with, he'd follow me to the creek, chattering. I needed to get a bunch of work done. Granny was leaving in a few days and I still had a lot of product to finish up.

"Go on," I said.

"Well, apparently Granny is trading our product for prices higher than ever. She shows up at the markets like royalty. She hardly deals with the dangerous people anymore. Alexander was pissed that he has to keep it professional all the time now."

I walked slowly away, cocking my head a little. That also had to be preposterous but . . . Alexander's reaction to it rang true. Given he was the one telling the story, though . . .

"Anything else?" I asked, stopping.

He hesitated, his body tense and his expression unsure. "Do you ever wish you could live on the Outside? Get out of here? I know we have everything provided for us, and we shouldn't complain, but . . . don't you find it a little restricting?"

"No," I said, walking again, and it was the truth.

67

Despite my wobble yesterday, I definitely didn't find this place restricting. I found it comforting. I knew who didn't want me within ten feet and who would tolerate me in their space. I knew who would sneak into my cottage for a little sexual relief and who would bash my head in if I so much as hinted at wanting to get intimate. Most importantly, I knew Granny wouldn't let anyone run me out or hurt me too badly. Here, I knew what tomorrow promised. My world was largely predictable. I took solace in that.

After a fast-paced workday, I'd gotten back to my cottage just after sundown. After chopping up meat and vegetables and throwing a stew together, I was just about to sit down and wait for it to be ready when a knock sounded at my door.

Frowning, I checked the contents of the pot, set to hang over an open flame. After stirring it, I crossed to the door and pulled it open.

A brawny man stood on my stoop, his weight leaned back onto his heels and his thick arms crossed over his chest. Alexander. His dirty blond beard reached down past his neck and his light brown hair was kept shaggy. Granny didn't much care about appearances of those in her employ and no one in their right mind was going to say *boo* to this character. All you had to do was look into his slightly manic eyes to know you had other places you'd rather be.

A thrill of fear zipped through me. It was not good news when this guy made house calls. Raz had learned that just this morning.

In the past, Granny had never let Alexander off the leash when dealing with me. I was more fragile than everyone else and didn't heal as quickly. Plus, I had work to do and didn't have a replacement. She'd always been on hand to ensure my punishments didn't get too extreme.

She hadn't shown up today.

Xarion had clearly told him I'd been listening to the gossip, and Alexander had come to ensure my silence.

6

AURELIA

I pulled all of my terror deeply inside of myself so that I was mostly a shell of a person. No emotion would show on my expression or color my tone. It was imperative not to show fear with this guy. He fed on it.

"Making the rounds?" I asked placidly.

His gaze moved down my body slowly, a feeling like spiders crawling over my flesh. "Joss mentioned that Xarion was *talking*."

I leaned against the door frame, the picture of disinterest. "Xarion is always talking. So is Joss." My tone conveyed a rock-solid confidence I did not feel. "So are you, it seems. I can't imagine that is a trait Granny is fond of in you."

He studied me for a moment, no doubt hearing my subtle threat. Unlike the others, Granny gave me an audience. She listened to me. I'd made myself invaluable for just such a reason. If he tried to shove me around, I'd tattle without reservation. Even if what he'd said wasn't true, and I suspected it wasn't, he wouldn't get let off the hook for saying anything at all.

He huffed, a little smile playing across his lips. He knew the score.

"Aren't you going to invite me in?" he finally asked, his eyes sparkling with violence.

"Nope. I have too many memories of the times you forced your way in. It's nice to have a choice this time." Assuming I did have a choice, anyway. That was still up for debate.

"You deserved those other times."

"Maybe, but that doesn't make this situation any more palatable. What do you want? If it's to tell me not to say anything, you don't have to worry about that."

"I know that I don't. I know you'll keep your mouth shut like a good little pet."

"Fantastic. So why did you come?"

"I paid your buddy Xarion a visit. Joss and the others, too. They'll know better than to talk about my business again. You're the only loose end, and we've already established that you know to keep your mouth shut about anything I might've said."

Hatred burned in my gut. "You've had a busy day," I said. "Imagine if you didn't speak when you should remain quiet, you'd have more time to relax."

"What would be the fun in that?"

"What fun, indeed."

He shifted his weight from one foot to the other and then back to center. "You don't need to hear about the Outside from those idiots, you know. You can get what you need directly from the source."

The sexual innuendo dripped from his tongue. He'd

made it very clear over the years that he wanted me in his bed. Thankfully, he would never force the issue, not with Granny watching over me. None of my punishments—no one's punishments—had ever been sexual in nature. That fact had been greatly relieving to many.

Even still, everything in me recoiled at his words. Somehow, I kept my tone light and disinterested. "Is that right?"

"I know that she shelters you, keeps you in the dark. I could shed a little light on things, tell you about the world." He paused for a moment, his gaze at my chest. "I tend to be very chatty after I come."

"Yikes, a little too much oversharing there." I straightened up. "Lovely offer, but I think I'll pass. I'm not overly fond of the outside world. If that's all?"

I grabbed the edge of the door, ready to close it.

He put his hand on the wood to stop me. "I got business with you."

My legs started to shake. Maybe she'd let him off the leash, after all. It took everything in me not to wet my lips in worry. Memories clambered for attention. Him pushing past me and into my little cottage. His fists connecting. His smile down at me as blood trickled into my eye.

"And that is?" I asked.

"I'm your babysitter for tonight. Granny said you had to go looking for flowers in the wood. She doesn't want you to stray too far and think about running."

And just like that, my tight hold on my unenthusiastic responses cracked. I wanted to reach out, grab his neck, and shake him.

"Seriously! I got off course one time and everyone

assumes I was trying to make a break for it. One time in fifteen years. Do you know why it is so fucking annoying?"

His brow furrowed. "I don't care."

"Oh no?" I stepped forward in a rush of anger and jabbed him in the chest. He flinched, stepping off the porch. "I'll tell you anyway, how's that? Quite frankly, I'm incredibly insulted that you all would assume, that *Granny* would assume, I was trying to escape, like this was some sort of cage. I get the reason for needing an escort to the Outside. I understand what would happen to me if the wrong people figured out who I was. I'm fine with all that. I've agreed to it. But to assume I would run . . .?"

Tears threatened to well in my eyes. It almost felt like a betrayal that Granny still kept on about my leaving the path, as though I couldn't be trusted. As though I'd just up and leave my family in the middle of the night. Because she was all I had now. She'd saved me, given me a home, and she was as close to a real granny as I'd ever had. It hurt that she would assume it meant so little to me that I'd walk away without a backward glance.

"I thought she'd had better faith in me than that," I finished, my lower lip trembling. "I'd thought we had better trust in each other." I hesitated at his intense look. "Granny and me, obviously. Not you. You'd probably brain me right now if you could, and smile while you did it."

"I'd fuck you first—"

"But her?" I shook my head, looking to the side.

"Why would I run? Forget that I have nowhere to go, but what would I be running from?"

I turned to look at him again, seeing the answer in his eyes. Him. The punishments. The parts of this village that were a little harder to bear.

"Well, whatever." I wiped my forearm across my nose. "I wasn't running. I won't run. Because again, I have nowhere to go, okay? Happy? This village is my home."

Alexander lifted his hands, his eyes wide. "Wow," he said slowly. Then, "Are you on your period or something?"

I dug my fingernails into my palms. "Fuck off," I said, turning and slamming the door in his face.

"Fine, but we still gotta get flowers," he said through the door. "How long you gonna be?"

I ate and cleaned up, wanting to take my time to annoy him but also wanting to get out into the forest and look for those flowers. The longer I wasted in my cottage, the less time for the flower hunt.

After packing a few random supplies, like a canister of water and a bit of dried fruit and nuts in case the night ran long, I grabbed my lantern and swung the door open. Alexander sat on my top step, looking out at the lane. Pati from up the way was passing by. Usually she'd glance up when I came out of the cottage and spare me a tight smile, but this time she hunched and looked down at her feet. Her shoulders were tensed, her whole body rigid.

"You're a big favorite around these parts," I said, stepping out and closing the door behind me.

He got up slowly, staring after her. "I had to pay her good-for-nothin' mate a visit the last time I was here. He was trying to smuggle out some—" He slid me a side-eye. "More to follow after you suck my cock."

"I'd better not. Small items are a choking hazard."

His eyes narrowed.

"Like you can talk, anyway," he said, following me. I knew exactly where I planned to start looking. "Anyone giving you the time of day in this village is only interested in one thing, your skinny little pal Xarion included."

"My witty banter, is it? My hilarious jokes?"

"Spreading your thighs. That's the only thing you're good for."

"Lovely. But untrue, right? My work gives you a job. My ingenuity affords your lifestyle."

He ignored me. Alexander was only good with his fists. When it came to sparring mentally, he didn't have any weapons.

"Shit detail, this," he finally said as we cut through the village. No one looked our way, their gazes directed downward. "Hunting for fucking flowers in the trees?" He spat. "Why we going this way? You have flowers near your hovel."

"My hovel?" I huffed. The guy lived in a shanty not far from Granny. Was he really throwing stones? "Because the Moonfire Lilies tend to group together and I want to go to the place I found the last one. Hopefully I'll be able to find a few that way."

He grunted and thankfully fell silent.

75

We reached the path that would lead us toward Granny's cottage. My lantern glowed in front of me and he stayed back a ways, not needing its light. The trees once again crowded in, leaning overhead, branches tangled along the sides. The longer we walked, the harder it became for the moonlight to reach the path, until it disappeared altogether, my lantern now the only light I could see by. It didn't take long for emberflies to drift in, sensing we weren't danger and dotting the path and between the trees with pricks of light. Too bad they didn't glow any brighter or maybe they could've filled in where my lantern struggled.

Halfway there, and not yet at the place where I'd had that vivid hallucination, I veered left, holding my lantern high so that I could slip between two slim trunks.

"It was somewhere around here," I said softly, scanning the ground.

"I ain't never seen as many of these bugs in one place as I do around this village," he said, his voice too loud for the serenity of the night. "They must like your stink."

"Or maybe they don't like yours. Hush now. I'm working and you can help." I described the pulse of the flower and where exactly to look, quickly mentioning that if he helped, we wouldn't have to be out here for as long. I knew that would shut him up. "If we wander, you'll know the way back home, right?"

"How do you not know your way around?"

"I do know my way around . . . when I can see more than a small ring around my feet. Otherwise, I have to rely on my directional sense."

"And?"

"I don't have one."

"What a shitty life," he muttered, tromping through the brush. "How can you live like that?"

"How can you make so much noise?"

We walked at a slow, measured pace. Emberflies dotted the way, occasionally going dark as they drifted behind trees, only to lazily pop out again.

"Have you noticed the emberflies kinda seem like they are keeping pace with us?" I murmured, not really caring if he heard or if he answered. "We're not really passing them. They seem to be moving with us as a horde. Usually they kinda drift on their own. I wonder what the deal is."

"They are keeping pace, yeah. It's fucking annoying. It's messing up my vision."

"How so?"

"My eyes keep trying to adjust to their light, as feeble as it is, and it's harder to see in the dark. It feels like I'm not able to peer through the shadows."

"My lantern can't be helping either, then."

"I can kinda . . . shield that a bit, but the bugs are everywhere."

"They have a name. Ember—"

"I don't give a shit. They're bugs. We need a bunch of birds to swoop down and eat the fucking things."

"I wish they had stingers," I muttered, "and an inclination to use them on you."

Onward we went, creeping almost. I walked at random, willing a flower to make itself known. The foliage was thick here, though, dense. Heavy leaves, vines and tangled moss could be caging in the light.

These flowers didn't shine like a beacon; it wouldn't be hard to contain their glow. Even if I was right on top of one, my indigo light would wash away the faded pink of the flower.

"Okay, new plan." I stopped. "I'm going to turn off my lantern. You'll need to direct me, okay? Maybe . . . get in front?"

"You can't see at all? Like . . . not even enough to walk?"

I rounded on him, my temper flaring. Work topics so often blotted out reason, eclipsing my fear of him. "Is pretending to be stupid your natural high? No, I can't see in the dark. You know this. Everyone knows this. Why do you think Granny got me this lantern?"

His power surged alongside his dissatisfaction at my insubordination. I was too frustrated with him and my situation to let it cull me. "She got it because it's a faerie lantern and you have some huge bullshit love of faerie shit. Keep you happy, keep our clients happy. That's why she got it." He paused for a beat, staring me down. "And because you can't see in the dark, yeah. But like . . . not at *all*, though? The moon is out tonight."

"It's barely a sliver!" I looked up at the dense canopy. Even if there was space up there between the reaching branches, the weak light from a sliver moon wouldn't do much to help me. "I need your help. It's why you're here."

He heaved a loud, exasperated sigh. "I see now why you don't have a mate."

"I've always seen why you don't. Come on, hurry up. I really want to find one of those flowers tonight." I reached out and took his arm, only to have him rip it away again. "Fine, move on your own. Just *move*."

"I hate this," he grumbled, stepping over a fallen branch and shuffling in front of me. "I still want to fuck you, because you're a nice slice of ass, but now I'll cover your mouth when I do it."

"Fantastic. Very charming. After I switch off the lantern, I do have to hold on to part of you for this to work, you know. Not your cock, either."

"Do you think I'm crazy?" he asked, half looking over his shoulder.

I wasn't quite sure what that was in relation to, since he'd been talking about cock-related topics since he'd first shown up on my doorstep, so I let it go.

"Just hold still," I told him, tapping off my lantern. Darkness rushed in to envelop us both, and while I did see a few weak patches of light way up in the trees and the soft glowing orbs from the emberflies, I couldn't see the ground or him in front of me.

"Here we go," I said softly, hooking my lantern onto my pack as I heard a foot crunch onto the ground. Then another. "Wait, are you moving?"

"You said go!"

"Did you fail to notice that I was not holding onto your shirt?"

"I thought you changed your mind." His boots crunched onto the ground again, coming back.

"You wonder how I go through life without seeing in the dark?" I reached forward, connecting with his shoulder. "How do you go through without a brain? I'm not the one people should be pitying."

"They're too scared to pity me," he growled. "You might take a hint."

"What's the fun in that?" I said, repeating him from earlier.

When he didn't start walking, I sighed.

"*Now* you can go," I said.

"Are you sure? I wouldn't want to walk away and leave you room to run for it."

My nails dug into him. His dark chuckle said he'd meant to affect me.

Finally he started walking, going just as slow as before. I stepped gingerly, my eyes scanning, ready to fall to the side if my foot caught rather than fall against him. I didn't want any more bodily contact than was absolutely necessary.

"What about that?" he said, stopping.

"What?"

"That!"

I scanned first one side for a glow, and then the other. "I can't see where you're pointing." I turned to look behind just in case. "I don't see any . . ."

My words drifted away as I noticed the emberflies begin to move. They started slowly, as though a heavy breeze were blowing them right. And then they picked up speed, getting out of the area, scattering every way but one. The way danger was obviously coming.

The events of the night before flashed through my mind. The emberflies scattering, the presence, the hallucination.

I dropped my hand from Alexander and took a step back. I could not imagine how I might've accidentally dosed myself, but just in case, I didn't want any touching. I wasn't sure what would be worse: danger finding me or sharing one of those hallucinations with Alexander.

"See it—" He cut off as a wolf howled in the distance. I heard the soles of his shoes scrape against the ground. He swore softly. "Run. Hide! Don't go home. Find a secure place and wait until I come for you."

"Wh-what?" I said stupidly. What sort of danger would keep me from going back to my cottage, something dangerous enough that even Alexander was afraid of it?

Something rustled, like fabric being stripped.

"What do you see?" I whispered urgently, alarm rising within me.

The emberflies cleared away and hands grabbed my arms. Foul breath washed across my face.

"*Go,* you stupid bitch. What are you waiting for?" He shoved me.

Not expecting it, my feet tangled in the vegetation underfoot, sending me to my hands and knees.

"Idiot," I heard before a sort of *whoosh*. Footsteps on a smaller scale pattered across the ground. He'd shifted into his wolf form and was hurrying away.

"Don't leave me! *Wait,*" I hissed, reaching around to grab the lantern from my pack.

I found it quickly and didn't waste any time in setting it to glow, getting up while I did so. Seen easily for a decent distance through the trees, it would act like a beacon. Without it, though, I was a sitting duck. I couldn't even hurry to get away, especially since I'd lost the thread of what direction we'd been heading.

The indigo glow highlighted the area around me. My breath was loud in the sudden stillness.

Hide? Where the hell was I supposed to go? Any shifter or forest beast would be able to smell me if I stayed outside. If I couldn't go home, I doubted I could go to the work shed. No one in this village would take me in, especially if danger followed.

There was only one place I could think of. Only one safe space I knew.

I took off at a jog, light held low, focused on the ground. I'd be damned if I would fall this time. My ankle had been miraculously healed the night before—the issue likely (hopefully) conjured by my mind in the first place—but I would not let it happen this time.

Trees seemed to ghost by me in the darkness. My breath came in fast pants. A few bushes caught my eye in certain configurations that looked familiar. Ferns were interspersed within the plants, and I recognized a bush with purple flowers.

Left! The path to Granny's was left.

I emerged onto it with a sigh that was short lived.

Vicious growls tore through the night. Baying. Loud whimpering-screams. They were battling somewhere to my right.

My heart shoved up into my throat. I worried they might've found Granny.

I dropped my pack and ran faster, with only the lantern now, the light bobbing and jiggling. Little shadows played across the path, hinting of uneven ground and rocks. I avoided them as best I could, hitting one but not going down. Around the bend and the trees started to thin a little, letting in a little of the weak light from the sky. Further along and they continued to clear, the moon and starlight giving me a shimmery view of what awaited me.

Granny's cottage sat in the little clearing, a stump outside with an axe sticking out of it. A woodpile was stacked neatly a little way behind it. Smoke curled up from the chimney and the area around it lay quiet. Still.

"Oh thank the gods their mercy," I whispered, not slowing. I chanced a look to either side as I passed, seeking out any hulking forms that might be waiting in the shadows. Looking for any evidence that the enemy had been here.

Nothing seemed out of place. I felt no strange presences or danger. No watchful eyes. Still, butterflies exploded through my middle in anticipation.

Nearing the cottage, I slowed and veered so I wasn't headed toward the windows. Closer still and I doused the lantern, just in case.

Then I grabbed that axe—also just in case.

I hadn't had to exert real violence in fifteen years and hadn't killed anyone in just as long. That didn't mean I wasn't capable of it anymore. I might not have genuine magic, but I had the innate ability to survive, and nothing, man or beast, would stand in my way of that. I'd proven it before, and I'd prove it again if necessary.

I hoped it wasn't necessary.

My limbs shook. My grip on the handle was too tight.

I put the lantern just outside the door, grabbed the door handle, and paused for a deep breath. A moment later I was action, ripping the door open and stepping through, expecting to see Granny in the chair by the fire or the room empty. Instead, several large figures crowded the space.

They turned as one just as I spied what they'd been looking at.

In the corner, with curled hair and a mangled face, lay the woman who'd saved me. Who'd taken me in when no one else would even speak to me. Who'd given me a home, a job, a *life*.

Her clothes were in tatters, ripped through with claws or teeth. A limb was severed. Blood had stopped flowing from the deep gash in her throat.

Dead.

My world spun in dizzying circles. The need to be sick clawed up my throat. I wanted to scream, to rage, to faint. All I could do was stand there, though, staring at the mangled and disfigured form of my last remaining family member. The only person in the world who had cared about me.

One of the enemies reached forward to grab me as emotional agony screamed through me. Adrenaline followed.

With a wordless howl, I launched into the small area. My axe came down hard, breaking bone and sticking into flesh. Blood splattered my face, my hair, painting my clothes like a scarlet canvas. The name Red would now take on a much darker tone.

I yanked the axe free as though my strength had doubled and swung at the next, who rushed toward me. I lodged it into his chest and punched over it, hitting his nose. His head snapped back, giving me time to yank the axe head free and throw it between the first two toward a third. It stuck in her chest and surprise lit her face. She looked down with her hands spread out, as though she couldn't fathom how the axe had gotten there.

I grabbed the nearest weapon I could find—unfortunately, just a knitting needle—and prepared to pay them their due. I turned toward the first guy, who was struggling to stand. These people were tough. Usually, the first vicious wound would send most people scattering.

I held the needle aloft as the door swung open behind me, a blast of air invading the small, musty space. With it came the most mouth-watering smell: sun-warmed sandalwood with hints of jasmine and peppered with forbidden sin.

Forbidden sin was not a smell, and yet, that's what my brain made of it, something I might have ignored when I thought I was hallucinating.

This was not a hallucination.

My stomach tightened but my muscles unexpectedly loosened as I turned, the other people forgotten. In my head, panic and dread and incredulity and disbelief all fought for dominance.

Large shoulders filled the doorway, the robust frame just as I'd remembered. Tall. Muscled. Powerful thighs I'd held onto while his hard dick fucked deep into my mouth.

What the fuck?

Last night hadn't been a hallucination. I'd fucked a stranger. An intruder.

The enemy.

The man whose people were responsible for killing the only family I'd had left. Because it was clear he was in charge. It showed in his confident bearing, in his air of authority, in the way he looked everyone dead on, not lowering his gaze for anyone.

I flashed my teeth and stepped forward, knitting needle at its zenith. This wouldn't kill him, but maybe if I could manage hitting his eye, it would maim him for life.

7

WESTON

*H*ere, with more light, I could see her in minute detail. She was so beautiful it hurt to breathe. Perfection in the flesh, my dream woman conjured up for just me to enjoy.

Her teeth were bared and pain showed clearly in her beautiful sunburst eyes as she advanced on me with some sort of long, thin object. It looked almost like a knitting needle, aimed for my face. Stunned by her appearance and aggression, by the exquisite feel of her presence, I didn't move.

"I got it, Alpha." Dante labored forward, blood pouring from a deep wound in his shoulder. He also held a weapon of sorts, something round and blunt. He swung it toward her before I could snap myself out of my stupor.

"No," I barked, reaching forward to stop him but it was too late. He crashed the object down onto her head with a sickening *crack*.

Bile rose up into my throat. I struck out before I'd thought about it, landing a hard blow to his wound. He sucked in a surprised breath, his knees giving out. He sank to the ground as I grabbed the crumpling woman. Her feeble weapon fell from suddenly limp fingers and tinkled along the floor.

"No one touches her," I growled, anger riding that command. I sank to the ground with her in my arms, one hand on her head to stem the flow of blood and the other arm wrapped around her back. Her skull was crushed in that area, the bone splintered. A shifter would come back easily. She would not.

Panic quickened my heart.

"Hurry! Tanix, get the Everlass elixir. The miracle worker."

"Yes, Alpha," Tanix said, yanking an axe out of Sixten's chest as he passed by. Tanix was the only one of the four in the room who hadn't felt my true mate's wrath.

I squashed down the pride. She wasn't *mine*. I had to remember that. She was a stranger, an enemy. She was nothing but a natural, magical connection that I had no control over. It didn't somehow make her the love of my life. It just made me want to fuck her.

"And protect her, and claim her as ours," my wolf said, and that was true, too. But none of that was anything I could give in to. My duty and my kingdom forbade it, as did all the people I was sworn to lead and protect.

"What's . . . going on?" Sixten said as Dante gave a ragged cough from where he still knelt, bowed in pain. "Why are we patching up the enemy?"

I gritted my teeth and thought about lying. I'd never

be able to hide this, though, not for any length of time. My body would respond to her even if I did not.

"First, because I have reason to believe she's one of the people we came here to find," I said, my voice filling the small space. "I cataloged her leaving the workhouse on the edge of the forest, by the creek. It's very likely she has a hand in creating the product we're trying to eradicate. Second . . ." I swallowed, not wanting to admit my connection to someone who'd done such terrible deeds. "She's my true mate."

Sixten sucked in a sharp breath. Dead silence filled the cottage for a long moment. The atmosphere changed, shifted, now heavy with uncertainty and shock.

"Are you sure, Alpha?" Dante said. "She's hot, but maybe—"

"Enough," I barked, rage spiking at his notice of her.

"Of course he's sure, idiot," Sixten murmured, her hand still palming her chest. Dark red blood seeped down to her belt line. "The second someone meets their true mate, they *know.*"

"And you saw her last night?" Niven asked, arms wrapped around the axe wound in his stomach.

"Yes. I knew then." I didn't elaborate about what happened after. "Her animal is suppressed. As far as I can tell, it always has been."

"Can you feel it calling to your wolf?" Sixten asked in a hush.

"Yes, but it'll remain suppressed. She's already deadly fast and agile. I assume she is, at any rate, given the state of you lot."

All three nodded slowly.

Dante said, "I didn't even have time to react, bro. She was wicked fast."

"Wicked fast," Sixten repeated. "She nearly sliced off a tit. I didn't see it coming and I was the third to get a whack."

Tanix hurried back in, both hands holding an elixir. He held one up. "Miracle cure or"—he held up the other —"normal cure?"

"Miracle," I said softly, bowed over the woman with one hand still on the bleeding wound and the other across her neck, two fingers feeling her pulse flutter too rapidly. She was losing too much blood. "Hurry!"

"I'm just going to sit over here and put my feet up for a sec," Sixten groaned, staggering to a rocking chair facing a smoldering fire. "Damn it, how does this lady not have a foot rest? What is this horrible place?"

Tanix knelt beside me. "Let her go, Alpha. I've got it."

"Bro, that's his true mate." Dante wiped his forehead. "How's he gonna let her go when she's all fucked up like that. Just give her the stuff."

Tanix's head didn't snap up to look at me as I'd expected. Instead, he nodded like he'd already known and pulled out a syringe. She was unconscious so she couldn't simply swallow; injecting the elixir was the best way to administer it, and would yield the fastest results.

I forced myself to unlatch my grip and pull back my hands, giving him some space.

"I need a numbing agent or something," Niven murmured, leaning hard against the wall. "Or that other elixir. She got me good. How the hell can she move like that without access to her animal?"

"She obviously has a shit load of power, fuckwad," Dante replied. "She's the Alpha's true mate. Have you ever met an alpha as powerful as him? No. Even without access to her animal, she's lethal." Dante issued a prolonged grunt, forming a ball on the ground. "Fuck this hurts. Like . . . this really fucking hurts. I want a numbing agent too. An *axe*? This is the first time I've been cleaved. Cloven? I don't even know the right term for it!"

"It sucks—that's the term for it. I just stood there and watched as it happened, too." Niven straightened up a little, his expression tight. "I saw her cut into you, then just stupidly watched her prance toward me with the edge dripping blood."

"She threw that fucking thing perfectly, that's my excuse," Sixten said, her head resting on the back of the rocking chair. "Well . . . that and she's seriously fucking beautiful. I was too busy being jealous—"

"That's enough," I barked, issuing a pulse of power within that command. "You four should've been watching for any enemy we missed along the perimeter."

"Yes, Alpha," Sixten said dutifully, though we were pretty well secured at this point. We'd taken out the sentries with no problem, as well as most of the patrol. They hadn't known when they were beaten, rising up against my pack only to be efficiently struck down. I'd roped the rest of their patrol into our pack bond, holding them for now. They'd be smuggled out of this kingdom and placed before the dragon king and queen for their part in the atrocities they'd committed. They'd have their day of judgment, and dragons were not so lenient as wolves.

"It felt like she stunned us," Tanix said, leaning back and looking at the woman. "Confused us might be a better term. It was like a whirlwind, almost. I knew something was happening but couldn't seem to react as I normally would have." He shook his head. "If you weren't sure she was your true mate, I'd wonder if she was even a shifter."

"She's a shifter," I said, doing everything in my power not to lean forward and cup her head. It was still gushing blood, pooling on the ground underneath her head. That elixir would heal her, though. Anything enhanced with the blood of a phoenix, a mythical and incredibly rare type of shifter, could bring people back from the brink of death. All we had to do was wait.

"What are we going to do with her?" Tanix asked me, his expression neutral and his eyes full of pity.

He was asking if I'd go through with this, knowing if they killed her, it would kill a piece of me as well. I'd feel her loss even though I didn't even know her. That's what everyone said would happen, at any rate. Given the tight knot in my middle at seeing her bleeding now, it was probably accurate.

I steeled myself. "I'm going to fulfill my duty. I'll deliver her to the dragon king and queen, as promised. She committed a crime against the people in my care. She will face judgment for her sins."

The room was quiet as I watched her face, my fingers on her pulse, feeling it struggle to keep going. I wanted to hug her to me. To carry her in my arms and secure her in our—no, *my* tent, watching over her until she got better.

I clenched my jaw. That was a primal response. It wasn't rational. I didn't even know this woman, and given what she did for a living, I didn't want to. I could not give in to nature's siren song.

"Put her in Hadriel's care." I pulled my fingers away from her and forced myself to stand. "The rest of you, get the healing you need and meet us in the village."

"Yes, alpha," they all said dutifully if not exactly sharply.

I rolled out my shoulders as Tanix scooped her up carefully and carried her from the room. I pulled my gaze away, refusing the suddenly overwhelming urge to rip her from his grasp and carry her myself.

"Anything of note in this cottage?" I asked when he'd gone, closing my eyes against the woman's lingering scent.

"Yeah. The axe wielder has been here before," Sixten said. "Someone stoke that fire. It's cold, isn't it?"

"No, you're just dying, thank the gods," Dante said, still curled up in a ball. "I'm tired of listening to you snore."

"Won't you feel bad if I am actually dying," Sixten muttered.

"No," Dante replied.

"There's only a few scents around this place, and hers is one of them." Niven pulled his crimson arms away from his stomach. He looked down at the wound, stitching together fast. "From what we know of Granny, she keeps her private quarters in the city for essential personnel only. It means the axe wielder was important. If she was in the workhouse, as you said, she's likely important in their operation. Does she also have a personal connection? That's the question."

"It's a good thing our fearless leader punched Dante where it'd hurt the most and ensured her survival," Sixten said. "Though punching him might've just been for funsies."

"We're going to see how you like getting punched for funsies just as soon as I can use this arm, how about that?" Dante bit back.

I picked through the various items around the cottage seeing very little of note. "Granny doesn't have personal connections. Anyone around her is expendable."

"Begging your pardon, sir," Niven said, "but that's true of anyone around her *in the city*. She could be hiding a relative away in this forgotten place."

"Forgotten?" Sixten huffed. "This place isn't forgotten. It's secludedness has been orchestrated. Don't you remember learning that Granny shut down all trade routes of the neighboring villages and forced those people to move nearer Ridge Town or starve? I'm not convinced she didn't kill a few people off to make the situation a threat, as well. That woman is ruthless. Then she fortified the territory boundary and populated the outer forest with demon beasts, magically kept to the area. I mean, for all intents and purposes, she made this town an island. She cut these people off from the outside world."

"And then people forgot about the village, yes," Niven said patiently. "I figured we could all surmise the *how* of it and skip to the important points."

"Like?" Sixten pushed, her attitude hard to manage when she was healing from a wound.

"Like the fact that there is a scent in Granny's personal space that we don't recognize from the city. The owner of that scent has been stashed in this territory for safekeeping, and she could be the key to this whole operation."

Silence rang in his wake. It was a succinct summary and my insides felt like they were shriveling in response to it.

She could be the key to this whole operation.

She could be enemy number two, second-in-command behind Granny.

"Let's see what Granny was hiding," I growled, leaving the cottage, needing air. The idea that my true mate could be responsible for the largest, most expansive drug trade in the magical world and the horror it had brought to so many sickened me. Her connection to me sickened me. The gods were punishing me—it had to be. Karma had come back around for the part I'd played in this very kingdom, stealing people, ripping apart families. How fitting that my true mate would be doing the same thing with the new-found blessing of the crown.

"Wait—dang that axe! I'll meet up with you—" Sixten was cut off as I slammed the door shut behind me.

Tanix in wolf form loped up in the quiet. None of the night creatures made a sound. They clearly felt danger in their midst, as they had last night, at least until the woman and I had been thoroughly engaged. Then they'd crept back in, the glow bugs lending an ethereal quality to the moment.

I shoved the memory from my mind and started walking in my human form. Tanix shifted immediately from a gray wolf to a brawny man with red-gold hair worn tight to his head, low eyebrows and a mean expression. He fell in at my side. I noticed his glance down at my rigid cock.

"You didn't seem surprised," I said.

"In the cottage, I recognized her scent from last night when you came back from checking things out. I'd figured you'd killed someone and didn't feel it necessary to let me know. When she came in, though, I knew it had to be something else. Something more . . . dire to explain your loss of control."

Dire. That was the right word for it. *Very astute, Tanix.*

He'd served time in the demon dungeons with me. He'd followed me to the dragon kingdom and stayed with me there, challenging to become my next in line. Not a lot got past him where it concerned me.

Just this once, I wished that wasn't the case. I didn't want him knowing my struggle to keep her at a distance, and I definitely didn't want him nervous that she would prevent me from doing my duty. Those were two things I badly wanted to hide from the pack.

"Last night I had been blindsided by her," I said by way of explanation. "Today I recognized her for what she almost certainly is—the creator. One of them, at any rate. We'll protect her until we can get her back to the dragons. Then we'll hand her over. They are not a forgiving breed. She'll see her justice."

Bile tasted acidic in the back of my throat. I swallowed it down. I would do what was necessary, regardless of how it affected me. That was what it meant to be an alpha, second in the kingdom only to the king and queen.

He was quiet for a moment. "Understood," he finally said. "For now, she's secure with Hadriel. I filled him in on the situation while I was tying her up. She might be fast, but she doesn't have the strength to break the ropes. She'll be there when we get back."

Damn it, I couldn't read his tone. What was he suggesting, that I wanted her there for personal reasons? Intimate, sexual reasons unlike any I'd ever experienced? To use her maybe, until I had to give her away, knowing she'd be using me in the process. She'd probably try to loosen me up, to work on my primal desire to protect her so I'd let her free.

Heat boiled my blood. I didn't care why, I wanted her to use me. It was a testament to how desperately I craved her. The last time I was used, it was against my will, my body languishing in a dungeon. I never thought I'd willingly give up that kind of control again. Yet here I was, wanting her to take what she desired from me, as many times as she wanted, drawing out her pleasure as she bobbed on my cock and then struggled to take my knot.

Butterflies filled my belly, but I shoved those thoughts away. "For questioning," I said firmly.

His pause was brief. "Exactly. For questioning."

This time I could read his tone all too clearly. He hadn't been thinking of anything more than our duty.

Fuck. She was so thoroughly in my head that I was even questioning those most loyal to the cause. He'd never want anything but to turn her over or kill her on the spot. I knew that. She'd been responsible for the death of his sister. He probably worried I'd grow weak and set her loose, allowing her to continue in her dangerous profession.

I didn't know what to say to secure his confidence, so I said nothing. I'd have to show him I would remain loyal to the cause, regardless of this trial. This punishment from the gods.

"One thing, Alpha," Tanix said.

"Go on."

"Is Hadriel not an odd choice to watch her? He only wanted to come on this expedition for a little excitement and to see his old kingdom. I know he was entrusted to watch the queen back when the kingdom was cursed, but he turned into her accomplice more than her jailor. He says himself that he's nothing but mediocre, something he's proven on this expedition."

"You haven't heard even a quarter of the stories. His ability to steer the queen and king through that dark time is commendable. To even survive in that castle when the demons ran it is exceptional. We didn't fare so well, as you recall. He's a lot more than he looks, trust me. He'll manage her just fine. She'll be there when we get back and he'll stay the course as befits the kingdom."

I didn't say it, because I hated that I even thought it, but men were his sexual preference. He would not be drawn to her beauty beyond appreciating it, like studying a piece of art. I might hate myself for it, but it didn't change the fact that I didn't want anyone else to touch her.

A travel pack waited on the path as though dropped and forgotten. I bent to it, catching her scent. She must've discarded it in her haste to get to Granny's cottage.

My fingers wrapped around the strap before I could think it through, pulling it in to my chest. Tanix's hand came out, offering to carry it. Him holding any items of note was standard procedure. He did it all the time. Yet this time, I couldn't help a low growl in the back of my throat, gripping her pack a little tighter. He backed off. Her things would stay with me.

We continued on until we reached the spot burned into my brain from last night. I'd dreamed of her, of my hands running along her curves, of working my cock deep inside her pussy. I'd fantasized this morning about doing it again, losing myself in her hard suction, her tight grip.

It made no sense how true mates worked. I shouldn't be this attracted to a perfect stranger. I shouldn't feel this pull to go back to her and ensure her safety. It wasn't natural. I didn't even know her name! Her very presence had the ability to undo everything I'd worked so hard to build, and I had zero say in it.

The path split off toward the village and I stopped, going over the timing of this invasion. By now, the pack would have secured the workhouse. They'd been instructed to go there first while another group took Granny's cottage. The garden should've been locked down by now, too, also a good distance away from the village. We'd scouted the locations ahead of time but hadn't stationed anyone close by in case they caught our scent or noticed any tracks. I'd need to visit both, collecting evidence from one and writing out detailed notes and getting samples from the other. The pack might not be within the village yet, quelling any rebellion.

"Should we check out the workhouse first?" Tanix asked, clearly doing the math as well.

Curse me, but I wanted to see where the woman lived. I wanted to look through her things and stand within that entrancing smell, unlike anything I'd ever experienced. This would be the only opportunity I'd have for a glimpse into her personal life. I wanted to get to it as soon as I possibly could, wading through any angry villagers if I must.

But that was stupid. Reckless. I had to maintain some semblance of rationality here!

I gave Tanix a curt nod and started forward again, toward the workhouse.

The path widened the closer we got until a clearing opened up under the pale moonlight. As expected, my people were there, though only a few of them stood sentry around the building.

"What news?" I asked as I approached, finding the door standing open and Nova stationed beside it.

She had pulled her dark hair into a tight bun but, like the rest of them, hadn't donned any clothing yet. We didn't know if we'd need to quickly shift and continue to battle. Granny's people hadn't posed much of a threat for an alpha like me or my detail, despite its small size, but the old woman was cunning. There was no telling what surprises might await us before we left this place with the prize.

No, not the prize. The villain.

"It was empty when we got here. No guards, no booby traps, nothing. No one has come by."

I furrowed my brow as she stepped farther away, giving me space. Why wouldn't they have at least one guard protecting the heart of their operation? That was odd.

The door moved on well-oiled hinges. A mostly clean and orderly work area presented itself. Tubs lined the walls, some with water and some with dried plants, not unlike the queen's workhouses. Instead of tables, though, they had three desks. One was close to the door and mostly bare, holding a few items that maybe didn't have a home elsewhere. Another was pushed against the back wall, a mess of plants and dirt and gardening tools on its surface, their placements haphazard and the tools not well cared for. The person working at that station didn't seem overly fond of the work. That, or they were a horrible slob. Maybe both.

The final desk, sitting in a far corner, held various canisters and jars. A tub sat next to that with vines soaking within. It looked as though everything was placed in a specific spot, as orderly as most of the work-house itself.

She was the boss—I'd bet my life on it. The one who called the shots and mixed the product. The operation's heart and soul.

"It's tiny," Tanix said, having walked in behind me. "For the amount of product they produce, I mean. I would've assumed their workhouse would be three times this size."

"Check with Nova to make sure we didn't miss any work areas. Maybe the garden has a space that we missed."

I found myself sitting at the desk in the corner

without remembering how I'd gotten there, her pack placed delicately on the floor beside my feet. I didn't need her scent to tell me she worked here day in and day out. It had her feel about it, her essence. From just two meetings I knew it like I knew myself, the feeling etched into my soul.

I placed my palms on the flat workspace and then traced a couple grooves that had been cut into the wood. The edges of those grooves were dulled now, perhaps having been a novice's mistake from long ago. No new scratches existed, demonstrating a mastery at work. The surface shone as though freshly cleaned, maybe tidied at the end of each day. Polished, too, though that didn't smell fresh.

I bent to peer in the little cubbies on the right side, each labeled with a delicate, loopy scroll. The left had drawers and I opened each one, breathing in her scent, envisioning her sitting here, completing her tasks. She was probably studious, missing no details, painstakingly getting each part of the process correct. A hard worker, diligent.

Did she smile while she worked? Did she sit there, humming a little tune, unbothered by the destruction she was creating in the world beyond?

Another thought flashed. Maybe she wasn't happy at all. Maybe she was forced into this labor, toiling at a job she didn't have a choice in.

But if that were the case, would she really try to defend her mistress? Take on a room full of warriors with nothing but an axe? Those weren't the actions of a captive.

Her tools were clean, well-tended to. The canisters

and jars stood in a perfect line along the side. I pushed one just a bit out of line and wondered if she'd immediately fix it when she sat down to work, or if she only straightened everything at the day's end. Not that I'd ever find out. We had her now, their drug maker. The brains behind this operation. The "talent." She was done with this line of work; I'd make sure of it.

Disgusted with myself, I pushed up to standing.

Tanix stepped back into the room after talking with Nova and I was glad he missed my overly detailed analysis of the workstation.

"Nova says they found a work area in the garden, but it's for pruning. Not for mixing," Tanix said, standing by the wall. "There's another little work area outside here, which we've seen, and the one by the creek, even smaller. Which we've also seen. Nothing else."

I nodded, crossing to the other desk. "The woman we caught is obviously the backbone of this organization."

"Is that her desk then?" Tanix jerked his chin toward the desk in the corner.

"Yes. This other desk has another scent entirely. It's habitually used, as well. We need to find the person responsible."

"The pack is spreading into the village now. We can place the other scents—the one from this shed and the other in the garden—once we have better access to the villagers."

"Good." I bent to the messy surface, pushing a pair of garden sheers out of the way. A note was scratched into the desk, the scribble looking almost like that of a child.

Grow eyes in the back of your head, son. She's wily. She'll stick a knife in your back.

8

WESTON

I looked behind me, half expecting someone to be advancing with a weapon. An axe, maybe.

"Check this out." I tapped it and stepped to the side, shuffling through the other items.

Tanix joined me, leaning over to read it. He looked behind, as well, and I couldn't help a grin.

"It seems the little axe wielder has her co-contributors nervous." I found another note and shoved an iron spike out of the way to read it.

They are her spies. Do not trust the glow bugs.

"Or maybe this guy is bananas," I murmured.

"There's another written on this side." Tanix knelt around the desk and then tilted his head to read it. "This one is warning about the moon flash boiling the blood." He stood, an eyebrow arched. "These are not the scribblings of a rational man."

"Mr. Gardener might be partaking in his own creations." I pulled open the door at the back, finding some sort of closet with shelves lining the wall. Broken glass littered the ground, and appliances, some smashed or broken, were scattered about. Only the top two shelves were intact, the appliances placed neatly in a line. By the woman.

I'd bet my life on it.

"Did they know we were coming, then?" I reached, taking one down. "Were they trying to quickly get rid of the evidence?"

"The blood is fairly fresh, but not entirely recent. Last night, maybe?"

"Before we invaded."

"But not before you saw the woman . . ."

I stiffened. He was correct. Not before.

"If my . . . slip up was the reason," I said, grabbing another mechanism and pulling them both out, "why not discard the top rows?"

Tanix shook his head, reaching for what I held. I handed those over and pointed back at the closet.

"Pack them all up, even the broken ones. We'll have the woman tell us what they do. The queen might be interested."

"Yes, Alpha." Tanix grabbed a broom from the corner and swept the glass away as he worked into the closet.

I paused near the hearth, finding her scent. I examined the baskets and various items there.

"More notes in here," Tanix called. "'The colors are dancing and blending like a cosmic symphony. That one's actually pretty."

"What'd I miss?" I heard as Dante showed up.

"'I've discovered the hidden pattern of nature'," Tanix read, having moved to another one. He paused. "This other one is written with the words all backwards. Weird. 'My mind . . . has dissolved into . . . a fragile illusion . . . of nothingness.'"

"It seems our gardener moonlights as a drugged-out poet." I spied the instruments Tanix was removing. They seemed to have clunky modifications, many taped on or glued, stuck together in odd ways. Whoever did this was no expert, and yet, despite most being broken, they were worn in, some with soot clinging to the sides or traces of dirt lining a pour spout.

"Sixten?" I asked Dante.

"She headed toward the village to see how that was going," he said, looking around. "This is it? Just two desks being used? No tables or anything?"

"Seems so, though Mr. Poet doesn't seem like much of a help, based on his work station," I said. "Maybe there's another workhouse in the village proper. They're checking it out now."

"These are . . . odd." Dante stood from the appliances Tanix had brought out. "Obviously used but not as intended. Someone's made alterations. Mr. Poet?"

I shook my head minutely, pausing as a faint light caught my notice. Pale pink glowed from within a small basket beside the closet door, strengthening slowly.

A solitary flower with a few discarded petals lay at the bottom of the basket. The petals themselves created the glow.

"Look at this," I said, picking up the basket and holding it out for the others.

Tanix took it, his face glowing pink as he peered in. "That's pretty. I've never heard of a glowing flower."

"Neither have I, and I've walked within the royal

garden with the queen as she mutters about her plants. She doesn't have any like this. I would've noticed." I gestured for him to keep it. "We'll need to ask Mr. Poet what it is, if we can find him."

"Or the woman," Dante said, standing by a small bookcase set by the front window. "She'd surely know her ingredients. Here we go." He held up a piece of paper. "We have our product order." He shook it. "This is quite a list. There *has* to be more workstations to fulfill this. Or else the axe wielder does nothing but work, day and night."

Nova poked her head in the door. "Alpha, we've got something. Looks like the finished product was kept in a storeroom in the village. The pack has it secured, along with the village. There was no push-back from the villagers."

"None?" I asked in surprise, collecting the woman's pack and headed for the door.

"No, Alpha," Nova said, waiting until I exited and falling in beside me. "Some stayed on their porches, watching us walk through, but most kept to their . . . cottages, we'll call them. No one shifted."

I frowned at that news. We had been expecting anywhere from a little to a great deal of resistance. This was a village of shifters, after all. Our kind protected their territories, and if not their territories, at least their homes. It was baked into our blood, part of our magic. We didn't throw out the red carpet to invasions. At least, I'd always thought that was the case . . .

"Let's check out the garden first, as planned," I said, continuing to ignore my desire to head to the village.

When we reached it, I stopped abruptly.

"What a . . . *mess*," Dante said in disgust.

"Our scouts don't know what they are looking at in terms of gardening." Nova looked everything over. "That's probably why they didn't mention the mess. But they did mention they'd found four scents. Two were those from the workhouse, and another two from here. All four they've found in the village."

"So they've found Mr. Poet, then?" I asked.

"Yes, Alpha."

Her tone was sharp. She didn't offer any other information. She handed me items to take notes with.

I nodded as I started forward again. Various plants grew somewhat wild, all mixed together it seemed, with weeds and grasses growing between and around. Garden tools lay discarded randomly, maybe used and left to the side? Tanix stepped on the end of a hoe he clearly hadn't seen, hiding in the weeds. It swung up and slapped him in the chin.

"Goat fuckers!" he exclaimed, kicking it. Dante guffawed.

"This cannot be the garden they use for their operation," I mused, taking samples and writing what notes I could. Nothing was labeled and I was no expert. We'd need the villagers to name the various plants. "It's chaotic. How do they find anything?"

"Something definitely seems off about all this," Tanix said, rubbing his chin. He pulled a clipboard from a small table within an overhang. "One person and a nutcase to create all that product with a team of drunk gardeners? It's not possible."

I handed off the items I'd collected to Tanix, glancing at the clipboard. Random drawings and strange symbols littered a faded and dirty page. Doodles only.

"Do we have the wrong village?" But even as I said it —somewhat hopefully, given the wrong village meant the woman might not be the drug maker she seemed—I knew it couldn't be. Dante echoed my ensuing thoughts.

"Granny has a residence here, as does her chief dog." He held onto the clipboard. "She cut this place off from society and keeps it in hiding. Most importantly, she stays in a tiny cottage and forces her dog to stay in worse conditions. This place is important. It's not like this is any sort of vacation home for her."

"Agree. But . . ." I shook my head again. "This just doesn't add up."

"The queen started in a little shack at first, didn't she?" Dante said. "She was able to work miracles from a home garden."

Tanix shrugged. "That's true. I've heard the stories. But that was only for her village at the time, right? She had help with larger areas. Now?" He blew out a breath. "She has a team of people and a huge, well-organized garden. The faeries do, too."

"And both of those produce double what Granny is."

"Still." Dante lifted his eyebrows. "Four or five times the staff and garden space but only double the output? Maybe triple? One sober person and a few high minions shouldn't be able to produce what Granny is putting out there."

"Let's check out that product storage area." I motioned for Nova to lead the way.

Walking through the village was a surreal experience. No one lay damaged in the streets, having attacked to protect their home. No one had even shifted. Some stood on porches and others at windows, watching us pass, mostly blank expressions. It was as though it didn't really matter that we'd come. Like it didn't change the trajectory of their lives. I'd never seen anything like it.

On the way to the product storage area, Nova had me stop in to see the person they surmised was Mr. Poet.

The man had been beaten to shit. His jaw was newly healed after being dislocated, his eyes were still mostly swollen shut, and his limbs were healing from obvious broken bones. He had access to his animal—Nova reported that everyone besides the woman had—and so his healing was progressing, but an incredible amount of damage had been done. He'd be down for several days.

He had no problem talking.

"You guys here to take that dud?" he asked immediately, his busted lip curling. "I knew she was trouble. People like her have no respect for normal shifter society. She dragged us all in with her, that's what she did. Ask my mate, Mindy. I said it as soon as Granny let that no-magic cur stay here. 'She'll drag us into the dirt,' I said. And she did." He'd huffed, wincing with the effort. "Lifted us out of poverty, my ass. I'd rather be poor and barely make ends meet than be trapped here by that old woman and her prized dud, doing shit I hate, punished for every Gods-damned thing. Take her. Get her out of here. Kill them both. Just leave us be."

I'd barely been able to breathe by the end of his tirade, shaking with rage. Everything might've been true. Certainly seemed so, at any rate. But calling the woman a dud, her suppressed wolf a natural pair to my own—calling her a cur, the biggest slight to a shifter there was—the primal part of me recoiled. I'd wanted to strike out to silence him. To do worse damage than the person before me, to teach him a lesson about how one should speak about my true mate.

Instead, I'd held my composure with everything I'd had, thanked him for his information, and left the rest of the questioning to Tanix. It was the best I could do. I knew no one would fault me for it. The strange bond of true mates might not make rational sense, but the primal element of it couldn't be denied. I would suffer her punishment for the crimes she'd committed, but I would not force myself to endure a small-minded narrative from someone who'd never given her a chance because she didn't have access to her animal.

I let Nova lead me to the village center and a small supply shed in the corner. Imagine, being distrusted and hated from the get-go, the sentiment never thawing even though two people worked in close proximity. What must her life have been like if the person closest to her fundamentally despised her for what she repre- sented—a shifter without magic. When her entire person, from day one, was reduced down to something she couldn't control.

Something *she* couldn't control. Granny damn well could've.

Granny had a good amount of power. Plenty to pull out the woman's animal, at any rate. The woman wouldn't need much, just a gentle tug from any decent alpha. Granny would've known that. She would've felt it. She'd purposely kept the woman suppressed, and in so doing, ensured the woman would be despised by her co-worker and likely many others in this backwards village.

What a fucking life.

With my heart now beating too fast—a warning that I needed to stop thinking about this or risk softening toward her too much—I took in the village center. There was a small play structure for the children amid a thick pelt of grass. That was nice, at least. A few benches ringed around the edge, all empty, and sheds lined the north side. Those appeared to be better built than the houses and were newer as well, a few with windows and counters, as though used to sell something.

"Is this what passes as their village market?" I asked as we headed to the end of the row.

"Granny supplies what they need, remember?" Dante said, shadowing Nova and me. "She buys in large quantities and ships it here."

"Yes, given that was how we found the location of this place, I am aware," I said semi-patiently. "But they must have a market for personally made items, little things to trade to keep their community going."

Dante grunted. "Probably, since they have a small setup for it. No idea what they'd trade, though. I looked over the supply manifests we managed to grab from Granny's estate. She had all the necessary needs met. Not a lot of any one thing, but enough. They wouldn't have needed to trade for supplies."

"Maybe just to keep people busy?" Nova offered. "Make them feel like they were still part of an active society, trading with their neighbors, offering some sort of value to their community?"

"Given the tirade of Mr. Poet," Dante said as Nova opened the supply shed, "it didn't work."

"Maybe not for him . . ." She stepped aside. "It didn't have a lock."

I paused before stepping up. "It didn't have a lock?"

"No. The doors had been closed, the contents as you see, but no lock."

"How does that make sense?" Dante asked, peering in. "It's in the village center where children play. Anyone could wander over and start up an addicting and potentially deadly habit, willy-nilly."

I shook my head, at a loss. Surely everyone knew what the product did and how dangerous it was, so they'd warn kids to stay away, but teenagers tended to do the opposite of what they were told. Not to mention the adults with poor decision-making skills, much like Mr. Poet, who sampled and got caught in the addictive snare. It didn't make sense to leave it open like this.

I looked over the small crates stacked on top of each other, the site lacking the precision of the woman. Clearly someone else managed this storeroom. Each crate had a name scratched in the side, like "hallucinogen 1," or "mild relaxant." None were names I recognized. Granny must've changed those for market.

"Have we found the packaging area?" I asked, picking up an elixir in a little glass tube. A green dot was painted on the side. It matched the other tubes in the crate, the only thing to identify the individual contents. "This is all very . . . rudimentary."

"We haven't found anywhere where they might do

packaging, no," Nova said. "There's nowhere nearly sophisticated enough. It must be done elsewhere."

"The woman makes the goods and someone else gets them ready for market." Dante pulled his lips to the sides. "We haven't found all the players in this scheme."

"The packaging people don't matter." I picked through another crate, then the next, seeing all the contents marked with a colored dot. "Cut out the root of the operation, and the whole thing will wither."

"Still, it would be nice to bring them all in," Nova said.

"The woman should know," Dante said. "We just need to get it out of her."

I couldn't help stiffening, but didn't comment. He was right. She'd know the ins and outs of the organization. They could force her to reveal Granny's secrets.

I took a step back. "Start moving this out and talk to more of the village. Let's see what else they know and what else might be of use to the dragon royalty. We'll see who needs to come with us and stand in judgment and who should be left to pick up the pieces of their lives. It's clear Granny forced this life on this village. They'll be useless without the woman and happily so. But let's reserve judgment until after we know what they have to say."

"Yes, Alpha," they said in unison.

"Nova," I said before she got to work. "Do you know where the woman resides?"

"Yes, Alpha. I'll show you—"

"No." I held out a hand. "Just give me directions. I want you to get all this squared away as quickly as possible. I can pick through her things just fine."

She rattled off some directions and I was on my way, looking at the little cottages on the lane as I passed. They were in a state of disrepair, with a few visible patches making them habitable. All of them, without exception, were tiny.

I knew her cottage immediately, not because it was bigger than the others—it was not—or because it was newer or better in any way—it wasn't. It was because of the care and attention she seemingly paid to every detail.

The quaint little dwelling sat nestled between two others, its rustic charm enveloping it like a warm embrace. Its walls were slightly weathered by time but washed clean and its window frames were freshly painted a pristine white to match the picket fence surrounding a patch of lush green grass. A few struggling flowers added a pop of color; saffron yellow, periwinkle and teal hugged the walls and partially outlined some of the porch. It was clear she wasn't any better at gardening than her counterparts. Even so, the dirt in which they grew was devoid of weeds and still moist, serving as proof she attempted their care as best she could.

I unlatched the gate and then swung it open as a neighbor peered out her doorway from the cottage on the right.

"What sort of a neighbor is this woman?" I asked, stopping in the middle of the walkway.

She pulled her sweater tighter around her as she stepped out gingerly, her face deeply lined with age.

She pursed her lips. "Quiet. She keeps to herself, as she should."

"And why is that?"

"Well, because of her . . . affliction, you know." She lifted her brow, the gravity of the situation evident.

"Her affliction?" I asked slowly.

"Didn't you do your research before barging in here? She's one of them duds. I thought everyone knew that. No magic. Not a lick. Now . . ." She squinted her eyes at me. "People say they's contagious, but she hung around with that Wilkens boy for a good stint and he never caught nothing. No one else has gotten sick with it and lost their magic, neither. I reckon that it's just a wives tale."

Contagious? Fucking hell, these people were certainly living in the past.

In this kingdom a long time ago, it had been somewhat taboo to be without one's animal. People feared that which was different, any situation they didn't understand. Someone without access to their animal was automatically considered to be without magic, something that was actually incredibly rare. Those "afflicted" were often outcast and usually despised for no reason.

When I left this kingdom—when I was forcibly taken by the demons—there were still some superstitions and prejudices against those without access to their animal, but overall people had been better educated about the situation. In my experience, anyway. Clearly in the forgotten places like this, that outdated mentality was still prevalent.

Rage simmered low in my gut.

"What makes you think she has no magic?" I asked, wanting to be sure. "Because she can't feel her animal?"

"Her mama didn't have no magic," she replied as though she'd unequivocally proved her case. "That gene is always passed down. They said her mama went to all sorts of alphas—one that got her with child, if you can believe that. Couldn't find no magic. Shame on her mother, but then alphas do have their wiles..."

Her eyebrow arched, a harsh judgment on me.

My stare bowed her spine. Her gaze snapped downward.

Magiclessness was rarely passed down. That was fear talking. Judgment. Superstition.

To have a person like this as a neighbor, constantly judging, always looking down on you?

The sentiment was still true. What a *miserable* fucking life.

"Thank you for your time," I told the older woman, my tone as harsh as my stare. "I am not here to use her in a similar ... field of ... employ. I'm here to escort her to her judgment. Her practices are unlawful. It's time she pays the price. Speaking of, is there anyone else that should stand in judgment for their part in all of this?"

The short answer was mostly no, except for Mr. Poet and a few of the lackluster gardeners. The "dud" was basically a one-woman show.

As she spoke, I realized the people here didn't have much choice in their lives. If they left the territory—if anyone left the territory—they'd need permission and to be escorted. At least one child would have to stay behind. Granny was holding hostages, using the children as leverage to ensure no one spoke about their tasks or their locations. It's how she was able to keep her secret so airtight.

Smart . . . and utterly disgusting. She deserved death.

"This woman," I finally said, pointing at the house in front of me, stopping the woman's rant about someone named Girdy and her light fingers at the weekly market. "What is her name?"

"Aurelia."

The name bloomed within my mind, so beautiful, so perfectly matching her essence. It was like a favorite song whose tune I remembered from my youth, but whose words I'd forgotten until just now.

"Thank you for your time." I offered the woman a slight bow this time.

"'Bout time justice was done." The woman sniffed and went into her house.

What a strange reception for an intruder who meant part of the community harm.

What a horrible village.

I reached the front door. It wasn't locked.

The smell accosted me first, a wave of a perfume so divine my knees about lost their strength. I sat in a single rocking chair facing the hearth, no other furniture in her sitting room. She clearly didn't entertain.

A pot hung over ashes and I looked inside. Confused, looking back at the kitchen, I realized they didn't have any sort of appliances for keeping things cold. Granny had all the modern amenities in her estate near the castle, but she was clearly keeping these people in the olden times, before a strange alliance between clever faeries and demons had learned how to leach energy from the human realm beyond the veil.

Why was Granny keeping this village locked in a time warp? To control them?

Figuring the woman, Aurelia, would've gotten rid of the contents if they weren't fit to be eaten, I hunted through the small kitchen and found a spoon. Reaching in, I scooped up a bit out of curiosity and studied what I'd found. Stew, it looked like. Carrots, potatoes, meat . . .

Hesitantly, I sampled the concoction . . . and then moaned, closing my eyes as the tastes exploded on my tongue. I'd had a million stews made by all manner of people, from those working for royalty to the mates of my pack treating me to a homecooked meal. Nothing—*nothing*—had ever tasted this good. It wasn't the ingredients, which were pretty standard fare, but the additions of . . . herbs, I guessed. Certain unusual spices? I couldn't say, only that it tasted fucking divine.

Before I knew it, I'd finished the rest of the (somewhat meager) pot and looked for more. Finding none, I once again returned to the kitchen, looking in drawers and marveling at how immaculate everything was. She'd gone out earlier not knowing an invasion would occur. I'd warned her, yes, but clearly she hadn't taken that to heart. She also hadn't told anyone about our . . . meeting the night before. The gods only knew how she'd rationalized it, likely not recognizing our true mate bond or maybe even knowing what that was. Those without access to their animals didn't usually get much coaching about shifter life or, like with true mate bonds in general, far-fetched possibilities. She'd left her cottage thinking she'd return home at some point.

My heart thumped against my chest painfully.

I'm ripping her away from her home. A place she clearly loves and looks after.

Breathing heavily against guilt I couldn't control, I glanced at the books stacked on a side table. Gardening mostly, but with a couple action-adventure titles randomly stuck in.

I ran my finger over the lettering on the spine. Action-adventure was a genre I gravitated toward, liking it above all others. Add in a little murder mystery and I was in heaven. I didn't recognize these titles.

I'd look them up when I got back to the castle. I didn't need to know her reading habits for this duty but fuck it, I wanted to. I wanted to know what made her tick. Who she was. Why we were destined for each other.

Honestly, I wanted to conclude that the whole "true mates" business was nothing but random, primal bad luck. That it had nothing to do with me personally. It would make my duty that much more bearable.

She had two bedrooms. I avoided where she slept for a moment, choosing instead the other room, the door closed tightly. Curiosity burned through me as I opened it slowly, feeling like I was entering a secret space. A private space, somewhere no one entered but her. And likely that was the case, given what was said by Mr. Poet and then her neighbor, two people who should've at least been congenial. Instead, they'd sounded like they'd wanted her to be taken away, both because of her "affliction" and because of her role in the community.

One of those I couldn't fault.

The door swung open fully exposing images that assaulted me in the best of ways. The walls held drawings made with pencil and charcoal; the room was crowded with art, each one more interesting and eye-catching than the last. I looked at every one, seeing a bird from an interesting viewpoint, a tree with such exquisite detail I felt like I was looking at the real thing, a fantasy land with a sense of longing. Every one of them sucked me in, leaving me captivated until I had to tear myself away again.

Shaken and unsure why, I finally entered the bedroom. Her smell was more intense here and her world much more chaotic. Despite the pristine organization of her work and home space, her bedroom was anything but—something I identified with. A glass of half-finished water sat on the bedside table along with another book, the page marked with what looked like a random slip of paper. Shoes lay on the ground by the door and slippers by the closet, as though thrown there randomly. A blanket was draped on a well-worn, overstuffed chair by the far window. Her sheets lay in disarray, rumpled and turbulent.

I paused as I looked at it and wondered if she'd dreamt of our meeting like I had. If she'd relived each slow, delicious detail. If she wanted to do it again but prolong it next time, joined together, me filling her up over and over again, lodged inside of her—

Sweat coated my forehead and I braced a hand against one of the four posters of her bed, leaning over in agony. My cock was painfully hard, the ache pounding through me. I wanted her here, now. I wanted admittance to those sheets and her body. I wanted to thrust into her tight depths until we passed out from fatigue.

Get ahold of yourself, I yelled internally, needing to find some sort of control. If I was like this when she wasn't present, what would happen when she was? How the hell would I control myself when she was living and breathing next to me, her beauty captivating me, her smell, her heat drawing me in . . .

Sucking in a ragged breath, I noticed a leatherbound book—no, a journal—laying closed in the center of a small writing desk in the corner. A quill and ink sat beside it, an archaic but romantic way to write out one's thoughts.

I crossed the room to it as though in a trance, then picked it up and glanced at the first page. Her words flowered in my mind, fresh and vibrant and expressive.

Before I knew time had passed, I'd finished the journal, and Tanix was entering the bedroom with a confused expression.

"Get out," I growled, surprising myself with both the ferocity in those two words and my reaction to another male in my true mate's intimate space.

Outside the bedroom, after a few more ragged breaths, I spoke to him again.

"I apologize. I—"

He held up a hand. "I can't imagine what you're going through with this, Alpha. True mates are supposed to be a clandestine, surreal meeting. What should've been the best surprise of your life has turned into a nightmare. I don't envy you this detail. If I can help in any way . . ."

I nodded with gratitude. "Thank you. And no, it's not ideal."

"We have information from the village. Did you find anything here?"

I pushed the bedroom door wide again, surveying

the messy interior and feeling a pang in my chest that I'd never get to know why she was so immaculate in everything but her most intimate space. Her wildness showed in her bedroom, as it had on the path last night. As it had when she'd burst in on four powerful shifters and struck them with an axe in Granny's cottage. I wanted to know more of that woman. I wanted to relish in her fierceness, but co-exist in the controlled, organized space she also clearly felt comfortable in. I lived a very similar existence but I hardly ever let the wildness show. Not like I had last night. It was something I never should've done—because it was something I could never, ever forget.

"I found her journal," I finally said. I didn't hold it out and Tanix didn't offer his hand. He clearly knew I wouldn't be turning it over. "Looks like there is a row of them on the bookcase in her bedroom. I've glanced through it. She had details on products she's created, information on some daily activities. Hopefully there'll be some information about the overall operation, as well. Regardless, the dragon queen will want to get these notes. Take all her books except the mundane gardening ones."

I did not dare mention I was enraptured reading the snippets of her very lonely life dispersed in between the work-related stuff. She wrote her feelings in such a raw way that I couldn't help feeling every slight at the market, every snub while taking her daily walk, every cutting remark she overheard as she passed. Visible amongst those, though, was her drive for perfection. If a word was spelled incorrectly, it had a strikethrough and the proper spelling next to or right above it. She either knew it was wrong after writing it, looked it up and changed it on the spot, or she went over her writing later, found the error, and corrected it.

At the end of the entry, every day without fail, sometimes the only entry that day, was a memory of her mother. How her eyes sparkled. The flowing dress she wore. Her steadfast resilience against the aggression directed at them. I assumed that was because of the no-magic situation. I could feel the love through the pages, and choked up several times reading these snippets despite not knowing either of them.

Aurelia had lost her mother. And it seemed as though her mother had been her only family; it was clear from the anecdotes in her journal she had no relatives in this village. She'd found Granny sometime after and been taken in, an act of mercy.

Hard to envision the Granny I'd recently learned about giving anyone mercy. After hearing firsthand accounts of her behavior and breaking into her lavish estate near the castle to catalogue her possessions, it was obvious Granny's actions were almost always self-serving. She didn't do handouts. She didn't offer charity. If she noticed someone, it was because they were necessary or special in some way.

I supposed it was possible she had a maternal desire to protect a younger Aurelia. But I wouldn't know for sure until I learned more.

"We need to move out," I said abruptly. "Pack up the books, and her drawings from the other room. She has a collection of spices, as well. Grab those."

I tried not to clench my jaw.

And failed.

We didn't actually need those drawings, and certainly not the spices but . . . I knew I was probably sentencing her to death, so there was no real point, but I wanted her to have them close, to maybe serve as a slight balm for having ripped her from her carefully cultivated world.

Before I regretted the decision, I stalked out of the house and headed toward camp. The others could handle things from here. I wanted to see the woman. Aurelia. I wanted to ask her—

I wasn't even sure.

Fucking primal instincts. I felt like my brain had been leeched out of my skull and all I wanted to do was fall into this desperate need to knot her. To claim her. To own her for eternity.

How the fuck was I going to question her *and* keep my senses?

9

AURELIA

I came to consciousness slowly, uncomfortable in my position but feeling strangely fucking amazing. All the tension in my body had magically released. No aches and pains plagued my limbs and the stiffness I always carried in my lower back had completely dissipated. Something bit into my wrists, though, holding them together underneath me. My face rested on something soft, a blanket maybe, and the hard ground lay beneath my body. Nothing stretched overhead. I was open to the elements.

Memories flashed within my mind. The emberflies, running, the cottage, Granny . . .

Pain began to creep in around the edges of my awareness so I needed to take stock before it blotted out my consciousness completely. I couldn't afford to lose myself to grief right now. I was clearly a hostage; I needed to assess my surroundings.

After wielding the axe I'd seen the stranger. The handsome, delicious-smelling, and incredibly real stranger. I'd moved to attack him, I remembered that much. Then everything went black. The attack had never landed.

I struggled to sit up, comforted by mellow yellow light emanating from two points overhead—lanterns, it looked like, suspended from the branches of trees in an unfamiliar area. A nightbird screeched somewhere off to the right, hidden within the darkness of deep night.

In front of me sat a person in a vibrant jacket with purple velvet lapels and matching velvet slacks. Shiny black shoes with a sort of tassel in gold adorned his feet, and a spear was hooked under his arm and leveled at my face.

"Good almost-morning, Highness. How did you sleep?" he asked pleasantly. Then he grimaced, a silly, pencil-thin mustache pulling tight over full lips. "Oops. Sorry, wrong job. Let me try again. Good almost-morning, prisoner. I hope your shackles are to your liking?"

I blinked at him for a moment, somewhat confused. I'd traveled a fair bit, driven from one home to the next before I'd found Granny, but those had always been poor villages and bankrupt towns. No one had ever had the sort of finery that existed in front of me. The man looked regal, despite sitting on a slightly wonky, battered chair in the forest of a humble, if well-provisioned village.

I had to say, the rich styled themselves very . . . colorfully. Or maybe he habitually used hallucinogens and his jacket was a constant source of entertainment. Either way, I wasn't quite sure what to make of things.

"Are those . . ." I squinted in the low light. "Do you have . . .penises stitched into your jacket?"

"My goodness, look at you! You wake up with your limbs tied, in a strange place, and you immediately notice the cocks littering my jacket!" He tsked at me, leaning back with a smile. "I can already tell you're going to push my limits." He turned his face to the side a little, still looking at me, his smile now coy. "Yes, they are dicks. I have forty-three dicks on me at present. Given you're a prisoner and have nothing else to do, I figured I'd give you a task while you wait for the alpha. Find all the dicks!"

His smile practically glittered and, strangely, it seemed utterly genuine. Almost comforting.

I said nothing. Showed no emotion. Everything I was feeling sank down into my depths, hidden away lest it give my captors more poison for the tips of their weapons. An easy trick, really. A learned trait, almost, something I'd been doing since before my teens. These people, no matter how extravagant, wouldn't get any information from me.

The man winked, as though we were sharing a joke. "Give me all you've got, love," he said. "It's been an absolute *bore* of a journey. I thought I might get away for a bit, knock out this detail and check in with my home kingdom. You know, just to see if it was still a piece of shit. It is, obviously. But the alpha is very . . ."

He made some sort of gesture and an expression that didn't do much to help me understand his meaning.

"But now . . ." He smoothed his velvet lapels with a slow hand. "This makes more sense, doesn't it? I think it does. I was in a demon sex castle—and then a demon sex dungeon!—for too long to live a sedentary life. Put me to the test, my darling. I am ready and waiting."

He crossed an ankle over his knee and pursed his lips at me, as though still conveying some sort of message.

My mind had stuttered over "demon sex castle" and now I just stared blankly. The only thing I could grasp was that this man's jacket would throw Raz for an absolute loop. He'd hate the very sight of it at first, but after using the product yet again, he'd be enraptured. With that jacket, he wouldn't be so worried about the glow of a flower . . .

A wave of pain and worry washed through me, wondering what happened to the town. To Raz. We weren't friends—he didn't even like me—but we'd been work associates for years. I cared what happened to him, to his family. I hoped he was okay and that they'd leave him be.

The memory of finding Granny swept through my mind again and I withered from the onslaught. I'd lost my only family. Again. With her, I would also lose the only community that had welcomed me, maybe grudgingly, but mostly peacefully. They hadn't run me out. That was saying something for someone like me.

An image welled up in my mind, threatening to pull me under. My mother's face. All the blood. The flames.

Run, Aurelia. Save yourself. Run! Don't look back. Don't think of me—of this—until you get to safety, do you hear me? Keep going until you finally make a new life for yourself. Her grip on my arms had been so tight. Her expression, blood trailing down her cheeks like tears, so urgent. *Only then can you think of me, do you understand, Aurelia?* Only then *should you remember me. Not before. Resurrect me in your memories and I will live again, but only if you survive this day. I'm counting on you, my heart. Run now! Please, RUN!*

I blinked through sudden tears, the man before me swimming in my vision.

He put his hand to his heart, leaning forward a little, peering at my face. The tip of the spear inched forward, still directed at me.

Keep going until you finally make a new life for yourself.

It was happening again. My world was burning around me.

Get to safety.

I was older now, though, and the experience of last time had hardened me. Alexander's punishments had sharpened the point and dulled my receptivity to pain. My mother would continue to live on and now I would carry Granny with me as well, keeping them in this world with my nightly prayers and moments of reflection.

I could survive this. I had to, or their memories would be lost.

First, I stoppered the tears. Crying was useless. It took valuable time, energy and brain power. It made me slow. I couldn't allow myself the luxury right now.

Next, I re-tucked away all irrelevant emotion and information. The pain of the past was nothing but a shadow. Only this moment mattered.

Finally, I allowed my anger to move to the forefront of my mind, where it quickly boiled to rage. In this moment, I was being held captive. Either they'd try to kill me soon or they'd take me for their own gains. Anger would make me sharp. They were the enemy, and enemy deserved no quarter.

"See?" The man removed his hand from his heart and pointed at me. He leaned back, crinkling his nose. "That, right there, is why I hold the spear. They said you don't have access to your animal?" He didn't wait for my response, not that I planned to give one. "Well, the last time something like this happened, that woman happened to be a rage-monger dragon and I was lucky she didn't take it out on me. Although . . ." He paused in thought for a moment. "I guess we had a lot more distractions at that time. Orgies and demons and pegging—it was a nightmare." He brightened up. "Cheers!"

"What?" The question escaped me despite having planned on not speaking.

"My last ward-turned-queen had a lot of distractions." He paused for a moment, one eyebrow arching.

"What?" The question leaked out again.

"Not impressed, huh? With the queen bit, I mean. Damn. I'd wanted to come back to this kingdom and gloat but I couldn't tell anyone and blow my cover. It was a cock softener, to be sure."

I couldn't wrap my head around his outfit, let alone the craziness coming out of his mouth. Having been raised in one drab village after another, the last full of dreary and sullen people who were slow to smile, my brain couldn't quite process the effervescent and boisterous man in front of me. I couldn't do much more than continue to stare blankly.

He took that as a cue to keep talking.

"Unlike back in the day, there are no distractions in this camp. Zero! I did not expect this. I know quite a few people on this detail, and when they are off-duty, they are usually a shit-ton of fun. Not here under the alpha's nose, though. Not even when it's their free time. I can't find *any*one to play 'open wide, here comes the cock' with! It's an absolute nightmare." He lifted his hand like he had a drink in it. "Cheers!"

Overloaded with things that were beyond my comfortable comprehension, my attention wavered from the man and instead took in the scene around me. Tent-shaped shadows loomed within the diminishing glow of lamplight near us. Those I could see ruffling in the breeze seemed plain, splotched with dirt or whatever else.

Beyond me, barely discernible, a large shape swished its tail. A horse, obviously. The rich had such things. They wouldn't want to walk and ruin their extravagant, shiny shoes. Or their finely tailored suit with the haphazardly placed penises, of which I'd so far counted ten.

"You know," he said whimsically, his gaze unfocused as he contemplated his thoughts. "I thought I'd be content living a calm and orderly kind of life. After we re-took the castle, I'd been happy to give up the alcohol and shenanigans and cocks everywhere I turned. But fucking hell, with the royal baby and the good leadership and no parties or danger or terrible-decision-making-turned-shame-fucking to distract me, I have to admit, I am bored out of my mind. Sure, sneaking out to bang a bunch of randoms in the woods was fun for a while, but none of them are random anymore. I know them. Most importantly"—he quirked a perfectly sculpted eyebrow—"I know how they perform." He spread his palm across his chest. "I am *not* a fuckboy trainer. Well, you know. You're what, twenty? Thirty? I'm shit with women's ages. Anyway, you're too old to go giving classes on how to properly fuck. We want our men to come preconditioned. If a guy can't figure out the right time for a hard asshole fingering, what fucking good is he, know what I mean?" He shook his head. "I just can't help him."

I felt my jaw slackening, my rage melting away into brain-buzzing confusion. It wasn't just his jacket that was colorful—and incredibly crass. I'd never heard anyone speak like this, not to mention what he was talking about. Orgies? Asshole fingering? What in the . . .?

"So I figured," he went on, "that I might join this detail and see the sights a little. A couple of the guys who'd agreed to go are really hot and had seemed somewhat cock-curious, so I figured I had that going for me. And if not, I could bang my way through the kingdom of my birth, you know? Maybe meet an old chum and rub my new position in their face. But that damn alpha runs a tight ship—understandable, but still, I've banged next to no strangers. And the cock-curious, you ask? They just wanted me to play with their dongs. They had no interest in reciprocation. Fuckers. Let the ladies deal with them, as I've got no time for one-sided sword fighting."

He was clearly distracted with his, uh, predicament. This was the perfect time for me to work at my bindings and figure out a way to escape. If I was freed, I could easily knock that spear aside and then swing my hand or foot at his face. He didn't seem like a person who was ready for spontaneous combat. He certainly wasn't a man who could run fast with those shoes. I could knock him aside and make a break for it.

The problem was, even if I could get free without his noticing, I didn't have a lantern. Those in the camp were all hanging relatively high, too high to quickly grab. Without light, I wouldn't get far. If I didn't knock him out—and it was unlikely I could given I didn't have a weapon—he would likely, and probably carefully, take off his colorful attire, shift into a wolf or other four-legged creature, and follow my scent trail. He'd be on me before I found the edge of the camp.

Besides, where would I go? This encampment couldn't be in our territory. Granny's people would've found it when heading to and from their sentry positions. Given the few times I'd been Outside in the last handful of years, I wouldn't even know which direction to go for help. Assuming anyone would help me at all.

No, I'd need to be patient. They had to move me to their home base. There'd be a time along the way for me to get free; I just had to be ready when it came.

"Then there's the problem of no dragons. Can you believe I even said that? But it's true. I am bored to fucking *tears*, like I told you." He chatted along merrily as though he hadn't had someone to talk to in ages. "Dragons are insane and are prone to extreme violence for no reason, but at least they give you something to look out for. They're unpredictable. This lot—" He jerked his head right and then followed it with a glance, indicating where the others had gone. Probably to my village.

A momentary pang hit me. Like with that fire those fifteen years ago, I would lose everything. I doubted very much that they'd allow me to go collect my things before moving me. I'd have to find my way back, someday. I didn't have much, but the few things I did have were precious to me.

Thankfully, the pain that should've overwhelmed me continued to be held at bay. It would consume me, if not in this headspace. I reminded myself there would be time to cry after I got to safety.

"They're all very . . ." He made a hand gesture, down in a line in front of him and then out to the side. I didn't know what it meant. "The alpha chose the best and the brightest. Do you know what that is code for? Boring and uninspired. They have no fucking sense of humor. Dick jokes? Lost on them. How is that even possible?" He widened his eyes at me. "A bunch of them *have* dicks!" He shook his head, clearly at a loss. "It's a fucking shame. They follow the alpha's command to the absolute letter. No stubbornness that the king and queen have to beat down, no veering out of their formation . . ." He slouched. "I'm the odd one out, can you believe that?"

I didn't give him a reaction, but yes, I definitely could believe it.

I was still trying to process everything when it dawned on me: they'd clearly gone through the village and found the supply. Of course they would have. It was a free gold earner.

"You've sampled the product." My tone was flat.

His eyes brightened with curiosity. He opened his mouth to speak, but then backed off and lifted a hand. "Let's just get the formalities out of the way, shall we? I've seen the towns where your product has run wild. I do think your operation is filthy and you're hurting a lot of people. You have a lot to answer for. Officially, I am a strong thumbs down to you and your operation." He took a deep breath, a smile flirting with his lips. "With that said, and given it is the dragon royalty's problem and not mine, I will say . . . I'm so fucking curious. Seriously."

He dropped his ankle from atop his knee and set both feet on the floor to lean forward to scrutinize my carefully expressionless face. The spear went a little askew.

He hefted it. "Do I need this?"

I didn't respond.

He studied me for a long moment. I couldn't tell from his expression what he was thinking. He nodded. "You're playing at calm—very clever. You don't fool me, though. I was drunk off my ass when I first met Finley, but I remember the wild look in her eyes. Very similar to you. You're dangerous, even with your hands tied. Don't pretend that you aren't."

Staying numb to the situation was not easy. It was like this man was battering me with his crazy. He permeated even my most unaffected, unemotional, and unfeeling state. I could probably get a limb hacked off right now and not feel it, but this guy? It was like he was burrowing into my mind and scrambling everything until I couldn't help but come to the surface to get some air.

"Anyway, that product you speak of . . ." He smoothed his little mustache, curled at the corners. "I am so curious about it. I'm going to be honest, I'd sample the shit out of it. I mean, I was a hair's breadth away from being killed by the curse. If it wasn't the demons, it was people trying to trick me into killing myself by talking about it. I made it though, didn't I? Mediocrity for the fucking win! I'm sure I can navigate a few recreational drugs. It would give me something new to do in my spare time. Besides, if I had a little *save me* elixir on hand, it would be fine. The addiction would be an issue, but Finley—the dragon queen—concocted something that greatly helps. I could work my way out of it, I know I could."

"What?" My head was going to pop off if I kept shaking it this much. Dragon royalty? What was he even talking about? "No." I breathed out in frustration.

"This is my fault." He sat back. "We've been tracking you down for months. Which means I've been cooped up with very square wolves for *months*." He gestured toward himself. "This bitch is a round peg. The situation just isn't fucking working. The only reason they let me don my professional attire"—he smoothed a hand down his lapel again—"is because I am reprising my role of mediocre guardian." He cupped his hand beside his mouth and stage-whispered, "I used to be a butler, but it would be absurd to call myself a butler in this situation." He winked. "But you make drugs! You've *got* to be more interesting than these people, right? I mean, I don't want to be your best friend or anything. The last very pretty hostage I governed got me into all sorts of horrible, life-threatening situations. I'm bored but I'm not *that* bored, you know what I mean? Plus, your fate is uncertain. You've killed too many people—you must know that. But between now and whatever terrible fucking atrocity happens later, I think we can be chummy without going over the top, don't you?"

I twisted my wrists, pulling at the binding. I didn't give a shit if someone found me later, so long as it was someone else. *Anyone* but this guy. I needed to escape this madness.

He nodded at me. "Go ahead. What's on your mind?"

"You're— What the— What is—" I yanked harder, twisting, the rope biting into my skin. "I don't make product that kills," I finally blurted in a rush of anger.

"I knew I still needed this." He adjusted his spear.

I ignored it. "I have personally tried every one of my products. Every single batch. My co-creator dabbled way too much, as did a few people in the village. No one has died. No one has even gotten ill. I built a few fail-safes into the product, as well, ones that can minimize the journey if the path turns toward nightmares. There are risks—of course there are—but none of those risks are death. You've obviously come for the wrong woman."

"I like that language—the journey and the path of nightmares. Yes, that sounds right up my alley. Now I'm desperate to try it. Damn it. Why'd you make it so dangerous?" He tilted his head. "You have, though. You do know that, right? Killed people. Unfortunately, you're the bad guy in this . . . journey."

"It is not dangerous!" I bit back. "It might be habit forming for some, but it is not dangerous. It's natural, all of it. It's made from plants and extracts. From fire and water. Air. It alters the mind, but it doesn't alter the body. If someone died it is because they had an ailment, like a weak heart or some other medical issue. That happens with healing elixirs all the time. That's not my fault. Is a person who made a healing elixir a bad guy because something went wrong and it killed the patient?"

"Except that person was trying to help . . ."

"*I'm* trying to help. You said it yourself—life can be dull. A hallucinogen gives people an escape for a time. People who are anxious can take a relaxant. People battling depression can get a lift. People with trouble focusing can clear away the fog. It isn't my fault if they take it irresponsibly or too often. Habit-forming doesn't mean addicting. It doesn't mean dependency. It isn't any different than ale in large quantities. And if you're traveling to dangerous areas, into shadow markets, don't you know the risks? Besides, in this kingdom, the king and queen have given approval for my product to be sold in the main market. Could it really be that dangerous if royalty are allowing it?"

I hadn't believed that last bit, but I would damn well use it to my benefit now until proven otherwise. Because honestly, if the product *did* have royalty backing, if Alexander was correct, then that essentially nudged it into the confines of the law. If that were the case, these people were the outlaws, not me. They were the bad guys.

His eyes had widened. "My goodness. You're very smart, aren't you? If I hadn't seen the addiction and death firsthand, I'd believe in your conviction. Sadly . . ." He frowned comically. "I have. We've nipped it in the bud in our kingdom—though the queen holds a grudge —but we'd seen it throughout our kingdom and heard about it in others. Why the king and queen here are allowing it, I don't know, other than they don't give two shits about their poor constituents. It's why I'd never come back—"

"If there is addiction and death, it isn't because of my product," I said stubbornly, noting that he didn't deny the royal backing. "You've got the wrong woman. Go into my village. See for yourself. I make the fucking stuff. Don't you think if there was an issue, my village would be riddled with it? We don't lock the supply shed. Anyone can get in at any time. If there was a problem, it would be here first."

"Hmm." He nodded slowly. "Mm-hmm. That *is* interesting. The alpha and his acting beta know the situation very well. They'll be able to figure out if you're lying." He leaned forward again. "I hope you aren't. Tell me, could I ride a horse while high? While on a journey, I mean. That would cut down on the boredom getting from place to place in this kingdom. It's incredibly spread out. It took *days* to get all the way out here."

I shook my head, looking away. Blood dripped down my wrist from the rope ripping my skin. "I have no idea. We don't have horses in this village. We've never tested that out."

"And you test everything?"

"As I already told you. Yes, every single batch. I make sure it is up to my standards and always try to think of ways to improve it."

He rested his chin on his fist. "I *really* hope this is all a misunderstanding. You'd probably get along really well with Finley, not to mention give Arleth someone new to share ideas with. But, sadly, in our experience with your trade, very few people tell the truth."

"I wouldn't know. I've never dealt with any of them. That was Granny's department."

He nodded. "Yes, pity. Sadly, we can't verify any of this because the person known as Granny is gone."

I gritted my teeth at his blasé attitude toward Granny's demise and the role this man's comrades played in it. He dared lecture me about killing people, yet here they were, infiltrating a village and taking out the residents within.

"Find Alexander," I bit out. "That swine knows. Ask him. He was with her all the time."

"Yes, he was." He clucked his tongue. "Well, this is fucking depressing. As far as first impressions go, I like you, but you'll need to do some serious groveling if you hope to sidestep the wrath of the dragon queen. She does not have a sense of humor when it comes to the welfare of her people. Not like this festering heap of a kingdom."

The anger inside of me was a living thing, lighting me on fire. "If you're royalty from another kingdom, you have no jurisdiction here. Unless the king and queen from *this* kingdom have given permission for you to capture and detain one of their constituents—and from what I gather, they most certainly have not— you're here without sanction. Granny was in good standing with our royalty, as was—*is*—our product. You're operating outside the law, just like I *was*. You have no right to invade, to murder, and to kidnap. You'll be hanged for this."

His smile pulled his lips wide. "You're *very* smart. And correct. We're going to have to smuggle you out of here—"

"Hadriel, that's enough."

The voice was like a whip-crack of pleasure that puddled in my core. I turned my head slowly to find the handsome stranger stepping into the light. Each movement of that stellar body was graceful and sleek, effortlessly hiding the coiled power contained in that robust frame cut with thick slabs of muscle. He didn't wear any clothes, nor did he exhibit any embarrassment or shame about that fact. It seemed he felt nudity was completely natural and free. I'd bet he was an amazing dancer; his movements were strong and sure but gentle, like his fingertips under my chin last night, lifting my face to look at him.

No, to be inspected by him.

I shivered with the memory. A moment later, though, I remembered what he'd done. Remembered what he had planned for me, the way he'd barged into my village like I was the criminal when he and his people were the ones not allowed. Bullshit, all of this.

And on the path with him? What the fuck was that? He knew he was going to abduct me and decided he'd get his cock wet while I was willing? While I was transfixed by this strange feeling pulsing deep within me?

What was this feeling, anyway? Why did it feel like his presence tugged at my middle? Yanked at me, more like. The sensations his proximity gave me felt like something akin to one of my creations. On the path I had been sure that it was. How was he creating this feeling? Because there was no way he could've administered something to me that night without me knowing. The Moonfire Lily was the only abnormal thing I'd been working with, and I was now sure it hadn't created these effects.

None of this made sense.

But then, it didn't really have to, did it? When traveling a journey on one of my stronger products, nothing ever made sense. It was important to flow with it, accepting what was until you could alter your reality.

I stared up at his startlingly handsome face, cataloguing all his features. Looking down at me from above were slate gray eyes cut from granite. Sharp cheekbones cut angles above his hollowed cheeks, and he had a small cleft in his strong jaw. His dusky brown eyebrows settled low, nearly touched by his long black lashes. His dark blonde hair held sun-kissed streaks and currently fell to the sides of his forehead and around his ears, longer than he liked it.

I had no clue how I could know that last bit. And yet, I'd bet a good fortune on that knowledge.

I'd walk in this criminal's journey, no problem, until I could alter my reality. When I did, only one of us would be walking away: me.

"Get up," he commanded.

He was the alpha of this pack, obviously. A man no one said no to.

I wasn't in his pack, and I didn't give a damn what he wanted.

I stared at him impassively, allowing myself to go numb again. He would feed off my anger, off my rebellion. I knew it. Instead, I'd give him nothing to work with. I'd give him a shell of a woman.

He stared back, his eyes heating until they were spitting fire. Currents of electricity sizzled between us, flowing over my body in a way that frazzled my mind. I didn't balk, though, pushing the feelings down with my emotions.

"Slap my dick and call me jumpy! This whole situation just got a whole lot more interesting," the man in the colorful jacket said, looking between us.

"Hadriel, you may go," the alpha said, his eyes not leaving mine.

"Goodie-goodie cum-drops." Mr. Colorful Jacket—Hadriel—set down his spear and stood from his chair. "She doesn't have a weapon, sir, but I'd watch her. I've known my fair share of wild women and they have this habit of conjuring weapons out of thin air. Access to her animal or not, she'll chop off your nuts if she gets half a chance."

"Go," the alpha growled. My small hairs stood on end with the viciousness in his tone. Hadriel shivered.

"Okay but . . . be nice to her," Hadriel said before turning. "You're not the judge. Keep her alive until she can grovel to Queen Finley. Finley is a lot more reasonable than you are when it comes to"—he affected a strange accent and tone—"duty and honor."

Now the alpha did tear his eyes away, his gaze finding Hadriel slowly.

"Fuck!" Hadriel flinched, hunching down on himself. "I haven't felt the need to terror-shit my pants in forever. What an unwelcome change." He looked at me and nodded a goodbye before heading away.

"This is the last time I will tell you." The alpha's focus came back to me. His cock was jutting out, hard and huge. "Get. *Up.*"

I remained unmoving, trying desperately to not

remember how that cock felt. How it tasted. How much I wanted to feel it again.

The air blistered with heat now, raking across my flesh. He felt it; I could tell. A sheen of sweat suddenly coated that fine body.

The rushing in my ears turned into pounding in my core. The desperate need to do what he said ate away my resolve. I didn't dare give in.

Instead, I did what I knew would incite him most of all. Nothing. I did and said absolutely nothing. I continued to kneel as I was, quietly defiant. Challenging him to a battle of wills. I was a prisoner now; I had all the time and patience in the world.

His left hand clenched into a fist. His pecs popped in frustration, knowing what I was doing. I felt his power curl through the air around me, goading me into following that command. Finally reaching the end of his tether, he moved, reaching for me.

10

AURELIA

I closed my eyes to keep from flinching as he leaned over me, expecting the pain that was sure to come. His large hand closed over my upper arm. He jerked me upright.

I straightened my legs, allowing him to set me on my feet. I again waited for the blow. Alexander sometimes liked to do it face-to-face.

His large hand now gripped my forearm.

"What is this?" he demanded, holding up my hands. His thumb trailed across the blood from the ropes. "Who did this to you?" His tone was vicious but his touch was soft, wiping away the blood. "Was this you, trying to escape? Did you do this?" He peered into my eyes, his expression pained. "Aurelia . . ."

Hearing my name on his tongue, said with that deep, sexy voice, sent tingles spreading throughout my body. Hearing the concern in his tone, feeling his touch on my skin . . . My knees weakened in response, though I held steady. Barely.

"You tie me up but then don't like the effects of the rope?" I asked in a flat tone.

A vein popped in his clenched jaw. He bent in a flurry of movement, grabbing the spear Hadriel had held and swinging it toward me. I couldn't help the flinch this time, jerking away from him violently. I'd never seen someone move that fast—much too fast for me to anticipate. He grabbed my wrist this time, holding my hands still and then driving the tip of the spear between them. The sharp edge of the metal sliced through the rope.

When he was done, he threw the spear to the side as though unworried I'd dive for it and ripped the rest of the rope away.

"Do not," he said, grabbing my shoulders and waiting until I met his eyes, "hurt yourself. Do you understand?"

I felt my brows pull together. "Why? So you can have that pleasure?"

His hard eyes were rimmed with fire. I felt my insides tighten with the power I saw brimming there, finding it hard to hold his gaze while also wanting to tip toward it and fall all the way in.

"I saw you flinch," he said. "I saw what was done to Mr. Poet. Did they do that to you? Did they hurt you in that village?" He paused for a beat.

I didn't know who Mr. Poet was, but I clenched my jaw tightly, refusing to answer.

Understanding lit his eyes anyway. I must've given away my affirmation in my body language.

"Who was it? That woman, Granny? Someone else in that village?" He studied me. "*Answer me. I'll end them.*"

I understood his reaction about as well as I'd understood anything Hadriel had been saying.

"Is there something wrong with you people?" I blurted. "You barged into my village, killed the only family I've known these last fifteen years, ripped me from my home, are unlawfully holding me hostage, and you're worried about me flinching from my captor? Do the dragons keep you around to make them feel smarter?"

His eyes narrowed slightly and he turned, jerking me along with him. We traveled through a well-organized sea of white tents, the lighting dim but still enough for me to see. The one on the end was the largest of all, almost double the size of the others.

People glanced our way—all of them nude, many dirty, and some bloodied. They'd been fighting. Killing people I knew.

Gritting my teeth against the desire to give in to the rising emotion, I staggered alongside the alpha. He reached the tent and stopped, shoving me inside. Expecting to be flung like Alexander might've, I was ready with quick feet and kept myself upright.

The tent's interior was surprisingly spacious, accommodating a large cot that could easily pass as a bed for a mated couple in the village. On the other side sat a moderately sized table with four chairs, the wood polished but worn. A blanket spread across the ground in the corner with cushions dotting the surface and a book had been left lying in the middle, a little ribbon denoting his place.

I wouldn't take you for a reading man. Or is that one filled with pictures?

The words went unspoken. Silence would needle him more than any barb. He was a man who wanted answers when he asked questions. Who took obedience for granted. I would give him none of what he was expecting.

He stopped just inside of the tent, his gaze intense. There was a sanguine quality to him, as though my proximity worked at every nerve in the most gloriously devastating of ways. Distracting ways. I knew how he felt and bet he hated it as much as I did. What I hated more, however, was not knowing what was causing it. His erection still stood proud, undiminished despite our walk. Everyone would've seen that. Did he care?

Did it matter?

He turned and unhooked the wooden toggle on the tent flap. It swung down, plunging us into near darkness, the only glow from one window with the flap still tied up.

Butterflies filled my stomach. This was what Granny had been warning about, my body being used as a plaything to anyone who captured me. It had revolted me. Terrified me.

I felt zero fear right now. Worse—much, *much* worse —was the kernel of excitement that sparked in my middle.

"I'm going to ask you questions, and I want truthful answers," he said in a tone that was low, soft, but imbued with a silent threat. He didn't step toward me. "There will be repercussions if you lie."

He paused as though I might comment. When it was clear I would not, his gaze flowed over me.

"Do you need to sit?" he asked, and I couldn't stop the frown at the unexpected question.

"What are your questions?"

Heat flared in his eyes, his gaze dropping to my lips and his eyes growing hooded. He flinched, and then snapped back to razor sharp focus. The air still crackled between us.

"Who do you work for?" he asked, both hands now fisted and his shoulders tense.

"You know who. You killed her earlier."

"Granny," he said. I didn't bother nodding. "When did she employ you?"

"She didn't, at first. She harbored me."

His brows drew together, his gaze intensifying. "When did you first start making drugs?"

"A year after I got here, she started working with me. A hobby, at first. When I showed promise, at about fourteen, she started teaching me the craft. I tried various products on the market, read books, and learned to duplicate. Over the years, I kept pace with other shadow market products—mostly—until she started bringing home some books and . . . documents to help me learn. She brought home apothecary supplies, as well, and explained how other people had altered them. In the last five years, I made the craft my own."

"And in the last three, you made your craft more deadly."

"I made the journeys smoother, I put in fail-safes, and I made the experience more pleasant. As I told your colorful accomplice, my product is not now, nor ever has been, deadly. I assume you toured my village. You should've seen that for yourself."

"How could I have seen for myself? Do you typically keep dead people on display?"

I opened my mouth for a rebuttal, but he had me there. We had quite a few empty residences since no new people had moved into our community in quite a few years. Old age had removed others. I didn't have the proof I was boasting.

"It isn't deadly or terribly dangerous for the mostly healthy," I grit out. "People here have taken my product. I have. No one has died from it. Do you assume we are some sort of ultra-powerful species that don't suffer the same way others do? I don't even have magic. If it was deadly, I'd have been gone a long time ago. I developed a more robust catalog as time went on, not a more dangerous one."

"Not dangerous—" He huffed, his eyes murderous. "Do you believe the lies you tell? Do they help you sleep at night?"

"Help *me* sleep at night? You invaded this village unlawfully. You killed and are in the act of abducting. Is creating a few hallucinogens worse than that? Worse than the murder of an old woman? Clearly the dragons *do* keep you around to make them feel smarter."

He took a step forward, anger vibrating his frame. I realized how much larger he was than me. At five-foot-two it wasn't unusual, but he was so much thicker. So much stronger. When I killed him, it would have to be by surprise. From behind, maybe. Something sharp into his neck so he couldn't heal before the job was done.

"The difference between you and me is I'm not going

after innocents," he growled, stopping right in front of me, leaning into my space. His proximity sent a flurry through my stomach.

"What part about people venturing into a seedy shadow market in search of unlawful drugs screams *innocent* at you?" I replied, my own anger now getting the better of me.

"And what about drugs slipped into drinks and given as gifts, wrapped up like little presents? Those pushed on children who don't know any better?"

"You think I travel the world slipping my product into the hands of the unsuspecting? What sort of awful place are you even from that those thoughts enter your head?"

He bent a little more, his face mere inches from mine. His fragrance wrapped my mind in a dizzying, delicious cocoon.

"Have a care with how you speak to me," he growled, his voice low and rough, sizzling across my skin. "You might not personally push those drugs onto people who have no idea what they are getting themselves into, but the organization you work for does. You're guilty by association."

"Granny sells to her network. She always has. She has no control over what they do, or what people who buy the product do. No one does. The only difference I've become aware of in the last three years is that the king and queen are now in on it, and that has *I think* been a recent change. Maybe you should take it up with them."

"Or maybe I should take out the source and wash my hands of it."

I looked at his lips, slightly parted as he breathed heavy. My core pounded with need I did not want.

Now it was I who spoke low and firm, straightening up as much as I could and returning my gaze to his eyes. Lust burned brightly there, very loosely controlled, much like my own. He was just as frustrated by that fact. I could feel it—feel him—in every cell of my body, as though he'd grafted himself to my flesh.

"Your threats won't make you right or just. You are a murderer and a hypocrite, and nothing you say will have any value to me."

A flash of pain raced through his eyes, so fast I half wondered if I'd made it up. "Who else works for Granny apart from those within this village?" His voice shook, his anger threatening to break free. "You create the *product*, fine, but who packages it? Where are they?"

"I have no idea."

"Don't lie to me!" he shouted, startling me into action.

I bashed his face with my forehead before shifting my weight and swinging up my knee.

He barely flinched, taking my head's blow in stride and almost lazily reaching down to stop my knee. He grabbed my shoulders and swung me around. I had the insane terror he'd bend me over the table and take me right then. The terror because I *wanted* it. Deep down to my core, I needed him in a way that wasn't natural.

Instead, he shoved me, only hard enough to make me stagger away.

"If you want to fight, then fight." He grabbed the edge of the table and flung it aside. It rolled across the ground and into the tent flap, a leg sticking out of the opening. He scattered the chairs next, leaving the space between us clear. "If you think that will somehow absolve you of your crimes, go for it."

His obvious display of rage, of violence, was strange in that it didn't terrify me as it should've. As Alexander would've. Deep inside, part of me trusted that he wouldn't hurt me. That he wouldn't treat me as Alexander had loved to do. It wasn't rational given his people had killed Granny, but right now that didn't seem to matter. Instead, his show of strength, of anger, incited me to heights I couldn't contain.

My control shattered, my frustration spilling over.

"I'm not looking to be absolved of my crimes, you block-headed jackass!" I yelled at him. "I'm trying to make you understand your hypocrisy."

I launched, throwing a punch. I hadn't learned how to properly fist fight, but I'd been in enough scrapes when I was younger to have a clue. Besides, what did it matter? I already knew I couldn't best him face-to-face. I could at least try to hurt him a little.

My fist connected and he let it, his hands at his sides, his chest rising and falling quickly. My wrist tweaked painfully; the man was made of bricks. I punched for his jugular, ready to dig my nails in and rip it out. He caught my wrist above the wound where the skin was already marked and raw.

I reached for his eyes, utterly without reason.

He caught that wrist as well, careful with the existing wound, and then spread my arms wider, pulling my chest toward his body. My peaked nipples scraped agonizingly through my thin clothes against his bare chest, sending sparks down to my core. His hard length pressed against my belly. I breathed heavily while looking up at him. His breath mingled with mine, his pupils dilating as he took me in. The air hung heavy around us, filled with anger and arousal. His grip was hard, and oh gods how I both loved and loathed being controlled and maneuvered. Being this close to him had my body at war with my mind.

"You'd be wise to pick your battles, Little Wolf," he said, and a hot dagger twisted in my gut.

I wasn't a wolf. I wasn't anything. He had to have known since I couldn't see in the dark. He was intentionally pouring salt in my wound.

I tried to head-butt him again, unwilling to give in despite the impossible odds. He twisted, catching my face in the crook of his neck, enveloping me in his scent.

My knees nearly went out from under me. My body melted toward him, my arms now using him for support. His grip tightened to keep me in place. I felt his hardness against my belly. Wetness made a mess of my undergarments. Anger made me irrational.

"I will kill you," I said into his skin, his taste salty and warm, delicious. My lips lingered there, my core throbbing.

"You won't get that chance," he said softly, without moving—and I had no idea why. His body was tight against mine, his cock pulsing. "You'll pay for your crimes, I will make sure of it."

I bared my teeth and sank them into his flesh, blood filling my mouth. He sucked in a startled breath and I relished in it.

He jerked back and grabbed my throat, tearing me

away from him. His eyes darkened menacingly. My newly freed hand swung down lifelessly, having not expected he would let it go. It slapped against his inner thigh. Brushed against his hard cock. Tore my last thread of sanity.

I grabbed his cock before I could stop myself. His hand slid to the back of my neck and he yanked me closer. His lips crashed down onto mine. His tongue delved deep, plunging. I groaned into his taste and stroked along his length, frenzied. His hands were at my clothes, pushing down my trousers and ripping off my top. He had me bared to him in moments, his lips leaving mine to trail down my neck. One hand ran down my chest to cup a breast.

I closed my eyes, shoving him backward, hating him so hard but utterly lost to the feel of him. His hot mouth replaced his hand on my breast, sucking in its peak. His legs hit the edge of the cot and he turned, pushing me down before him and then quickly spreading my thighs with his big body.

He reached down and hooked a forearm under my knee, hoisting it up. He threaded the other hand into my hair, his kiss deep and sensual.

I wrapped an arm over his shoulder, my nails digging into his back as the other hand reached between us, finding his length and running it up and down my slickness. His growl of pleasure sent me over the edge and I thrust up, lifting into the air. His tip crested my opening and then he slammed down, filling me in one glorious, hate-filled slide. I didn't care; I needed this. I could have regrets after I'd climaxed.

He pounded me, hard and fast. I went to pull my

hand from between us but he stopped me by grabbing my elbow. He broke our kiss so that he could put his lips near my ear, his voice raspy, our bodies colliding with a wet smack.

"You're going to help yourself come all over my cock, Little Wolf," he said, his movements changing. He lifted up a little, his hips still swinging but giving me a little space to work. He shoved my elbow again, pushing my hand down, my fingers gliding against myself and sending me shivers of pleasure. "That's right," he cooed, looking down on me now, watching me enjoy the sensations. "Good girl. Work that little pussy while I shove in deep."

I should've been livid with the nickname and the praise, but fuck me if it didn't curl through my body in delicious shivers.

He did as he said, swinging his hips and then grinding into me. I felt the bulge in his cock grow, slipping easily in and out for now. It grew bigger, though, starting to catch. Butterflies filled my stomach and my body answered, pushing up to him. Helping him work it in. The liquid magma poured down my middle. Lights danced behind my eyes. My nerves were on overload, craving this, craving the slick slide of our bodies crashing into each other.

"I'm going to fuck this knot into you," he whispered softly, propped on an elbow now with that hand wrapped around my shoulders. His other hand was at my hip, holding me in place while he strove deeper. "I'm going to lodge it in, good and tight, and you're going to stew in anger as you come on me, over and over and over again. Tomorrow you're going to hate me as you leak my cum all down your thighs and shiver with the memory of how it got there. I can fight dirty, too. The next time you decide to knee me in the balls, you'll remember this moment."

My eyes snapped open with his dark chuckle, anger rolling through me. It was too late, though. Even if I hadn't been too far gone, desperate to get him closer, needing his release, his knot was already trapped inside of me. It kept expanding until now it was getting uncomfortable. Then it was painful, a hard ache, stealing my breath.

I whined, my legs uncoiling from him, trying to push him away now.

"Work that clit, baby." Despite his intentions, his voice became oh so soft. His arms came around me, holding me tightly. "Work that clit and relax for me. You need to relax or it'll be pain the whole time. Let your body adjust to me."

I held onto his neck with one hand, my face tight against the other side, my fingers working myself. He held totally still, allowing me time to adjust, filling me in a way no one else ever had. The size of the knot must grow with the power of the wolf, because I'd never experienced one I couldn't get away from with a little effort. And certainly not one that I'd needed coaching to endure.

"That's right," he cooed, the pain easing into merely being uncomfortable again, my ministrations helping. "Keep going. That's my good girl. Almost there."

I pulled back from his neck and found his lips, thankful for once that he had this weird effect on me. He moaned, and while he might pretend this was some sort of payback, he was just as wrapped up in this feeling as I was. His control was equally nonexistent.

The uncomfortable feeling gradually fell away and as it did, the pleasure started to build again. I moved a little, gasping with the drum beat of decadent sensation that vibrated up my middle. His slow smile was dazzling, intimate, and then he was rolling his hips in a way that enhanced the feeling. I closed my eyes and bowed my head a little, working myself, feeling his movement.

"Fuck, baby, you feel so fucking good," he groaned. "Work that little pussy around my cock."

I tried a little move of my own, his knot tugging on me, a splice of pain through the pleasure that made him moan deep and low.

"That's right," he said before sucking in my bottom lip. "Use me. Fuck this big dick deep into that little pussy. You are pure ecstasy."

I moved a little more until the pain eased again, my body winding tighter until I was rocking into him, him twisting and turning in a way not usual for sex but that lit me on fire all the same.

"Fucking . . . hell," I said against his shoulder, squeezing him tighter with my legs. "Holy . . . fuck-ing . . . *he—*"

My climax exploded, making me shake and quiver against him. He continued to move, rolling his body within mine, hitting places I didn't realize could feel that way, could consume my focus so totally.

He reached down and yanked my hand away. "You won't need that anymore. My knot is going to make you come all over your alpha's thick cock."

A sunburst exploded behind my eyes, another wave of pleasure slamming me home. Still it built more, his movements getting more erratic. His breathing became heavier until he held me hard again, pumping deeper into me, never pulling back enough to cause me pain. His cock rubbed just right, like it was meant to fit there. His teeth took little bites at my neck before he sucked in my fevered skin.

His hips jerked harder. I groaned within the sensation. He fisted my hair, grinding deep.

"Fuck *yes*," he swore with his release, filling me with a heat that made my eyes flutter. Another climax tore through me, this one the biggest yet, making me shudder against him and rake my nails down his back.

"Oh fu—" I said as I rode it, wrapping around him as much as I could.

He shook again, utter bliss, before his kiss turned languid.

"Hold on, baby. We've got a while before this will subside, I think." His upper body peeled back. He grabbed my hands and pulled me with him, wrapping one around my back to steady me and turning us over. He lay back down, me on top of him, before putting his hands behind his head.

I looked down on his beautiful, beguiling face, his smug smile one I didn't much care for. His cock was still a huge swell inside of me, not yet diminished in the slightest. I'd heard some wolves took a few moments to go down, but it was almost always soon after their climax.

A throb of pleasure stole my breath. It was not a climax but kick-started me into building toward one again as though I was actively working for it and not merely sitting atop him. I knew my confusion showed clearly on my face.

"You're with an alpha now." His smug smile grew. "I derive pleasure from locking my release deep inside you. It creates a constant sort of hum until the knot fades. You'll derive pleasure from the same thing, except you also have bodily stimulation. I'll climax each time you do, and I get to sit here and watch you writhe, desperate to be away from me but equally desperate for more. Isn't that right, Little Wolf? Hatefully trapped in pleasure as your tormenter watches you struggle? As I said, there is more than one way to fight dirty."

I stared down at him, my stomach tightening.

He was right, of course. The passion that led me to make this terrible decision was receding, and with its departure came cool logic. The last thing I wanted was to sit here impaled on the cock of a man that intended to unlawfully rip me from my home and take me to the dragons to have me killed. A man who had destroyed my life anew and killed the last person I thought of as family. I'd rather cut his dick off than get pleasure from it—something I should've remembered *before* I grabbed his cock or accepted his knot.

However, logic wasn't without its rewards.

He thought I was scum. A killer of innocents. He hated me as much as I did him. Whatever feeling was altering my mind was working on him, too, making him lose control. An alpha like this, a leader who had his camp in perfect order with all the tents in a crisp line, and his people following his direction to the letter—he'd hate that slip. He'd hate that I'd gotten to him. He was probably kicking himself that he'd locked me like this, realizing his desperation at the time, complete with flimsy reasoning, was now a punishment for *him*.

Instead of admitting fault for this fucked up situation or allowing himself to feel the guilt and degradation of the moment, he was shoving it back on me.

Well, I'd be damned if I let him get the upper hand while using my sexuality to embarrass me or make me feel smaller. If he wanted to watch, I'd give him a show that would result in fever dreams for years to come. Every time he thought of me it would come with blind lust. I'd lean hard on this weird feeling and follow this journey to its conclusion.

I called upon my learned and practiced ability to lie to call his bluff.

"You thought," I said, bracing a hand on his chest and bending with laughter. "You thought that I'd be . . . what, embarrassed to come repeatedly? Why the fuck would that embarrass me? I don't know if anyone told you, but women fake their climax a lot of the time. You fuckers aren't even a quarter as good as you think you are. So if your *alpha* body is built to give me pleasure? Go ahead and relax, I'm used to getting myself off when a guy won't do it for me."

His smile slipped and I got right into it. Oh yes, I'd walk this path so that my journey didn't take a sharp left turn into a nightmare, but after that—after I was free of his body—I was done. I would never, *ever* let this happen again.

11

WESTON

"What's the status?" I asked Tanix at the east end of the camp, the sun at its zenith and the need to be out of here tugging at me.

Despite my plan playing out to the letter and locking that village down early, some of the enemy had escaped. A few had slipped from our lines and somehow evaded our control. They'd know we had their prize. They'd come for her, I knew they would. In order to salvage their operation, they'd have to, and I knew they wouldn't hesitate to go through us to do it.

They'd also, almost assuredly, inform their royalty of our actions. Aurelia had elevated this kingdom to one of the hottest markets in the magical world. Royalty here, as disreputable as they were, would surely want to retain their market share, if not increase the growing dependency of other kingdoms on her product. They'd want to rescue her for their own needs, and this would provide the perfect opportunity to do it.

If they caught us, it wouldn't just be our heads.

They'd either pull the dragon court into war or demand unrealistic compensation for catching us meddling. I had sworn I could get this done without putting our kingdom in that position, and it was a promise I intended to keep.

"The pack has an hour of rest time remaining," Tanix said, sitting at the last table in what we thought of as the common area of the camp. The rest of our seating and supplies had been packed away, ready for transport. He studied a pile of papers spread out over the surface. "We need to make fast time out of this kingdom and I don't want—" He glanced up and then did a double-take.

I couldn't imagine what he saw. A man that felt like every nerve in his body was still firing with exquisite pleasure and hating-while-loving every fucking moment of it? A guy that had watched a beautiful woman get off on his cock for twice as long as he'd ever been in that position? Or maybe a usually balanced and in-control alpha with a suddenly dark and turbulent disposition.

I'd completely lost control last night-turned-this-morning and I'd gotten no information while doing it. I had to do better.

"Is there a problem?" I growled. It happened. Fine. Time to move on and forget it.

"No, sir. I was just saying that the closer we get to the sea, the greater the need to move fast and stay vigilant. I want to give the pack adequate rest. We're a long way from the worst of the danger way out here and I think we should make the most of it. Anyone intending to intercept us will do it when we are closer to civilization."

I nodded, looking toward the village. "Agreed. You got the product?"

"The drugs?"

Many years of showing no emotion kept my flinch hidden. I'd used her vague term for it.

"We did," Tanix said when I didn't comment. "They are loaded in the carts. The pack knows not to touch it. The sheer quantity of it suggests that this is, in fact, the sole origin. The woman must do little other than make it."

"Just not package it."

"Doesn't seem so. We spoke to a great many of the villagers. Once they realized we meant them no harm, and that their territory borders were now open, they had no problem answering questions. Certain villagers take the crates to the border in hand-pulled carts. They leave them for the patrol or whoever to take over. We found hoof marks at that location."

I furrowed my brow, adjusting my stance as I processed. "They made the villagers tote the crates all the way out? Why not have the horses come in and collect it?"

"I have no idea. It didn't seem like these villagers had seen a horse within the boundaries in years. Over a decade."

"Yet they were being used to transport the drugs to another location."

"The tracks suggest they were."

"And no one knew where that location might be? The details of what they did there?"

Tanix shook his head. "The villagers didn't have a clue. Not about Aurelia's operation, Granny's—

anything. Occasionally Alexander would let slip some things that happened 'Outside.' They used the term 'outside' like it was a specific place. The most recent incident got several people punished. I guess punishment for rule breaking is severe here—beatings, whippings, cut with tools."

I shivered with the memories of when I'd endured such treatment in the demon dungeons. I knew exactly what these people had been through.

"Is there anyone we need to take with us?" I asked.

Tanix pulled his lips to the side while slowly shaking his head. "I really don't think so. Mr. Poet was the closest to the woman's—Aurelia's—operation. No one else worked in her vicinity. He never actually helped her, though. Didn't know how. He just learned what plants she'd need next and made sure she had them. He seemed to be her errand boy, mostly. Granny's as well. He dreaded delivering both of them things—Aurelia because of her lack of magic, Granny because she was prone to bad moods. Apparently, Granny's bad moods had the potential to result in punishment at any time."

"Did you get any sort of history from him?"

"Yes, as a matter of fact," Tanix said. "It seems that when Aurelia advanced in her craft, Granny quickly shut down the borders. Alexander let slip around that time that their business was taking off and Granny needed to protect it. This, too, was years and years ago. The villagers let it happen because Granny brought in gold to fix up dwellings and the village square, and offered them more food than they knew what to do with."

"They didn't look like people that had more food than they knew what to do with."

"Offer them plenty so that they will choose to enter the cage. After they are trapped, take it away. By the time they realize what they've done, it's too late."

That was true.

"Mr. Poet remembers Aurelia entering the kingdom half-starved," Tanix said. "Only a kid. This was before the borders closed. He learned quickly that she didn't have any magic and from that moment on he—and most of the village, it seemed—didn't much trust her. What quickly befell the village ensured no one would warm up to her. She was an outcast while also being Granny's prized worker. The village around her was collateral damage. She has no friends here."

"I gathered that." I inflated my chest with a deep breath.

She'd been just a child when she'd come here. A child without her mother who'd obviously fallen on hard times. When she'd needed support and love, she got the censure of a village and put to work by a calculating woman. I couldn't help thinking how heartbreaking her life was. She'd been set up for the loneliness I'd read in her journals. She'd been trapped in it by an unfeeling person who wouldn't pull out her animal and make her part of the village. She'd been kept separate on purpose.

"Terrible fucking life," I murmured. "Why would she care about those she's hurting when she doesn't have a friend in the world to protect?"

"With Granny's help, it certainly made her dangerous."

"Indeed."

"There's something I've been wondering . . ." Tanix snagged his lip in his teeth. "If she's your true mate, that obviously means her animal is just suppressed. And powerful, we'd have to guess. I can feel it and I'm not even an alpha."

"Very powerful," I supplied. "It is pulsing within her."

"It wouldn't take much for you to yank it out, right?"

"Correct. I've almost done it by accident a couple of times." I didn't elaborate, unwilling to admit that it had been at the height of pleasure. I'd barely known my name, drunk as I was on the euphoric feeling of her pulling me into her climaxes. I'd never experienced an intimacy so overpowering.

"You never got close to Granny," Tanix went on, "but we've always heard she's a fairly strong alpha."

"Why didn't she pull out Aurelia's wolf?" I said, surmising the question. Tanix nodded. "I honestly have no idea."

"Do you think it was about control? Keep her weak, keep her an outcast, show her the only kindness she's liable to get, and thus keep her dependent. Do those things and you maintain control of the prized asset."

"It's very possible. Aurelia must've seen what was going on within the village, though. She was helping to cage people. That and making the types of drugs she does—drugs ten times more dangerous than any of her competitors— remain inexcusable. She needs to stand in judgment, and if this disgusting kingdom won't do it, ours will."

He stiffened. "No doubt, alpha. I wasn't trying to let her off the hook. I was just trying to understand is all."

I nodded, needing that reminder myself.

"Were you able to get anything out of her?" Tanix asked before I could turn.

"No. The situation got away from me."

"I figured." He looked down at his papers. "I heard about the table and the . . . noise. I could always try, if you had other matters to attend to? We still have some of the truth elixir Queen Finley sent with us."

Yes was on the tip of my tongue. I wanted nothing more than to shrug her off on someone who was better able to handle her. As much as I wanted to, I couldn't seem to keep a straight head where she was concerned. But the idea of them possibly getting rough with her, or gods forbid, hurting her, raked down my middle with razor tipped claws. I wouldn't be able to endure someone else touching her, not for any reason.

"I'll use the elixir. We'll have ample time when we get moving. Did someone bring her clothes?"

"Hadriel grabbed something for her at about dawn. He was wearing his castle clothes."

"I saw." Yet another fucking hassle. That wolf was wily. He'd picked up too many traits from the dragons. The second you thought you had him in line, he went and threw everything into chaos. If he wasn't so damned good at information gathering and making the right sort of friends, I'd send him home. As it was, he was a valuable member of the team, just one that constantly tested me.

"Do you want me to send him her way?"

"Don't bother. I'll grab them both."

. . .

Nearly an hour later, as the pack was getting ready to tear down the rest of the tents and get moving, I stood outside of my tent with Aurelia's attire. I'd washed myself off and changed clothes so that the scent of her body wouldn't linger on my skin. Doing so had cleared my head enough to get my affairs in order and would hopefully keep me steady during this meeting.

She lay on the bed with her wrists bound to the frame, the rope just under the marks she'd caused from last night. Her eyes were closed and the sheets rested just above those luscious breasts. Her pert nipples stuck up through the material. My mouth started to salivate with an overpowering urge to rip off that sheet, take one of those taut nipples into my mouth, and tease a moan out of her.

Struggling for control, I approached the bed. I could just bark *wake up* at her, but the memory of how she'd been treated in that village still rubbed my heart raw. She might be on the road to her death, but the least I could do was make it a decent journey.

"Hey." I stopped beside her, shaking her hip gently. "Wake—"

She flipped to her side and a foot came out of nowhere, fluttering the bedsheet and kicking me in the balls.

"Fucking—" I bent and backed up, cupping my dick. "Fuck!"

She adjusted and kicked out again, for my head this time, faster than she should've been without the help of her animal.

I dodged, the movement eliciting a fresh stab of agony in my groin.

"I was trying . . . to be . . . fucking *nice*," I grit out, standing with effort.

"Tying me to a bed is very nice, yes." Her sunburst eyes, beautiful with their flare of golden yellows, fiery oranges and soft browns, were brilliant and brimming with violence. "I kicked you in the balls as a thank you. Now we're both fucking *nice*."

"I tied you to the bed to keep you from running off." I flung the clothes at her face. "You're a captive, remember?"

She shook her head to get them off. "The epitome of nice, yes." She quirked an eyebrow at me. "What a gentleman you are."

I moved around to the frame and untied the rope. "There. Freed. Run and you'll be punished. I hear you're familiar with that."

"Are you going to punish me with your fists or your dick?" She pulled her wrists apart and threw the rope away before yanking the sheet back over her breasts with a glare. Too late. The picture of her nudity was re-burned into my brain. My cock was painfully hard.

"You made it pretty clear last night and into this morning that my dick was not a punishment. Come on, get dressed. They need to pack this tent up and get everything stowed away. We're due to head out."

Her eyes flicked back and forth between mine. "You have zero guilt that you are tearing me away from my home, huh?"

My chest tightened but I didn't show it. I had a lot of guilt, yes, but duty and justice didn't give a shit about her feelings or mine.

"None." I lied smoothly, and then couldn't help a

little dig as retaliation for my aching balls. "Especially since removing you means the people of this village can go free. Their cage has been pried open. I'm a hero."

"You're delusional, is what you are." Her fists balled. "A hero doesn't murder villagers."

"We left all the innocents alive, darling. We only killed or captured the poison in this place."

Her eyes narrowed. "This village is anything but a cage. Is that how you sleep at night? By inventing your own reality? The people here stayed because they have food and shelter and a good life for their children. If not for Granny, they'd still live in poverty, their children uneducated. Now they're obviously going to have to leave because you killed their provider and are abducting the one person who could still find a way to keep them in their lifestyle."

I stared at her incredulously. "Do you seriously believe that? Granny's people wouldn't let anyone leave without an escort."

"I know. A couple months ago I was punished because they thought I'd tried to leave—it was a misunderstanding. We're in a dangerous line of work. We need protection when we venture out, me most of all. We can't risk anyone knowing our location because they'd invade and do exactly what you did—kill Granny, take me, and steal the product. Congratulations, you proved her right and validated the rules we live by."

I held up a hand, the surge of rage taking me unexpectedly. "You were punished? *You* were?"

Her chin tilted up a fraction. "Yes. I live by the same rules as everyone else. I'm not special."

"They punished you even though it was a misunder-standing?"

"Yes. I did something stupid, and to keep the peace, I accepted the punishment."

"To keep the peace . . ." I huffed out a sardonic laugh and turned away for a moment, the rage still pumping strongly. I couldn't seem to make my way around it. "Who did it?" I asked softly. I turned back to her. "Who hurt you?"

Her eyes widened a little and a flush crept into her cheeks. "It doesn't matter."

I stepped toward her, each word clipped. "Who. Hurt. You?"

Her breath came faster. She wet her lips and I real-ized she was aroused. She was responding to my primal need to kill anyone who laid a finger on her.

"Alexander," she whispered, desire filling those beau-tiful eyes.

"Did he hurt you as badly as he did Mr. Poet?"

"Who?"

"The man who worked with you."

"Raz. I don't know, but probably not. Granny always supervised my punishments so I could heal within a couple days. I heard that Alexander hadn't been super-vised for Raz's latest punishment."

Her words died away, still watching me, no doubt seeing my struggle for control.

"He'll die for what he did," I ground out. "I'll ensure it. And someday you can explain to me how you think it is okay to punish people for wanting free will. How you turned a blind eye to villagers not being allowed to leave because of a dangerous profession they were forced to take part in. How you're so fucking naïve that you think it's okay for Granny to cage a village of people under the threat of pain using rules they were tricked into agreeing to. But that can wait. Right now, you need to get your fucking ass up and get dressed. We need to get underway."

"First of all—" she started, her eyes dipping to the clothes that currently lay on her lap. "Wait, these are mine."

"Well now, it seems you *do* have powers of observation. I guess you just didn't care what you and Granny were doing to your village. The dragons won't spare you long."

Her glare was now accusatory, holding up the garments. "Stop saying that. You're twisting things." She shook the clothes. "I mean that these were pulled from my cottage."

I crossed my arms over my chest. "They'll fit you. You're welcome."

"You looked through my things?"

"Yes. I look forward to reading your journals."

Her face paled. "You wouldn't dare."

"Why? Afraid I'll have proof of your lies?"

"I'm not lying," she ground out, getting off the bed. The sheet pulled away and I refused to let my gaze wander from her eyes. "I have personal stuff in those journals. Private stuff."

"You also have work stuff. Recipes. Procedures. I can only assume you'll have organizational notes, people visiting the village you've talked to, things Granny said—"

"I'll tell you whatever you want to know."

175

"I don't believe you. Get dressed. I'm leaving for a moment. If you run, you will be caught immediately. You'll ride with Hadriel today. I don't need you well, I need you barely alive. You'd be wise to remember that. I can make Alexander look like a puppy."

She stood mute and rigid, a kindling of fear in her eyes. My gut pinched and I turned away. I hated even bluffing about hurting her. I hated the situation she continued to put me in. I hated her for making this all so fucking miserable. For making *me* so fucking miserable.

Today I'd stick her with a babysitter so that I could skim those journals and see if the packaging and organizational information was easy to come by. If it was— and I hoped to fuck that it was—I could stick her on a cart and ignore she even existed. If I kept her at an arm's length, it wouldn't be so easy to be affected by her.

If not . . .

I gritted my teeth.

If not, I'd need that truth elixir to pry the answers out of her. One way or another I would shed light on the entirety of Granny's organization, including the parts we hadn't yet uncovered. We needed to make sure, with one-hundred percent accuracy, that Aurelia was the only creator. It would also be nice to bring in any other co-conspirators to stand in judgment with her.

I would do as I'd promised and bring this drug-running operation to its fucking knees. The woman, my true mate or not, would not stand in my way. I wouldn't, under any circumstances, lose my control around her again.

12

AURELIA

"*K*nock, knock," I heard at the closed tent flap. It sounded like the man from last night. Hadriel.

I remained silent, sitting in the lone chair in the tent where the table had been. The alpha must've cleared everything else away this morning while I was still asleep, drugged out on bliss and frustratingly, deliciously sated.

"Please say you're in there," he said. "I don't want to peek in case I accidentally see you naked and get killed by the alpha, or in case you are waiting in there to harm me in some way. This is a nice outfit and blood would absolutely ruin it."

I tried to practice the vague calmness of a composed woman . . . and ended up shaking my head and looking away to keep from smiling. His humor was so crass and dark, it easily knocked me off balance.

"Okay. It seems you are not responding." I saw the shadow of a foot at the bottom of the tent flap. "It is either that you are trapped under something heavy, like the weight of your conscience, or you are doing a wonderful job of ignoring me. The third option would be that you have escaped, leaving me the terrible task of informing a slightly manic alpha of your disappearance. Let's hope it's not that one. So. I am going to come in. Please do not stab me. I'm not the bad guy here." He paused. "Except for unlawfully abducting you and taking you to—okay, I am kinda a bad guy here. Let's join forces and rule the world, shall we?"

I didn't respond. I wasn't going to make this easier on these people, even if this one was oddly amusing.

"Gods tickle my balls, please be in there and not naked," he murmured, pushing the tent flap aside and peering into the gloomy space. Very little light filtered in through the window, the flap closed. The alpha had done it to preserve my privacy, it seemed. Which was . . . thoughtful, actually. It hadn't diminished the flaming embarrassment of what I'd done with him last night.

Hadriel's gaze found me and his bearing relaxed.

"Thank fuck," he murmured as he stepped in before raising his voice. "Well, hello and good afternoon to you." He bustled toward me with a steaming mug. "Look at you." He gestured to my plain brown shirt, tucked into faded brown trousers that I'd worn into the ground. "Drab *chic*, I love it. Who needs fashion when you have that face, am I right? Now, here we go. Let's drink some tea and make sure last night's bad decision doesn't evolve into a spot of trouble for life, hmm?"

Ah. The pregnancy tea. How antiquated.

"I have my own remedy if you'll just let me go back to the village and grab it."

He clucked his tongue. "I don't think that's a possibility, I'm afraid. We're moving out in the opposite direction today." He held the tea forward.

It had been worth a shot.

I studied him for a moment, wondering if they'd put something in the brew. Would they want to knock me out to make the journey easier? Or maybe the alpha had too many regrets about losing control last night and decided to cut out the problem.

"Is this intended to kill me?" I asked, sniffing it.

"And rob the dragons their chance to torture you gruesomely? Not likely." He grinned at me for a moment before the twinkle left his eyes. "Sorry. Gallows humor. In the not-so-distant past, we lived each day wondering if we'd see the next. At first we joked to cope. Or I joked to cope, anyway. What's the point without a sense of humor, you know? Then reality got all fucked and twisted, as did my humor. I forget you're normal. No, it's not poisoned."

There was something about him that made me want to trust him. To believe him. He was odd, no doubt, but he seemed completely genuine.

Regardless, I doubted very much I had a choice. Either I took it with him voluntarily, or the alpha would likely be brought in and force me.

As I drank it, my soft *ugh* of disgust couldn't be helped. This stuff tasted like the inside of a sweaty shoe.

"Okay," he said once I'd finished, taking the empty mug, "let's get you up and out there. You'll be riding with me today."

I stood, my hands clasped as though still shackled, trying to keep my voice from showing how uncomfortable and awkward I felt. He seemed incredibly blasé about riding in close proximity, but I knew from experience how uneasy I made people. How afraid they were of catching my "affliction".

"I should probably give you some distance," I said. "I'll walk."

He turned a little sideways and narrowed his eyes dramatically at me.

"What've you heard?" He lowered his brow. "Who was talking, Kurt? He gets all his information from Liron, that cornholing dickface. Are you really going to trust a guy who doesn't know which hole he's sticking his dick into? No. Besides, that rash had nothing to do with the orgy in the woods. Well, it did, but that was because I was on hands and knees leaning over the wrong bush. When the railing from behind got a little extreme, I leaned too far down into the bush and suddenly I'm a sexual pariah. It was the plant that gave me the welts! The *plant*! Finley patched it up in no time. I wasn't even contagious! Besides, it's gone now. You have nothing to worry about."

"I—" My brain filled with static. I blinked rapidly. "I—"

He waited patiently for me to get my thoughts together. It was not easy.

"I didn't hear anything about you, no. I was just trying to make things easier on you."

"Oh good, that's a relief." He reached out to loop his arm through mine, probably so that I wouldn't run. I shied away and he stuck out his hands. "Look! It's gone!

Seriously, the rash is gone. It wasn't even contagious! It was *months* ago. You're blowing this way out of proportion."

I knew my lips quirked as I struggled with the budding smile. "I believe you. We have plants like that here. No, it's not that. It's just—"

"Oh, my horse? Because Jenkins can take more weight, don't worry about him. He's a feisty stallion prepared to hold the likes of the largest dragons. You're a waif who needs a little more nutrition in her diet and I'm lean. He can easily and comfortably hold more weight than us."

I blew out a frustrated breath. "I know the alpha wants me watched, but I'd be a real idiot to run in the middle of the day with wolf shifters all around me. I wouldn't get far. So I'm fine to walk. You don't have to share air space."

"Listen, love, I have no fucking idea what we are talking about, but I do know we are wasting time. The alpha is impatient to go and you holding things up is just going to enrage him. I do not want to deal with an enraged alpha wolf. Sure, *usually* I'm pretty sure he won't lose his mind and accidentally kill me, but today he's acting a bit manic. I don't want to put him to the test. Get your cute little ass sashaying to the door, please. Let's go."

"It's just . . ." I flinched away when he tried to loop my arm again to head to the tent flap.

Before I could spell it out—because he did not seem to be getting that I was letting him off the hook—I noticed the group of people waiting just outside the tent. They stared at me, one and all, their gazes curious or hostile, a few taking a step back as I neared.

My body had gone rigid. I could ignore this type of scrutiny in the village; it was something I'd grown used to shrugging off. But these were powerful strangers. Dangerous warriors. Their hostility made me freeze up, worried about what they'd do and reminding me of a violent past that had sent me running.

"I'm not contagious, either," I murmured with a tight jaw, passing the onlookers by. "But I understand you wanting to keep your distance. It's nothing new. I'll walk."

"Ooh, what's this now?" Hadriel hurried to get closer. "What sort of sexual affliction did you catch, how did you get rid of it, and what were you doing when you got it? Tell me everything!"

I couldn't get a handle on this guy. Was nothing he said ever normal?

"Not—no," I said quickly, a wave of heat rolling over me as my mind replayed the many things I'd done with the alpha last night.

I followed his directional gesture toward the horses, their leads tethered around poles that had clearly been set up recently. When we neared, I turned to him angrily, embarrassed that I had to spell this out. Usually people were relieved when I let them off the hook like this.

"I know I make people uncomfortable," I said. "You won't lose your animal because I don't have one, but I get the concern. I can walk, it's fine."

Understanding spread across his face. He barked out a laugh before planting his hand on my upper arm, refusing to allow me to pull away this time. "My darling, I don't give two shits about your animal situation. There are things much worse than not feeling the stubborn basket of cocks you have lodged in your person, let me tell you. In fact, here, get on this horse and Uncle Haddy will tell you some stories about when my animal was suppressed and what it was like in the demon sex castle. Those stories are sure to curl your cunt hairs."

I choked on my spit at the verbiage and spooked the horse with my coughing.

"Also," I said through wheezing, "I've never ridden a horse. I don't know how."

"That's easy. I'll teach you. I just have to remove the saddle and get things ready for two riders. The dumb as rocks stable boy surely won't be able to do it. He'd probably try to fit two saddles and wonder why it didn't work."

He didn't just prepare the horse we'd ride, though. He ended up helping the flustered stable boy get all the horses untethered, organized, and ready to go. It was clear he knew what he was doing, much more so than the boy.

I waited off to the side in the trees, watching the riders take to their horses. Not all the people in camp would be riding, it seemed. Some would walk beside horses and donkeys laden with saddle bags or pulling carts. Others seemed like they'd be carrying a pack themselves, walking in a group. Still others shifted into their wolf forms, taking to the trees, their movements lithe and graceful in a way I had never seen. Hunters, all. The only thing that came close was Granny's patrol and sentries, but they couldn't hold a candle to the beauty of movement I saw before me.

My insides curdled as I remembered Granny. Thinking about the patrol and everyone who'd perished. It wasn't right, marveling at the people who'd been responsible.

I turned my back on them, wandering away a little. I hadn't been lying to Hadriel—I wasn't so stupid as to assume I could make a run for it. They'd follow me easily. They'd then surely punish me, and any injuries I received would hinder me from other, easier escape opportunities.

I scanned the area, looking for landmarks I might know. Sadly, everything here was entirely foreign. It had to be outside of our territory, or close to the perimeter.

A small thread of guilt and worry wound within me. I couldn't shake the innate feeling that I was doing something wrong. I'd lived with Granny's rules for so long, afraid of what would happen if I strayed outside of her protections. It felt like a freefall to be this far out. It felt like I'd have a punishment to look forward to, regardless of whether it was my fault or not.

But she was gone. She wasn't in control anymore. I'd better get used to my new normal.

My meandering carried me a little further still, though I made sure I could hear the chatter and shouts of the pack so I wouldn't get turned around and lose my way. I looked through the plant life below me, hunting for the reclusive Moonfire Lily and thinking about my creations. I needed something to occupy my mind beyond what that man had said about there being worse things than a suppressed animal. I'd never heard anyone say something like that. People might feign indifference, but no one laughed off my affliction. No one stayed in my presence so easily, tried to touch me so often, and looked me straight in the eye as though he was fascinated by what he saw. It was . . . perplexing.

Warmth blossomed in my chest and then started seeping down my middle. My nerve endings sizzled, like fire washing over my skin. I recognized that feeling . . .

I turned around slowly, butterflies filling my stomach.

What I saw stole my breath.

A massive wolf stood twenty paces away, larger than any I had ever seen. His slate gray eyes matched his pelt, trained on me with intense focus. He stepped forward slowly, his head lowered a little.

Unsure, I took a step back.

His lips pulled away from large canines and he growled deeply.

I froze, my flight instincts going active but the magma now gushing in my middle, wrestling my control.

The alpha wolf crept nearer, still showing his teeth. He circled me, as though assessing. I didn't dare turn to watch him, unconfident I'd keep my position if he wound closer.

My heart beat rapidly as he entered my field of vision again, having closed half the distance to me. I could smell his mouthwatering scent, even in his wolf form. Feel his proximity now as he continued to circle. He stopped mere feet away, his shifter form intimidating. His eyes sparkled as he beheld me, holding my gaze for a long beat, and then he shifted.

The man stood from a crouch, towering over me, his heat blanketing any exposed skin.

"What are you doing out here, Little Wolf?" he murmured, his voice deep and rich. Butterflies fluttered faster through my stomach. "Are you trying to run from me?"

My head was tilted up so that I could sink into those deep gray eyes. His taunt, *Little Wolf,* sounded more like an affectionate term this time, said like it was something precious. His power radiated, making my bones feel like jelly.

"You can, you know," he murmured, his hand coming up slowly, as though I might spook. "Run. I'd like it if you did. It's in my nature to hunt. To bring you down like prey. When I catch you, I'll do with you what I like."

My eyes hooded. Damn me, but I wanted that so fucking badly. I wanted the thrill of terror as he closed in, then the thrill of pleasure as he used me to his liking.

His fingers wrapped around the base of my neck, holding me in place.

"Or maybe I'll do with you what I like right now." He bent, his face inches away, his eyes jogging back and forth between mine.

I should've run. Fought. At the very least I should've told him to fuck off. A simple "no" even.

Instead, I stood there, frozen, heart racing.

With a little smile, he continued to bend until his lips grazed the edges of mine. Lightning sizzled between us. He traced my jaw with his tongue before sucking in an earlobe. I groaned in miserable delight.

His lips grazed down the side of my neck and then stopped briefly at the line of my top. His hand slipped from behind my neck, his fingers hooking into the fabric. He pulled it away enough for his lips to travel along the surface of my shoulder and back, just a little past the crook of my neck. He sucked in skin and then grazed his teeth over the sensitive location.

My stomach clenched, wanting it. Wanting him to bite down and mark me in a way that would never go away, that no one else would ever be able to cover. No one would be strong enough. Powerful enough. I didn't know much of the Outside, but I had a feeling there weren't many, or any, more powerful than this shifter. I'd be his, forever.

"No," I moaned, but tilted my head away to give him more access. My body wouldn't stop contradicting me.

"No?" he murmured against my flesh, scraping with his teeth and making me shiver.

"No," I whispered, my hands at my sides.

His wanton tone matched mine. "Are you sure?"

I didn't answer him with words. Couldn't tell him to stop.

My head fell away that bit more, a silent plea for him to continue.

He ripped the fabric of my shirt, making me gasp. One of his hands was free to grab my neck, holding me in place again, and the other slid down my front. He pushed it into my trousers, down until his fingers found my wetness.

I moaned, standing still like a good girl, wanting to

hear that praise again. It was a strange sort of fetish I realized I was very much into with this powerful shifter. I could hate myself for it later.

"Hmm," he said, the word vibrating across my skin. "You're so wet for me."

He sucked on that sensitive spot in the hollow of my neck. Ran his teeth over it, making me shiver again. His fingers delved into me, his thumb circling my clit and making me dizzy.

"I think you'd let me," he said, his teeth digging in a little more. My head felt light. I did nothing to stop him. "I think you'd come as I claimed you, wouldn't you?"

His fingers worked me fast. His hot mouth felt so good against my skin.

"Not yet, though," he whispered, so faint I could barely hear him. "Not until we can all participate. We'll compromise this time."

I didn't know what he meant. Couldn't focus on what he was saying. A delicious heat was building in me as his fingers worked, capturing all my attention. His grip on my neck tightened, and I liked that, too.

He moved fast. Sharp pain barely registered as his teeth cut into the flesh at the side of my neck. His fingers plunged in and out quickly and his thumb continuing to circle. He sucked the offending spot so hard a normal person would've probably wriggled in pain, first scoring my skin, and then bruising it. His mark in that spot wouldn't be forever, but it would be a mark all the same. For an alpha, it meant that if anyone else dared touch me, it was a challenge to him. He'd kill them without blame.

I should be utterly pissed, fighting him off.

I closed my eyes, gyrating my hips as he finger-fucked my pussy. My moans increased in volume. My fists tightened.

"Oh gods," I groaned, putty in his hands.

"No," he said, pulling his face up even with mine. His eyes rooted me to the spot. "You don't call on the gods when I'm touching you. You're *mine*," he growled, his fingers against my neck tightening a bit more. "You use my name. Weston or Alpha. Now come for me, Little Wolf," he commanded.

Like a damn bursting, pleasure exploded through me. I cried out with the sheer power of it, this time using his name and earning an approving growl for my efforts. My knees weakened and I clung to him.

He dropped his head to rest his lips right beside my ear, pulling out his fingers and then rolling them around my clit. Aftershocks rippled through me.

"Good girl," he praised, and his electric heat sizzled across my skin. "This was a warning. The next time you wander away, you'll be on your knees, worshipping my cock."

Tingles flowed over me. He pulled away, leaving me standing there panting, my eyes closed. I didn't hear him leave but felt his growing distance as though part of him was still attached to me. In a moment, when the feeling subsided, I let my eyes drift open.

Hadriel stood in the clearing with his hands braced on his hips and his colorful jacket catching and throwing the sunlight.

"Well," he said, not coming closer. "That'll teach you to wander off, hmm? Looked like a nice little fingerfuck you had just there. I see you have a darkening mark to show for it. I sure hope you didn't intend to fuck any more of your captors, because there's no way that's going to happen now. No one is going to come near you."

"They wouldn't have, anyway." I shivered with a lingering aftershock.

"I suppose you're right. No one's stupid enough to touch an alpha's—never mind. Come on, let's go get you a new shirt. It's like he thinks we have an endless supply of your drab attire. What if you have to start borrowing from other people? I'd bet you won't know what to do with yourself if you slapped on a little color, not that there's much of it around this place."

I followed after him like a lost little lamb, not really sure what to say for myself. What *could* I say for myself? He was right. I'd just let my captor, the guy who'd I'd sworn not to touch again, finger me until completion. And though he hadn't claimed me, he'd marked me for all to see. I was his prisoner in body and now in flesh. Worse, whenever he was near, I was his in spirit, too. It was like every time he came close, he gave me a drug that stripped away my rationale. A drug I couldn't chase away with my mind.

A drug I really fucking liked.

Maybe that was why people were getting so addicted —assuming I could believe my captors. They loved the experience my product created. They didn't have the mind power, or the threat of Granny's punishments, to balance out the temptation.

I wasn't sure what I could do about that, though I guessed it didn't really matter, anymore. Granny was gone and her organization with her. Unless he handed me off to another distributor or his dragons decided to forgive whatever wrongdoing they thought I was a part of and jump into the trade, my days of making product were over.

Getting back to what he'd said, I chose the most obvious to focus on.

"You watched all that?" I asked meekly.

We wound through the trees.

"Of course I watched all that. I got there late but absolutely stayed for the end of the show. You were standing in a fucking field, getting off on him manhandling you. I was riveted."

I grimaced, expecting embarrassment or outrage. Instead, a strange sliver of heat wormed through me. A weird sprinkle of pride that he should witness me with the alpha.

What in the hell was going on with me? More importantly, what could I do to stop it?

"I bet his wolf was leaning on him hard. Sometimes our animals have a way of influencing us. Too bad Leala isn't here," he murmured. "She'd help you work out your kinks. Seems like you like a little dominance play, huh? You like being . . . maybe not submissive, but a little passive? You should try enraging him next time and letting him take out his aggression on you. You might like that. You'd probably get the bang of your life."

In the space where the camp used to be, people were waiting atop their horses, the shiny and well-groomed animals swishing their tails. Other people waited near them, holding supplies or standing with donkeys. The alpha—Weston—was nowhere to be found.

Hadriel walked past and I followed, noticing people look my way, their gazes once again tracking my movements. It wasn't my lack of magic they were gawking at this time—it was the prisoner with the ripped shirt and intimate mark on her neck.

"What the fuck am I doing?" I murmured, my face heating.

"Making very delightful, if somewhat questionable choices." He plucked at my shirt to get me moving faster. "I wouldn't worry too much about it. You might as well have a little fun before the end, if that is what's to come. I know all about that. I lived that for sixteen years or so. Just please, love . . ." He stopped and faced me, his expression serious. "Stop before you reach shame-fucking. That's a very slippery slope. Learn from your ol' pal Hadriel. Hate fucking is fine. Getting off on the power play of captor and prisoner? Sounds fucking amazing, and I'm definitely going to roleplay that as soon as I can wrangle up some kinky fuckery. But shame fucking? No. You've gone too far." He started walking again, leaving me sputtering awkwardly. "I promised you stories and I will absolutely deliver. You'll see what I mean. By the way, did you find all the dicks on my jacket, yet? I wore it again today since you didn't have enough time to see them all last night. Wasn't that nice of me? Now, where the fuck is that fucking supply wagon?"

As my mind tried once again to process his words, my gaze dutifully fell to the back of his jacket, quickly spying several dicks sewn into the design. Various carts and wagons gathered in the middle of a forming line, many of these pulled by a sturdy horse or two.

"Ah, here we are." Hadriel ran his hand over the rump of a black horse with white spots before stopping at the cart it was attached to. A man off to the side glanced his way and then noticed me. He saw my ripped shirt and then the mark on my neck, his eyes widening a little.

"What do you need?" he asked Hadriel, his surprise not coloring his tone.

"A shirt for her. She had a tryst with her enemy and ended up coming all over his fingers."

My face started burning but the man seemed to take it in stride. Apparently Hadriel's manner was no secret among the pack. It meant he wasn't putting on an act for me, something I appreciated.

"The alpha is acting fair peculiar with her, ain't he?" The man helped Hadriel unhook the latch and pull open the back of the cart. He stood back, leaning against the edge of the cart as Hadriel started rifling through packages neatly stacked inside. His gaze took in my face and drifted down my body, sticking on the mark again. I did everything in my power to stop from fidgeting at the appraisal. "I get the appeal—she's stunning—but it isn't like him to let down his guard like that. She's a murderer, for heaven's sakes. She took down my mate's friend's nephew. Our alpha can't stand the things she's responsible for. You'd think he'd kill her himself, not take her to the dragons. He's got that personal grudge against it, you know? Why wait when we can just be done with her now, that's what I say. I can't stand the sight of her, let alone want to have sex with her."

I lifted my chin and turned my face away a little, muscle memory for when people were saying nasty things about me within my vicinity. It was more common than I cared to admit. Ignoring it was now second nature.

Hadriel straightened up with an incredulous expression. He stared at the man for a brief moment.

"Real fucking nice, Chuck, you miserable weeping cock." He threw out his hand to indicate me. "She's standing right fucking there. If you're going to bring up a possible execution, at least have the class to joke about it." He shook his head, moving packages out of the way to get deeper into the wagon. "Who taught you social etiquette, the fucking demons? Next you'll be trying to give her a dick flavored lollipop."

The man straightened, crossing his arms over his chest. "I never much liked you."

"I know, you tell me that every time you see me." He opened up a package and pulled out a shirt. Holding it up, he nodded and then held it out to me. "Drab as they come. Just like you like it."

"It's better not to stand out," I mumbled, taking it. "People think you're putting your lack of magic in their faces if you stand out."

"I get that," the man said, studying me again. "That's not the sort of thing you need to advertise. It makes people nervous."

My gut twisted but I kept the familiar pain from showing on my face. He wasn't wrong.

"Spank me and call me mama," Hadriel muttered as though talking to the gods. He stood, facing the man again. "That is the dumbest fucking thing you have ever said, and given you say almost exclusively dumb things, that's an achievement."

A swell of gratitude rose in my middle. No one had *ever* stuck up for me like that. Granny had never made me feel inferior, unlike some in her employ, but she'd never backed people down when they said something like this man had. His opinions were common, as good as fact. No one had pushed back on someone saying what everyone was thinking.

Until now.

"With her face, she can't help standing out," he finished. He rumpled his brow at me. "Is that why you starved yourself, to try and erase all your curves?"

"I didn't . . ." I looked down at my loose clothing. "I've always had plenty of food."

He quirked an eyebrow at me, as though knowing it was a lie and wanting the truth, as though willing to actually listen to the truth, like he cared what it was.

Something uncomfortable tightened me up, realizing he was right. The lie was so well-rehearsed, said confidently whenever Granny asked, it had kind of stopped feeling like a lie at all.

Another part of me, though, had loosened within this exchange. He'd just defended me, a non-magical stranger—a prisoner, of all things. He'd done it so vehemently. I felt like I owed him that truth.

Or was that a lie, too? Did I actually just want someone, *anyone* to hear my pain? Pain I hadn't been willing or able to tell Granny without her doing something to make matters worse? Writing it in my journal was therapeutic, but it hadn't ever been completely enough.

I shrugged, a little uncomfortable, opening my mouth to respond.

He held up a finger. "Hold that thought. We don't

need this butt plug listening in and passing it around. He's an awful wanker."

He pushed the package back into the wagon.

"You're one to talk," the man said, bristling. "How many times did you get caught whacking off behind a tree?"

"Not as many as within the tents, I'll tell you that. If only someone with a firm grip would take over, I wouldn't have to do it myself. Do me a favor, Chuck. Go stick your head in a pond and try to breathe. That would save us all a lot of heartache."

The man's chest puffed out, his arms flaring at his sides. "Get bent, you little runt."

"Fuck a cactus." Hadriel closed up the wagon and ushered me in front of him. "Come on, love, don't worry about him. There's a reason he's back here tending the supplies. Mediocrity would be a step up for the likes of that cock drip."

At the end of the line of supplies, he pointed me to a grouping of thick-based trees. "Just pop behind there and change your shirt really quickly. Please don't run. My nerves are fried, and I really don't want to chase you. I certainly don't want to deal with a feral alpha."

I did as he said, handing back the ripped shirt when I was done.

"And thanks," he said, ushering me toward the front of the line again.

"For what?"

"For letting the alpha finger bang you. I would've gotten my ass chewed for letting you wander away. Here we go."

It took Hadriel and someone else to get me onto the

horse. There was only a padded sort of blanket, something he mentioned had to do with two people. I wouldn't fit in the saddle with him.

After he was up, I spied the alpha—Weston—at the head of the procession, strong and handsome, sitting atop a fierce-eyed, white stallion. The sun highlighted streaks of blond in his hair, sparkling as though a halo. His people, waiting around him patiently, sat tall, regal and confident, on horses just as fine. Their clothing wasn't colorful, as Hadriel had hinted, but was made with fine fabrics and sewn with an expert hand. It was clear the alpha led a very rich and powerful pack.

Another spark of pride worked through me, as though I had a right to it. Even if that wasn't so hopelessly fucked up because of my situation, all I'd done was fuck him. If I'd had magic, I still would never be in high enough standing for anything more. Not for someone like him.

His head was bowed just slightly, engrossed by something he held.

As though feeling my gaze, he suddenly straightened and turned to me. Butterflies exploded in my middle. His deep voice uttered something, his tone low, said to the person at his side and a little behind him. I was too far away to hear it. Then he tapped his heels to his horse's sides, starting forward.

"Okay now." Hadriel tore me out of my focus. "Let's go over how we keep you on this horse, shall we? You're going to hold me around the middle, but don't hold too tightly or the alpha will freak out. Definitely don't grab my cock. I wouldn't really mind, but the alpha would.

Tweaking my nipple a little would be great, but only when he's not looking."

I spit out an unexpected laugh.

"Oh good, you have a sense of humor. This will go swimmingly."

I did hold him too tightly. I clutched onto him like I would fall to my death at any moment. We were just so high up and it all felt so unsteady. At one point, the animal stubbed its toe or something. It had jolted forward, as though ready to tumble or buck or roll over. I didn't know which, all I knew was that I was halfway off its back and ready to dive to my safety before being crushed under its dancing hooves.

Hadriel had been able to steady the animal and grab me simultaneously, hauling me back up. I'd nearly crawled across his back when I'd been righted, only then noticing Weston not far away, his eyes filled with murder.

"I've got her, sir," Hadriel had said jovially. "Just a little slip is all. We're all fine here. She'll get the hang of it."

He didn't say a word, just about-faced and headed back to his horse. He must've hopped off and run back when I was struggling to jump or climb back on or just throw up the white flag in defeat.

Before he'd re-mounted, he bent to pick something up. A brief flash of what it was had my blood boiling.

One of my journals. My private thoughts, ransacked from my home.

Taking me was one thing, but that sort of flagrant violation of privacy was another completely. Worse, in the hour or so we'd been traveling, he had hardly come up for air. He'd looked up once, to spy something in the trees, and then went right back to reading all of my most intimate thoughts as though hating to tear his focus away.

My insides shriveled in embarrassment. In rage.

There had to be a way to find out where he stashed those things and burn them all. Maybe I could arrange to do it when he was knocked out cold in the same vicinity. I had a product that would put him into a deep sleep, I just had to get to it.

WESTON

"*It should be you who is riding with her,*" my animal accused, my heart still racing as I swung my foot up and over the saddle. "*It should be you she is clinging onto. You who teaches her to ride. It's your duty.*"

"This is my duty," I said, getting underway and flipping open the third journal so far. I was flying through them, finding most of the entries about her life, her day, the people around her.

"*Trespassing in her thoughts?*"

"Skimming these pages and finding out what she knows."

"*Skimming.*" His laugh held no humor. "*Is that what it's called when you go back and read a passage for the third time?*"

I flexed and unflexed my fingers before opening to the page I'd left off on. Instead of reading right away, though, I looked out to the side. He was right, of course. I wasn't skimming, not even hardly. I'd meant to, I'd tried to . . . but I just couldn't stop myself from reading every single word, sometimes two and three times, feeling the moment through her thoughts, feeling rage well up at each slight she'd endured. If I'd known how her co-worker had treated her, I would've killed him when I'd had the chance. Alexander was a fucking dead man. I'd make it slow, too. He'd feel every ounce of fear he'd caused her. He'd feel more pain than he could believe was possible. And then I'd throw him to the dragons to drop his broken carcass from a great height, filling his final moments with terror. That childhood sweetheart turned almost-friend would've been chased away easily, Aurelia clearly too naive to realize he was looking for the courage to make her his sidepiece. And Granny . . .

Rage tinted the edges of my vision red. There were no words.

It was clear Aurelia had held her up on some sort of pedestal. Granny had taken her in at the tender age of twelve and apparently saved her life. Aurelia had been on the run. From what, I didn't know. She'd been starved, though, that much I'd gathered. Scared, near death. No one would open their home to a dirty, magic-less shifter, not even a child. Or so Aurelia had thought. I couldn't believe that was the case, but that was the reality as she'd known it. It was the reality Granny had certainly allowed the girl to believe. Manipulating her must've been a cinch, especially with the way the village of small-minded people stuck in their ways treated her.

The journal held my focus. My gaze swung downward helplessly, picking up the next entry.

July 9

I talked to Granny about the rancid food order last week. She promised to talk to the suppliers.

She's usually so good about looking after the village but this is the third time this has happened, and her response was exactly the same as the last two times. I get that I'm supposed to stay healthy because the village relies on my ability to make product, but several families didn't get enough. Little Maggie was crying at market a couple days ago because she was hungry. I can't, in good conscience, get my fill while others go hungry. If more doesn't come as Granny promised, they could be in trouble.

The day ended as all the others had, with a memory of her mother. This one was of a rare feast they'd enjoyed like kings after her mother had found a gold coin in the street. I got the impression Aurelia hadn't had constant and plentiful meals when in her mother's care. They seemed to move around a lot, their homes never consistent. Had they been on the run, even then? Had whatever killed the mother then followed little Aurelia?

Curiosity ate at me.

I flipped another page, desperate to find answers to this enigma.

August 11

Alexander paid me a visit today. My ribs hurt from where he repeatedly punched me. I don't think anything is broken, but it hurts to breathe. I guess it's a good thing no one talks to me because I won't be surprised by any jokes. Laughing would hurt like hell.

I shouldn't have told Granny that I've been giving some of my rations away when the food comes in rotten. I wasn't prepared to lie, though. I hadn't realized I'd lost weight.

I get why I was punished, because yes, I know I need to make the product, but honestly, this situation cannot go on. It <u>can't</u>!

Granny got all stony when I told her that. She doesn't like when I get angry and likes it even less when I push back. But it had to be said. Everyone else in the village is too scared to say anything.

What's really frustrating is they won't take my rations if I hand it to them. If I take what's mine and then distribute, they won't accept the food they need. They'd rather let it go off than take it <u>for their children</u> from a "magic-less cur." So I have to just take what I need to keep most of my weight on and let them have the extra.

At least they are distributing it how I most likely would have. The end result is the same, I guess, but come on, really?! No thank you? No acknowledgement? They won't even take the fucking food because it was me who gave it? It's such bullshit.

Sometimes this village just seems like a soulless, unforgiving place. A hollow place, filled with empty smiles and passionless chatter. People seemed really happy when Granny first started her business and was fixing things. There was a lot of food and new products and stuff for everyone then. Now, though, people don't seem as thrilled. I guess hunger will do that to a person.

Granny needs to fix this food issue. It's the main reason

people were excited for this new setup. I remember that. Until then, I guess I'll get really good at stretching food resources.

There wasn't a memory that time. Just a simple and heartbreaking: *I miss you, Mom. I miss our happy home, wherever it was. I miss your cuddles and your stories. I'm lonely. Maybe someday soon I'll see you again. More and more, I think I'd like that better than this.*

I flipped the page, oblivious to my surroundings. Trees passed, scents floated by, but I didn't notice any of them, so intent I was on the next passage.

September 20

    I guess it wasn't just me that got punished this time.

    I've lost more weight and Granny was concerned. Alexander really took to me today. I have two black eyes, definitely a broken rib, and bruises all over my body. Xarion came and visited. He brought me some broth.

    Five other people got a visit from Alexander. All women —the mothers of the families that often got the extra rations. I guess they said they didn't get it from me, that it was just what was left over and the kids needed it, but Granny didn't believe them.

    Plus side: <u>this</u> was why they wouldn't take the food from me directly. They didn't want Granny to find out they were taking what was mine. I don't know why they couldn't just *tell me that instead of calling me a slur, but whatever. At least it isn't me. Not totally, at any rate.*

Bad news: I'm getting preferential treatment over <u>children.</u> I can't accept that. I won't.

I see a lot more punishments in my future because fuck Granny. I won't take the food. If she doesn't send enough, she'll lose her prized drug maker. I made that very clear to her. I shouted at her, actually. She can have her dog punish me as much as she wants, it won't change my mind.

Mama, I'll probably join you shortly. I will not yield in this.

December 19

Not dead yet.

Plus: I don't feel pain like I used to. Alexander has to really work for a reaction, and often that gets too close to killing me.

Bad: It's taken a lot of beatings to get to this stage.

Fuck them both.

January 1

New day.

New year.

I won.

Granny fixed the food situation. She needs me working and when I'm all busted up, I can't work. She's also agreed to go back to how things started—fixing up the village and keeping people happy.

I'm pretty well-hated. For a while, she thought punishing villagers, including children, would make me come around. I held firm for the greater good. Even Granny has limits, it seems. Alexander never worked over the children much at all. Spankings and a few bruises. That helped me stay strong. Everyone else has accelerated healing. It helped them to hold out until we got what we needed to live.

I wish I could just leave, but I have nowhere to go. Beatings are still living. Life means mama keeps living through my memories. If I leave, I'll be killed and so will she. Hopefully it'll get better.

Her handwriting was hardly legible by the end, simply ending it with "love you Mama." She must've been deeply in pain, broken nearly beyond repair.

My entire body coiled as I struggled with a rush of rage so extreme I could hardly think. My wolf prowled within me, desperate to go back to that village and level it, kill them all. She was so young. Seventeen, judging by the date. Alone. Hated because of how Granny had singled her out and focused on her. Hated even though she was sacrificing herself—her body and her dignity—for that village. It was disgusting. Heart-wrenching.

The lengths she went to push back against the alpha of the village, to her detriment, was awe-inspiring. Her courage was incredible, her morals noble. She was willing to be beat to death to ensure the people and children—children who weren't even hers—had what they needed to survive. More, she held strong even when others were dragged into the beatings with her, knowing they all had to stand united, unbending, unyielding, against the tyrant in order to claim their victory. Battle commanders hardly had that clear a purpose, nor leaders of great packs, of kingdoms. And she'd been only seventeen with no experience and no training, just her conscience.

Everything in me wanted to go to her now, pull her from her horse and wrap her in my arms. I wanted to ensure she would never, not *ever*, be harmed like that again. I would protect her, mind, body, and wolf. I would hunt for her and feed her, tend to all her needs, worship her body, make sure she never wanted for another thing as long as she lived.

But that was impossible. I was doing exactly the opposite, now delivering her to a punishment she likely wouldn't walk away from. Granny had cultivated the problem, and to fix it I had to damn my true mate.

My thoughts and feelings were so fucking conflicted. I hated that I could see both sides of this, not sure which tugged at me more. I had to remember that she'd killed people. She'd saved her village but damned many others. She'd gone through hell—I couldn't even think about it without the uncontrollable rage—but put many others through hell at the same time and for years to come. She was not innocent. There was a reason I'd been sent to find her.

But gods help me, reading her words, walking in her shoes . . . I didn't fucking care. I couldn't stand it. I couldn't even understand it. Beating children so Granny could get her way? Serving people rotten food? Incomprehensible. What kind of monster ran that village?

Also incomprehensible was the change in Aurelia's

outlook. She'd seemed to hate Granny in these passages. It didn't seem like the same woman who had burst into Granny's cottage with an axe and faced four powerful shifters without flinching. To know her now, one would assume she had a great love for her benefactor. If nothing else, then loyalty and pride in her job. What had changed? How had Granny worked her back around?

I reached for the next page, waiting to hear my wolf grumble. Instead, he was silent. He wanted to know, too. He wanted to piece all of this together, because right now, my heart went out to young Aurelia. She'd had nobody on her side, but she still held firm for the greater good. She believed that their happiness was a direct result of her performance.

I shook my head, sweating a little, knowing I wouldn't be delving this deeply into her past if it didn't affect me directly. Fuck it, though, I had to know. I had to know if she'd been corrupted in the end, or if she'd been maneuvered so thoroughly that she honestly believed the things she had been telling me. It mattered. To me, it mattered. Her life ending might happen all the same, but at least I'd know my true mate wasn't evil to the core. I wasn't sure how I'd handle the knowledge that my supposed mirror was as rotten as I'd once feared myself to be.

14

AURELIA

"*T*here are forty-two!" I told Hadriel as we wound through the trees. I'd leaned forward against him, my cheek on the back of his shoulder and my hands randomly exploring his jacket. I could feel the threads creating the dicks, giving me something to do as we traveled. I didn't dare uncurl my arms. A while ago I'd almost abandoned horse again. It had stepped on a rock that rolled a bit and the horse adjusted gracefully.

My reaction was anything but.

I'd almost truly fallen by the time Hadriel had caught me, gripping my wrist as I half dangled over the side. This time Weston was useful, his hands on my ribs firm but the way he handed me back up to Hadriel gentle. He waited for me to get my leg back over then grip Hadriel tightly, watching me without a word. When I was settled, his acute focus switched to Hadriel.

"What is happening that she keeps falling off?" he asked, his tone scary, made evident by Hadriel curling over and his ass and thighs clenching. I was that close that I could feel it.

Hadriel had stuck up for me. I'd done the same for him.

"Only a fucking idiot would think it was his fault that I can't stay on a horse," I said, my anger evident. "I've never done this before and I'm traveling without a saddle. It's terrifying up here. If you'd let me walk as nature intended, we wouldn't be in this mess."

"And what mess is that, exactly?"

"The one where my instincts tell me I'd better save myself from being rolled over by a horse and trying to jump to safety."

Weston's expression did not change, his face utterly blank. His eyes started to sparkle, though. "You're worried about the horse somehow rolling over on you?"

"In the moment it's really hard to tell what, exactly, I am afraid of, actually. But yes, that would be terrible."

"And you think falling off the side, onto the ground at its feet, would somehow prevent this horror?"

"Look, I don't know. This horse could decide I'm a nuisance and buck me clear off. I'm ready to just do it a favor and get off by myself before that happens."

He stared at me for a long moment before shaking his head. "Please don't. Hadriel is an excellent and experienced horseman. His horse is well-handled and well used to that handling. You are in no safer hands. Trust him. I wouldn't have put you up there if I didn't think you'd be safe."

Hadriel straightened up, clearly preening. He'd liked the praise. Job well done.

"I'll do better," I told the alpha out of habit, something I'd said to Granny after every call down. It seemed to appease her, the quickest way to get me out of her angry glare.

Weston didn't move, the glimmer in his eyes dulling. He studied me for another moment, his hand coming out to rest on the horse's rump. Without another word, he walked back to his stallion, bending to pick up the journal he'd dropped when hopping off, then pausing to retrieve another from a little sack he had on the side of his saddle.

I turned my face to the side and leaned against Hadriel again, not wanting to watch Weston read my innermost thoughts. I went back to tracing the dicks.

"Fucking hell," Hadriel said softly as we got moving again. "Thanks for defending me, but I thought he might brain the both of us with how you did it." He blew out a shaky breath. "Only you would be able to calm him down like that."

"Because I'm a captive?"

"Something like that. And yes, you're right, there are forty-two dicks on this jacket."

"You said there were forty-three."

"On my person, yes."

I paused for a moment, watching the trees slowly drift by. Darkening shadows gathered near the bases and deep within the branches. The evening waned, the light bleeding from the sky, an issue for the horses as well as me. We'd have to stop soon. My aching butt and legs could sure use the reprieve.

"On your person," I said slowly, mulling that over before leaning back and nearly yanking my hands away.

"Gross. You mean you counted your actual dick in the forty-three?"

His laughter was loud and jubilant. People glanced back, making me slouch behind him again. He didn't mind the contact at all. He'd never once flinched away or tightened up. I could've been his best friend for how comfortable he was with my touch. I found I liked it—the easy, friendly closeness.

"Usually I don't spell it out so clearly," he said, still chuckling. "If I'm flirting, the hint is sexual. If it's a new person in the castle, I might be more lewd."

"But with me?"

"I'm obvious and your reaction is priceless. Welcome to debauchery, my darling. We're going to have a whole lot of fun. Now, quit stalling. It's your turn for a story. I told you about my scary encounter with the Mighty Vagina that had teeth. You tell me something from your life."

His stories were so insane that they all just seemed like crass fabrications of reality, like a never-ending party with unlimited product at his disposal. He'd take my concoctions in stride. I'd told him so. They might not even be enough to compete with his past.

Then he'd mentioned addiction and dying and we agreed to disagree. Because while maybe I would allow that people were getting addicted based on their desire for the effects, they were *not* dying. We'd never had one fatality. Not one! It's why I'd put in fail-safes. It's why I'd designed the product a certain way. If people were taking hallucinogens and dying from them, they weren't taking my product. End of story.

Hadriel hadn't pushed like Weston always had.

Instead, he listened to a story that didn't at all relate to my village, Granny or my job. I told him about my mom finally scraping enough money together to buy a forever home for us, and how we'd created a vegetable garden and planted flowers.

"That sounds lovely," Hadriel said when I'd finished. The light continued to decay around us. "I love flowers. I'm absolute shit at keeping them alive, but I love them."

"I'm not great, either."

"And where is your mom now?"

I leaned harder into him, resting my cheek on his shoulder, my fingers stilling in tracing the dicks on his jacket. "The townspeople didn't like that we'd moved in. They used to throw things at us and call us names when we shopped. I remember someone standing on the other side of the lane from us as we walked home one day, yelling that we had no business in the shifter lands. We didn't belong."

"Why is that?"

"Because we had no magic."

"Your mom was suppressed also?"

"I'm—we aren't suppressed. *She* wasn't suppressed. She didn't have magic. She was a dud. I'm sure you've heard the term."

"Riiiight . . ." He drew out the word. "But many people call shifters duds when that shifter is just suppressed. A strong alpha can usually pull out the animal. It doesn't even need to be the same shifter type. A dragon pulled out my wolf."

He'd told me stories of his animal being suppressed by the demons, their whole kingdom cursed and living without the magic that made them shifters. I believed

213

him when he said he knew what it was like not to feel an animal inside or have the benefits of healing and strength. Weston, too, it seemed, had lived for a time without his animal.

"She went to the strongest alphas she could find to try and pull out her animal. It didn't work. They couldn't even feel one inside her. The last alpha apparently made me, and when she'd told him she was with child, he banished her from the kingdom."

"Wait." Hadriel half turned to look back at me. I clutched onto him, worried I'd slide down the side of the horse. "Wait, wait, fucking stop. Stop. Everyone just calm the fuck down."

"What?" I glanced around but no one so much as looked over. "Are you talking to me or the horse or . . .?"

"Banished her from the kingdom?" Hadriel asked, still trying to turn and look at me. "That's not a thing unless you're royalty."

"She was anything but royalty. She grew up poor. Her family didn't have much, including power."

"And the alpha that put something in instead of pulling something out?"

I spit out a laugh and then snaked my hand between us to wipe him down. "Sorry."

"Don't worry about that, spit is the least of the terrible substances that have been sprayed on me. Talk faster, love, I'm dying from curiosity."

I shook my head slowly, trying to remember the scant things she'd said about it. I'd never pushed, seeing how much it hurt her.

"I don't think the alpha was royalty, no. But she did go to the court to ask for help, and I think she was granted an audience by one of the staff or something. She was really beautiful, my mom. Really lovely. She had this . . . way about her. Men could be calling her a name one moment, and then asking her over the next. She never went, not that I saw. I get why. It's demoralizing when all they want is your body and then are disgusted with themselves after they have it. I had to learn that the hard way."

"I feel for you, love. I do actually know what that's like. With me, it was guys influenced by the demon magic who just wanted to fuck. They didn't care what. That's what that magic does to you. The next day, though, when they realized they'd been with me—another man . . . We'll just say that the fall-out wasn't pleasant."

I nodded. Different situations with the same result. I hugged him a little tighter and he put his hand over mine, sharing our pain. Sharing a moment. I felt my eyes prick with tears knowing someone understood.

"She was with the alpha from court for a few months before she realized she was pregnant. I think it blindsided her that he didn't want me. She'd been desperately in love, and it seemed like she'd thought he was, too. When he sent her away . . . It crushed her. She couldn't talk about it without breaking down. I think that's why she went. He'd torn out her heart and she didn't have the will to fight. She took the money for passage and a little coin for starting a new life and left. She rarely talked about it. It was just us after that, town to town, house to house."

"Why did you move so often?"

"Chased out, usually. Our forever home was her

finally saying she planned to stay, come hell's fury. I think she did it for me. I hated moving. I hated having no friends and no consistency. But hell's fury is exactly what came." I swallowed thickly. It felt like a confessional, telling him this way, talking to his back, not seeing his eyes. It was why I continued, hopeful he would understand. Hopeful his open mind would give him some inkling of understanding this, like he had understood the other part. Because then I wouldn't be so hopelessly alone in dealing with it. "In the middle of the night a bunch of men broke in, beat her until she couldn't stand, and lit the house on fire with us in it."

"Stop." He ran his hands through his hair. "Wait. Fucking hell, give me a moment. Now, I know in the rural places people can be horrible to those suppressed. Those without magic usually move to the cities. I'd heard of this kind of brutality but as some sort of . . . I don't know, urban legend. Like the way things used to be before we all had more awareness."

"I assure you, the fear of those without magic—the raw hatred stemming from that fear—is alive and well. People in my village worried they'd lose access to their animals if I got too close."

"Good-fucking-grief. Fine. That's horrible, I have fucking tears in my eyes, but fine. You were in the house, though? I've never heard of violence toward a child, or a family with a child. Not even for this strange sort of fear-induced-mania."

"My mom had rejected one of the guys. I think people in the town taunted him about it. 'Can't even get a dud to spread her legs for you, huh? What sorta man are you?' That festered until he turned it into violence.

They were killing her. I couldn't stay hidden like she wanted."

"What did you do?"

My breath shuddered as I sucked in air, remembering that night. Remembering my terror and emotional agony. "I got knives from the kitchen and I stabbed as many as I could. I was young—I couldn't do enough damage. It must've brought them to their senses, though, because they took off. All except the main guy. He slapped me so hard I blacked out. When I came to, she was lying in a broken heap and the house was roaring with flames."

Pain unfurled in my middle, rising up until it dragged me under. Flames danced in my memory, blood pooling, my head pounding, my heart shattering.

"I ran," I said as sobs made my body shake. "She told me to run, so I ran. She told me to stay alive so that I could remember her. I couldn't move her—she was too heavy. I couldn't drag her out. Trying made her cry out and she begged me to stop. It was so hot in there. She told me to run, so I ran. I should've helped her. I should've saved her."

"Hey, hey." The movement under me stopped. I felt Hadriel's hands grip mine and hug them awkwardly, pulling me tighter against his back. "It's okay. Listen, you're not going to like this, but let him comfort you. It'll help the best, okay? Give in to his comfort. Trust me."

"Give her to me," I heard, the voice heavy with command.

"No," I said weakly as strong arms pulled me from the horse and crushed me close.

217

"Give in to it, just this once," Hadriel said, and because his tone was riddled with pain on my behalf, and because I truly felt like he was trying to help, I did. I relaxed against the alpha as he carried me to the side, barking orders at his people to stop here for the night and set up camp.

"I'm here," he cooed, his tone deep and comforting, his arms tight around me. "It's okay to let go."

Leaves brushed my hair as I buried my face into his neck. He carried us into the trees and away from the noise of the others. I heaved with sobs.

"Let go," he coaxed, still walking us away until I couldn't hear the clamor and chatter of the pack. Until all that existed was us and the surrounding nature scene, the birds singing overhead and little critters scurrying out of the way.

"I couldn't help but overhear your story," Weston said, his voice so soft, his embrace firm. "She wanted you to live, above all else. That's why you had to run. You *had* to, for her. You did it for her. It was brave."

He sat, situating me on his lap before rocking me gently, his cheek resting on my head. I cried against his chest, the electricity buzzing between us, a soft warmth throbbing in my middle. That strange mind- and mood-altering drug I felt when he was near helped me now, grounding me in the moment. It seemed to help smooth out the pain, rounding out the corners and sanding away the worst of the agony.

"I miss her," I whispered, tears soaking into his shirt. "I miss her so much." He rubbed my back as he rocked me. "I still wake up with nightmares. I shouldn't have left. I should've tried harder."

"She must've known you would've died trying. She wanted to save you. I'm sure it gave her great comfort that you lived."

I was quiet for a long time. Crickets began their slow, mournful throb. Emberflies filtered in around us. An owl hooted somewhere overhead.

"If I think about it," I finally ventured, "I know that you're right. I did as she said, and I cherish her memory because I know that's what she would've wanted. But when I think of that scared little girl that left her mommy to die—"

His arms constricted around me. "Let's forget our situation for the moment. What can I do? How can I help?"

"Make love to me. Give me a distraction to help pull me out of the darkness."

I'd said it before I'd thought about it, and then fell into it once I had. He wasted no time, but he wasn't fervent like before. He kissed me deeply, standing with me to remove my clothing and then his own. His movements weren't frenzied or stormy but slow and gentle, methodical. Comforting. He pulled me with him as he walked backward, our lips devouring each other, the feel of his body stealing my focus until all I knew was him, his taste, the feel of his embrace. He settled in a soft, mossy spot without breaking our kiss, directing my thighs to either side of his. He ran his cock along my wetness before wrapping me in his arms and pulling me down onto him.

His groan matched my own, the sensations heaven. Without regret, without thinking about my oath to stay away from him or what I might feel about our situation tomorrow, I began rocking my hips over him, taking him deep and then stroking back. His breath became labored, his hands all over me, mine on him. The base of his cock began to swell, butting up against me.

"Do you want it, Little Wolf?" he murmured against my lips, his tone tender.

"Yes." It wasn't even a question.

I ground down onto him while working my clit. He growled, his teeth raking up the side of my neck and his lips stopping at the shell of my ear.

"*Mine*," he said possessively, pulling down on my shoulders as he lifted his hips, fucking his knot into me.

Tingles worked up my spine as he continued to swell, his movements different now, grinding it deeper, locking us together. Being so new to his size meant an inkling of pain still registered along the edges of my awareness, but I didn't care. I was so wet it dribbled down between us.

"That's right, baby," he groaned, holding me tightly so that I couldn't get away. One of his hands fisted in my hair, his teeth raked my neck again. "Take it. Take your alpha's knot and keep all my cum locked deep inside of you like a good girl."

Holy fuck, I loved when he talked dirty.

"Fuck it into me," I moaned, joining in, throwing my head back. "Mark me as you fuck it into me."

The sensations expanded as he did, overwhelming me. He adjusted so that he was on his knees, my legs around his waist, my arms around his shoulders. He rolled his hips and twisted me, his cock deep, his teeth at my neck. His arms still held me, his strength and power wrapped around me possessively, his hold firm but gentle.

"Do you like when I fuck that sweet little pussy?" The language sent me spiraling.

"Yes," I groaned, moving on him with abandon. "Please . . . almost . . . there . . ."

His movements were small but so fucking perfect. I kept building, so high I started gyrating wildly. A flash of pain stole my breath and he crushed me to him, one hand on my ass and the other tangled in my hair—keeping me from hurting myself by pulling away. The swell of his cock had trapped me on his dick. Even if I'd wanted to escape, I wouldn't have been able to. I was completely at his mercy. For some reason that made me vibrate with indescribable pleasure.

"Please . . . I need . . . to come," I panted through labored breaths.

His lips were near my ear, my body in his control. He relieved one hand from my back and circled my clit with his fingers before giving it a sharp tug.

"Holy—" I cried out as I shuddered against him. My pussy tightened around his cock with the waves of my climax and a moment later he groaned, filling me with heat like he'd promised.

The thought made me start building again, wanting my alpha's seed lodged deep, the need primal and maybe a little nasty but fucking delicious at the same time. I'd never been talked to like this, or pumped and gyrated so hard just to hear the wet sounds of sex we made. It was perfection, consuming.

"That's right, baby," he said as I neared another

orgasm. "Use me. Think about nothing else but this. Get lost in the moment."

Feeling grateful, I did exactly that. When the next orgasm came, I rode it with exquisite shudders, then did the same with the next, his knot pulsing all the while. The swell didn't diminish as I worked, his body holding strong during my need.

By the time I'd exhausted myself, full night had settled around us. His dick still lay huge and heavy within me, but the pulse had slowed. He held me tightly, leaning back against a trunk so that I could lay across his chest.

Emberflies drifted around us, more than I'd ever seen. Their lazy movement through the air was mesmerizing. Ethereal.

"How long can you stay like this?" I asked, my eyelids heavy, his warmth radiating around me.

"As long as you need."

"No, I mean your cock. How long will it . . . lock us together?"

He was quieter this time. "As long as you need."

"I didn't think you had control over it."

"I don't. My body is responding to yours, I think."

I sat up and scanned his face. "I didn't know that was how it worked."

Weston shook his head slowly. "Me either, but here we are. You have a need. It seems my body's response is to fulfill that need for as long as you require. My cock has never lasted longer than a half-hour after completion, max. Yet last night it lasted over an hour and didn't subside until you'd passed out. I'd been worried you'd drain all my fluids before you were finally done with me."

I stared at him mutely, wanting to argue. I wanted to accuse him of trying to put last night on me again. But right now, his body inside mine felt too good and I didn't want to jeopardize losing it. Right now, I did have a need, and I did want him to fulfill it. Whether it was my doing or his, I didn't really care.

I laid back down against his chest. He rubbed my back gently, gliding his fingers along my skin. His release of breath seemed tranquil. Maybe he needed this, too. Maybe it was both of us responding to each other in this moment, forgetting the horrible outside world.

"Do you want to stay here, or would you rather settle in a bed?" he asked as I watched the emberflies.

"Are you uncomfortable?"

"I'm not worried about me."

He must've been, though, on his knees, leaning back against a tree with no real support, his muscles bulging to keep the position. If I hadn't known anything else about him, I'd think he was a true gentleman. A saint, maybe, sacrificing his own comfort to ensure I was looked after. Someone that would put my needs above his own.

Sadly, that was the stuff of fairy tales, and my life was anything but. In reality, he was just ensuring I didn't have a breakdown before he delivered me to the dragons.

I pushed off his chest and pulled the back of his neck to get him upright again. At least I could relish in the

K.F. BREENE

journey before the harsh light of day burned away all the pixie dust.

"One more," I murmured, pushing my breast toward his mouth. He sucked in the peak, swirling his tongue and making my eyes roll into the back of my head. "Then bed," I whispered.

If he was allowing me to control this, I'd get my fill. His cock now, and then his body wrapped around mine protectively as though I was some sort of priceless treasure he was scared to let leave his sight.

If I was going to dream, I'd dream big.

15

AURELIA

"*N*ow, love, how do you feel?" Hadriel pushed into the tent with a steaming cup of the horrible tasting tea in his hand.

I was dressed and ready, having woken up with the big alpha curled around me, just as I'd wanted, his lips against my bare shoulder, his arms holding me close. He had laid me there last night, the two of us merged as one.

As predicted, of course, the morning brought its troubles. It hadn't taken long for him to roll away and for my situation to become real again. We'd had a moment, yes. But that moment had passed.

Still, it had been great while it lasted. The sex had been fucking amazing. Out of this world. The only awkward part had been when he was carrying me through camp, only one tent setup. Everyone else would sleep under the stars in wolf form, as was easier for a pack on the move. He'd had me put on my shirt, had covered my bare ass with our remaining clothes, and had even held me in a somewhat awkward position as he strutted to the tent, confident and strong and somehow not at all mortified. He'd barked at everyone to turn around at our passing, giving me the respect of whatever privacy could be managed. It was chivalrous and kind, and if he'd stayed that way, my heart might've melted just a little bit towards him.

Unfortunately, this morning he was back to being an insufferable prick. He'd barked at me to get up and get dressed. The sooner he could get me to the dragons, the better. My time for emotional turbulence was over. There were clearly more important things to do, like hurry me to my death.

"Fine." I stood and reached for the tea. "Sorry about yesterday. About . . ." I motioned to my eyes. "You know."

"Don't you dare, you horrible creature." He frowned at me comically before handing me the mug. "I had a good cry as well. Then I asked the hottest guy in this mini-detail for a pity lay."

I nearly spit out the tea I'd sipped. "How did that go?"

His lips pulled wide, stretching out his little mustache. "Not amazing. He told me to suck it up or it would be his foot in my ass, not his cock. I, of course, told him I could work with whatever got him off. He did not find that joke amusing, especially when he realized I wasn't joking." He shrugged. "It was worth a shot. Okay, here we go. We have a lot of ground to cover today, and I am hoping to do it without you jumping horse, so to speak."

He ushered me to his beautiful horse who I was positive glanced back at me with an ill-suffering look. Poor thing. I felt bad for it. Weston sat at the front again, his head bowed, reading. Prick.

"Have you ever heard," I said softly, leaning close, "that an al—"

"Nope." Hadriel waggled his finger in my direction.

I leaned back again, closing my mouth, wondering if he'd decided chatting with me was not a good way to pass the time after all. It hadn't really worked out well for him the day before.

After the procession was underway, though, he glanced over his shoulder. "Sorry about that," he murmured. "I figured it might be better for more noise and a softer voice. You were planning to ask about the alpha, were you not?"

"Y-yeah."

"I thought so. You had that scandalized tone to your voice. Shifters with access to their animals have excellent hearing. Clearly you don't realize how good."

"Clearly." I tried again, this time in a whisper. "Have you heard that an alpha's knot is dependent on the female?"

"What do you mean?"

"Like, it stays . . . big for as long as the female wills it?"

"No. But then there might be a different dynamic for your situation."

"My situation? People without magic, you mean?"

"Uhmm . . ." He adjusted his seating as though uncomfortable. "No—well, I just mean that maybe he knows you need it, and is responding to that need . . .

Actually, you know what, let's revisit that another time. Without hitting a pressure point, we've discovered that your mother might not have had any magic. That, or it was so suppressed that she couldn't find anyone strong enough to pull out her animal. But what's your deal? Why do you assume *you* don't have any magic?"

I started tracing the dicks on his jacket again, this a different jacket than the other. "Do all your jackets have dicks on them?"

"No. Some have vaginas. The seamster, Cecil, is a horrible jackass. Answer the question."

"Oh. Well, my mom didn't have magic, and that trait is always passed on."

"It almost never is, actually. It's quite rare not to have one's magic flower, but every person born a shifter still has the genes. But I see what you're saying. You've always assumed you don't have magic because your mother doesn't, then?"

I furrowed my brow, shaking my head a little. "I've always heard that a parent will pass on magiclessness. And anyway, Granny is—was—a pretty powerful alpha and she said she couldn't feel an animal in me. She tried every year just to appease me. You know, because sometimes there are late bloomers."

He went rigid.

I leaned back a little to give him space. "Sorry if you thought I was just suppressed. Do you want me to walk?"

"Aurelia, my darling, don't dip your toes into the absurd. That is not your journey. Granny told you that you didn't have an animal?"

"Yes. She tried numerous times. She said she'd be able to feel something even if she wasn't strong enough to pull it out."

"She certainly should've been able to, that is true. And obviously, without magic, you'd have worried that life outside of Granny's village would end in the same sort of trauma you witnessed as a child, but this time it would be targeted at you. And while you seem like a determined, stubborn sort of person who wouldn't back down in the face of adversity, I imagine you worried that if the tormentors succeeded, you'd fail in keeping your mother's promise in remembering her?"

It was silent all around us but for hooves thumping against the ground and the squeak of carts farther back. Weston's head had come up, clearly having heard me and Hadriel talking, this apparently more interesting than my other issues and hurdles over the years.

I hunched a little, my gaze finding the ground, still so far away. "You're pretty astute."

"I'm incredibly good at reading people, love. It makes me unbelievable at sussing out information through gossip."

"Which is why you are my babysitter, I take it? You try and pull information out of me through idle chitchat while Head Dick over there reads my most intimate thoughts and feelings from over the years."

"Something like that, yes." He patted my leg. "I'm enjoying my time with you, though, if it's any consolation."

At least he was honest. I supposed that might've been the reason I didn't take offense to it. That, and I was enjoying my time as well. Most of it, anyway. I enjoyed his easy banter and his effortless proximity. I liked that he seemed to actually care about my stories and worried I might break my neck from jumping off the horse.

Maybe it just boiled down to the fact it felt like he actually cared, and I craved that. I was big enough to admit it.

I shrugged. "Is that so hard to fathom? Granny kept me safe. She kept us all safe. And look, what she said would happen if I got captured came to pass. Imprisonment, taking me away, the leader using me for sex . . ." She had failed to mention I'd like it. "She tried to protect me from exactly this. And you killed her for it."

"Phew." Hadriel braced a hand on his thigh. "This is a juicy onion. I have water works with each layer."

"It's just . . ." My voice was firm, knowing Weston was listening. "You've been suppressed, fine. But, number one, you knew you had magic, and number two, you were in the same boat as the whole kingdom. You were all in it together. I don't have magic and I'm on my own. I'm the only one. My mom looked for help and look where it got her. She tried to settle down, look where that got her. Right now, I have—or had—a forever home. I have flowers and a semblance of a garden. I have a life. A community. They might not like me being there, but at least they tolerate me. They don't try to force me out. All of this without magic. I had it pretty damned good for my situation, and I know that from experience." I paused to take a steadying breath. "So yes, I'd go against the law as long as it wasn't hurting anyone—and it isn't, by the way. I dealt with the punishments from Granny when I stepped out of line because you know what? My life with her was a helluva lot better than the alternative. Even being punished or killed by your dragons is better than what I've already been through. These streaks of white in my hair are from trauma--being chased out with pitchforks when I was four, or seeing my mother get stoned in the street, barely able to escape, or hiding in wet bushes, freezing, starving, hoping the dogs from the nearby village I'd stolen bread from didn't find me. I am not going to apologize for my choices. I am only apologetic for not killing the alpha when I had the chance."

"And the other villagers?" Weston asked, interjecting into the conversation. His hand was braced on his thigh, looking out to the right. "They wouldn't have those problems living elsewhere, yet they aren't allowed to leave."

"Of course they are allowed to leave," I spat, angry. "People come and go all the time."

"With an escort."

"Yes. We've had this conversation. Our job is danger-ous. Granny provides them protection. And before you say otherwise, they cast a vote in favor of Granny's organizational goals. They gave their consent to stay there. I was young, but I remember that vote. I partici-pated in it. Someone from the village tallied it up. Notes of that would've been in one of the journals you were reading so closely yesterday."

"It was. As was what you were all promised for that vote," he replied. "Those promises must've seemed like heaven to the impoverished. But then she started slacking in her duties, didn't she? You wrote that, as well." His tone turned harsh. "You pushed back and were punished for it. For *months* you were punished. You thought they'd kill you. Children were beaten to get you to come around. To get *you* to come around. *They* didn't matter, not even the kids. It was you Granny needed to cull. Her drug maker. The key to her whole operation. She needed to keep *you* happy, Aurelia, and while she worked on that, they were trapped in hell. A hell without end, it seems. It looked to me that they had just enough to get by. Are they really much better off than they started?

"Regardless, they no longer have any freedom of choice. They can't even move to a neighboring village—those are all gone. Granny made sure of it. Even if they weren't, what gold do those people have? Besides what we left for them, of course, the offering one they seemed over the moon to receive. Without me, they'd have nothing. Isn't that right? That isn't all written in your journals—so far—but it doesn't take a genius to connect the dots." He paused for a moment. "Or don't you remember what you wrote?"

I opened my mouth for a rebuttal, ready to say how absurd that all was. Granny did look after everyone. She always mentioned the special things she was doing for the children. She talked of special treats she was working on procuring. Every few months we were all spoiled with enough haunches of meat and extra loaves of bread for a feast.

Before I could utter a word, though, memories long forgotten rose to the surface. I'd been young, fresh in my new role and just getting traction. I'd been working hard on belonging in the village, creating a situation where they needed me and couldn't get rid of me on a whim. Weston was right; Granny had reneged on her promises for a time. Food had come in rancid. Bread was moldy or rock hard. She promised she'd fix the issue and never did. Everyone had been starving and no one would take my rations unless I just left them behind. I remembered the beatings—oh, how I remembered the beatings. They'd been constant and brutal.

I did think I would die, then. I'd wanted to.

My eyes teared up and I looked away. Granny had been callous and unforgiving. Cruel sometimes. I'd hated her then. I remembered that now. I'd hated everyone; I'd tried to help and they were horrible to me. But what had been the alternative? For me, only death. Death there, or death elsewhere.

I'd stayed firm to help everyone, or so I'd thought. Now, as I looked back, had I really? Or had I been helping myself, ensuring they would all stay so I'd have a place to live without fear of waking up in a burning house? I knew Granny would not only protect the borders, she'd protect me as well. She wouldn't let the villagers turn on me. She'd said so often enough. She even enquired after my sense of safety periodically.

I'd never once wondered why no one had left. I didn't wonder even a couple days ago, either, confident it was because they had more now than they did before Granny brought in food and supplies.

But honestly, I had no idea if that was true. People wouldn't tell me how their day was going, let alone their lives. I knew Raz was unhappy, but figured he stayed for his kids. Did he, though? Was that why he dealt with a job he hated and a co-worker he despised?

My mind churned, thinking back. The past was foggy, unfocused. So much of my life had been about survival. About negating danger. Anything not directly related was hard to call up and analyze.

Didn't we have some of the same problems now as we did back then? Not nearly as often, I supposed, but sometimes food was lean. Sometimes roofs weren't fixed. Sometimes we didn't get the supplies we were promised. It was never bad enough to really be a concern, and I'd never had to push back so hard again, but it wasn't as good as in the beginning—of that, I was almost positive. Plenty good enough by my standards, but not the avalanche of goods and materials like in the beginning.

It should've been the opposite, really. I worked harder now than I ever had. I produced more product— better product. Granny was in the main trade markets, for gods' sakes. The gold should've been pouring in.

The village didn't see any of that coin. *I* didn't see any of that coin.

The most obvious issue that I'd never bothered to reflect on hit me in the gut.

None of us had ever been paid in gold. Not ever. I was given gifts and they were given supplies, but we never got more than a pittance to spend in the Outside, and that was allocated only when we were actually traveling, a long journey to and from the nearest town. The villages that used to be close had dwindled until they were ghost towns.

Our village never got raw materials from which to

make goods, either—those goods came already made. Even if people wanted to trade their wares for some sort of savings, they couldn't. Without that job and that village, I had nothing. Literally nothing. The clothes on my back. The journals Weston had stolen.

My stomach churned, bile clawing up my throat.

"No. Stop. Just . . ." I struggled to get away from Hadriel. "Stop, let me off—"

I slipped off the back of the horse and fell into a heap on the ground. The horse danced away, probably freaked out at the lump of human that kept dropping off its side. My mind spun as memories bombarded me, each more damning than the last. My stomach heaved now as I tried to process, dizzied as I swam in guilt.

"Whoa, wait a minute." Hadriel steadied his horse. Those to the sides cleared some space, the path suddenly filled with stomping and dancing hooves.

I darted out from between two large beasts. One reared, whinnying. Its owner struggled to stay on.

"Sorry," I mumbled before I was through the trees, gripping a trunk and losing the meat and cheese I'd eaten on the trail.

I flipped back through those hazy memories, adding a new lens crafted of age and experience.

"Did you know she wouldn't allow a whole family to leave at the same time?" Weston stood somewhere behind me.

I closed my eyes, leaning heavily against rough bark.

"If a family wanted to leave the village," he said, "one child would have to stay behind. Did you know?"

"What?" I asked, head still spinning. I sucked in deep

breaths, my stomach threatening to upheave again. "That's absurd. That can't be."

"Multiple people in the village verified it. She wasn't providing escorts for them, Aurelia. She wasn't providing protection. She was monitoring them and keeping a hostage in case they tried to run."

"In case they tried to run?" I asked, my knees suddenly weak, remembering the things the patrol had said to me when they'd thought I was trying to escape.

You trying to run, little girl? You stupid enough to think you'd get past us?

"The drug trade is dangerous," Weston went on, though he didn't venture any closer. "But not in the way you're talking. I've never heard of a drug maker being abducted. Or killed, even. They might've tried to poach you—tried to offer you gold and a better living situation to entice you away from Granny, but I've never heard of them outright abducting someone. They certainly wouldn't take *you*, not with your royal backing. She was manipulating you, Aurelia. She saw your predicament, knew your limits, and was using you."

"No!" I squeezed my eyes shut, my heart aching. "No. She took me in when no one else would. When I didn't have a penny to my name. She hadn't known what sorts of abilities I might have. It was only later she learned how good I was at making product. She wouldn't have done that if she didn't care. She wouldn't have helped me set up a new life if she hadn't cared!"

But she'd beaten me to within an inch of my life. She'd starved me. She'd tried to force my hand once she learned what I was good at. Her caring clearly had limits, limits my mother never, ever in her life, would've had.

Tears threatened to fall and I sank to my knees.

"Please," I begged, the memories coming faster now. A black hole inside me stretched wide. "Please," I whispered. "She's the only family I had left. You've already taken her from me, please don't tarnish her memory as well."

16

WESTON

I watched Aurelia's perception of her life crumble around her.

"Go to her," my wolf said on a whine. "She is a product of her environment, you must see that. She's crying out for help—can't you feel it?"

Of course I could feel it. Her agony pulsed through the air, pounding at me, begging for mercy. For help. The sheer power of it almost brought me to my knees. No magic, my ass. Even without the help of her animal, she was able to affect those around her. Maybe her mother hadn't been totally honest about her history. There had to be some other sort of creature mixed up in Aurelia's genes, because no shifter I'd ever encountered could do something like this.

Was this why Granny had taken her in? Had she felt this magic and either succumbed to it—hard to believe —or realized its uniqueness and wanted to see how it developed?

Unlike her mother, though, Aurelia's animal *had*

budded. It just hadn't risen to the surface. Was that by Granny's design—she had demon connections and could use their magic to ensure Aurelia's beast stayed hidden—or because Aurelia believed it didn't exist at all? Either way, the lack of appearance by an animal had helped Granny manipulate this woman. When sheer force hadn't worked, Granny switched tactics until she'd found something that had.

I took a step forward, my whole body taut. My true mate huddled at the base of the tree, hugging herself. The bond that united us yanked at my middle, demanding I look after her. Demanding I make this right.

Duty was a hard master.

Wrestling for control, I stepped backward again. We couldn't waste any more time fucking in the trees and staying entwined for half the night. The best I could do would be to give her a minute and stop tormenting her with the reality of who Granny really was.

Shouts and yells echoed through the trees. Wood clanged and horses whinnied. Donkeys sounded what I'd come to recognize as an alarm.

A thrill of adrenaline went through me.

"Alpha!" Tanix shouted. "We've got a problem."

"Aurelia, hurry." I ran at her as she turned around, her brow pinched and confusion evident. Her eyes were haunted.

I grabbed her under the arms and hoisted her up like a child.

"What's happening?" she asked in a small voice, her fingers digging into my shoulders.

I held her tightly so that she didn't jostle as I reached Tanix, who was visibly coiled for action.

"They escaped," he said as we jogged out of the tree line. Horses danced and stomped their hooves, sensing commotion and ready for battle. They'd been bred for warfare.

"All of them?"

Hadriel was still on his horse and his attention was directed our way. I didn't dare leave her with him in case this was the enemy's first attempt at coming for Aurelia.

"Hadriel, with me," I called out, just as Tanix said, "Yes."

Tanix directed us toward the rear of the procession.

"Who?" Aurelia asked with alarm, struggling against my hold. "Who did you take?"

Her ability to pivot for the sake of her community or for survival was awe-inspiring. I'd just turned her world upside down but she was ready to face the next obstacle. Knowing how shitty her life must've been up to this point, it was no wonder she took terrible situations in stride.

"We captured some of Granny's patrol," I quickly told Aurelia so she'd stop struggling. "In wolf form, I can suck them into the pack and force a bond with them. It gives me complete control. When I'm in human form, a few powerful wolves in the pack can hold the bond I created and consequently hold my control. Only in human form could they have the free will to walk away." To Tanix I said, "How'd they get free?"

The horses back near the carts were visibly agitated. The donkeys had their ears back, tension wound through their withers, clearly wanting to bolt but held in place by the harnesses. People ran here or there, clothes were scattered on the ground. Wolves darted through the trees.

Instead of answering, Tanix stopped in the area where the prisoners had been kept, grouped together and flanked by two pack members. Nova turned from talking to one of the pack and stepped up quickly, her eyes tight. It meant she didn't have a handle on things and was likely angry at herself because of it. I never needed to reprimand this wolf, she did a great job of that on her own.

"Alpha," she said, shaking her head. "We were in position, same as yesterday. Our people didn't notice any real change, just that suddenly the pack bond seemed a bit slippery with one, then the next prisoner. Then the other few. Nothing came of it, though. There was no change in their demeanor."

"Why wasn't I alerted?"

"You were, uh, otherwise engaged." Her gaze flashed to Aurelia.

"I instructed them to monitor the situation closely," she went on, "until you could be reached. The moment we stopped, though, the prisoners scattered. One blink and they were gone. They barely needed to flex to rip the pack bond. Grasping at them through it was like running fingers through water. Speaking of water, there's a creek that runs parallel to here. It's wide and shallow, and they all ran through it. We have yet to pick up their scents outside of that creek. We're still looking."

"Dante, Sixten?" I asked.

"Organizing the search effort," Tanix responded, his clothes at his feet. "The prisoners escaping shouldn't have created this amount of chaos with the horses." The look he gave me was pointed, meaning there was a large predator out there, helping to create a diversion by scaring the animals.

Fuck. I set Aurelia down quickly and shed my clothes. If the escaped prisoners met up with those who'd evaded capture, they might think it an ideal opportunity to try and pick off some of my pack, one by one.

What they didn't know was they were about to run up against the big bad wolf.

"Guard the woman," I commanded Nova. "Pull everyone together. Group them tightly around her and the supplies. Wait for my return."

I ran to the side and shifted, waiting for the flash of pain to subside before feeling the pack bond stretch out around us. My wolf took hold of it, quickly getting a feel for where everyone was and effortlessly structuring them. Tanix was sent in the opposite direction with a team accompanying him, just in case the prisoners running toward the creek was a diversion.

How had they broken my bond?

I dashed through the trees, my wolf calling others to us as we ran. They fell in line as my wolf caught the scent of the prisoners.

He bared his teeth as he stepped in the creek, the pack spreading out around us, with Sixten flanking us to the right and Dante quickly joining my wolf's other side. Issuing cues through his body movements and pushing his will through the bond, my wolf steered both

Dante and Sixten to break off and go up the creek. We took fewer people with us down the creek. If we ran into the enemy, it would be easy for my wolf to force a bond and protect our people. The others might need to fight, and therefore needed the numbers.

Currents of scent drifted through the air. I thought my wolf caught a faint, familiar whiff, but not one from the prisoners. Slowly, he tried to catch it again but it was elusive, older. He couldn't quite place it. Continuing onward, he had our people spread out a bit, most on land, hunting for a sign that the prisoners or anyone else had come this way. Nothing.

After about a half hour, with no alarms pushed through the bonds from anyone else, we called everyone in and headed back.

"That was a very well-executed escape," Tanix said when we met back up, just out of the creek. "*Very* well executed. We wasted no time in going after them, but they were just . . . gone. Vanished. We didn't pick up any scents stepping out of the creek."

"We had people stretched out along the banks, too," Sixten said, her hands on her hips in obvious frustration. "Nothing."

"Think it was magic?" Dante asked.

"I've never heard of magic like that, and we know the most powerful of faeries," Sixten replied. "We know the new demon . . . thing, whatever it is he's calling himself—"

"Lord," Dante supplied.

"Lord, whatever. He doesn't have that kind of magic."

"The woman ran into the trees at near the same time

the prisoners escaped," Tanix said softly, his gaze on me firm. "They took off in the opposite direction."

I felt a pang in my gut, knowing what Tanix was suggesting. His account of the timing was correct.

"Did she try to run?" Sixten asked, looking between everyone. "Didn't she just wobble into the trees some?"

"Yeah, bro, look," Dante told Tanix, "I get where you're going with that, but she didn't bring up that line of questioning. That was all Mr. Dick Jacket and the alpha. That chick has taken an emotional beating these last two days. She's sloppy and unstable—no offense, Alpha. She didn't execute this plan."

I gritted my teeth, not commenting, kicking myself for being distracted by the woman yet again.

"I'm just pointing out the coincidence," Tanix replied.

"You're pointing out when the alpha was distracted, which was a perfect time for the prisoners to take off," Sixten said. "Any idiot can see she's a product of Granny, not a team member. I'm not saying she isn't a guilty party, because we all heard that she has no reservations about what she was doing, but she is just trying to stay alive." She paused. "I was in the demon dungeons —I know what that's like. I'll tell you something else, if part of my group escaped and didn't bring me with them, I'd escape later out of spite, track them down, and kill the lot of them. She wouldn't want to stay behind if she didn't have to, good sex or not. No offense, Alpha."

"Real eloquent," Dante murmured.

She punched him. "Shut up."

I took a beat to balance myself, thinking through this logically. I couldn't allow my leadership to be affected by that woman. She'd done it too much already and now the prisoners had escaped. Whether she'd planned it or not—and I didn't think for a moment that she had—she was still responsible for pulling my focus away. One of my people could've died. I needed to take greater care.

"She sacrificed herself so children could eat," I said, still looking out at nothing. "She would sacrifice herself here to help her people go free. Any good alpha would, even if she doesn't know she has that kind of magic."

"How could she not see how fucked they all were this whole time?" Dante said, bewildered. "Like . . . we clearly saw her figure it all out. I was watching that shit. She's not good at hiding her emotions. I felt like I could *feel* her horror. Broke my fucking heart, I'm not gonna lie. But she's smart enough to have seen this before now."

"Sometimes we ignore the truths that contradict our worldview or our ideals," I said. "I'm not saying it's right, but it is a distinctly human thing to do. If she didn't ignore it she wouldn't have been able to live with it, and then where would she be?"

"She survived at the cost of a village," Tanix said.

"Yes, she did." I sighed. "I hear your concern, Tanix, but this escape wasn't her design. Her life is small. She works mostly alone. She doesn't manage people. She would never be able to pull off this kind of escape, not without some extensive training. This was done by someone with experience. Someone who runs patrols. We're being shadowed, of that there can be no doubt. My question is, why didn't they free her? Why didn't they include her in their plans?"

"Simple," Dante said, quirking an eyebrow. "She's being watched closely by a powerful alpha. The others had a lot less people paying attention to them. They just had to break the bond to get free."

"True, true." Sixten nodded slowly. "Kind of lucky, then, that there's a true mate situation—"

This time Dante punched Sixten. "Lucky for the dragons getting their woman, maybe," he ground out, "but un-fucking-lucky for the alpha, hey? Have a little common decency."

Sixten grimaced and looked at the ground. "Apologies," she murmured.

"The question still remains—how did they break that bond?" I started back to the others. "They shouldn't have been strong enough."

"Is it possible they've brought in another powerful alpha and just ripped the bond away?" Tanix asked. "The strongest of us were in human form. We weren't on hand to solidify it."

"No," I said. "They said the bond weakened. They would've felt someone taking it, even in that state."

"Can't be Aurelia," Sixten said. "Even if she wasn't suppressed, she didn't shift."

"She didn't know we had other prisoners," I said. "We've kept them apart and as you all have clearly viewed, yes, she's been watched closely. Besides, they aren't the first of their patrol to break the bonds. We lost some when we invaded the village."

"True." Dante looked out at the trees. "They'll be back. We've got their prize."

"And now that prize knows she has backup," Tanix said. "All she has to do is get free of us and they can snap her up. Once they get her, they can head straight to the royal court. If that happens, she'll be beyond our reach."

Something like panic gripped me at the possibility of losing her. Of someone taking her to a place where I couldn't see her again. Of hiding her from me.

Heart racing, I sought her out immediately, ignoring someone offering me my clothes. The crowd in front of her parted and her eyes, tight with worry, found mine.

"What is it?" I asked, and through my concern I forgot to be suspicious.

"She thought she felt a presence," Hadriel said, holding her hand. I stilled a flash of rage at the contact, backing down my wolf. Well, trying to.

I took her hand from Hadriel only to have her pull away. "What kind of presence?" I asked, letting her.

"Alexander," she said in a firm voice. That tone was practiced, intent on hiding fear. I could feel her fear, though, like I felt her begging for help earlier. Like I felt her begging for my touch the first time I set eyes on her. "I can't be certain. I didn't see him or anything, I just always feel a kind of . . . uneasy, crawling sensation when he looks at me." She shivered. "It felt like he was watching me."

"From where?" I growled.

It was Nova who pointed, the opposite direction the prisoners had run. "We'd already sent people that way when she spoke up. They didn't find anything. No scents, no tracks."

"Neither did we," I replied. "Mount up, let's put some—"

"I found this, by the way." Aurelia held out a little square tab of paper.

I hesitated before taking it, glancing at Nova. She shook her head infinitesimally. Aurelia hadn't brought it up before now.

"And what is that?" It felt like cardboard, thick but somewhat pliant. The edges were slanted, one side almost looking torn.

"Don't you recognize it?" She gave me a haughty look. "That's one of my evil products that apparently kills whole villages." She pointed at the ground near where she'd been standing. "I found it on the ground. Clearly your people have been sampling the merchandise. Very reputable, your outfit."

I yanked it nearer my face so I could get a better look. The surface was lighter in some places than others, the other side equally nonuniform. The slanted edges and ripped area looked like a child had cut it out. The coloring was almost anemic and overall, it didn't seem at all appetizing, not like the colorful, symmetrical candy-coated looking tabs I'd seen in badly hit towns and villages and all through the cities.

"This is part of your product?" I held it out to make sure she'd had a good look.

She rolled her eyes. "I know what I make."

"Is it a new product? New to markets, I mean."

"Not even remotely. It's done really well without a lot of modifications."

Dante practically leaned over my shoulder to get a look. "Do you have kids working in your outfit? Because that looks like a kid cut it out."

She stared at him for a beat. "I don't have help and I have a lot to get done. I cut them in the doses best suitable for the batch and toss them in the bin. A few villagers collect it and store it, and a few others take it to the property line when its time. Granny's people pick it up and take it to market."

"Like that?" Dante reached over me to point at it, clearly forgetting himself. I wanted the answers, though, and she didn't tend to give those to me easily.

"For this product, yes, like that. For others, I have to separate them into sheets for storage. Others need to go in little packets or they corrode. Obviously you can just look for yourself since you clearly took the supply. I'm surprised you haven't already."

"The cart holding the product is behind us." Nova jerked her head toward it. "It hasn't been touched. None of the crates have, either. I checked when you were looking for the prisoners, Alpha. The crates we took out of the storage shed are still covered and tied down exactly like they were when we pulled them out, save the couple we checked to figure out what it was. I could be wrong, but they don't look like they've been disturbed." She lifted her brows slowly. "I will have everyone searched, but I can't imagine anyone would take the chance."

I agreed with her. Only a fool would dabble in the drugs coming out of this village. We'd looked in a couple of the covered crates but in the haste to get moving, hadn't dallied with the details. Everyone was wary of that product's dangerousness, no one wanted to dig through it.

"You found it on the ground?" Dante asked, looking around the ground at his feet.

Turned out, there were more. Some ahead, some behind, scattered in the dirt with enough space between them that they could easily be missed. And they had been, obviously, except by Aurelia, who knew what it was, and by the prisoners, who knew what they could do. That product must've somehow loosened the bond connecting those shifters to my pack.

"Walk with me." I motioned her on, needing more info but also needing to get my people on the move. I didn't want to give the lurkers time to organize and surround us. Without my ability to capture them with a pack bond, we'd be in trouble, especially if they outnumbered us.

"Sir." Clothes were given to me and this time I took them, handing the drug to Nova. "Mount up," I told everyone. "Let's move out. We'll need more feet on the ground. We're being watched. Stay vigilant. Sound the alarm if you see or smell anything."

Once near my horse, I quickly dressed and swung into the saddle. I reached down for Aurelia, who had Nova at her back to make sure she didn't bolt.

"Oh." Hadriel paused near his mount. "I'm riding alone now, I take it?"

"Not even a prisoner should be subjected to your jokes for too long," someone murmured.

"Cute, Kurt. I can see why you never developed a sense of humor—your mother was all out of jokes after she had you."

"Ooooh," a few people said as everyone started laughing.

Aurelia ignored all that. "But . . ." She pointed at the saddle. "You don't have much room at the back of that."

It was true, but I didn't have time to mess with it.

I continued to reach for her. As though on impulse,

she took my outstretched hand. In the next moment I swung her up in front of me, chest to chest, guiding her leg over my thigh.

"Ohmmm," she said, her surprise turning into a soft moan. "This isn't going to be comfortable."

Her arms constricted around me, clutching onto my shoulders. Her face tucked into my neck, her lips touching my skin.

I begged to differ.

"This is a bad idea," she whispered, crawling up a little more, her groin over mine. She wrapped her legs around my waist and settled, almost melting down around me.

I realized my eyes were closed, reveling in the press of her body, in the feel of her breasts pushing up against my chest and her lips resting against my neck.

Fuck, this was heaven.

"We need to get out of here," I said gruffly, starting the horse forward. "I know of a place we can stop and regroup. We'll ride like this until we can get there. If it gets to be too much for you, we'll figure something else out—"

"The horse will be okay? You're much bigger than Hadriel."

"You're a waif." A pang of unease hit me, remembering her stories about food in the village. I needed to ensure she had plenty. "Tell me about that . . . product you found. What does it do?"

"If I'm honest, will you stop reading my journals?" She leaned back a little so she could look into my eyes.

My breath caught as I took in her beautiful face. Those gorgeous eyes held a sunburst of golden browns, honey, threads of green. She wet her plump lips and it took everything in me not to lean forward and capture them with mine.

"I really want to say yes," I replied honestly, "but you had a couple passages where you wrote down names Granny had mentioned in passing. Another one where you detailed what Alexander had gossiped about when he returned from one of his trips. You give time frames when you note Granny coming in with various presents." I lowered my voice, falling into her gaze. "I need that information, baby. I need those details. You aren't the only part of this outfit. If we want to stop this operation, we need to find the other part of it. It's not stuff you'd be able to remember off-hand."

Her gaze drifted down to settle on my lips. Her thumbs absently stroked my shoulders. "Don't call me baby."

Not yet.

The answering thought was so quick it shocked me, then unsettled me. I felt my brow knit together.

"I apologize," I said stiffly, my cock painfully hard. "I need the contents in those journals."

"What if I go through and point it out to you?"

I studied her for a long moment, unable to tear my eyes away even to see our surroundings. Hopefully my people were doing their jobs, because I certainly wasn't doing mine. I couldn't help it, I was entranced.

"Do you really want to?" I asked her softly. "You've written about some dark times in those journals. Do you really want to go back and remember them?"

Her eyes clouded over, sadness permeating the air around us. She didn't comment.

"What did that . . . product do?" I asked again.

She tightened her left arm around me so that she could reach down with her right, digging into a pocket. She pulled out another of those tabs. "This one wasn't far from the other. It's a relaxant. It works best on shifters and goblins, but Granny made an off-handed comment about vampires buying them for some reason, as well. She didn't give me any further info. It smooths out all the rough edges. Rounds the corners, so to speak."

"I don't know what that means."

"It helps to calm anxiety, basically. It helps to de-stress." She popped it into her mouth.

A shock of alarm ran through me. I pulled the reins to stop the horse before I grabbed her face, squeezing her cheeks to pop her mouth open. I dug in my fingers, searching for that drug before she swallowed it down.

17

AURELIA

"Wh—" I slapped his hands away, twisting in his grip.

"Spit it out," he barked at me, what sounded like terror dripping from each syllable. Other horses stopped beside us. "Spit it out!"

I jolted forward, head butting him above his right eye and then trying to wiggle out of his grasp. His arms came around me, holding me tight, his grip much too strong for me to break away from.

"What is wrong with you?" I shouted.

"Don't eat that, it's dangerous!"

"Oh for the love of—" I pulled back until he could see me and opened my mouth, sticking out my tongue. "It's gone. I chewed and swallowed it. For the last fucking time, it's not dangerous. You'll barely even notice the change in me. I'll be a little spacy at times but that's it. Don't worry, you'll have a living body to deliver to the dragons."

He put his hand to the side of my cheek, waiting

while I tried to lean away from it, and placing it there again when I settled. His eyes darted between mine, his worry evident.

I wrapped my fingers around his wrist. "I promise you, Weston, I will be fine. More than fine. I'll be a lot calmer riding on this animal. It'll be okay, I swear."

He let out a slow breath, stroking a thumb across my cheek. A moment later he nodded, though I could tell he was not appeased.

"You should take one, too. It would make things a lot more pleasant between us," I said, adjusting my seat so that I was comfortable again, my groin over his hardness, my body draped around his. Hadriel was fun and funny and I enjoyed riding with him, but this just felt so fucking good. If only I'd liked this guy, nothing in the world would've been more pleasant. I wouldn't have needed a relaxant at all.

"What does the drug do when taken in wolf form?" he asked, kicking his heels to the sides of the horse to get it walking again.

"I don't know. I haven't ever heard of someone consuming it like that. Occasionally people in the village would take it and then shift into wolf form. It negates the effect of the relaxant, which is the fail-safe for shifters."

"Fail-safe?"

"Yeah, I bake in ways to stop the journey."

"The journey meaning the high, correct?"

"It's not always a high, like with this relaxant. But sure, the high. If the journey takes a sharp turn and lands you into a nightmare, you'll want to get yourself out. The fail-safe isn't always the same for each product.

With this one, for anyone who can shift, it's just that—shift. The effect goes away almost completely, and when you shift back it'll be gone. That's why there is really no point in taking it if you're planning on shifting, like to hunt, for example. I would assume that eating it when in wolf form won't have much of an effect at all."

He shook his head, half twisting to try and look behind him, probably to get the reactions of his people, following behind. "I hadn't heard about that."

"Maybe the instructions didn't make it to you on your high horse."

"Drugs don't come with instructions."

"They do if the trader is knowledgeable in any way. Granny always passed on pertinent information about anything I made."

"News to me."

I quirked an eyebrow. I'd wager most of the shadow market world would be news to this guy. He was clearly a rule follower, wound tightly and always on the straight and narrow. I wondered if he ever actually lived, or if he was too busy being a good guy all the time.

Although . . . did good guys really take women hostage and then fuck the sense out of them?

"That's all that the drug does?" he asked. "Relaxes you?"

The product's effect started to take hold, unwinding my muscles and smoothing out the tension in my shoulders. I sighed and slunk down a little more, moving my arms to encircle his waist and resting my cheek against his shoulder.

"That's all I know, yes."

"No one mentioned that it would dissolve a pack bond?" one of the guys behind us asked.

I thought back to when I'd first made it and we were testing it, getting feedback from various people in the village. "People always tested it in human form. Finding out about the effects when shifting was an accident. I wouldn't know about a pack bond. Honestly, I don't even know if my village was a pack. Granny would've been the alpha, I guess, but she didn't engage much with the village. We didn't have a mayor or anything. No real leadership besides her."

"You mentioned they hunted," another guy said, the one I hadn't been able to cleave in Granny's cottage. "Did they all hunt together? The same people, every time?"

My muscles unwound further and a tranquil hum settled within my body. Weston's heat enveloped me and I could feel his heartbeat, slow and steady. My thoughts were just as slow, drifting along, taking in the day, warm and pretty, the sun a buttery yellow.

"I don't think it was the exact same every time, but always a similar grouping," I said, letting my eyes drift shut and snuggling a little closer into Weston. "The idea of hunting has never really appealed to me, but I wanted to go along with them. They always came back so refreshed, with their hair mussed and their eyes sparkling. Energized, you know? They would always joke with each other and nudge. They did seem like they had a bond, though I'm not sure who the alpha might've been. They didn't really seem to have any kind of structure. They just seemed . . . happier. Included."

I knew my voice held the longing I felt but thanks to this product, I didn't care.

"I've never taken this product under duress. It's incredibly pleasant. Good job, me."

"You'll have no more of it," Weston growled. "It's a wonder you're not addicted already."

"I am not a person who forms habits out of my products. While this is nice when riding atop a handsome stranger I don't like, it would get in the way of my being productive. The fear of failure makes me thrive. Remembering the stakes in my life keeps me producing. If I stopped caring about those things, my world would fall apart."

"Fuck, lady," the guy who'd taken an axe to the shoulder said, slouching a little. Dante, I think they called him. "Every time you give us a slice of your life, I feel a little more depressed."

"You're ripping me from my home to have me killed in a land far away by a creature I've only ever heard about in books. Is that not already plenty depressing?"

"Not when you put it like that, not really, no," he replied. "Sounds exciting, except for the death part."

"Doesn't it just." I pulled a hand from Weston's waist and felt it up his hard chest to around his neck. I ran the edge of my thumb along his jaw, feeling the stubble. "You need to shave."

"So do you. I'd happily do it for you," he murmured, his deep voice vibrating in his chest.

"That is judgmental and wildly inappropriate," I said, though I wasn't actually offended. I smiled against his neck. "But I am very curious."

"Did that group of hunters ever take that *drug* and

shift into a wolf?" the one who escaped the axe said. Tanix, maybe?

"Speaking of judgmental," I drawled, chuckling. "Don't like what I do, hmm?" I kissed Weston's neck softly, my desire starting to pulse.

"Did you ever notice any of them losing interest in the others?" he pushed. "Maybe not caring about hunting as much, even if just for a while?"

I sucked in Weston's fevered skin, feeling his arm tighten around me, while I thought back. I'd watched that group of hunters often enough, feeling my loneliness keenly every time they started out. That feeling always ramped when they'd returned. I'd wished I could have such easy camaraderie with someone. Wished, with everything I had, that I could take to four legs and sprint through the trees in a pack. I'd lived in a community, but I'd still been very much a loner.

"Damn it." I pushed off Weston's chest, his arm around me resistant to let up. "That's the problem with this product. You really need time to be lazy with it. It dulls the mind. Give me a moment, Mr. Judgmental, and I'll shake off this journey. I think I remember something to that effect."

"What do you mean—"

I didn't hear the rest of what Weston said as I entered a sort of trance, feeling the areas where the product was altering me and imagining washing it away. Slowly the effects receded. As they did, the tension crept back in, the stress tightening my muscles.

"If I still had a job, I'd start working on that one again," I said, fluttering my eyes open. "There has to be a way to—"

I paused, realizing Weston's hands were on my cheeks, his expression panicked as he looked at my face. The horse was stopped and several others gathered around, all looking at me in concern.

"What happened?" I asked, confused. "What's the matter?"

"Exactly—what happened?" He put the backs of his fingers to my forehead. "It felt like you were having a seizure. You were shaking and burning up and then you just kinda slumped down, like . . . like you'd died." He swallowed heavily.

I felt my brow furrow at his reaction. At the strange sadness that welled up as I thought about parting from him. Then I pushed that strange feeling away. It was worse than any product I made because I couldn't fucking get rid of it.

"I was shrugging off the effects of the relaxant. It feels great and really does the job, but it's too hard to think deeply on it. I don't like my mind being cloudy when I need to use it." I pushed his hands away from my face.

"You were—you mean, you made it stop working, just like that?" His tone was incredulous. He clearly didn't believe me.

"I test every batch and don't have time to walk each journey. Some of the hallucinogens will keep you going all day. It's a lot of time to waste and I'm not overly fond of the things my imagination sometimes conjures up. Can we get moving again, please? The sooner we can switch things around the better. Hadriel didn't fuss nearly as much."

"She likes me better," I heard from somewhere in the throng.

"Yeah, good idea," someone else responded. "Go ahead and keep poking the alpha. I'll enjoy watching him turn you inside-out."

I grinned and leaned against Weston so he'd be forced to quit staring at me in alarm.

"I did notice some of those things," I told the guy who didn't get axed. "I'm sure of it."

As we continued, I recounted several times when a member of the hunting party, or several, would come back without smiles. They'd seemed frustrated and aloof, walking on the outskirts of the group, not connecting like before. Now that I looked back, it had always been around the times various batches needed testing. A few people from the village always volunteered. I couldn't remember how long that had lasted, though. I wasn't always around to watch the hunting party set out or return, not when things started getting busier. It hadn't been forever, that change. I noticed throughout the years those few people always got back in the groove of things eventually.

"Huh," Dante said, looking at the other guy as the horses walked. "It really does sound like that drug can weaken pack bonds."

"Why wasn't I told?" I asked, peering over Weston's shoulder to look at the ground. In his strong, tight grip, I didn't feel any fear I'd fall. Not with him. "Alexander clearly knew about it if he sprinkled it on the ground for the patrol. Why wouldn't he mention that to me?"

"I wonder if it is strong enough to keep you from bonding them again?" Axe-less said, looking at Weston.

"It has to be somewhat safe if she ate it, right?" Dante said. "Maybe we should test it out when we rest tonight to see what we're dealing with."

"Did she actually eat it?" Axe-less asked, his suspicion evident. "Or is she a fine actress? Because I don't buy just shrugging off a drug like that."

"She wasn't acting when she was on it," Weston replied. "I felt her body relax. It hasn't felt that way since I met her. Now her relaxation is gone. Something clearly happened, and now it's over."

"I'll take it," Hadriel called from the back. "If she says it's safe, I'll take any of it. These trees are boring the balls off me." I could just see Hadriel put out his finger to a guy on the horse somewhat beside him. "Don't bother making a comment, Kurt. I can tell you're dying to, but we all know you are absolute shit at witty banter."

Weston stared out to the right. "We'll take two tabs from the batch in the cart. She will eat one, Hadriel can eat the other." He turned to me, his voice low. "I want your word that it is safe."

"What does my word mean to you?"

"More than I'd like it to."

I rolled my eyes and dropped my cheek to his shoulder again, this time my face turned away. "It's safe. All of it is. I've told you this."

The traveling dragged on. Where I might've thought the landscape would interest me, not having been this far away in, well, too many years, I was disappointed with the lack of variety. Nothing much changed. No animals scurried out of the way and the flora was the same as in my wood. The sun glinted above, playing peek-a-boo behind the leaves and reaching branches. I thoroughly understood why Hadriel was bored to tears. Hours passed as I stared out into the trees.

The feel of Weston's body continued to give me a strange sort of comforting pleasure and I found myself slipping a hand into his shirt so I could feel the smooth skin and cut muscle. He didn't seem to mind, his gaze scanning side to side, quiet as we continued on.

Finally, boredom got the better of me.

"Why do a bunch of wolves ride horses?" I asked. "Wouldn't you cover more ground in wolf form?"

"We have supplies. We'd only be able to go as fast as the horses and donkeys walked, anyway. This way we save our strength in case we need to fight."

"Most of you. You're not all on horses."

"The more powerful among us, those that tend to do the heavy lifting in battle, are on horses."

An image of him coming out of the trees, flanked by his people, drifted through my mind. They'd all been perfectly in sync, graceful in that way only predators could be—sleek and dangerous. The sun had sparkled off their strong bodies, Weston the most stunning of all.

The bond of this pack was incredibly strong, I could tell that easily. It wasn't just whatever magic shifters had, either. These people respected their alpha. Trusted him. It felt homey, this pack. Inclusive. The foundation felt solid.

Something else occurred to me, though, forgotten when I'd felt Alexander's presence lurking.

I leaned back in a rush, only getting so far before he tightened his arm to keep me put. He released it slowly, then, in control.

A thrill of heat arrested me and my stomach fluttered with the implications.

As usual, I ignored it.

"You talk to me about trapping a village, and yet you trap your pack in a bond you control. You trapped those prisoners. You don't need walls and patrols to keep people caged—you use your magic. How is that any better?"

His gaze was guarded. "If anyone wants to leave, they have but to ask."

"If anyone wanted to leave the village, they had but to ask."

"People leaving the village had terms. They weren't allowed to be gone for too long, and they weren't allowed to stay away forever. If people request to leave the pack, I sever the bond completely."

"But you're in control."

"Yes. That's how an alpha's magic works. The stronger the alpha, the stronger the pack bond."

"Are you in control of the people?" I lifted my eyebrows at him.

"When I need to be, yes."

Damn that wave of heat! It was fucking annoying.

"And when is that?"

"When I'm on the job. I organize the pack in very complex ways. The pack bond helps an alpha direct his or her people. It's vital. It also helps form that sense of togetherness you've noticed. It creates unity. A pack is a family, and the bond is our connection."

"Granny didn't want people to leave." I gritted my teeth against the emotion that welled up, still not having totally processed what I'd learned. What I now realized had been going on all those years, completely obvious and yet unnoticed. "What will happen when you don't? What will happen if you become corrupt and you don't want to sever the bond?"

"I've been down that road," he murmured, looking past me now. "I was from a prestigious family, presented to the royalty of this kingdom early. When they realized how much power I had, they advanced me within the hierarchy. I unified their royal pack with ease. At their behest, I also traveled to other lands— other kingdoms. My job was to seek out the most powerful shifters, wolves, and to bring them back. Those people might not have wanted to come with us, but once I'd chained them within the bond, they had no choice. I ripped them away from their lives and delivered them into the hands of the king and queen. They didn't get to leave when they wanted, either. They stayed until the king and queen let them go, which wasn't often—especially if they were powerful."

His face was granite. His jaw clenched.

"I was their jailor." His gaze met mine and I saw the pain there. The guilt. "I didn't think to wonder if it was wrong. I was doing this with my parents' blessing and by the king and queen's orders. I never once stopped to think about the morality of it, so wrapped up in titles and prestige and the gold they were throwing at me. It wasn't until they ordered me to keep my brother trapped within the bond that my sense of duty started to waver. It wasn't until it affected me directly—affected my family directly—that I thought about what I was doing."

"Why did your brother want to leave?"

"He wasn't as powerful as the rest of us. He was often overlooked, ignored by our parents. He was withering. He needed to get out and do his own thing."

"If he wasn't powerful, why'd they want to keep him in the pack?"

A nerve in his jaw danced. He unclenched his jaw. "For his pedigree. They wanted first crack at his brood. He'd be nothing more than a stud."

"That's horrible," I breathed. "What'd you do?"

He looked away again. "I walked away from my post. I broke that pack wide open, freed my brother, and walked away."

"And they let you?"

He huffed out a sardonic laugh, that turbulent gaze darting to me. Power welled up around him. "They didn't have a choice. I was the most powerful alpha they had. No one could bond me without my consent. I took my brother to a remote area and established my own pack. When they sent people after me, I killed them. Eventually they stopped trying to wrestle me back."

"Was that before the demon dungeons?"

"Yes." He inhaled and held it for a moment. "Not a day goes by that I don't regret the things I did for this kingdom. Every day I think of how disastrous it would be if I lost my way and turned into a tyrant. You said you put safeguards into your product. I put it into this position. The dragon king and queen monitor my efforts with the pack. If I lose my way, they'll ensure the people are freed."

"How will they free them?"

His eyes were steely. "They'll kill me. I would expect no less."

Pain nearly stole my breath at his admission. Confused by it, I pushed it away.

"We're not so different," I said softly. "I wasn't the jailor, but it was because of me that the village was jailed. I see that now." Guilt welled up within me, and with it came a sheen of tears. I blinked them away. "I will forever regret the part I've played in all of this. I was blind to it because I was focusing only on myself. For that I should stand in judgment. I will accept my punishment, without hesitation."

"For trapping them, but not for making the drugs?"

"No, not for that. You have it wrong when it comes to that. I see the parallel between your past situation and mine—don't think I don't. It's the same king and queen, after all. They clearly don't care about what is right, they care about how it benefits them. They want the gold from the products I make, and so they approve of it being sold. But while some things I wished were still only available in the shadow market because they aren't for the unsuspecting, they don't have the level of danger you claim. I can prove it. I'll take each one right in front of you."

"No, you most certainly will not. *I* will prove it. There are plenty of towns we can detour into as we pass. I'll give you a tour of the destruction your products have plagued the magical world with."

"Look, maybe people are mixing stuff in ways I haven't thought of or intended. Their misuse isn't my fault, but I would've fixed it. If there had been a problem, Granny would've mentioned it because it would've affected sales. And I would've fixed it. Sales are higher than ever. If people were dying in droves, how would sales continue to increase?"

"Addiction keeps sales on the rise."

"My village tested batches all the time, but Raz was the only real habitual user. He wasn't addicted, though. A small thing like punishment kept people from forming a habit. That's it. Wouldn't widespread death and danger keep people away?"

"Do you not understand what addiction is?"

"I don't make chemically addictive drugs!" I yelled at him. "For the last fucking time—"

"I'll show you," he cut in, crushing me to his body to get me out of his face.

My core pounded. I wanted to punch him. I wanted to fuck him. Electricity surged through me and heat burned my middle, dripping down in that way it did when tensions with him rode high. I clutched onto his shoulders, my breath shallow. I could feel his heart racing against mine, his hardness pulsing against my core.

I would not give in. Not this time. I would not rip off his clothes and bang him right here. I would not!

18

AURELIA

*I*t was the longest day of my fucking life, and with a past like mine, that was saying something.

I didn't give in. That was the one win I could claim for the day. I did not reach down and slip my hands between us to capture his hard length. I didn't devour his lips or sink my teeth deep into his neck to mark him. I didn't even gyrate against his unbelievable body to relieve the tension. I sat still in broody silence and stared out at nothing, silently dripping with pleasure as the horse jostled our bodies against each other.

We did stop once, as he'd said we would, but it was for a quick meal and a bathroom break before we were back on the road. He didn't let me ride with Hadriel. He didn't even take off the saddle so I could ride behind him. Nope, I was back in his lap, leaning against his chest, both hands in his shirt to have skin-to-skin contact and pretending like it was a normal thing to need to touch someone so badly.

Now, with dusk fast approaching and my body feeling like it was a jigsaw puzzle with the pieces put back in all the wrong places, we finally stopped. He gave me a curt command to dismount.

"Can't." It was the first word I'd uttered since our argument.

"What?" he asked as the rest of the pack dismounted and began making camp.

"I can't dismount. My body is too stiff. I'd fall off."

"Why didn't you tell me—" He cut himself off in angry frustration. His fingers dug into my back, both crushing me close and clearly displaying his annoyance with me. "Fine. Hang on."

His hand slid down to my butt as he stood in the stirrups, pulling me up with him. He leaned forward, bracing one hand on the saddle and keeping my chest flush with his before swinging his leg over the horse and basically jumping off. He landed gracefully, both arms around me now, one under my butt and the other across my back.

I waited for him to put me down onto my feet so I could stretch or bend or just fall down and stay there. Instead, he ensured my legs were still wrapped around him as he followed the others to the right and into a little clearing.

"Don't you worry about how it looks when the alpha carries a prisoner around like this?" I asked in bewilderment. "Or rides with her like you were. Or . . ." I thought back to when he carried me through the camp, his cock stuck inside me, our activities incredibly obvious. "Or walking around in the middle of fucking?"

"No. They trust that I'll do my duty."

"But they're not concerned about the moral dilemma of fornicating with the enemy?"

"No, because of what I just said."

That didn't make sense to me at all. They were pretending to be the good guys, but they were cool with an alpha participating in morally gray activities? I mean . . . fucking the enemy? They should not be okay with it. They really shouldn't. I mean, *I* wasn't okay with it.

And maybe that was actually the crux of the problem. Because Granny had filled me with stories of alphas capturing women and using them to their liking. That wasn't new. The issue was I liked it. Not rationally, obviously. Logically, I was not okay with any of this. I did not want my body intimately reacting to the man who had abducted me, killed my family, threatened my community, and was unlawfully keeping me prisoner. It was wrong, ass-backwards, and it was seriously, unequivocally fucked up. I just wished my stupid body would get on board!

He reached what seemed like a random spot and stopped, delicately uncoiling my feet from around his waist and setting me down gently. Weston was back to the chivalrous gentlemen so at odds with the vicious alpha marching me to my doom.

His hot and cold routine had me spinning in circles. I couldn't handle the dichotomy of him hating me one moment and treating me like gold the next. I didn't know what to do with Weston, the kind, caring man. It weakened my resolve to hate him and then I was left angry and hurt when he switched back to being Alpha. I was left ashamed and embarrassed when I remembered he was the bad guy.

I wanted to scream in frustration. My nerves were frayed from being in his proximity for so long without relieving the overwhelming sexual tension.

Or hell, maybe I wanted to cry. My heart hurt from the revelations about Granny and my village, I was scared about my future, and felt beyond frustrated that these people would not believe the product wasn't dangerous.

Basically, I was not handling this abduction very well. Not even a little. I was at my breaking point. Someone was going to go down with the ship. It would not be me.

"You're no better than Granny, you know that?" I shouted as he steadied me, standing close and with the utmost patience even though I could see a crowd of people standing by, waiting for his direction. I jabbed him with a finger. "You're really sweet and amazing some of the time, but otherwise, you're a huge asshole. Just like Granny, apparently. She gave me gifts and made me sticky buns. And then, yes, she punished me, but only when I broke the rules. You said she was keeping me caged? Well, what are you doing? And let's not even go into you hate-fucking your prisoner. You're using me just like she did. The only difference is you're just doing it for your own pleasure."

I winced as I said it, my heart feeling ragged. I doubled down on my anger to compensate.

"She kept me in the village to make product, and now you've captured me with the intent to kill me so I'll stop.

She at least consulted me about the product. She listened to me about it. You? Not a chance. I've proven it is not dangerous. You've seen my village; you know it isn't running rampant with addiction and death. Yet you will not listen to me about its properties. You want to kill me, and come hell or high water, you plan on doing it. So how different are you, really? I said it before and I'll say it again, *Alpha*, you are not the good guy in this story. And like when you worked for this king and queen, stealing people and ruining families, you're not the powerful guy who is just. You're just the guy with power."

He leaned down until he was directly in my face, his body coiled tightly and his breath coming quickly. The air heated between us with his wavering restraint, his lips inches from mine but coming no closer. He was barely in control of himself.

I was not in control of myself. Not at all.

"She gave you presents to keep you happy. She punished you to keep you in line. She spent all her time manipulating you, obviously so. I have not done any of that. I don't give two shits if you're unhappy. As far as how I'm handling you, I have my reasons."

"Screwing a prisoner you constantly threaten with death is a pretty immoral fucking situation."

"If I was forcing her, sure. I'm not forcing you. You screw me of your own free will."

My face burned red and I balled my fists, my core pounding and the energy between us zipping with fire. We were so close our breaths mingled. Our chests rose and fell quickly, each of us teetering on the edge.

"You do care if I'm unhappy," I ground out, fighting

fire with fire. "You make that abundantly clear when you put in the effort to make sure I come. Repeatedly."

His gaze burned into mine. Lust sparked hotter between us, growing like a brush fire. Passion coiled within me as my unbearably wet core throbbed.

He didn't respond. Instead, he about-faced and walked away, taking his heat and mouth-watering scent with him. He started barking orders at his people with cool efficiency. His authority and command couldn't be rivaled. It wasn't only his magic, but an obvious natural talent. A love for his pack. I realized that I admired him for it, for the way his people revered him. For the community he fostered and unity he nourished.

I stood alone in the aftermath, suddenly chilled and silently nursing the sting of his dismissal. I was so horribly turned around. Upside-down. Confused. Despite our situation, it felt like he was chipping away at my hatred of him. The more I learned about the alpha and his people, the more I grew to like them. The more I forgot about the precarious situation I was in.

Was this how captives ended up falling for their captors? Would he show me just enough kindness, ply me with orgasms, and slowly sap my will to survive as he delivered me to my doom?

Weston

Tingles fired along my nerve endings as I directed the pack to setup a perimeter and organize the camp. My heart thundered in my chest, trying to hold onto my control. It took all the restraint I could muster to not turn back and make her see that no way in hell was I like Granny. I had repented for the life I'd lived in this kingdom and now paid close attention to the leadership I followed, needing to respect them and trust their morals.

But when it came down to it, she was right, wasn't she? She hadn't gotten a say in her fate—not when she was under Granny's influence, and not now. When she tried to talk to me about her creations, I could only think of the towns and cities I'd seen destroyed, the lives I'd seen lost. Personal lives, of those close to the pack. That she wouldn't even *contemplate* any of that being her fault . . .

I saw red. Every time.

"Well, you wanted her to talk to you. You got what you asked for," my wolf said accusingly.

I'd tried to re-engage her after our argument, desperate to return to our easy yet poignant conversation where I'd shared parts of my past that I didn't usually talk about anymore. I'd breathed a sigh of relief when she'd understood my pain, connected to her in that moment in a way I'd never connected with anyone else.

She hadn't taken the bait. I'd mentioned the various flora we'd passed, pointed out colorful birds, even commented on the cheese she had when we'd stopped to eat and rest. Nothing.

The bitch of it was, I respected the hell out of her stoic silence. No one else would've so thoroughly ignored me. She was traveling on my fucking lap, with her fingers tracing the grooves of my sides, chest and stomach, and she didn't bother with so much as a grunt. It was as infuriating as it was commendable. She had a backbone of steel when she needed to.

I was so fucked. So hopelessly, unbelievably fucked where it concerned her. How could I even pretend at this point? Her light touch had kept me enraptured. My arm around her had never slackened, keeping her close, my cock constantly hard as she jostled on my lap. Occasionally I caught myself rubbing her back with my thumb or resting my lips against her shoulder and breathing in her scent. She must've noticed my lapse in control, but she never said anything.

"Of course she noticed," my wolf said. *"Didn't you hear the part of her many accusations where she accused you of using her body? She probably thought you were making her ride with you so that you could manhandle her."*

"So that I could manhandle her?" I answered in incredulous frustration. *"She was the one with her hands on me. She didn't say a word about that."*

"And she also doesn't know what's causing that. You're keeping important things from her, just like Granny did."

I gritted my teeth and stopped where I was. Dante halted his approach and quirked his brow as I stared at the ground in frustrated rage.

"She doesn't know she has an animal, and because of that, she wouldn't understand true mates. She can't have access to her animal right now because she'd probably want to shift, and we don't have time to walk her through it. It's dangerous to shift without help. She could die. Even if she didn't, she'd need time to acclimate. Time we don't have."

"What if she consented to avoid shifting until we could help her?"

"Then she'd probably try to run and the enemy who escaped today would easily scoop her up. You know all this! You know it as well as I do. Nothing has changed."

"Everything has changed," he spat.

"Only our regard for her has changed," I said, suddenly exhausted. *"The death toll hasn't. What her products have done hasn't. We have changed, nothing else."*

And I'd give anything to change back, to shrug off my contradictions and go back to being resolute in the knowledge that performing our duty was just and needed. That we were, in fact, doing the right thing.

"What do you need, Dante?" I asked crisply.

His pitying expression cleared. The pack had been watching, had seen my struggles with this. I half wondered if I'd been lying to Aurelia when I said they trusted me to do my duty. Was that still the case?

Did I trust myself to do my duty?

"We've got company." He shifted and waited for me to do the same.

I hurried out of my clothes and made way for my wolf. His heightened senses surveyed the area as he followed Dante. The dappled sunlight played against the crushed leaves littering the forest floor. Richly textured bark adorned the towering trees around us as my wolf cut between the trunks. Various scents drifted by. The earthy, musty scent of rich, dense soil competed with the stale aroma of an old rodent den. Sage mosses clung to sharp rocks, shining with moisture as they neared what would become a perimeter line.

A familiar scent caused my wolf's hackles to rise and he burst ahead of Dante. Fresh, as though it had just been laid, was a territory marking announcing the presence of the enemy. This one I recognized as one of the prisoners that had worked her way free earlier that day. Two others I didn't know, indicating our former prisoner had clearly been joined by a larger pack. They'd followed us.

My wolf sent communication through the pack bond, pushing certain wolves out to the perimeter to relay what they found. He roamed a little farther, catching another marking with one of the same scents and two others. Another, just beyond. They were trying to entice us farther and farther out.

A moment later, my pack members all came back with the same findings. The enemy was trying to draw us out, spreading out our people, leaving gaping holes in which they could push through. A disorganized pack would fall for the bait, recognizing the enemy by the few they knew and going on a chase. With us scattered, the enemy could dart in and grab their prize.

It was as obvious as it was rudimentary. Only untrained or untested alphas would fall for something so obvious.

"*How could they think this would work?*" I asked as my wolf brought everyone back in and tightened up our defenses. We'd pull the perimeter in a little and cut down the space between sentries. The rest of the pack would cluster in the middle, keeping Aurelia at the center. "*We hit their village hard and fast with an excellent strategy. They should know the experience level they are dealing with from that alone.*"

"*They walked out of our line earlier today and disap-*

peared without a trace. You might've been checking on our true mate, but the rest of the pack was on hand. Standing around. Didn't matter. We didn't even smell them on the trail as they left their little breadcrumbs for their packmates. They might very well think this would work. Now they know it won't. An enemy can still learn something from a failed attempt. The question is, what will they do now?"

Those were all good points.

My wolf headed to check in at each new station of the perimeter. We had to ensure there were no holes in the defenses. When he was done, and after a final check to make sure all was well and there were no new markings, he headed toward the supplies. We'd need to organize those in a way that protected the animals and the carts. A raid had the potential to be just as devastating as an attack.

As he did, he said, *"When we get back, you are to make good with our true mate. She is hurting. You've ripped her life apart. It is your duty to support and help her. Stop pissing her off and chasing her away."*

If only our circumstances didn't make that so damn difficult.

19

AURELIA

"*H*ello, darling. Good journey?" Hadriel sidestepped someone hurrying by before reaching me, his mustache a little mussed on one side and his hair standing on end as though he'd repeatedly run his fingers through it. He quirked an eyebrow at me. "I'm your monitor once again. Thank the fucking gods and their kinks, am I right? I was bored out of my fucking face today. Come on, sit down. Let's get some wine and be merry, shall we? We have to wait a while for everything to get setup before we can tuck into that product of yours. Be honest with me." He gave me a side-eye. "You're being truthful about its safety, right? You seem like you believe it one hundred percent. And you just popped that one thing you found on the ground into your mouth. That could've come from anywhere and you just chucked it right in. Are you some sort of ethereal being that isn't affected by the woes of mortals? Is that why your product doesn't kill you?"

I twisted to try and stretch out my back before kneading my legs. "I'm definitely not ethereal. You'll be okay, I promise. And if half of the stories you told me are true, you'll be more than fine. If you step into a nightmare, I'll be on hand to coach you back onto the right path. I have a lot of experience guiding people through a rough journey."

"I love the lingo you've devised. Great marketing technique." He motioned for someone hurrying by. "We need wine. Alpha's orders."

He got a funny look, but the woman nodded and changed direction.

"A little white lie for his favorite prisoner." He patted my knee. "While we wait, tell me a story. A happy one, for a change. You do have a happy story that doesn't end in a horrible situation, I trust?"

As it turned out, I didn't have very many. Not that appeased him, at any rate. Things I found solace in, for example, made him unbearably depressed—his words, not mine. Recounting little highlights of my day made him grimace at me. Having lived a life as colorful as his, I could see how my small victories and the little nothings that made me grin would seem lackluster in comparison.

After we'd gotten our wine—it was delicious; I'd never had anything so fine—a man with a pot belly and dirty apron set up a few cooking contraptions that weren't much more than a pot set over an open fire. He set up a table as well, cutting vegetables and fresh-looking raw meat I assumed had been hunted recently. I didn't see many herbs, and when water was brought to him and as he prepared to get his cooking underway—a stew, I presumed—it was clear he didn't have much concern for the taste of his end product.

"No." I was up before I'd realized, putting out my hand to stop him from turning for the pot with the items he'd just picked up. "No, no." I hadn't meant to intercede, but I motioned for him to put the items down again anyway. He took a step back in confusion. "No, you don't just throw it all into the pot and hope for the best. Here, let me help."

Helping essentially meant I took over completely. He didn't seem to know which herbs to use and which ones he was missing entirely. I found it hard to believe they'd have such amazing wine but sit down to a flavorless meal.

"Did you guys happen to steal my supplies from the work shed?" I asked Hadriel as the meat seared at the bottom of the pot with the few spices they had on hand.

"Uh . . ." Hadriel looked around, wine glass in hand. He hadn't bothered to get up when I'd decided to take over the cooking operations.

It turned out they had. The alpha was very thorough in procuring my belongings, and not just from the work shed, either. Dante walked up with the spice rack from my kitchen and I wondered if the alpha had thought it was meant for the product. Why else would he have grabbed it? Given the state of their cooking setup, I could see the confusion.

"My dirty uncle, what is all this?" Hadriel asked when the spices were delivered. For some reason, the alpha wouldn't release any of the dried herbs he'd taken from the work shed. He probably thought I'd create some sort of plague with a bit of basil.

"I like to cook," I said as I grabbed what I needed and turned toward the pots. "That's putting it mildly, actually. My favorite thing to do when I get home from work is to look around at what ingredients I have on hand and use them to make something. Granny rarely gave us anything exotic, only on special occasions, and sometimes the meat was too tough for anything besides stew. I've gotten very good at stew—"

"You realize she is rolling in gold, right?" Hadriel said, standing next to me now and watching my efforts. "She's swimming in it. She could give you enough food for daily feasts if she wanted to. It'd be a drop in the well."

I held up my hand, closing my eyes. "Please, I'm not ready to hear any of that. I need to process it, and I can't do that right now, not in this situation. Let's just pretend my reality hasn't changed, okay? I need that."

"I'm sorry," he murmured, bracing a hand on my shoulder. "Of course. She really outfitted you with spices, though, huh?"

"Yes. It was a gift. She knew I liked to cook so she brought me back this set. She replenished it whenever I needed anything." I paused, cracking my neck. "No, she didn't do anything like this for anyone else. Not to this extent. Raz got a couple things, and a few other people got nice alcohols and whatnot, but my gifts were more thoughtful." I popped out a hip, chewing my lip to keep the emotion away. "Honestly, I'd always thought it was because I was like a daughter to her. I mean, I know part of it was because I worked hard and I got her product orders filled on time, but . . ." I shrugged, my vision blurry with tears. "I'd thought she'd done a little bit extra for me to . . . take care of me. Everyone else had families to look after them. I only had her. I thought she reciprocated the affection." I shrugged again. "She paid attention to the things I liked best and went out of her way to get those things. She could've just gotten me a bottle of fine wine like you drink, but instead she got things that were special."

He nodded with an understanding look as I quickly wiped my eyes and continued to work. Maybe I was a fool, but some of the things she got me really did seem personal. She'd always watched me closely when she gave them to me, pleased at my reactions. She needed me happy and she needed me working—I'd always known that. And yes, now I saw the actual state of that village in a way that shriveled my insides. I was stupid and selfish to have been so blind, duty-bound like that alpha, not questioning the motives or repercussions. But fuck, she'd really seemed genuine in giving me the truly special gifts. She really had.

"Anyway." I made short work of putting together the rest of the stew and checking the fire beneath. "Done and dusted. She's gone, and if you all are to be believed, I don't have long myself. Might as well enjoy what's left of my miserable existence."

I thought he might comment on my self-loathing sarcasm. Instead, he lifted his glass and said, "It's a nightmare. Cheers! Let's get drunk, then we'll get high, you'll get hate-fucked, I'll play with my ding-dong, and we'll all have a great night for once."

An hour later, though, as the stew was bubbling away and almost on point in flavor, the alpha showed up with five people in tow. Their gazes were stern and their demeanors intense, their movements brusque with a certainty that screamed *warrior*.

Four of them had been in Granny's cottage when I'd descended with the axe. The fifth was a woman called Nova, a very intense sort of person with an eye for detail and a firm handle on her duties. If she'd been in Raz's place, we would've gotten twice as much done and had a ton more time for leisure activities.

Hadriel shoved me, looking up at all of them. "Quick, Aurelia, get your axe!"

"We're almost ready, Alpha," the cook said, a man whose name I'd forgotten because Hadriel kept calling him Burt. I had no idea why, only that Burt gave him a flat stare every time he did it. "Just a few more minutes—"

"An hour would be best for that meat, but it'll be edible in a half hour," I corrected.

Weston blinked at me for a moment, turned and glanced at the pots, and then down at the wine.

"She requested the wine." Hadriel pointed at me. I spit out laughter.

"Let's go," he said, turning back. "We need to try your . . . product. We need to see what effect it has on pack bonds. Hurry, I want everything settled before full night."

Hadriel bounced up in a flash, somehow avoiding spilling the wine that was now sloshing around in his glass.

I leaned over so I could brace my hand on the ground only to have Weston reach down to help me. I let him pull me up and then drank in his proximity. My body vibrated pleasantly from the alcohol, draining away my woes just as the relaxant had earlier. Within that lovely hum, I could feel his power beating through me. Into me almost, enticing me closer, daring me to take that leap.

"Okay, let's go." I stepped back.

The fleeting sun cast long shadows across the ground as we reached the carts. They'd been grouped together with the horses and donkeys stationed not far beyond. I felt more than saw wolves within the trees all around us, blending into the darkness as though made of shadows. They waited, their presence lethal, their duty to keep us safe. Well, keep the camp safe, I guessed. I was to be contained.

Weston stopped beside one of the carts and pulled back a tarp. Within the cart were the crates of my product, all of them unopened save two, and those had been tied back down.

"Not a very curious bunch," I murmured, surveying them all. "You want the relaxant, right?" I got a nod. "Can I also get out the concoction I made for staving off pregnancy?"

"You have the tea. You don't need your . . . product." Weston slung his big arm over the edge of the cart, waiting.

"The tea is only mostly effective. It can be prepared wrong, and the effects can diminish if it isn't consumed in a certain amount of time. The properties of the creation might not be in prime shape—there is a lot of room for error, and given the size and stamina of your locking ability. . ." I circled my finger, indicating his crotch. "I'd rather be safe. It's no fun to kill a pregnant woman, after all. That might be a little too gruesome, even for someone as duty-bound as you."

"Great gods, I fucking love this woman," Hadriel said with a goofy smile. "Hits you right where it hurts."

Weston's jaw clenched, his body tightening up. "What is the concoction you made?"

"It's edible, it is precise, and it gives you a little fizzle of joy when you eat it—like a high five for getting laid. Most importantly, it works. The people in the village have been using it for years. They don't consume the tea at all, and given how little they like me, that's saying something. It has worked far better than the tea did in the past."

"I haven't heard of it."

"Granny hadn't been sure how to sell it. People don't tend to take leaps of faith where pregnancy is concerned. They want what they are sure works. A couple months ago she said to get it ready, that she might have a marketing tactic." I shrugged. "I made more and here we are. This was the trial crate to see if she could sell it. Well, one of the crates in there is."

His gaze bored into me, unsure.

"I wouldn't gamble with a child, Weston," I told him softly. "Not ever. You've read my journals. I've always ensured the children had enough. They were always my first priority, and I always made sure Granny made good on her promises where it concerned them. I wouldn't bring a child into my world, not even to save my life. I wouldn't pass this curse on to another."

He flinched, his eyes flickering. Then he nodded.

"Good." I turned toward the cart. "because that tea is gross as fuck."

20

WESTON

*H*er admission felt like a gut punch. It was a hard dose of reality.

I'd always wanted kids. Maybe not right now, as I was still helping to build the kingdom and flesh out the pack, but . . . someday. I'd always thought I'd find someone compatible, who'd complement me and who I'd complement in return. A partner.

Here I stood, looking at my true mate, and the barrier between us was as insurmountable as ever. It had never been clearer than when she said she wouldn't dare have my child. That thought had me withering away. It curdled my stomach. I hadn't even been thinking along those lines, but now that I had, this situation was ten times bleaker.

"Get this done," I growled, standing too rigid. Feeling too rigid. I didn't want this duty anymore. I didn't want to be dealing with any of this. I wanted to go home and pretend like none of this had ever happened.

I couldn't, though. Nor could I pretend that settling for an imperfect fit would ever be enough. After having met Aurelia, I knew that it wouldn't. I'd never met someone so . . . intoxicating. No one's touch had ever felt as perfect. No one had yelled at me with such fervor, or spent an entire day so thoroughly ignoring me. No one had ever dared to. I liked that Aurelia wouldn't give in when she'd hit her limit. I liked that my power and position had no bearing on her.

I also liked how soft she could be, how pliant, letting me dominate when I needed to. I liked when she melted around me as though she couldn't help herself, and how she gave in to her primal need even though she clearly wanted to throttle me. I just wished we could see eye-to-eye. She wouldn't backpedal. She wouldn't apologize for the drugs she had created. She had no remorse. The dragons would never grant her a pardon if she saw no blame in her creations.

Now here we were. I was going to allow my pack member to sample that product while a threat possibly existed somewhere out in the woods. Tanix and I had scouted the area. We'd found scents and followed them until it was clear they had taken off, but still, that didn't mean they were done. They could double-back at any time. Had I lost my fucking mind?

But what choice did I have? We needed to see if I could form a bond with a wolf after they had ingested those tabs. Our strategy for protecting ourselves depended on it.

At least we had the healing elixir from Finley and her brother Hannon. We didn't have much, but if something happened to Hadriel, we should be able to pull him out of it."

Aurelia looked in the cart. "Granny said she'd name the pregnancy one. I just called it Project X."

"I like it." Hadriel finished his glass of wine. "Which one is the hallucinogenic one? I want to try that one."

Aurelia turned but I stopped her with, "Just the relaxant."

"Poo," Hadriel grumbled as Aurelia stepped aside.

Her eyebrows climbed slowly. "Well? What are we waiting for? I'm the hostage—I shouldn't have to pull the crate out."

"Right you are. Here, hostage, have some more wine." Hadriel stepped up with the wine bottle.

"Dante, Sixten, get the crates," I said, stepping aside. "What's the name of the relaxant?" I asked Aurelia.

She frowned at me. "I thought you were supposed to be the expert on the horrors of my product. Don't you know their names?"

"I know their market names, yes. What did you call them?"

Her frown increased. "They should be the same. Granny never asked me to change my labels."

I sighed. "Did you turn a blind eye to literally everything outside of your little bubble?"

"We talked about this," my wolf admonished as Aurelia said, "Uh, yes. I focus on doing my job. When the product is finished, I hand it over. I'm not the manager of this outfit, I'm the worker bee."

"And you didn't know Granny had changed all the names?"

"No." She looked into the cart again, squinting with

the dying light, trying to see through the encroaching gloom of the forest. "I wonder why . . .?"

"Tanix, run and get her lantern to help her see. She can pick them out for us."

Her face lit up, gratitude seeping into her eyes. "You saved my lantern?"

"Love," Hadriel said, "he brought your fucking spices. Of course he brought your lantern. He probably pawed through your drawers, sniffing —"

My *look* cut him off. The dragon king and queen allowed this wolf a lot of leeway and I honored their looseness, but I had my limits.

"Why did you bring my spices, by the way?" she asked me, for once curious and not accusatory.

Thankfully, before I could answer, Sixten asked, "Do you think she kept you in the dark in case you got captured?"

"She never mentioned if she did, but she definitely did not like me sticking my nose in. If I asked too many questions or pushed too hard, I was punished for impertinence."

"And you were cool with that?" Sixten asked, crinkling her nose.

Aurelia shrugged. "I didn't have any other choice. Granny could be funny about certain things. You just kinda learned when to butt out. Given most of her affairs didn't concern us and she let me know if something was ever amiss with my product, I just kinda . . . bumped along."

Tanix jogged back toward us and held out the lantern. "I couldn't figure out how to turn it on. There's no switch."

"It's magic." Aurelia winked at him before explaining how it worked.

He did as she directed, trying a second time when it didn't work. He shook his head and handed the lantern over.

She followed the same instructions with a smile and in a moment, a bright indigo burned within the glass.

"See?" Her smile widened and the light twinkled in her eyes.

I stared, entranced. I'd never seen someone so incredibly lovely in all my life. Her happiness beamed from within her, like a beacon.

"What kind of lantern is that?" Dante asked.

"A fairy lantern. It was a gift from Granny." She turned and held the lantern up so she could better see the labels. "I've always been intrigued by fairies. I'd always dreamed of one day traveling to their lands and finding a handsome fairy mate with all his riches."

Dante looked at me out of the corner of his eye. Everyone else looked straight ahead, suddenly stiff.

I let it go. Her comment hadn't sparked even a kindling of rage. She didn't really mean it, I could tell. More importantly, my wolf could tell, knowing her heart wasn't in it. And then she glanced at me, nothing more than a quick look, and I knew why. Any other mate would be an imperfect fit, and now, after having met me, they would never do. She was in the same situation as I was, thrown together by some force of nature, unable to rationalize a way around it.

What a shitty fucking situation—her shitty life matched my terrible fucking past. We deserved each other.

"Here." She pointed at one of the crates. "That's the one. And then this one . . ." She lowered the lantern, pointing at the crate on the bottom left. "Product X. I hate naming things. She clearly thought I was no good at it if she changed all the names for market."

Dante and Sixten got to work, moving things around so that they could pull out the crates she needed.

"No, don't—" She jumped into the cart, reorganizing before looking into the crates to check their contents. "Some of these need to be stored in a specific way or they smush together and mess up the doses. The doses need to be precise."

"No one is going to be taking them," I growled. "They might as well go into the fire."

"Someone will take them. As soon as you see that they aren't lethal, people will want to try them."

I pursed my lips and didn't bother arguing, instead turning my attention to the crate Tanix was unwrapping. The same sort of tabs I'd seen earlier were piled in, all a slightly different shape but the same size. Tanix stepped back, still looking down on it all, as Aurelia finished up and then checked her Project X.

My stomach clenched and I turned away, unable to stop thinking about her carrying my child. Unable to stop the yearning. My wolf did the equivalent of whining in misery.

"Right." Aurelia dusted off her hands and bent to the crate of relaxants. "How do you want to do this, Hadriel? Should I take half of one, and then half of another, wait a minute to prove I won't die, and then you can take the same ones?"

Hadriel snaked between the others and then bent next to her. "You promise I'll be okay?"

"I still promise that, yes. You'll be fine."

"Take it in wolf form," I advised, turning back and avoiding looking at that other crate. "That's how they did it."

"Right-O." Hadriel handed off the nearly empty bottle of wine, set down his glass, and quickly stripped.

"Good gracious." Aurelia spun away to keep from looking.

"Sorry, love, I forgot you're bashful." His shift was fast, then he shook himself out before opening his mouth and sticking out his tongue.

"Just a thought." Aurelia bent to pick up one of the tabs. "There were quite a few sprinkled on the ground. How do we know they took just one?"

She placed it on Hadriel's tongue.

"There you go, good boy," she said with a laugh, patting him on the head.

He growled a little, making her laugh harder, before eating the tab. I shed my clothes, tossing them away and noticing that Aurelia did not turn around this time. Instead, her eyes slowly drifted down my body, stopping on my cock. It twitched with the notice but I didn't wait for the results of my rush of desire. I shifted as the others backed away, dwarfing Hadriel's wolf with my own.

The bonds of the pack were all there, waiting. A quick check-in regarding the perimeter showed all clear. No sightings, no scents, nothing to cause alarm. All good news—for the moment.

Hadriel's connection to the bond dimmed, turning

elusive. My wolf reached for it, feeling it try to slither away from our touch. Nova was right, it was like running your fingers through water. My wolf tried again, mustering our power and determination, getting ahold of that bond and reeling it in tighter.

"He's got it," Dante said, reading my wolf's cues.

"Ain't no hiding from our alpha," Sixten said with a smug grin.

"Should we try another tab?" Aurelia asked. "He can have up to five before he might throw it all back up. Five was my limit."

"You tried five of those things at once?" Tanix asked her.

"Six, actually. I needed to see how my body would react if I took more than the recommended dose. I have been on some truly nightmare journeys with the hallucinogenic product, let me tell you. It's what inspired me to learn that trick of shrugging off the drug's effects. I didn't want to keep subjecting myself to multiple doses without an 'out.'"

Hadriel stuck out his tongue, ready for more.

My wolf rose his hackles but we let it happen, watching as she placed the tab on Hadriel's tongue. He consumed it and we waited, our hold consistent but tenuous. In a handful of minutes everyone looked at me, then back to him. Nothing had changed. More minutes trickled by and still nothing changed.

"It should've happened by now. Another, or are we done?" Aurelia looked at my wolf. "If there was any sort of change, I'd suggest trying another. If there was zero change, I doubt you need to try more. Either the effect will be compounded or not at all. I'm guessing, obviously, but that stands to reason."

She was so confident when she spoke about her product, so authoritative. So fucking sexy. I could tell she took pride in her work and knew every detail. I trusted her when she administered it and believed her when she spoke about its properties. The problem was, her small world view didn't line up with the larger picture. There were some things I'd seen in person, and she had not. Not yet, anyway. We'd see what she had to say for herself when she did.

I made ready to take over, expecting my wolf to shift out of his form and hand back control. Instead, he looked at her, at her beauty, savoring her tantalizing scent and feeling that deep pulse within her calling out to him. Her wolf waited for him, and would ache to be with him once she was allowed out of the darkness. We both knew it. It's how these things went, I'd heard.

His need to meet his true mate rose. He leaned a little harder toward that pulse within her and yanked, bringing it forward.

"*What are you doing?*" I hollered at him. "*We talked about this!*"

She gasped, grabbing at her middle. Her power throbbed, pulling everyone's attention. Hadriel's wolf stiffened, feeling another alpha in the vicinity.

"*No!*" I scolded my wolf. "*She's already unnaturally quick and vicious. If you let out her wolf, there'll be no stopping her if she runs when we're not looking. We can't do this here. We have to wait until we get to the castle. You fucking know this! Stop thinking of yourself and think of her.*"

"If she runs, we'll be able to chase her." I could hear his excitement and matching desire.

"Not if the enemy grabs her first. If she runs, we could lose her forever."

It was only that which backed him down, I knew—the threat of losing her. I wouldn't be able to shift when the dragons made their verdict. He would never let them hurt her. Despite his agreement that he'd do our duty, I knew when it came down to it he wouldn't be able to. He'd sacrifice everything for her. Before being with her and getting to know her, there was a chance he could have resisted. But now—after smelling her, tasting her, burying inside her—the primal urge was too strong. I'd need to handle this situation with pure, rational thought. There could be no other way.

My wolf gave up control and I resumed my human form, straightening up slowly, watching her warily. Her power still throbbed within her, bleeding into the space around us. The others stood rigid, wary, probably ready to defend themselves if she reacted.

Seconds ticked by. Aurelia's brow had pinched tight and then lowered, her hand tight to her chest. Her head cocked to the side and her eyes found mine. An accusation burned within them, and then slowly the power drifted away, her wolf plunged back into the abyss.

My wolf whined within me, hating that we had to do this to her. There was nothing worse than the feeling of your animal, your power, slipping away until only a void stood in its place . . . except maybe trying to use it without training.

"That was all on you," I told him angrily. *"I don't want to hear one more lecture about hurting her. You can only hope*

she hasn't realized what that was. Otherwise, she's going to know we kept it from her. More importantly, she's going to know Granny did. Talk about ripping her life apart little by little. She's going to think we're monsters by not going through with freeing her animal. If she knows, there'll be hell to pay."

"Well then," she said slowly, her gaze piercing into mine. It looked like she wanted to peel back my forehead and have a look inside. "I guess that's us done." She bent and retrieved a tab as Hadriel shifted into his human form. "Maybe I'll partake."

She quirked an eyebrow at me as though daring me to argue before slowly slipping it into her mouth.

"I'm in." Hadriel struck out his hand. "I didn't feel a damn thing in wolf form except a sort of disconnect from the pack. I'll tell you, Alpha, I didn't much like that. It felt like my lifeline was disintegrating and I was left hung out to dry. Even when you managed to hold on, communication through the bond was hindered. Did you feel that? It felt like you were barely holding on."

"That's exactly what was happening." I watched Aurelia, watching me back. "That drug is dangerous to a pack."

"Only if you get power hungry and people want to break free, hmm?" She handed Hadriel the tab. "You won't have the same power over people if they take that *product*. Does the thought of losing control scare you?"

A strange tone had entered her voice, as though she were speaking about something else. It probably had something to do with whatever had happened in that moment when her wolf had come to the surface, teetering on the edge of being pulled out entirely but unable to claw free. The human part of her had been kicked around and managed all of her adult life. She'd been scarred and scared during her childhood. Her life had made her somewhat pliant, willing to accept a harsh reality just to keep living. Her wolf, however, would be brand new. Fresh. There was no telling what sort of creature would emerge, and how that might change Aurelia's willingness to calmly accept her current situation. Her wolf might've said something before being thrust back into the darkness, something that would clue in Aurelia to her situation.

I answered her as though I didn't suspect any turmoil. "The thought of losing control of the pack does scare me, yes. It should scare everyone. I keep us together. I keep us operating smoothly. Through my bond, we are united, and when we are united, we are stronger. When we are at our strongest, we are at our safest. That bond is important to protect this pack, and jeopardizing it with chemicals jeopardizes us all, including you."

She huffed, her eyes narrowing. "Jeopardizes me? You're taking me to my death. How much more could I possibly be jeopardized?"

But a shadow moved behind her eyes. She feared something worse than her predicament with me. I wondered what it was.

I knew better than to ask. She'd shut me down hard and fast and probably never speak of it again. I was learning when I could push, and when I shouldn't. She might often be pliant, but she could also be stubborn as all hell.

"Is eating going to ruin whatever this drug—excuse me." Hadriel put his hand on his chest. "This *product* does to me? I'm starving."

"No." Aurelia started away, looping her arm in Hadriel's and tugging him along with her. "Let's sit, though. You're about to get very lazy."

"I love lazy," Hadriel replied.

I hung back, hands at my waist, looking at the crate of tabs at my feet. The others were quiet, watching me.

"Thoughts?" I prodded, my mind scattered.

"What, uh . . ." Dante cleared his throat. "What happened there?"

"My wolf pushed when he shouldn't have and I had to talk him back. He's grown . . . fond of her. He wants to meet his other half."

They nodded in understanding, but their stances were still uneasy.

"What else?" I pushed. We needed to have this out. Things were getting too complicated. They needed to know I was still fully in line with our goals and my duties.

"She has a lot of power," Sixten said.

"Of course she does. She's my true mate. She'll match me."

"If she shifts, will she then be able to affect a bond like you do?" Tanix asked. "Because, assuming you can't talk your wolf back one day, we'd have some serious problems if she ever tried to disrupt the pack, which she might do out of spite. Or to get away."

I took a deep breath. "In theory, she won't be able to mess with the bond without training. There is a quality to being an alpha that is instinctive, but many of the details need to be taught. I've studied since I first shifted. She shouldn't be able to do much damage right away."

They nodded again, the tension of the group starting to drain away.

"This product is dangerous to the pack," Tanix said, nudging the crate with his toe. "It sounded like Hadriel didn't much like it, but it still weakened the bond."

I nodded, looking down on it. "I have questions. Can it be tossed into a stew, for example, and fed to us without knowing? Can it be slipped to us in another way?"

"What happens if it's you who takes it?" Tanix asked. "If it is slipped to you in your sleep?"

"He wouldn't be in wolf form in his sleep." Dante frowned at Tanix. "That's a bit too far along Paranoia Lane, don't you think?"

Tanix bristled. "Is it? If I were her, I'd do everything in my power to break this pack down and get away. We're not dealing with a morally sound individual. We're dealing with a woman who was just handing out drugs mere moments ago. She refuses to take account-ability for what she has done, and she constantly pushes back on the alpha. Do you really think, when given the chance, she *won't* do everything in her power to disrupt the pack and escape?"

"She doesn't even know she's magical," Dante said. "Since we've taken her in our custody, she hasn't tried to hurt anyone. She's joking and having fun with Hadriel, for fuck's sake. She's not acting like a normal criminal."

"Because she's been dazzled with a true mate

connection, most likely, and it hasn't yet sunk in that we're going to kill her—"

"Enough." I held up a hand, closing my eyes. "Enough. Pack this product away and make sure *no one* is allowed near it. Make sure someone is watching our food and water. This product is dangerous to our way of life, and we need to account for that."

"Can I just . . .?" Sixteen raised her hand. "Can I just point out that she has popped a random tab into her mouth on two occasions without flinching? She offered to take half of the ones Hadriel would eat. Is it just me, or is she not at all concerned with how dangerous they are?"

She wasn't—not even a little bit. Her confidence in her creation was unparalleled. Even Finley, master plant worker, would sometimes pause when under scrutiny of a potentially dangerous mixture. Not Aurelia. She believed one-hundred percent that her creation was safe, validating it by taking it personally.

"Is it at all possible . . ." Sixteen said haltingly, offering a small grimace, "that we possibly . . . have the wrong drug maker?" She held up her hands. "I know we found Granny's lair, and I know the shoe fits as far as location and isolating these people and product supply quantity, but . . ." She grimaced again. "It's just—this product looks a mess, doesn't it? What we've seen in the market looks a lot different. Some of that is packaging, but . . . the color of it? The sizes? Those are different. So far this stuff really doesn't seem dangerous. Their patrol ate it off the ground. The names are even all different!"

My breath caught with the implication but I wouldn't allow any hope to surge. I couldn't. If I let my barriers soften and opened my heart, I would be just as lost as my wolf. Not even my sense of duty or rationality would save me.

Dante stepped back into the cart, opening the crates and exposing the various products. All were a little lopsided, cut by hand or ripped, some resembling the color of those in the marketplace but all a little—or a lot —off.

"We already knew someone else was doing the packaging," Tanix said, "and she's only been blasé about the one drug. Who's to say the rest of this stuff isn't exactly as dangerous as we've seen?"

Sixten fell silent. That was a very good point.

In the back of the group, usually silent and reserved until it was time for action, Nova slowly raised her hand. "You shifted before Aurelia's power dimmed. You pulled that animal close to the surface and it took a bit before it slipped back. I'd bet anything it was struggling to get the rest of the way out."

"It had to be," I affirmed.

"She would've felt that struggle. She might not know exactly what it is, but she'll know something isn't right."

"And if that animal spoke . . ." Dante quirked a brow. "You might be in for a rough ride, Alpha. She won't be pleased if she knows what's up."

There was no telling how she'd react. Or if she'd even figure it out. All he could do was wait and watch.

21

WESTON

I left the others to put things away or get back to their defensive positions while I shifted back into wolf form and checked in with the sentries. Still, no one had seen or smelled anything.

With my people accounted for and the borders of our encampment solid, I returned to the center where people had congregated for food. Delicious scents wafted over the clearing, much more complex than was usual around dinner time.

Everyone sat around various fires, relaxing after a long day's ride. Soon we'd need to do without fires, to avoid advertising our whereabouts. For now, we'd soak in the luxury.

Sylvester stood beside his preparation table, soup ladle at the ready next to an empty bowl. It was customary for the pack to wait for me to be ready, ensuring that everything was seen to. I nodded at him as I approached, reaching for the bowl and following him to the first pot simmering over the flames.

He ladled the contents in, filling it up.

I paused. "Only half is fine until everyone has eaten, same as always."

"Yes, Alpha, it's only . . ." He cleared his throat. "I had help tonight, and Aurelia was able to stretch the ingredients into a larger amount of food. I have no idea how —it's the same ingredients—but . . . we have plenty. We might even have enough for seconds."

I glanced back to where she was sitting with Hadriel, a wine glass in hand, her eyes heavily hooded. Something—the drug or the alcohol—had gotten a hold of her. Even still, her eyes were rooted to me, her gaze pensive.

Nervousness stole through me that she was working out what had happened at the supply crates.

I nodded at Sylvester before turning away from the table. Usually, I'd remove myself to the outskirts of the gathering, eating in solitude while watching the pack, on hand in case anyone needed to talk something out or voice concerns, but not stressing them out with my presence. It was hard to relax when in the vicinity of a commander.

This time, though, I headed for Aurelia. I told myself it was because I needed to stay close to her in case the enemy attacked. Or to monitor her because of the stunt my wolf had pulled. The truth was, though, that I couldn't help myself. I wanted her proximity. To hear the sound of her voice. I couldn't prevent myself from sinking down beside her near the main fire in the middle of the pack.

She glanced over when I did, and a rush of joy flashed across her face a moment before her brow lowered and frustration dulled the sparkle in her eyes. Our connection, our chemistry, versus reality.

"Come on, my darling, let's get some grub." Hadriel plucked at her arm to get her to stand up.

"Oh no, it's okay. I'll wait until everyone has some."

"Nonsense. You helped make it. They're probably all wondering if you poisoned them. You'd best show them you didn't."

Usually Sylvester would take his next, as the cook. Surprisingly, he let Aurelia go first, stepping in before Hadriel could go after. The rest of the pack looked on, probably confused by the fact that a prisoner was not only helping cook the meal but getting priority in eating it.

"Slap a tit, Aurelia, this is delicious!" Hadriel groaned and leaned back, face pointed at the sky. "Fucking hell." He leaned forward again, his attention focused on the contents in the bowl.

It was delicious. Not as good as the stew in her little cottage, but certainly the best camp dish I'd ever had. I'd bet most of the pack felt the same. Soon sounds of groaning drifted over to us as people nodded, looking at their food. Chatter died down and the only sound was that of wooden spoons scraping against bowls.

"It needs a little something," Aurelia murmured, only halfway through hers by the time Hadriel and I had finished. "Well, I mean, it needs a bunch of stuff, but I missed the mark on spices."

"Rubbish." Hadriel shook his head. "It's delicious. I want more."

So did a lot of people. Before Sylvester would serve them, though, he looked at me.

"Do you want seconds, Alpha?"

"No." I held up my hand. "I've had plenty. Give it to them."

Aurelia glanced over at me, gingerly taking a bite of meat. A little juice caught on her lower lip before her tongue swiped across, licking it away.

"I tried the stew in your cottage," I blurted like a dummy. "I brought the spices because I figured to have that sort of talent, you must love cooking. I figured you'd want your tools, at least those we could provide."

She finished chewing, studying me. Her eyes were calculating, as though working things out.

Another wave of nervousness stole through me. She knew about her magic, she must. She was naïve, but she was not stupid. She'd be able to put two-and-two together.

How terrible would things be now if she knew I was keeping such an enormous truth from her? Knowing I was intentionally keeping her suppressed.

Guilt ate at me and I cursed my wolf his carelessness.

"Thank you," she said slowly, "though I don't really understand the point in bringing my spices if this is my death march."

Neither did I. I didn't much understand the point of any of it, anymore. My duty, this task, this horrible situation.

I turned away from her assessing stare.

"Fucking delicious, my dear," Hadriel said, taking her bowl and standing to return them. "I am raving."

"I'm glad you liked it. It was a little watery because there were a lot of people to feed."

"It was perfect. Everyone would tell you so if the big alpha wasn't scaring them away."

That was probably true.

I glanced back at the small tent she and I would share, the only one standing. I should probably retire and let the pack wind down. I had reading to do, anyway. Today was lost to the sensation of her body resting against me; I'd had no inclination to read her journals over her shoulder. I'd been somewhat callous about them, but even I had limits. Hadriel would be fine to watch her, and the sentries knew not to let her escape if she were to sneak away.

She took that moment to sway, though, the wine affecting her balance. Her shoulder bumped against mine and sent a thrill of delight through my body. She smiled at me, having felt it, and that smile made me lean back a little. I rested my hand behind her, leaning toward her, my positioning an obvious declaration she was mine.

If bad decisions were gold coins, my behavior toward her would buy the world.

Aurelia

The relaxant washed away most of my tension and worries, a hefty task. The issues just seemed to keep piling up. This most recent was a real fucking doozy. The lava I'd often felt when in Weston's proximity had turned into . . . something else. It had almost felt like something had stretched into my skin with me.

And that something had talked.

"Help me the rest of the way. I'm almost there. Don't let that alpha call the shots and stuff me back. I can tell he's thinking about it."

What . . .? I'd frozen.

Was I going crazy? Because with that voice had come a rush of power. My sense of smell had increased until I was picking out complex weavings of the things around us. The light from my lantern? Distracting. I'd nearly been able to see details in the dark. Oh, and yeah, Hadriel's wolf had called to me. I couldn't even describe how, just that I felt his joy, his pull, his desire to fall in line and go for a run through the trees. Not as I was, but as I could be if I'd just let that entity continue expanding until it filled me entirely. Until I gave in to it.

I knew how all those things lined up. I wasn't an idiot. I knew what they all had to mean. But if they did?

I swayed, bumping up against Weston and letting him stabilize me.

Weston always seemed to create the feeling. He created the lava, and this time, he brought out what was attached to it.

Brought out? Pulled out, more like. From within me . . .

I breathed deep, slightly panicked breaths.

It couldn't be what I was thinking. It couldn't. I would not allow my hope to rise and overwhelm me. Because Granny had tried. She'd sought out an animal within me many, many times. She'd never felt anything.

Maybe she hadn't been as powerful as Weston, a small voice murmured. *Maybe all I needed was more power...*

I swayed again into Weston, my stomach churning from my emotions mixed with a lot of wine.

"Don't let that alpha call the shots and stuff me back. I can tell he's thinking about it."

Why would he be keeping my animal from me if I actually had one?

Control.

The word floated up immediately.

I couldn't see in the dark so I couldn't easily escape at night. I wasn't as strong as a shifter—my axe didn't penetrate far enough. I couldn't heal, I couldn't scent. Without more power, I was vulnerable, and that made it easier to keep me caged.

Hell, they weren't even bothering to cage me. They just kept me within sight so that they could easily pick me up if I ran. Two legs wouldn't get me far enough away, not with four legs chasing me.

Give me my animal, though, and watch me run.

"Let's get you to bed, Little Wolf," Weston whispered, his lips against the shell of my ear.

Little Wolf...

A storm of adrenaline and emotion rolled through me.

He'd called me that a few times. Once or twice it had seemed like a taunt. Sometimes, he'd said it almost intimately, like now.

My heart started to sprint.

It was true, it had to be, and he'd known all along. He must be able to feel it, because he caused that lava effect in me. He tugged on the thing inside of me but never far enough to pull it out fully—not until tonight, when his wolf had been in control. The wolf had backed off, but not before whatever was inside of me was teetering on the edge.

Little Wolf . . .

"Hadriel, not too late," Weston said as he gathered me into his arms and stood.

"Right-O, Alpha," he replied as Weston carried me back. "Don't worry, tomorrow I'll be rarin' to go."

"I can walk," I murmured, my words slurred as I wriggled in his arms.

"Yes, I'm sure you could get to the tent. You'd probably cover twice the distance going side-to-side, though, and you need your sleep. We have another long day tomorrow."

I didn't say a word until we reached the tent, letting him put me down gently so that he could walk us in and close the flap behind us.

"Why are you so nice to me when you know you'll have to kill me?" I said, afraid to ask what really mattered.

Pain flitted across his expression. "I'm hoping it doesn't come to that. You will stand in judgment, yes, but your sentence is not yet set. The dragons are fair. They'll hear your story and decide how you should pay for your crimes."

"And you? Did you pay for your crimes?"

"More than you could possibly know."

"The dungeons, right? The demon dungeons?"

"Yes. I ended up there when trying to save a pack member. They snatched me from the beach and punched in my animal so that I was helpless. Then they

311

did things to me that—" His eyes turned haunted in the low light, a solitary lantern glowing in the corner, not mine. "You wonder why I hate what you do so much? It's because, as I was rotting in that place, they juiced me up with their magic and loaned me out to their people. Their magic acted like a drug. They made me want to fuck, anything and everything. I begged for their filthy dicks. I pleasured their women and let them pleasure me, my mind controlled by their magic. By their version of a drug. And the next day? I swam in shame for how I'd acted, felt dirty for what I'd done. But then they'd come the next night, and the next, and I knew I'd have to do it all over again. When I wasn't being forced to have sex, I was beaten and tortured to fuel their beasts. I thought I'd die in that place. I'd hoped I would, sooner rather than later. Your drugs are influencing people that way. They are altering minds and locking people in cages of addiction, doing things they would never normally think of doing to afford the next high. I've suffered for my sins, but innocent people who shouldn't be are suffering because of you."

My chest constricted with empathy I wished I didn't feel, especially not now. When Hadriel told stories of the demon dungeons, he'd always spun it so that it didn't seem real. It didn't seem as dark and haunting, as traumatizing. Now, hearing it from Weston, seeing the pain in his eyes, the darkness of his past evident in every line in his body, I couldn't help but be struck deep. He was hurting from that encounter still, I could see it. He probably always would. I understood where he was coming from. I understood that pain, so similar to mine.

But he refused to see the truth staring him in the face.

"I have proved to you that my product is not doing those things. You saw how it affected Hadriel. Me. It isn't the same! There is no addiction, and if they are consuming the product in the first place, they are not innocent!"

His eyes kindled fire and I knew it matched mine.

"Don't you think I have paid for my sins?" I fumed. "I paid before payment was due. That payment started me on this path in the first place. Now *I* am the one who has been snatched, taken from my home. By you. And—"

I took a deep breath, swallowing hard. Here it was, the moment of truth I'd been circling.

I lowered my voice to a whisper. "You are keeping me suppressed, too, aren't you? That's what I felt earlier, isn't it? An animal. *My* animal. I have magic, don't I?" My whole body started to shake. "I do, don't I? That was the voice. The heat, the power . . ."

His face closed down into an unreadable mask—but not before his eyes flickered. For that brief moment, his confirmation of my accusation showed clearly.

The realization I had magic sapped the strength out of me and I sagged, unable to believe it. Unable to wrap my head around it.

All this time, I'd had an animal tucked inside me? It didn't seem possible.

My mind spun with the implications and the larger picture came into focus.

"I suppose you will continue to keep me suppressed and helpless." Tears leaked from my eyes and I couldn't tell if they were because I was happy I had magic, sad that I'd spent so much of my life without experiencing it, or frustrated that he was keeping it locked away from me. All three emotions boiled within me. "You snatched me, caged me. You'll keep me in your bed, on your lap, in your sight and use me to your heart's content, just like those demons used you. And in the end, you'll deliver me to my death, like you'd hoped they would deliver you. I really don't see, Weston, how your situation is any different than mine. But somehow you assume you're in the right and I deserve whatever I get. What an extraordinary twist of logic."

I had to get out of here. I had to escape. Thanks to my sleight of hand around the crates earlier, I finally had a way out. I just needed to time it correctly.

I bit back the tears as I shrugged out of my clothes, folding them up neatly and setting them on the ground in the corner. "Those will be fine for tomorrow."

I approached him then, needing to focus on the goal. If I wanted to escape, I needed to maintain our proximity. I could use him just as he was using me—had to, as a matter of fact. I needed to lull him into security with my perceived complacency and then take advantage of his trust. I was now convinced it was the only way.

I grabbed the edges of his shirt and pushed them up.

"What are you doing?" he asked, letting me.

"What do you think I'm doing? I want to kill you and I want to fuck you. I can't do one without more power, so I may as well do the other."

He shook his head slowly, waiting until I pushed down his pants before grabbing my upper arms and stopping me from dropping to my knees.

"No. Not like this," he murmured.

"Not like what?"

"You're mad, Aurelia. You're hurt. The truth? You do have magic, yes." My heart thumped so hard it was almost painful. "Granny would've been able to feel it. Any alpha would. And yes, I will keep you suppressed *for now*. I hadn't ever intended to keep you suppressed forever."

"Just until my sentence."

"Something along those lines, yes. You can't shift for the first time without help—it's dangerous—and we don't have the time for that now. Not when we're on the road."

I narrowed my eyes. "Not to mention the fact that I'd be harder to contain."

"There is that, yes. I won't hide that fact."

I slapped away the angry and frustrated tears. All my life I'd been kicked around because I'd been different, because I'd been without magic. I'd been sneered at, spit on, or like in Granny's village, avoided and side eyed. But all this time, I'd just been suppressed.

I had an animal. I had magic! *All this time.*

My knees weakened and I nearly dropped to the ground. Weston caught me quickly, holding me tightly as he directed me to bed.

"No," I said, trying to struggle away.

Granny would've been able to feel it. Any alpha would.

"No." I shook my head. "Granny couldn't have known."

He was my captor, I would expect something like this from him. But Granny? She'd been my family. She'd saved me. She wouldn't have kept me—

Helpless. Dependent.

The truth felt like a slap.

Prior to the last few days, I wouldn't have believed Granny capable of it. I would not have trusted this man to be telling me the truth, not over her. But now, after taking a hard look at other aspects of my life . . .

Without magic, I'd had to stay in that village. I'd been very clear about that. I welcomed her walls, her cage. I learned to make her product and do it exceptionally so that she would never have cause to toss me out. I had apparently helped trap a village in fear of the Outside, out of fear for my life. All that time, it had been a lie. She didn't pull out my magic for the same reason she hadn't paid the village in actual gold: she wanted us to stay there and continue working.

I went limp in Weston's arms, letting the pain come. It felt like he was ripping my life apart, little by little, and leaving nothing but wreckage in his wake.

He settled me into bed and slipped in beside me, gathering me up into his arms. I sobbed against him, tears dripping against his skin.

Had Granny ever actually loved me? Why had she saved me, only to betray me like she had?

This last shredded piece of my life tore into my heart. I'd never get those answers. She'd never be able to explain herself. Not that I could trust what she had to say, but gods help me, I wanted her here to make this better. I couldn't handle this pain.

My body shook, taking the comfort from him I so desperately needed until I could calm myself once more. Despite how badly it hurt, and how ardently I wanted to give up and let him take me to the dragons for a bittersweet goodnight, I'd promised my mother. There was still surviving to do, no matter how desperately I wanted to fail.

At least I had magic. That was something—a big thing. If I could just get away from him and find another alpha, I could have that magic pulled out. It was my only chance at a brighter future.

My cheeks were still wet but my resolve hardened. I pulled Weston's face toward mine and captured his lips. I slid my hands down his chest, aiming for the hard cock I could feel pulsing against my thigh. I craved the abyss that sex with him could give me.

"No, Aurelia." He gently grabbed my wrist, pulling my hand up to his heart. "You'd regret this."

"I always regret being with you. What would make this time any different?"

"I don't want you to regret it. Not this time." He paused. "Because *I* wouldn't regret it this time. I had a nice time tonight, it's why I allowed the wine to flow. I can't let that happen again because soon we're going to head into more dangerous areas. I also can't ignore the things you've said. I want it to be clear I am not drugging you, or taking advantage of you. You are in control of your body and your mind. You've given your consent to me each time we've been together, but tonight, you're under the influence. If or when we have sex again, I want you to have a clear head."

"Anger is a clear head?"

"Compared to your product and wine? Yes. You get more lustful on your product. Probably on alcohol, too."

The thing was, despite everything, I'd had a nice time tonight, too. A really nice time, with his strong, comforting presence so close and Hadriel's jokes so funny. I'd felt included in a way I never had before. Weston had been incredibly patient, stabilizing me when I laughed too hard and nearly fell over, or adjusting how he sat so I could lean against him. He'd been watchful as well, never partaking in the wine and often looking this way or that, making sure he checked out every little disturbance he heard or felt or even just imagined. It was the kind of protective diligence I'd craved since my mother had died, the kind I thought I'd found in Granny.

None of that mattered, of course. Not anymore. I needed to get free of both my old life and Weston's shackles. I'd have sex with Weston again, hoping to incite him enough in lust or anger to accidentally bring my magic to the forefront, but I wouldn't take my eyes off the goal. Now I could claim my freedom in a way I never had been able to before.

22

AURELIA

The next night, Hadriel led me to the center of the clearing we'd be bunking down in. The cook was setting up and others were preparing to erect the tent I knew was for me and Weston. He was off seeing to the sentries and setting up a perimeter to guard the pack as they slept. I had wanted to go with him and see where he was positioning people—it was knowledge I'd need to get out of here—but I couldn't find a non-suspicious way to ask. I'd be better off just asking about it later, maybe during pillow talk or when he had his guard down.

Besides, though there hadn't been any reports of Alexander or his people dogging our heels today and they hadn't picked up any markings or scents when we stopped, I worried they would still be out there, waiting. I didn't want to make a run for it until the coast was clear. Hopefully, it would be soon.

"I have to go look after my horse, love," Hadriel said, stopping near the cooking station. "Why don't you take over for Burt so that the food is edible." He patted me. "We'd all appreciate it."

Burt—whose name was actually Sylvester—glowered at Hadriel as he walked away. He didn't shrug me off, though, saying that he planned to make chili and asking if I had any input. I did, of course, quickly taking over and using poor Sylvester as more of a sous chef than cooking partner. By the time the pack had everything squared away and were ready to eat, the chili was nearly ready and Weston was standing close, watching me work.

"Almost," I said, stirring the pot and taking a taste. I passed the spoon onto Sylvester. "Here, see what you think?"

He did as he was told, nodding adamantly. "Best damn chili I have ever tasted. Jessab is going to be mighty threatened by you."

"Who?"

"The royal cook. He'll be worried you'll steal his position."

"I'll be too busy getting my head cut off," I groused with a smile, and Hadriel barked out his laugher as he sat patiently to the side. To Weston I said, "Go ahead and eat. Ten minutes won't make or break it."

He nodded, stepping up and spooning some into his bowl, filling it only halfway.

"You can take your fill. There is plenty to go around," I told him, my heart swelling that he would repeatedly take less to ensure his people had enough. I used to do that in the village when the food was meager.

He did as instructed before Sylvester shooed me up to the pot. "Your turn. Let's go, they're all hungry."

"I'm pretty sure no one thinks it's poisoned this time." I tried to step away. "I'm a prisoner. I'm fine to go last."

"You're the cook. You go first." Sylvester gave me a shove and everyone stood around us, waiting for food while nodding their agreement.

Unlike in the village, it was clear there was no use arguing. Face flushed and fighting a pleased little smile that they'd insist, I filled my bowl and turned for Hadriel, only then surprised to find that Weston wasn't there. Instead, he was walking away, finding a little spot by himself and sitting down.

"Was it something you said?" I asked as Hadriel stood to get in line.

He followed my gaze. "Yesterday was a strange occurrence, him joining us. Usually, he sits on the periphery to eat and then heads off early. Unlike some alphas that lord over everyone all the time, making them nervous, he heads out and lets the pack relax."

"But . . . he's not very intimidating. Why can't they relax when he's here?"

Hadriel gave me a funny look. "A great many people find him plenty intimidating. Besides, he's in charge. It's hard to really let your hair down when the boss is looking over your shoulder. It's fine, he's used to it. Sit there, I'll be right back."

Weston looked off to the right, chewing, a solitary figure set back from the pack he ruled. A pang of sadness hit my heart. Maybe it was because I'd distanced myself throughout my life, always removed from those around me, or because I constantly had to eat dinner alone, but I sympathized with him. He just seemed so lonely. So isolated, with no one to talk to. It was his choice, but he was doing it to give his pack some peace of mind. That was commendable. I was angry as hell with him, but the humanity in me recognized that he shouldn't be rewarded for his sacrifice with a companionless meal.

His head snapped toward me as I moved in his direction. He watched me approach, chewing.

"Hey." I sat down beside him. "Thought you might like the company of a person you don't make nervous."

He didn't respond but his gaze didn't leave me. He took another mouthful as I took my first, focusing on the flavors for a moment before breathing out and getting a bit more comfortable.

"Dinner was always wind-down time," I said to fill the seemingly expectant silence. "I looked forward to it all day—I thought about what I would cook, what drink I would have with it, if I'd have a fire or sit outside. I'd play with the flavors, try new things, and then sit in peace as I finally ate and wound down."

"This dish tastes like heaven," he finally said, going for another bite.

Emberflies started blinking into existence, hovering in the trees as the light faded. They'd been around last night, too, though I hadn't paid them much notice. It had been the rest of the pack that marveled at their presence, apparently never having seen them in the area before. It was probably because the emberflies correctly assumed they were dangerous. I wasn't sure why they would hang around now, but I enjoyed their glow.

"It could use a few things, but it's decent for what we had available."

"You don't give yourself enough credit."

I shrugged, continuing to eat. "What will you do when you can no longer have fires? Sylvester said we'd only get a few more nights since we were still somewhat remote? I hear we're taking the long way."

We'd seen some people on the road today looking at our procession in confusion, but not many travelers walked these lanes and roads. There were bigger thoroughfares leading to closer villages and the somewhat-still-distant larger towns and cities. Our path would take longer in order to remain less conspicuous.

"We'll smoke some meat to tide you over until a couple of us can go into the nearest town and buy some cold meats and other supplies. The rest of us can hunt and eat in wolf form."

I hadn't even known that was possible. I'd never heard the people in the village eating raw meat when in wolf form—not that I had ever asked about it.

I ignored the burning frustration and betrayal about the magic situation. In a few days we'd get close to those larger towns and cities. I could wait to exercise my freedom until then, when it would be hard to find me in a bustling crowd.

I focused on the food, starting the winding down process again.

"I can organize a ground roast, if you want?" I finally said. "If you guys can hunt for a wild pig or something, I can cook it overnight. We can do it the night before we have to go to cold food. It'll still taste good cold."

His spoon scraped the bottom of his bowl. "That sounds like a rare treat." He put the bowl to the side and leaned back, looking out as the pack got their food and settled down to eat it. "I've asked you this before, but things were . . . more strained. Do you remember Granny saying anything about who packaged your supply? Where it went after you?"

Things between us were still plenty strained. It was good for me that he didn't seem to realize it.

I took a slow bite, really thinking back. "Granny almost never talked about her side of things unless she was telling me what needed to change about a product. Even then, it wasn't specific to the operation, only the product itself. Alexander was the one that leaked Granny's business stuff. He liked to brag. I always heard it second hand." I shook my head. "He did mention right before you guys came that they'd started getting fancy with how they packaged the product. Again, I heard this second hand, so I don't know specifics. It was said in conjunction with being in the royal market. I'm not sure if it's a new thing or he's just now bragging about it. Either way, it sounded like it was very upscale, what-ever they were doing. I suppose they did need to take it somewhere to have that done, though I can't for the life of me remember him ever talking about it. It always sounded like they were taking the product *in*. I thought 'in' meant to the city, I guess, where Granny kept her affairs."

"Did you write that down in your journal?"

"No. I heard it the day after we, uh, met." I looked away for a moment, a rush of heat coming over me. "We went looking for the Moonfire Lily that evening and then you guys showed up. I didn't get a chance to write anything down."

"Moonfire Lily?"

"It's a glowing flower that has some amazing properties. It's rare and hard to find. It's easier at night because it glows."

"Was that the flower you had in your workhouse?"

"Of course you combed through the work shed." I hunched over my bowl. "Yes, it was. I picked that flower a couple months ago and though the stalk has withered, the petals are miraculously still perfect."

"Granny's product is purple and black. The packaging, I mean. Does that ring a bell?"

I looked over at Weston for a long moment. "Only because purple reminds me of fairies, and purple and black is my favorite color combination."

His eyelids fluttered and then blinked twice in quick succession. This time he didn't turn into stone, unlike when he was trying to keep the knowledge of my magic from me.

"Yes," he said, his tone deep and thick. "You had purple accents running through your cottage. Your bedroom was purple, your furniture black."

"And you scoped out my bedroom. Fantastic," I said sarcastically.

"Obviously. It's where I found your journals. You didn't help Granny with the design?"

"No. I would've, but she never asked."

"Was she ever in your cottage?"

"Of course. She bought it for me and visited from time to time. I was the only person she called on for tea. It was another thing that made me feel special. Not work special, but that we had a—a connection."

He nodded slowly. "Did you ever show her your art?"

My gut tightened. I needed to look away, suddenly wishing I hadn't sat down with him. "No. The art was just for me. I didn't show that to anyone. She respected my privacy, getting me what I needed without asking why."

"You were the enemy, Aurelia. The drug maker. I needed to see what you had stored in your house."

"And now?"

"And now . . ." He cleared his throat. "Now you're the prisoner."

"You like to dive right into the fire, I see." Hadriel sat down next to me, forming a line rather than a circle, Weston on my other side. "This chili is fucking divine, my love. My asshole is puckering with how good it is."

"That's not—" I giggled helplessly. "That's not normal, I don't think?"

"It's certainly a strange compliment," Weston murmured, sitting forward and taking my empty bowl. "I'll leave you to your night. Hadriel, bring her to the tent when she's ready. Don't stay out too late. We have an early start."

The crowd parted as he walked through, everyone going a little quiet and nodding at him respectfully. He placed the bowls down in the dirty dish area, said a couple things to those close by, and excused himself. He stopped by the tent, shed his clothes, shifted, and drifted off into the night, presumably to check in with the pack still working. Maybe to relieve some of them so they could eat.

"He doesn't take time to relax?" I asked Hadriel.

"No. All work and no play makes Alpha a very dull boy."

"Before I forget." I pushed to one side and dug into my pocket, feeling what was there and choosing the item I was after. I put out my hand, the item cupped in my palm. "I swiped this for you last night. Don't get caught."

His brow knit as he took what I offered. Upon seeing it, a smile spread across his face and he slipped it into his pocket.

"It's the hallucinogen," I explained. "Yes, you'll be fine. No, you won't get addicted. You'll see things, though. Take it with caution. If you get into trouble, curl into a small, dark space or just come find me, preferably without the alpha being present."

"I cannot . . . fucking . . .*wait!*"

I rubbed my temples and just decided to put it out there.

"Did you know?"

He paused in eating.

"Did you know I had magic?" I elaborated, choking up a little with emotion. It was such a big deal for so, *so* many reasons.

He lowered his spoon slowly. "Do you want a comfortable lie or the truth?"

"The truth. Always." I furrowed my brow. "Why would someone ask if they wanted a lie?"

"To feel better about a shitty situation. Yes, I knew. Even Tanix can feel it and he's not an alpha. Before you ask, the reason I didn't say anything is because it is between you and the alpha. This is his show. I'm just a stage hand."

Now I put my face in my hands, wanting to cry

again in frustration, or joy, or just overall fatigue with this awful and life-altering journey.

"I don't know how to feel," I finally murmured.

"Bittersweet, I imagine. Right? Happy and relieved to have it, sad that so much of your life was spent being told you didn't."

It felt like those words speared my heart, sending blood seeping down in the wake of destruction. Tears welled in my eyes. That was a pretty succinct summary.

"And then mad, probably," he went on, resuming his dinner, "because now that you know you have it, and after finding out in mostly a bullshit kind of way, the guy who could help you . . . won't."

Another very succinct summary.

"You know what they say," I murmured. "If it wasn't for bad luck, I'd have no luck at all."

He bumped my shoulder in support. "What do you plan to do?"

"What do you mean? I'm a captive. What can I do?"

He huffed and said very quietly, so low I could barely hear, "You don't fool me, love. Just don't kill him. The kingdom greatly needs him. He brought all the animal shifters together in a way they hadn't been before. He's a good man who sometimes has question-able judgment."

"You think that excuses him?"

"No, so I'm asking as a favor. Beat the shit out of him? Fine. Nearly end his life? More power to you. But as a gift to me, please don't kill him."

· · ·

A while later, when a few people had come to join us, everyone laughing and chatting, telling me how much they liked dinner, I noticed Weston slip into the clearing again. He hugged the tree line, mostly, his great wolf head swinging my way for a moment. When he reached the tent, he shifted into his human form and ducked inside, leaving the flap open. A small pool of light flickered on, spilling across the ground. The invitation was clear: he was waiting for me.

I hugged my knees, looking at my feet. The desire to go to him yanked at my middle, drying up any interest in hanging out with these members of the pack. Part of me hated to leave, though. I felt included right now. They listened when I talked, laughed at my jokes, and told me to stop telling stories because they were depressing, which made me laugh so hard I wheezed. It shouldn't have been funny, but the way they said it, with dark humor, tickled me.

But as much as I enjoyed having the easy camaraderie, even as a prisoner, I couldn't deny the overwhelming need to be near Weston. It was maddening. He was the man who kept me hostage and had no guilt about ripping my life apart. He continued to keep my magic from me. I should want to torch the bed he slept in.

Instead, I just wanted to curl up with him and feel his warm skin. To receive his kisses and his attention. To feel his body moving within mine.

Fuck this strange pull.

Is this what love feels like?

It couldn't be. I didn't know enough about him to

feel love. This had to be something else, another little secret he was probably keeping from me. It *had* to be.

Telling myself it was to strengthen my escape plan, I finally relented. I excused myself and made my way to the tent. Once there, I hesitated at the opened flap.

He sat on the ground next to the cot, using it as a back rest, reading one of my journals with a pencil in hand, making notes. He looked up as I was deciding if I'd leave again and placed his thumb in the spine of the journal to keep his place before closing it.

"Come in," he said softly.

I eyed the journal.

He caught the look, lifting it for a moment. "You were twenty-two here. Granny got you a cake for your birthday. You seemed really happy and fulfilled in this passage. I can see why you thought she was family. She did seem to notice the details of your life in a way I've never heard of her doing with anyone else."

I took the step inside the tent, choosing to sit on the ground beside him. "She noticed everyone's details. I realized that when we were traveling earlier today and I was talking to Hadriel about my depressing life." I smiled remembering his comments as he'd squeezed my knee in support.

"She knew Raz's favorite liquor and when his mating anniversary was. She often surprised him and his mate with something special because she knew how much they each loved the memory of their mating day. Alexander got a lot of gifts, the disgusting pig. He boasted about them all the time."

"Yes, I've seen your comments about all that. She kept her people happy. There is nothing wrong in that."

"As an employer."

He lowered the journal again. "You can't know that specifically. As you said, she took you in before she knew how priceless you'd become to her organization."

It was nice of him to say. I clutched on to the sentiment, hoping it was at least partially true.

"I'm skimming, Aurelia." His tone was hushed. "I am looking only for the bits of information that can help me. As much as I can, I am skimming. I'm trying to preserve your privacy."

"Yet you're reading about the birthday that she surprised me with a cake."

He looked at me for a long beat. "Sometimes I can't help but get snagged. Maybe you can share this story. Then maybe it won't be so very depressing."

I huffed out a laugh, leaning into him. "You've got jokes, too, huh?"

"You'll fit right in at the castle, that's clear."

My smile drifted away. He was so sure he'd get me there. He was resolute in making me stand judgment, even knowing I could receive a life-ending punishment.

I couldn't think about this anymore. Hadriel was right—my life was so fucking depressing. I might as well give in to the things I enjoyed, regardless of how toxic they might be.

I pushed the journal away and swung a leg over Weston's lap, sitting down onto him with a release of breath. His cock hardened quickly and his hands came around me, the journal forgotten. Despite all logic, I did crave this man. I always had. Despite his betrayal and my anger, I wanted him. I might as well make the most of it and forget the stuff that would bring me down, at least for the moment.

"My head is clear," I breathed, taking his lips with mine. I ran my tongue along the seam of his mouth and was rewarded when his opened and his tongue danced with mine.

His hands slid up the inside of my shirt but I pushed off him, needing to take my clothes off by myself. The items in my pockets needed to stay there without being discovered.

I closed the tent flap and undressed quickly, folding my clothes and putting them to the side before crawling onto the bed and spreading my thighs, running a finger through my wetness before circling my clit.

He rose slowly, taking me in. Still nude from shifting, he knelt onto the mattress, ducking down to lick.

"You shouldn't taste this good," he groaned, getting more comfortable and doing it again. "You shouldn't taste like candy until we've imprinted. But here we are . . ."

He sucked on my clit as his fingers started to move. I groaned, jerking my hips with his pace. He took his fingers away and fucked me with his tongue, now working my clit. After switching again, I gyrated my hips rhythmically, fisting his hair. He growled with the treatment and the extra vibration sent me over the edge. I called out his name, shivering with release.

He kissed up my body slowly, taking time to focus on my nipples before his lips slid to my neck. He kissed and sucked as he pushed my legs out wide to accommodate his size. He fisted the base of his cock, sliding its head up and down my slit.

"Tell me how much you want your alpha's big cock in your tight little pussy," he commanded, his voice rough and sexy, his words deliciously dirty.

"Yes, Weston," I mewed, straining up to him. "Please, fuck me."

"I'm going to fuck you deep and hard until you beg me to come, and then I'm going to fuck you harder."

I grabbed his shoulders, trying to pull him nearer. His cock stroked along my seam, catching at my opening before slipping by again, driving me crazy with anticipation.

"Do you want me to fuck you, baby? Do you want this cock?"

"Yes," I groaned as his teeth ran along my neck.

"Tell me. Beg me to fuck your tight little cunt."

He circled my clit with his slick cockhead and in moments I was utterly lost to him.

"Fuck me, Weston. Please, fuck me hard. Mark me. Make me yours."

He moved his lips against the shell of my ear, his cock paused at my opening. "You're already *mine*," he growled and flipped me over, yanking me back until I was on my hands and knees. "I will brand you with my cock until you are ruined for anyone else."

He thrust in deep, taking me from behind like he had our first time in the woods: rough and feral and deliciously dominant.

"Yes, Weston, please, *yes!*"

His pace was hard and fast as he slid into me with wild abandon. His chest touched down over my back, his hips pumping. I felt his lips on my neck, sucking in my skin before his teeth bit down.

Incredible shivers rolled over my flesh, and I groaned with the sensations. It was all so much better than that first time. We knew each other's bodies now, what the other liked. He knew what I could take and no longer went easy on me like I realized he had then. I knew how I liked being dominated, his strength pinning me in place as he rammed his cock deep inside. I shoved back into him, desperate for every thrust, my shoulder tingling with the need to feel him bite deeper, to make the mark last longer. Forever.

"More," I groaned, so wet it dribbled down my thigh, so full of desire, of pleasure, I saw lights dance behind my eyes. "*More.*"

He complied eagerly, gripping my waist so that he could pummel me, his movements possessive. I was lost to the sensations, the hard swing of his hips, the comforting feel of his skin and proximity, knowing I was safe no matter how hard he took me. And I wanted it hard, bruising. I wanted him to whisk me away from this life and suspend me in pleasure, to reduce my point of focus down until he was all I knew.

He pushed me forward, pulling out and swinging me around. He yanked me closer again and wrapped my legs around his hips while he stayed up on his knees. He held me there while he thrust up into me, his lips crashing down onto mine. I devoured him, savored his taste. My groan expressed the depths of my pleasure and he answered as though starving for the feel of me, needing more, to be closer, to couple harder.

"You feel so fucking good," he groaned, his thumb moving against my clit, his lips pressed against mine. "Perfect. Like you were meant to be fucked by me and me alone." He held me tightly, fully in control of my body, driving my desire higher. "I'm going to fuck you to the limit." He rammed his knot into me, the friction so intense, the electricity between us crackling. "I'm going to make you forget everything but this cock rocking hard deep inside that wet little pussy."

I groaned, my head lolling against his shoulder, my pussy stretched gloriously around him.

"Tell me," he commanded, his power ripping through me. "Tell me how bad you want this. Tell me who you belong to."

I panted with the rising sensations, utterly lost in the moment. Lost to him.

"Holy fuck," I cried, hitting a plateau and grinding my teeth as my eyes fluttered, my body needing release. Needing to jump off this incredibly high precipice. "Oh fuck, Weston, *fuck*—"

"Who?" he demanded, dominating me with his size, with his body.

I vibrated against him, consumed. Overcome. Fucking demolished.

"You, Weston!" I cried, clutching his shoulders. "You," I said, over and over, the words tumbling from my mouth, needing him in a way I didn't even understand. "You, Weston, I'm yours. Take me. I'm yours!"

I kissed him with everything I had, with everything that I was. My focus narrowed to just his hard thrusts, his arms around me, his heat.

"Take my knot, my Little Wolf," he commanded as he fucked it in harder. "Take it deep." The stretch nearly undid me. "Tell me again. Tell me who you belong to."

"You," I whimpered, my eyes fluttering, the sensations almost unbearable. "I'm *yours*."

An explosion of pleasure rocked me to my core, soaking into every cell in my body. He roared through his release, clutching me hard, branding me with his pleasure.

I shook against him as his movement slowed, still holding me tightly.

"That's right, baby," he murmured as exquisite shivers from the retreating climax rolled through me. "Take all that cum." He sucked in my fevered skin, his movements small now, rolling that knot within me. "I'm going to keep filling you up until my scent is seared into you. Everyone will know you belong to the alpha."

I whimpered with desire. My breath was heavy from exertion. He worked that knot, joining us, rubbing against all the right places.

I mewled with increased pleasure, all my nerve endings firing, my pussy so full. He pulled and pushed so the friction between us increased as his cock started to pulse. Our joined sex was wet and slippery, the sounds erotic. I started building again immediately, drowning in these feelings with no desire to find the surface.

"I'm going to fuck you raw," he said darkly. "And when I'm done, you're going to beg me to do it again."

All I could do was cry out in pleasure as he made good on his word, taking me to new heights until all I knew was him.

23

AURELIA

*S*o sure, I'd gotten a little carried away last night and ended up with marks all down my neck, one on my inner thigh, and one on my forearm of all places. I needed to stop taking his knot so that I could slip away when needed, but last night any sort of restraint had been lost almost immediately. I'd wanted to ignore my life . . .but then accidentally slipped into insanity a little bit.

Telling him to make me his? I'd done that right out of the gate. What kind of fool was I? If he claimed me, I'd be fucked. With all his power, people would immediately know the caliber of wolf scented to my body. If his people were looking for me, it wouldn't be hard to track me down. Oh, the dingy woman with the powerful mark? Yeah, I saw her run down that alleyway just there.

Stealing things? Forget about it. If people didn't actually see me slipping from here to there, they'd smell me. Correction: they'd smell *him*, the alpha of all alphas. The commander.

Another suitor? Laughable. I might not even get someone willing to pull out my magic.

Bottom line, I needed to stop asking him to mark me. To make me his.

I certainly needed to avoid ever telling him again that I belonged to him, regardless of how fucking hot that had been at the time and how fucking hard I had come.

At one point, the lava had flowed down my chest again. I'd tried to push him just that much harder so as to release my animal. Unfortunately, he was ironclad in his control. The man had things locked down. I needed to appeal to the wolf, which the man clearly knew because in the days following our coupling, his wolf had never been even remotely close to me.

Fucking Weston.

The following days did at least go a bit easier on the horse. I got to ride with Hadriel again and got much better at hanging on. Weston picked through my journals, randomly twisting to look back at me as we traveled. I could never tell if it was because of something he'd read, or because he wanted to make sure I hadn't jumped off and started sprinting away. He used a pencil, making notes and dog-earing pages. Every time I noticed, I had to look away. The good thing was it constantly reminded me of our status—jailor and prisoner.

I started assisting with dinner every night, often taking over soon after we started. I even orchestrated digging a pit where we would roast a wild pig in the ground overnight. The next morning, we had some for breakfast and then stored the rest for the first fireless dinner that night. It was a fan favorite and soon so was I. People nodded at me and called me chef. They began sitting down to dinner with Hadriel and me or stopped to chat as camp was getting setup or taken down. I'd never felt so included in my life. I hated to give it up.

I reminded myself, though, that even if I were to stay on, this wouldn't be forever. We were traveling now and making the best of it. They were on a break from their usual routine, and I was another odd thing in this new situation. If I was brought to the castle to stand in judgment, this easy camaraderie would quickly dry up. They'd go back to their lives and I'd go to the dungeon. Whatever my outcome, this moment in time was just that—a moment. Temporary.

The good news was that all evidence of our lurkers had seemed to dry up. The sentries hadn't spotted anything during our travels or at night. The wolves doing sweeps for smells or tracks didn't, either. I never felt Alexander's or anyone else's presence. It was like they collected what was left of their patrol and buggered off.

That fact made me wonder if the product Granny sold was actually mine. I mean, I knew she sold my stuff, but maybe it wasn't the product these people were talking about. Hadriel had mentioned that the others didn't think it looked exactly like mine, and the stuff I'd snuck him hadn't made him crave more or feel sick in any way. Basically, it had had no lasting effects—like I kept saying.

Not like I could use that as proof. Even if they did

believe me—which I doubted would ever happen—they'd know I'd snuck other product. I couldn't allow myself to be searched. Tonight was the night. It was time to go.

Our winding trip through the countryside was at an end. Our route would now straighten out as we neared a large town, headed toward the sea.

To get out of camp, I'd rely on the bits and pieces of information I'd collected about Weston's perimeter guard. Hadriel had been the most helpful, always happy to chat away merrily whenever I asked a question. Once, I'd overheard the others talking to Weston about it, and last night Weston had been grumbling about the setup, not knowing I was already in the tent. I roughly knew the formation. It would be enough to slip through if I was agile and quiet.

I really hoped I could be agile and quiet.

Weston had even started letting me carry my bag from my village so that I could collect plants and colorful rocks along the way. Apparently, he'd found it along the path to Granny's and had hung onto it. I didn't give a shit about rocks and those plants were useless, but he didn't know that. I just needed the bag and a reason to keep it. I would empty everything out before I left and replace it with things I could use.

My lantern was brought into the tent every night and used for us to see by. I'd requested it because it shut off on its own. Neither of us would have to get up to turn it off after we were finished with whatever we were doing, which was usually having sex. I'd grab that once I was ready to head out, though hopefully I wouldn't need it much. The sky was clear and moon almost full. I should have plenty of light to see by. The only thing left to do, besides spring the plan into action, was to say goodbye.

"Heya, chef." A man named John nodded at me as I made my way toward the cooking station.

I'd been granted a small fire tonight, one single line of smoke that would not be unusual for this area, so close to a large town.

"Hey," I replied, smiling at him.

Only Sylvester waited near the cooking station, working at getting the flames going. The rest of the pack would be out hunting, most of their meals lately eaten in wolf form. Weston would bring back a fresh kill for me so that I could eat. He was the only one allowed to do so. It didn't take a genius to know why. His marks had faded and he'd given me no new ones in the past few days, but he was still making his claim. I was his. He'd provide my meals and keep me close at night to protect me.

Shivers worked through my body every time I thought of it. That, and the other nice things he did for me—like give me massages when traveling made me stiff, clearing my empty plate or bowl, helping me up or letting me lean on him—had constantly made my resolve wobble.

If only this had been a different life. Maybe just a different situation. Wouldn't that be a dream? A strong alpha staking his claim on me, providing for me, protecting me. If I could ignore that he was my jailor, suppressed my magic, and continually dragged me toward my punishment, I would daydream him being my rescuer. Or a handsome prince come to take me away to a charmed life full of love and laughter.

But no, in his eyes I was still a drug maker, a killer of innocents. Dragon food.

It was definitely time to go.

"Sylvester, how was today's ride?" I asked as I neared. He'd get leftovers from the other wolves, way more than he could ever eat. We'd then spend the evening cooking and cutting the offerings into appetizers so that everyone could get a taste. It was clearly why they brought so much.

"I'm tired of trees," he groused. "Trees for days. It didn't take us half as long to get to that village. I want a town with lively music and a pretty little barmaid to sit on my lap."

"Does that happen?" I helped prepare the meager vegetables we had left and the roots I'd found at our lunch stop. "Do barmaids really sit on your lap?"

"They do when I tip them well."

We worked in silence for a moment. Someone brought us a pot of water before wandering away again.

"I didn't see a tavern in your village." Sylvester straightened from his crouch with a wince. He looked to be in his mid-forties but sometimes he acted much older. "Did you not have one?"

"No. I think there may have been one when I first arrived, but it went under at some point. I don't much remember those early years."

"What did you guys do for entertainment?"

I wiped my forehead with my forearm, scooping up the chopped vegetables and putting them into the pot. "I didn't ever have time for entrainment. I ate, I worked, I slept. Whatever time I used for art or writing or my flowers came out of sleep or work time. Other people gathered together, though. They had dances occasionally and I often heard laughter and what not when I walked home from work. People provided entertainment for each other."

"You were never invited?"

"I don't have magic—" My words hitched. "Or, you know, I thought I didn't. They thought I didn't, which I think is more important. They didn't invite me around." I shrugged. "I didn't have time, anyway. It was nice to hear the laughter on my way home."

He shook his head as the first person arrived with meat. He was careful to reach around me and hand it to Sylvester.

"I heard you learned about . . ." He twirled his pointer finger in my general direction. "You know. The thing. With the alpha." He cleared his throat. "We're not really supposed to talk about it."

"I'll talk about it. Apparently, he knew I had magic the whole time and didn't say anything. It took his wolf accidentally pulling said animal halfway out, and me confronting him about it, for him to 'fess up. And he didn't even really 'fess up at first! If I hadn't been watching his face closely, I would've missed the little eye flicker. 'Little Wolf,' he calls me. Clearly that means I've got a wolf hiding in me somewhere. I can't meet her, though, because—"

I made an exasperated sound and cut myself off. There was no point in venting. It wouldn't change anything. I needed to find someone to help me, and that person wouldn't be in this camp.

"No, I meant—oh gods. Aurelia!" Sylvester snatched my wrist and held up my hand. Only then did I realize I'd nicked myself. "Shit. Here, let's put water on it."

"It's fine, honestly." I tried to pull my hand away.

"It's bleeding all over! It must be deep. Here—"

He wrestled the knife out of my other hand and grabbed the pot with the vegetables.

"Don't you ruin that food with my blood." I yanked my hand.

"Doesn't that hurt? Stop struggling, I'm trying to help you!"

"What is going on?" Weston's voice slid deliciously across my flesh.

He walked in our direction, his movements fluid but hurried. Crimson smears crossed his bare torso and down one of his legs. His eyes were feral, vicious.

Sylvester let go of me and put his hands up, backing away. "I was only trying to help her, Alpha. She cut herself."

"It's fine, seriously." I looked around for something to use to stop the flow of blood. "It's just a little nick. I'll live."

"She didn't even seem to notice it." Sylvester licked his lips in trepidation, gaze rooted to my hand.

"I cut myself all the time. Get as many beatings as I have, and you don't sweat the small stuff," I joked. Neither of the men cracked a smile. "No, but seriously, I barely feel it. Honestly. It doesn't even hurt. My pain tolerance is pretty extreme."

Weston reached for me, his movements so fast I thought he'd snatch at my wrist. Instead, his fingers wrapped around me delicately and he stepped closer, looking down on the cut. Bright crimson seeped over the edge of my pointer finger, dripping onto the work station.

"It won't kill me," I said, my words having zero effect on these guys. "Weston, honestly—"

I cut myself off with a moan as he sucked my finger into his mouth. His eyes weren't on fire, though—they were concerned.

"Fuck, even your blood tastes good," he muttered a moment later as he stepped forward and reached, grabbing Sylvester's shirt and ripping it off his body. "Make a couple strips from that," he ordered Sylvester.

He again sucked away the blood on my finger before wrapping it tightly in one of the proffered strips.

"You didn't need to ruin his shirt," I whined, watching him tie off the fabric. "You guys are really overreacting here."

"You didn't feel that cut?" Weston demanded, in my space, his anger raw and wild.

I gulped. "No, honestly. I really do cut myself all the time." I showed him my other hand. "I have the scars to show for it. Look."

He did, turning my hand over and tracing one of the scars on my palm with his thumb. "You not feeling pain —is that because of what Granny has done to you?"

"Alexander gave me the beatings. You've already made it clear that you read about it in the journals."

"This needs to be voiced in the present. You need to hear it and let it sink in. Granny ordered those beatings, right? The ones that took you to the brink?"

I knew anger swirled in my eyes as I stared at him mutely. Anguish swirled in my gut, his words poking at the brutal truth that my whole life had been a carefully constructed and maintained fabrication. I didn't want to dissect this now. I couldn't allow the reality of my past to disrupt my goals in the present, which were to escape, to claim my magic, and attempt to find safety in obscurity.

He nodded, knowing he was getting to me. "They beat you so often and so badly that you don't feel pain, Aurelia." He held up my hand. "This cut is deep. It should be throbbing. It should hurt badly. Hold onto Granny as family, fine, but beating someone within an inch of their life is not the action of someone who loves you."

I ripped my hand away, breaking that little bit more. "What the fuck do you care? Worried I'll spoil the goods for your dragons? That they won't have an able body to punish?"

His jaw clenched. He didn't respond.

"Yeah, you and your precious duty. Concerned about me as you march me toward death. That makes real sense." I unwrapped the strip of fabric, already soaked through, and grabbed another. "Let's not forget, my tolerance for pain enabled me to take your knot the first time," I seethed, wrapping a "clean" strip around it. Who knew how long this shirt had been worn by a man who usually sweat over open fires. "You remember, when you were trying to punish me with it? You could help me cure this right now. Just pull out my animal and I'll have access to faster healing."

His eyes were the customary granite. He didn't respond.

I issued a sardonic laugh, holding my hand out for Sylvester to tie the strip of fabric.

"Fuck off, why don't you," I spat at Weston. "Keep your fucking kill. I'll eat vegetables and leftovers. Or nothing at all, it doesn't really matter. I've gone without plenty of times. Doing it here or in my village makes no difference. It's a cage all the same, just a different tyrant as my jailor."

Pain—regret?—flashed in his eyes. He stared at me for another tense beat. It was to Sylvester he finally spoke. "Get someone to properly clean and sew up that finger."

He strode away, parting the crowd that had gathered, everyone with bits of meat in their hands. They watched him silently, their gazes then swinging back to me, having heard all.

I didn't care, but I needed to. In order to get out of here tonight, we had to follow the same routine we had the last few nights. I'd need to apologize to him and make it believable. He needed to drink his glass of wine as we chatted in the tent. If we didn't stick to that routine, there was no way I'd be able to escape.

I wanted to cry in frustration with the unfairness of it all. It didn't matter, though. One final "good girl" act and I could go. Fuck him and his hypocrisy.

"I can deal with my finger later," I said, taking up the knife again. "Your shirt is already ruined. There's plenty of fabric in it."

"But you're bleeding pretty heavily."

"I'm bleeding from a finger, Sylvester. Get ahold of yourself. I'm not going to bleed out from a cut in my finger."

He didn't argue and Weston didn't come back to force the issue. In fact, he didn't come back at all. Sylvester and I finished dinner, me ignoring absolutely everyone who told me I didn't need to make them anything, that I should sit down, that someone should take a look at my finger. I sampled items as I prepared them and the person who told me to eat what the alpha had killed never opened his mouth to me again. It had just been a *look*, but that look promised plenty of violence. I was at my wits end—with this journey, with my life. All of it.

It was only when all the food was cooked that I allowed the pack to baby me, to sit me down and hand me water and look at my finger.

"Gross. Love, that's deep," Hadriel said, massaging my shoulders as he peered at my finger. He'd stayed right behind me all through dinner, watching me closely, helping with anything he could. He didn't utter a word, not telling me to sit down or to stop, just supporting me in case I should need something.

To say my heart had swelled during all this would've been an understatement. I hoped someday, when I had a different identity and life, that maybe I could see some of them again. Maybe we could reunite and reforge the bond we were creating on this journey.

Or maybe I tended to make everyone into family whether that was their intention or not, even those who wanted to hurt me. It was a hard truth to face. A hard reality that constantly threatened to spill tears.

"You really didn't feel it?" the woman doctoring me asked, bent over my finger as the blood welled up. It wasn't bleeding nearly as much as before.

"She didn't even know she'd done it." Sylvester stood behind her, looking down on the proceedings.

The woman looked up at me, her gaze intense. "You need a few stitches. I don't have anything to reduce the pain. We've used it all and we haven't had a chance to get more."

"Would any of your product work?" Hadriel asked, his fingers stilling on my shoulders.

"It's fine, really. We don't have anything to dull pain in the village. Granny thought we should endure the effects of our punishments from beginning to end."

"Fuck that place," someone murmured.

The woman doctoring me just shook her head. "Do we need to hold you down? Do you want a leather strip for your teeth?"

I laughed. "Just get it done, will you? This is taking forever."

She did, and while I felt the gouge of the needle, I never flinched or pulled away. I hadn't been lying—this was not a unique situation, and as someone who didn't heal quickly, I'd had to have stitches from time to time.

After it was over and my finger was wrapped in gauze, the group around me sat back and collectively heaved a sigh of relief.

"How long will it take to heal?" someone asked.

"It's clear you've never been suppressed. It'll take ages," Hadriel told him before sitting in beside me. "Now, darling, what will lighten your mood?"

"How about a couple stories, and then I think I'll get some wine for me and the alpha and head to bed."

Hadriel's eyebrow arched but he didn't comment. He launched into a raunchy tale, many people hanging around to listen and interject, the evenings apparently a lot more lively for him with me here. Looser, he'd said. He'd even gotten into the pants of someone he'd been pining after. He'd never dwelled on it long enough to really explain, though, and once he started a new story, I was swept up and forgot to ask.

Now I listened to him sadly. I would miss him. It had been such a short time, but I realized I'd liked him from the get-go.

The night waned and finally I knew it was time. I felt my eagerness to get going and finally claim a future for myself rising. I would still be running away like the last time I'd had to set out on my own, but this time I wasn't scared. I was older now, more experienced. Better at lying. Besides, if I could survive at twelve, I had to be able to survive at twenty-seven.

"Let's get you that wine." Hadriel rose with me, not rushing me when I gave a few lingering goodnights. He reached under the cleaned-off table we used for food prep and grabbed the half-bottle left over from the night before. Everyone knew not to touch the alpha's stash.

"Thank you, Hadriel." I hugged him tightly. "For everything."

He handed over the cups and then held onto my upper arms, holding my gaze. "You were never meant to be in a cage, even one that hands out orgasms like they're silver nickels." He squeezed my arms. "Take care of yourself, my darling. Be careful. From the back of the tent, aim southwest for a half mile. Then watch out for yourself. The town will be beyond."

"Wh-what?" I asked stupidly.

"Please leave him alive. Remember what I said? Our kingdom needs him."

"I . . ." I licked my lips, my heart racing at his intuitiveness. "I'm just going to bed."

"Aurelia, just so you know, he doesn't want this duty, anymore. He's been leaving a hole in his sentries every night. It leads directly to your tent. Whether he means to or if his wolf is somehow hiding that fact from him, there has always been a way out for you, and a way in for danger. He wants to let you run free, and he will face the danger head-on to give you that opportunity. He's not a bad man—exactly the opposite, actually—he's just in a bad situation. Visit one of the drug riddled neighborhoods and see for yourself. There is a reason we're here, and Granny's clues all point at you. If you could shift the blame where it belonged, none of us would be in this mess."

He hugged me again and kissed my cheek and I could hardly speak after what I'd heard. Weston had been leaving me a way out? Even if subconsciously, it meant there was a part of him that did care what happened to me. Part of him that was pushing back against duty, against everything he thought he stood for, to see me safe. I didn't know how to feel, or what to say.

That Hadriel had known all this time, only telling me when he intuited I was finally ready to leave . . . It was all too much.

"How did you know?" I finally asked, my voice barely a whisper.

His grin was sly. "I guarded the dragon queen, which really just amounted to flying by the seat of my pants as she did what she pleased. I recognize danger, and I recognize a person hellbent on surviving. With you, it was only a matter of time."

"Yet you didn't say anything."

"Of course I didn't say anything," he said, scandalized. "I don't snitch. Besides, I've tried a few of your products over the last few days. You're exactly right— they're tame. I mean, they're fun, don't get me wrong. Last night I had a great time wandering through the trees. Apparently one of the sentries got a lot of entertainment watching me. It was like a really cool dreamscape. Anyway, some of that stuff seems almost medicinal. Whatever is sold in the market has been altered. It's giving you a bad name, as I said." He lifted his eyebrows. "If I were you, I'd be pissed."

"How'd you get more of my product?"

He huffed. "I don't help out simply because I'm a nice guy. You think you're the only one with quick hands?"

I chuckled, my eyes tearing up. "I'm going to miss you."

"This isn't forever, Finley—sorry, Aurelia. How embarrassing. I just see so much of her in you. In your wilder parts, I mean. You're a lot more balanced than a dragon. It's been a real pleasure. I hardly ever have to be on my toes."

"I'm not sure that's a compliment."

"Trust me, darling, it is. Now run along. Your alpha went without dinner tonight. If I'm not mistaken, he's hating himself for how he's treated you. It won't be hard to make up with him." He tilted his head at me. "Remember, don't kill him. I'm counting on you."

I was intensely curious to meet a dragon. They sounded crazy.

I paused in a little corner of shadow near the tent, setting things down and pouring the wine. Weston's glass got an extra ingredient, and I left the bottle where it lay. Someone could grab it in the morning.

He sat where he had the last few nights, journal open as usual, no pencil to take notes this time. He was still reading, engrossed, his legs crossed and clothes rumpled.

"Hey," I said, putting the cups down so I could close the tent flap. It was time to make the apology that I didn't feel.

He shut the journal and glanced up, his gaze open and eyes haunted. "Hey," he replied, holding out the journal.

Confused, I picked up the wine glasses, handing him his before taking the journal. I took a sip of mine before sitting down next to him.

"Is this a terrible memory? I'm really not in the mood for one of those."

"It's the last memory you wrote. You thought I was the product of your imagination. An effect of a drug."

I definitely wasn't in the mood for rehashing that night.

I sighed. "The product of a flower. My favorite flower, if that makes you feel any better."

"I wondered why you gave in to a stranger coming out of the shadows." He paused, expectant. "Don't you want to know why I did it? Why I walked out of those shadows to you?"

"Honestly, no, I don't. If it's okay, I'd like to just have

a few quiet moments together and then go to bed. I'm sorry for the things I said—"

"Don't do that," he replied, his voice so soft, his gaze pointed at his feet. He took a big gulp of his wine. "Don't say something you don't mean. Not to me."

My heart hurt even though it shouldn't. I looked away. "Okay."

"*I* am sorry, Aurelia. I am sorry for everything. I am sorry for how your life has gone up until this exact moment and I'm sorry for whatever will follow. I'd thought the demon dungeons were my penance for decisions I've made, but maybe it is this situation with you that is my true punishment."

I furrowed my brow, now trying to read his face. "I don't understand. Why go through with it if you don't want to?"

He slouched a little, the first time I'd seen him do so. "Because it is the only way I will be able to live with myself." He drained his cup dry and then held it up. "I am assuming your products didn't suddenly become dangerous, correct? Will this kill me?"

I stared at him with a slack jaw, then I was back to stammering. "I— That's just— What?"

"Will it?" he whispered. "I will need to write out instructions for the others if so, and you'll need to hurry. I assume Hadriel told you the best way to get out? He's been watching me pretty closely. It's no secret that he likes you and thinks my treatment of you is unjust. He's not nearly as mediocre as he likes to claim, he just has to want to do a job to do it superbly."

I was struck mute. I'd been so careful, so sneaky.

His smile was sad. He put his hand to my cheek, his

thumb stroking my skin. "I watch everything you do, Little Wolf. Every movement, replaying every detail when you're not near me. I can't help myself, I'm a man enraptured. You've been more calculated these last few days. I knew the storm was coming, and tonight was the final straw. I saw it in your face, in your bearing."

He could read me so easily.

"You took product the other night, right?" he asked. "You've been keeping it on your person? Or in your bag?" He waited for my nod, not much more than slightly tilting my head. "Will it kill me?"

"You took it without knowing that answer? How'd you know it was even in there?"

"It is not tasteless, whatever it was. I've been expecting your retaliation. I have a lot to answer for. You're a woman who needs help, needs kindness. I felt that the first time I met you. I have given you neither. I've torn into your life and told you to shoulder the fallout while I marched you to your doom. My actions have been unforgivable. My wolf is no longer speaking to me. But please, I need to make preparations if this will kill me. There's the pack to think about."

I shook my head slowly, recognizing the sadness in his tone, his eyes.

I set my wine down. "It won't. It's just a sleeping agent. Why are you letting me go?"

"I'm letting you go because it is the right thing to do. You're right, things aren't adding up. I am certain you are telling the truth and your journals are further proof. Product is definitely coming out of your village, but it is getting a makeover. How and where, I don't know, but Granny must have changed the properties of the product. With Hadriel's prompting, several people have tried your creations in those crates. They informed me of this earlier tonight, after you cut your finger. I think Hadriel wanted to prove your story and as the others got to know you, they wanted to help. No one has felt sick or even dizzy. No one has had a craving for more. Someone took it yesterday while we were traveling and I didn't even notice. That is not the case with product sold at market."

"Honestly, they might crave it if they keep at it. It can be habit forming if they do it enough."

"That's the thing—in the market, it might take just twice before people begin chomping at the bit. Or they die. It is those scenarios that brought me to your village, but you are naive to both. I can't, in good conscience, hold you any longer. I won't, in good conscience, deliver you back to that village, for your sake and theirs. You need to be set free."

"Why are you allowing yourself to be slipped a sleeping agent instead of just wishing me well and watching me walk away?"

"Because Granny's drugs have killed people dear to those in this pack. Some still want you hanged as a representative of Granny's organization. They are not moved by your circumstances. They want our duty fulfilled. This will appease them. We'll go hunting for you tomorrow. Hopefully, we will not find you"—his eyes lit with determination and pain—"and we'll start working on finding this other organization. I just ask that you please stop production."

Hadriel was right, Weston had been giving me an opening with which to walk away. He was letting me go even though it went against the commands he'd been given by his royal crown. He'd known, and accepted, what I'd planned to do. He was pushing back against his duty. For me.

Conflicting emotions roiled within me. He was ready to sacrifice his life to help me take control of mine. Thank you wasn't enough—he'd listened; he was protecting me in the only way he could. He was granting my freedom and allowing me a future.

Sorrow filled me at the realization that this was where it would have to end between us. I couldn't express my newfound admiration for this alpha. For this man. I couldn't express the regret that our journey had started so dark and had to end so bittersweetly.

"Clearly I can't read you as well as you can read me," I said, scooting closer and leaning against his chest. "I had no idea you knew any of this. And I said such awful things to you."

"They were true, all of them. I needed to hear them. Everyone needed to hear them. Lastly, about your animal, and then I'll need to head to bed because the agent is starting to work. Note for the future, I would've had time to tie you up before this drug took hold. You'd want to get your captor really good and drunk before you slipped him this."

"We would've been in bed dozing off by now if you hadn't thrown me for a loop."

He smiled, so handsome. "That makes sense." He resumed his seriousness, talking faster. "Any decent alpha can pull out your animal. You have a lot of power. For anyone looking, it's a shining beacon pulsing inside of you. Wait to ask someone to do it, though. I know that is a lot to ask, but it will be dangerous for you to expose your animal without the correct backup. A lone wolf packing that kind of power, without training and with your extravagant beauty, would always need to watch herself, but in this kingdom they'll hear about you and rope you in whether you want it or not. Let my past be a lesson. There are many types of cages, and some of them are gilded, but they are cages nonetheless. Keep that animal bottled up until you have powerful protection or are on the shores of another kingdom— maybe a fairy kingdom. A strong fae can easily pull out your magic. You'll have the life you've always wanted. Now, let's get to bed. Can I undress you now that you've used what was hidden in your pockets?"

My eyes teared and the breath left me. "You knew about that, too." My heart ached to hear these truths, to realize the lengths he would go to in order to make amends.

"As I said, I can't help but watch you. It's like you dance with each movement. It's so beautiful. I wish I could see your wolf. She'll be so graceful, I bet. So sleek. The beauty to my brawn."

"You're plenty beautiful," I said, closing my eyes as he pushed up my shirt and circled a nipple with his tongue.

"Yeah, we gotta hurry. This thing is taking me down fast. Strip yourself, love, I want to feel your skin against mine one last time before this takes me under."

We barely got him settled before his eyes began drifting shut.

"Please, find happiness," he whispered, already breathing deeply. "Stay safe, and find your happily ever after."

2 4

AURELIA

$\mathcal{I}$ lay curled up in his arms, breathing in his scent and basking in his heat. The voices in the clearing were quieting as people drifted away to their beds, shifting into their wolves and curling up. The lantern still glowed, bathing his strong jaw and straight features in the warm light.

I traced his full lips with my fingertips and then his shapely eyebrows. The pad of my finger drifted along the ridge of his nose, along his chin and then down his throat. His even breath washed across my face, so peaceful in his sleep.

For once I felt entirely tranquil beside him. I wasn't his prisoner any longer. He was letting me go.

My heart swelled with overwhelming gratitude as I took in his handsome face. He was easily the most attractive man I'd ever seen. The most charismatic, too.

Maybe it is this situation with you that is my true punishment . . .

It occurred to me that the situation he spoke of

wasn't taking me to the dragons. If it were, letting me leave would absolve him of that hardship. It wasn't foregoing his duty, either. How I left would clear him of that, not to mention my innocence of the crimes in question. No, it had to be me leaving him at all that was his true punishment.

I gasped out a struggled breath that rustled Weston's hair. It was time to go.

I bent forward and kissed his lips softly, lingering there for a moment. Gods help me, I no longer wanted to walk away. Now that I had the ability, I didn't want to exercise my freedom. I couldn't stay here, though. If I stayed, he'd have no choice but to do his duty.

And it sounded like it might not be in my best interest to meet the dragons.

After quickly getting dressed I grabbed my bag, hearing a tinkling in the bottom. Confused, I opened and reached down, finding a little sack with hard objects inside.

Gold.

My eyes widened as I looked into the pouch.

Inside was more gold than I'd ever seen in my life, though in fairness, I had rarely ever seen one coin, let alone several. Weston had known with certainty tonight would be the night even before I'd given him that wine. He wasn't just letting me walk away, he was ensuring I could do it easily. Safely. He was providing me the necessities to start a life on my own, something Granny had never done.

The tears filling my eyes overflowed this time.

He didn't have to do this. Letting me go was plenty, providing me an escape path was beyond expectations, but this? My heart swelled again, so big I nearly choked on it.

I wasn't going to waste his generosity. I tucked the pouch back inside my pack, on top of a pile of my clothes. He'd put those in, too.

Last was the lantern. I took it from its hook and then stopped next to the cot, bending to press one last kiss to his forehead.

"Good-bye," I whispered, my voice quivering.

With the lantern doused for the moment, I wasted no time, quickly and silently slipping out of the tent and around it to the woods beyond. Wolves lay in groups, sheltered at the bases of trees or opting for the soft grasses. Emberflies moved through the air in a lazy drift, sparkling above them.

This time my heart constricted. I'd made friends here. Well, the closest thing to friends I'd ever had, at any rate. I'd made allies; Hadriel was clearly in my corner. I'd remember them, always. I'd remember that, despite how we'd met, they'd eventually helped me get a fresh start in life.

Beyond them and through the trees, the bright moonlight dappled the ground, cutting down on my visibility. There was nothing for it but to push through. I couldn't use a light until I was away from sentry view. There was a hole in their coverage, sure, but I doubted that would extend to a great glowing beacon. All I had to do was keep my current direction and I'd be fine.

It took about an hour and a half to finally step out of the trees, and I stood there for a moment, a little shaken. I looked back, seeing nothing but darkness and shadow in my wake. I felt no presence lurking in the shadows, felt no eyes watching me. No one waited.

Good news.

I ran my fingers through my hair and straightened my clothes so that I looked presentable. Once upon a time, a starved and frightened child stumbled up to gate houses and along thoroughfares of towns like the one in front of me, looking for help or shelter. Looking for food. Sometimes it had been in the middle of the night; I'd been bedraggled and wild and begging for help, eventually explaining what happened to my mother and revealing my magic-less status. Those had been nails into my coffin, the guards completely unbothered if I were to stagger away somewhere and die.

Not this time.

With my head held high and an air of importance swirling around me, I walked with confidence along the path leading to the town. Given the hour and the apparent size of the town, the large wooden rolling gate would still be closed. A little viewing station sat beside it, currently empty.

"Hello there," I called up, my lantern glowing and my pack secured on my back. I had a few coppers in my pocket for easy reach. Weston had thoughtfully given me change. Flashing around a bunch of gold would only bring the wrong sort of interest. "Hello!"

A sleepy face showed in the cut-out window with no glass. A man on in his years rubbed his eyes and then ran a dirty palm down his face. He blinked several times and then looked down on me again.

"What are you doin' here at this time of night?" he

asked, looking around me as though someone might jump out of the bushes.

"Please forgive me my intrusion," I said with a gracious smile, bowing a little. "My horse went lame on the road and I dared not stop for too long. The roads can be dangerous at night. Unfortunately, it took me way longer than I could've expected on foot. Please, I'm tired and my feet are sore. I need an inn and a hot meal or warm bed—"

The sound of hooves and the clink of metal interrupted my rehearsed speech. A light danced down the road, a bright lantern showing the side of a wagon, a ruddy sort of face with long whiskers, and the silhouettes of a team of four horses.

"Well what's this, now?" the gatekeeper demanded, his accusation plain.

I didn't bother answering, instead stepping to the side and further into the shadows. I knew that wasn't part of Weston's pack. What I didn't know was if these newcomers had any connection to Alexander. He might not have been lurking these last several days, but that didn't mean he wasn't traveling the roads. Maybe it was a long shot, but I knew better than to take chances, especially with him.

"Whoa," the whiskered man said as the horses drew near. "Whoa!"

The horses whinnied as metal clinked and leather groaned.

"You there!" the man shouted when he was within earshot. "Open the gates!"

"By whose authority?" the gate keeper shouted in return.

"I've got supplies here and a new shipment of tradable goods. We got some of Granny's Special."

A thrill coursed through me and I stepped a little further into the shadows beside the gate, lowering my lantern as much as I could without making it seem like I was trying to hide. Hopefully the light, now coming from below, would distort my visage somewhat, hiding my identity.

"We don't need none of that Granny bullcrap," the gate keeper growled. "We've got too much as it is. It's ruinin' this town, I say. That stuff is pure evil."

"It's not for you to decide what this town needs," the stranger snarled. "This order was placed by the mayor. Open the fucking gates. I'm already way behind schedule. You're holding me up."

"The mayor is getting a cut of it, that's why," the gate keeper said, leaning out a little more. "Crooked, the lot of them!"

"That's the way the world works. Hurry up."

Continuing to grumble to himself, the gate keeper disappeared from view. The man on the wagon looked down at me, his light shining against his glass eye.

"What are you doing all by your lonesome at this time of night?" He looked me over. "A pretty thing like you shouldn't be traveling all alone."

"That's why I'm here," I answered smoothly, if a little defiantly. There was no hint of the frightened girl I remembered. "I was waylaid. My travel companions are inside."

"That right." His mouth worked for a moment before he spit off to the side. His gaze trailed over me, noticing my lantern and then the pack on my back. "Fancy lantern. It don't seem to match your cheap clothes or that dingy rucksack."

I huffed and looked away as though annoyed. My legs shook.

"Not that it is any of your concern," I replied haughtily, "but the lantern was a gift and outlasted my travel lantern. It is the only reason I use it now." A latch clinked beyond the wooden gate. I turned and applied the same scrutiny to the stranger. "As far as my attire . . . well, you're in no position to judge, are you?"

He paused for a moment as the whine of a crank began. His smile showed a few gaps in his teeth.

"Feisty. I like that," he said as the gate started to open. "When you get tired of your travel companions, I'll be at the Red Lion Inn. You know, in case you run out of funds. Hah!" He snapped the reins, getting the horses moving.

I was pretty sure that last bit was meant to be lewd—an offer to pay me for my services. Charming.

The gates were wide open by the time the wagon was through and I slipped in after it, darting through the shadows and ignoring the "Hey!" from the gate keeper. If memory served me correctly, he wouldn't be bothered to get down to chase me. Even if he did, he wouldn't catch me.

The town didn't so much as open up before me, more like it gathered around. A couple banners flailed limply from spires off to the sides of the modest gate I'd just walked through, a greeting for those visiting or returning. Each featured some sort of creature I couldn't decipher, maybe mythical, but probably a sigil of the mayor or whatever noble essentially ran this place.

Cobblestone streets wound in various directions, snaking around stone houses and wood-framed shopfronts. Oppressive stone walls encircled the outskirts.

The stranger had gone straight on, probably to the heart of the town or maybe just cutting through to the other side. He'd been headed for an inn. Given the size of this town, I assumed there'd be more than one but felt it likely they'd be grouped together.

I hurried forward, sticking to the edges of the lane, no one sharing the walkway with me. The horses and wagon moved through the glowing streetlamps ahead, spots of light rolling over the bobbing horse heads and a hunched human frame behind them. For the moment, he didn't seem to be looking around or looking back, intent on his destination and his meeting with me forgotten. If he never saw me again, I doubt he'd remember the meeting at the gate at all.

I'd just have to make sure he never saw me again.

The lane widened as more store fronts dotted the way, leading to a central square featuring a large stone fountain. The creature in the middle—a badly carved wolf, perhaps?—was different than the banners, probably built with the town or shortly thereafter, a noble etching his or her name into the bones but the family unable to stand the test of time. No water poured from its mouth or pooled in the shallow surface.

More banners flew here and I noticed the wagon stopping at the stable beside an establishment with a roaring lion on the sign. Obviously he wasn't lying about where he was staying. There were others, though, one with a five-legged horse, another with a teddy bear —no, wait, that was a toy shop. Still another with a . . .half-horse and half-fish? That just seemed wrong.

Anyone checking in right now would be suspect. A woman my age checking in right now would garner unneeded attention.

I slipped into the alleyways, surprised to find bodies huddled along the sides or laying spread out on tattered sheets and other sleeping items. Those on their backs or sides were obviously sleeping, obviously without homes and unwelcome in stables, but the ones huddled, or the guy standing at the far side, stooped and staring, mouth hanging open with drool dripping down, seemed . . . not lucid. It almost looked like he was in a coma while standing up.

I slowed as I passed, lifting my lantern a little to make sure he was okay. His pupils were blown wide and hardly contracted in the glow. He flinched, his movements jerky, before his expression creased in anger.

"You dare return, creature of the night?" he rasped in a broken voice raw from too much screaming. "You dare to seek my soul?"

He lashed out, attempting to strike a non-existent enemy.

"Unhand me, you fiend!" he shouted, growling as he continued to wrestle with nothing. He backed up against the wall, bounced off it, turned, and bent under the force of an unseen foe. "I will not go with you! Do you understand me? Oh!"

He froze . . . and then straightened up in halting movements. His head cocked to the side, his eyes focused on an invisible target about ten feet from me. A wicked gleam pulled at his lips.

"Is that how you want to play it?"

This man's behavior reminded me of Raz when he'd spun in a nightmare for too long and couldn't find his way out. He'd threaten to kill me or just blindly attack, and I'd have to shove him outside or into the supply closet. This man was much wilder than Raz, his movements not right or natural, but with the same sort of wild mania. He'd taken a similar product.

An uncomfortable feeling crawled through me.

"It's going to be okay," I said in a soothing voice, lowering my lantern to look at his feet. I had no idea why I'd thought to, or how I'd known exactly what I'd find.

A crinkly wrapper lay not far from his toes, discarded and forgotten. It refracted my lantern's glow in some places, and the color was off because of the indigo light, but it was familiar to me all the same. Purple and black in a design I'd created when I was younger and had given to Granny as a card for her birthday. I'd created a dancing little fairy in the middle of my art, but this wrapper's design showed a butterfly in flight, the fairy wings I'd drawn used for the insect's.

"Breathing will help defeat your foe," I told the man, circling around him to step among the rags and debris lining the wall of the alley at the back or side of a business. "Suck in your fuel and breathe fire onto the enemy."

I picked through his things as he froze, his head cocking to the side as my voice infiltrated his hallucination.

"You must become the mighty dragon to defeat the knight," I said, finding another wrapper mixed in with his bedding. "Suck in the fuel, man," I commanded, half paying attention. "Suck it in!"

I heard his deep intake of breath.

"Now . . . *fire!*"

The man exhaled loudly, and while he was distracted I gathered up all the wrappers I could find. He had a couple others I didn't recognize, other competitors probably, scant in comparison to those from Granny. His other trash came from food items or other living necessities. I gathered that up, too, before straightening out his bed clothes.

"Almost there!" My voice was lofty. "Seize the day. Suck in that fuel. You are mighty."

I folded his rags, the scraps of cloth apparently being used as his clothes, and put them to the side.

"Fire!" I shouted.

I looked around for something larger than these few items, finding a tarp down the alley—and another person who'd been hunched, now following my instructions. My heart pinched.

"Suck in that fuel." I made my way over to the second man, this one not nearly as animated as the first. He was near the end of his journey. "Are you okay?" I asked him softly so that the other man wouldn't hear. If the other man thought about it, he'd render himself definitely *not* okay and all hell would break loose.

The hunched man looked up at me and I moved the lantern away a little so it didn't blind him. His skin sagged and his eyes were dull as they looked through me, not at me. The torn clothing adorning his body hung from him, much too big but well-worn, as though he'd owned them when he'd had twice the body mass.

"Have you come to take me to the gods?" he asked in a frail and shaky voice.

I shook my head sadly, laying a hand on his shoulder. "The gods do not want you, yet. You have more life to live. Tell me, how can I help you?" I turned toward the standing man quickly. "Fuel, man! Suck in that fuel! If you don't, they'll get you."

"Are you an angel?" the hunched man asked me, his eyes clouding a little.

"No," I whispered, sparing a moment to shout, "Fire!" over my shoulder. My hand stayed on the hunched man's shoulder and I spied a discarded wrapper within his things. The butterfly in the center taunted me. "Quite the opposite. I think I am the bringer of hell."

The man's eyes seemed to clear a little and looked over my face. "No," he replied, his face stretching into a smile. "No," he said again. "I see the light in you. You are hell's nemesis." He issued a wary sigh. "I think I'll go to the gods now. Thank you for coming."

With that, he closed his eyes and laid down, curled up on his makeshift bed. His pulse still beat, thank the gods. He'd just sleep.

"Suck it in," I said as the man in front of me drifted off to sleep. "Fire!"

I stood, looking down the alley at the others, not paying attention to what was happening at this end. Who was helping them? Were they all taking Granny's product?

My product?

A sinking realization had sweat beading along my brow.

"Can't be," I murmured, dread pitting in my stomach.

Weston had listened to me in the end. I'd never listened to him, so sure in my product and my relative innocence. I'd trusted Granny implicitly to handle my product with care.

Hadn't Weston showed me that I couldn't trust her at all? Not with my life, not with my wellbeing, not with an entire village of people. Why hadn't I stopped to think that maybe, just *maybe*, I shouldn't trust her over him in this, either?

"Fuck," I murmured, my chest suddenly tight.

Dread coiled in my belly, rapidly turning into threads of panic. I returned first to the standing man, who was now breathing deeply on his own and in the process of calming down. With gentle firmness, I directed him to the side of the alley and helped him hunker down on his pile of rags, his bones too sharp and his movements too clunky. This wasn't something that had happened overnight. He'd been on a slow decline to this state for a while.

I covered him with the tarp I'd found, the smell a little musty but no worse than the man's odor. He tried to push it off, but I held it down and then tucked the edges around him.

In a moment he stilled. His exhale was telling. The tarp started rising and falling with his breaths.

Granny had told me one time not to bother with the fail-safes, that no one else did something like that. I hadn't listened and she hadn't pushed because changing it would've taken time—a resource she hadn't wanted me to waste.

The fail-safe worked. Of that, there was no doubt. This man was clearly in throes of something that had my product as its base, but he reacted in more extreme ways, suggesting the product had been altered after it left the village. Raz had never stopped and stared with his pupils that dilated. No one in the village had. He'd never drooled like that, or essentially powered down while standing upright. At his worst, he'd attacked.

Tingles washed through my body at what this meant as I checked the other people in the alley. I was shoved away from a man I thought was sleeping. A woman told me to fuck off, but I collected the few wrappers I could find anyway. Almost all of them were Granny's. Almost all of them showcased my design, created as a child, created to thank her for taking me in. I think I'd been thirteen. Fourteen? Weston would know. He'd probably read about that card in one of my journals.

The people in this alley must've taken quite a bit if there were this many wrappers. That, or they didn't consume food as much as they consumed this. Judging by the way their bodies wasted away, that was likely the case.

Gods, I hoped it wasn't. I hoped their need for my product wasn't stronger than the need for sustenance. That wasn't what this product was made for, though I feared this was exactly how it was used.

With dread crawling into my heart, I exited the alley making a mental note to return in the daytime. Hopefully they'd be cognizant and able to chat then. Hopefully they'd want to. I wanted more information. I *needed* more information. The implications of what I'd just witnessed in conjunction with the things Weston and his people had been saying worried me.

I also wanted to see if I could help them in any way, maybe to find proper lodging. I had more money than I needed and could afford to help these people get a leg up and out of their current situation.

I didn't know what I would do if it turned out Weston had been right all along.

25

WESTON

I knew she was gone before I even opened my eyes. I could smell her delicious scent, but it merely lingered, the source no longer by my side.

My heart ached and I rolled onto my back. I finally opened my eyes and looked at the ceiling. I didn't want to see her empty place in my bed. It was a hole that no one else could ever fill, I knew that as surely as I was breathing.

"You did the right thing," my wolf told me. It was the first time he'd spoken to me in days.

"I know," I replied, *"but it hurts."*

"At least you got to hold her and feel her. You got to speak to her and learn about her. She is in your memories. I never got to meet her wolf. You denied me that."

"You know why. Would you have us put her in more danger? Do you have any idea what the royalty of this kingdom would give to have someone with her power? They'd rope her in and try to breed her immediately, aiming to create another one like me."

He didn't respond, conceding that fact. Without me to protect her, without a pack to support her, she was vulnerable. I hadn't been lying; a lone wolf of her stature was always in danger. I'd preyed on them in the past.

Thanks to Aurelia's journals, we had a few leads—names we recognized but that we hadn't found any other information on. Granny had hidden those connections a lot better than she'd hidden Aurelia. That had to be by design.

As I laid there mulling over the situation, I thought about getting up. But we didn't need to hurry anymore. We were back to searching for the creator of the dangerous drugs stamped with Granny's name. Aurelia had designed their base, that was clear, but we needed to find who was altering them.

Speaking of Aurelia's product, I felt fucking amazing. I hadn't slept well since starting this journey, concerned for both my pack and the kingdom. If the royals of this kingdom caught us, it would pull the dragon kingdom into debt or war, and I would very likely be killed in the crossfire. The royals of this kingdom would make sure of it. They'd been trying to get rid of me since I walked away all those years ago. They hated that the dragons had me in their employ.

The sleeping product had lulled me into a deep slumber for the whole night. I felt utterly refreshed. My body had been able to heal from various aches and pains completely, and then fill up my cup, so to speak, with the needed downtime.

I finally let my head fall to the side, my gaze

lingering on the empty space beside me. My heart constricted.

What if she needed me and I wasn't there?

What if I never saw her again?

"Knock, knock." Hadriel called out to me from just outside the tent flap. "Rise and shine."

After a pause where I still said nothing, his head slowly pushed through the flap. His gaze darted around the interior before he stepped in, slipping the flap back down behind him.

"I'm going to pretend I am waking you up now, yes?" he whispered, moving into the space. "We have a duty to this pack and to Aurelia. We need to play this off. You have to feign outrage at being drugged and we have to storm the town to look for but not find her. I have no clue how we are going to pull that off because she is not great at being sneaky, but I'll come up with something."

"How'd you know it was a sleeping agent?"

"I had a little listen at the side of the tent, obviously. I wanted to be prepared for today and also make sure no one else was eavesdropping. Come now, up we get."

I didn't move to get up. I couldn't be bothered.

"Sir, you need to keep up pretenses. Doing so will help protect her." He nudged my arm.

"Is this what you do to the dragons? Annoy them until they do what you want?"

"Yes, but it is never what *I* want, it is what is necessary. I often worry their tempers will flare and one will bite something off that I love, like my cock. They're spiteful like that. You're a wolf, though—a calmer, more balanced species that can see the duty he must perform and doesn't explode in a temper when asked to perform it."

"What if she gets in trouble?" I ran my hands through my hair, gripping the roots in frustration. "What if she needs me and I'm not there? It feels wrong to let her go."

"That woman is also a wolf, right? And your true mate? She is certainly a balanced sort of lady who is only prone to explosions when incensed--by you, usually—but I have no doubt she'll rise to the occasion as necessary. She has lived through some extraordinary circumstances and survived despite terrible odds, through both her childhood and Granny's reign of terror. She will prevail, and if she needs help, she'll ask for it. She'll find you again, sir. Give her a chance to clear her name and then she'll find you again, I know it. At the very least, she'll find me. I was the favorite, obviously. She and I have a connection, you see. She'll definitely seek me out when she's ready."

I didn't know why, but that last part was actually reassuring. Even if she hated me, she might still find him. Given he served the same court I did, it was quite possible I'd see her again.

Gods, how I wanted to see her again! I'd been awake mere minutes and already I missed her fiercely. I'd rather her be by my side and hating me than forgive me and not be here. It was selfish, but there it was.

I sighed and sat up.

I wouldn't allow myself that luxury at her expense. Her happiness was the most important thing, and she hadn't been happy here with me; she'd made that abundantly clear.

"There we go." Hadriel stepped back. "Fantastic. A wonderful start to a dismal day. It could be worse—you could be back in the demon dungeons, being loaned out on a nightly basis."

"Do not bring that up again."

He shivered at my release of aggressive power. "See there? I proved my point. It could be worse. Like the terror shart I might've just released. Not ideal to shit oneself right before we cause an uproar about a missing prisoner. I'm going to go ahead and check things out, probably change my knickers, and then I'll be right back. You just roar and growl and wander out there in your fabulous nudity and get the show started. I'll be back momentarily."

He dashed out, holding his ass. He was such a strange wolf, but he did know his stuff.

Stopping myself from reaching for my clothes, I then conjured up faux frustration and anger and stormed from the tent.

"She's gone," I shouted, gathering everyone's attention. "She drugged me. Aurelia left sometime in the night."

Tanix jogged up with his brow furrowed, Sixten with him. Nova stood from a crouch near the breakfast station where Sylvester was chopping fruits, the cook not looking up.

"Start getting the camp broken down," I told Tanix in curt tones. "Get everyone ready. I'll send a few people into the nearest town to hunt her down. The rest of us will continue on our path slowly, waiting for the hunt to return with her. She's not worldly—she shouldn't take long to recover."

They nodded and jogged away, shouting instructions. Nova grabbed something off the table and walked right, her gait unhurried. Ordinarily that would cause me to yell after her, something I'd never had to do before. Something I didn't do now. She was incredibly good at reading the situation, she must know something was up. Given she went through the motions anyway meant she was playing along.

The woman was due for a promotion.

"Alpha." Dante jogged over to me as I ducked back into the tent to grab some clothes. He stepped into the tent with me, the flap closing behind him.

I glanced at him in confusion. He didn't usually enter my living quarters unless invited. "What is it?"

"I thought I should inform you that I saw Aurelia last night," he murmured, his voice too low for anyone hurrying outside to hear.

Pants on, I turned to give him my full attention. "What's that?"

"The woman has absolutely no sense of direction. She was angling my way instead of toward the town, making enough noise to rouse the dead." He clasped his hands behind his back. "I pointed her in the right direction and then shadowed her for a bit to make sure she got there. She went off course again—she has literally *zero* sense of direction and is apparently hard-pressed to follow straight lines—so I guided her until she was close to town and then drifted away."

My face was a hard mask to hide my surprise. I couldn't believe what I was hearing.

"You guided her?" I finally asked. "Why?"

"The same reason the dozen or so people she

must've passed didn't stir as she tramped by and are currently feigning surprise at her disappearance. She's had a hard fucking life, Alpha, you must see that. We needed her journals and her knowledge of her products but she's no more at fault for what's going on than that gardener poet or anyone else in that village. She was a product of her environment, trapped there like everyone else. She didn't know what was going on outside the village and she doesn't seem like a person who would be okay with what her product has become. She's not one of them, Alpha. She's one of us. She doesn't deserve to be on trial for Granny's sins—she deserves a fair shake at a life that isn't so gods-damned depressing. How can that woman find it in herself to smile, you know? Her stories have given me nightmares. I kinda hate hearing about her life. What a shitty existence."

"Who else knows you helped her escape?"

He shrugged, looking uncomfortable but determined. "I didn't see anybody else. Not sure if anyone noticed I wasn't at my post for a while."

I pulled on a shirt and grabbed the few things I'd need for the day's ride. "You'd do best not to tell anyone else. There are a few people who would not understand. They want justice. The memory of their loved ones makes them irrational."

Dante half bowed. "Yes, Alpha." He hesitated in leaving, tone still quiet. "You let her go, correct? The weak sentry line was on purpose. Right?"

"Is that why you're telling me of your involvement? Are you insinuating I played a part in her escape?"

His shoulders straightened, his head high. "No, Alpha. Of course not."

He knew that I'd let her go. I assumed he also knew I couldn't admit it. Only Hadriel would ever hear that confession, because I knew he'd keep it to himself for her sake. There was no one more trustworthy than Hadriel when he was helping someone he cared for.

"I would never relinquish my duty. Our kingdom is counting on us."

"Yes, sir." Still, he hesitated. "Just so we're on the same page, in case no one says what they're thinking . . . Going after the actual problem and not the decoy is your duty. Letting Aurelia go *is* doing your duty. We'd just be wasting time looking for her. Her journals are the sum total of what she knows, and we still have those. I see one just there. She can't help us by being here anymore."

"Thank you for your input, Dante. You may go."

This time he did leave, and I heaved a sigh of relief. Ordinarily, no, letting her go was not part of my duty. The dragon royals had initiated this assignment and they should get the final say on Aurelia's fate. As their commander, though, I had to be allowed some liberty to determine which leads to chase. As her true mate . . . I couldn't stomach the idea of them hurting her, for any reason. She wasn't evil, I was sure of that. She should not be punished for what were ultimately Granny's sins.

The camp was pulled down and ready to go in no time. Those who'd go into the nearest town to look for Aurelia had been chosen, Hadriel among them. With him was Dante and Nova and a few others who held positions of power but had softened to Aurelia's plight. Hadriel would tell them the goal and ensure Aurelia was not found.

To keep her safe, this was my goodbye.

26

AURELIA

"*H*ey!"

Something hard slammed into my ribs.

I jumped up before I'd realized what was happening, grabbing a boy by the neck and twisting him until he was bent backwards in an uncomfortable headlock. His arms flailed and his boots—probably what had just hit my ribs—scrambled for purchase.

Horses grunted as they shifted below and hay scratched at my neck and was probably sticking out of my hair.

"Sorry." I let him go and then dusted him off.

He slapped my hands away, staggering backward and falling into a pile of hay.

I'd slept in the hay loft of the inn stables last night, the one with the horse-fish on the sign, intending to get up near dawn and inquire about a room. Instead, I'd clearly slept a bit later than intended and been found out. Whoops. Such were the hazards of traveling at night.

"Sorry," I repeated. "I just laid down, waiting for a respectable time." I held out my hands to show I meant no harm and bent slowly to reach for my lantern and pack, both of which had been laying at my side. "I meant to be gone by now. I'll just go check in."

"They had rooms last night," the boy said, cross now that he knew I wasn't going to continue hurting him. He pushed up to standing. "You should've just gone and slept there. We don't allow people to sleep in here."

"Definitely. Totally. I get that. It's just . . . kind of odd for a woman to wander in in the middle of the night, you know? I didn't want them to refuse me thinking I was some sort of, I don't know, bad news or something."

He rolled his eyes. "Not around here. We get women coming in here all the time, trying to sneak their snacks or waiting for their misters to sleep it off so that he don't raise the fists." He took in my clothes and scanned my face. "Which are you? You've got no bruises but you have all your teeth. New to the snack box, I'd reckon, right? Which one has you on the hook?"

"No, no, it's not that, not at all. I'm just passing through."

He huffed, his grin knowing. "We got plenty of them, too. I swear, we might as well claim heavy tourism for how many people come through looking to buy." He shook his head. "Excuse me to say it, ma'am, but you should try to resist until the urge goes away. You're still pretty. The hunger will come back if you can just resist that hook for a while. That lantern is real nice. I'm sure you'd get a good price for it. Use that to buy the dragon elixir that kills the hook. I reckon you'd be able to buy enough to get you off. Then stay off, you hear what I'm telling you? I live around it. I see it all the time. All roads lead to a bad ending on that stuff."

"Wait." I shook my head, my palm held up gesturing for him to give me a second. This was all new lingo, and I needed a few breaths to organize my thoughts. "When you talk about the snack boxes, do you mean Granny's, or just . . . you know, in general?"

"Yeah, Granny's. None of 'em hook you like hers. Someone should've said that. It's the best around, I heard, but it comes at a steep price. If you get a bad dose, it'll kill you."

"There are no bad doses at market," I said without thinking.

The knowing glint in his eyes dimmed, a little bit of sadness seeping in. "Trust me, I've seen it. It's bad stuff. They shouldn't allow it. The mayor is getting a little action from it, though, so . . ." He shrugged. "You know how that goes. The people in charge don't care about the commoners if someone is greasing their palms." He stepped back. That was my cue to go.

"The dragons make the cure for the hook expensive?" I pulled on my pack and waited for him to go first.

"Yeah, ain't that a bitch? I hear they wax poetic about the dangers of drugs and how horrible it is to be addicted but don't they have their hands out, too? They're gettin' rich, same as that Granny. Same as the royals. Everyone is profiting off somebody."

Indeed.

"And . . ." I waited for him to get to the bottom of the

ladder before I started down. "Losing one's appetite—that's common?"

"Yeah. It's a side-effect, I guess. Some people do it just for that, I heard. Might just be a tall tale, I don't know. Pretty dumb, if so. A bit o' meat on your bones is better than what you'll end up looking like after too many snacks, know what I mean? You haven't lost too much weight yet. You'll be okay. You just gotta resist. It's really hard, I hear, but you'll thank me later."

He walked me to the front of the stables and nodded at me.

"Best thing for you," he said, "is to take that money and spend it on a good night's sleep." He pointed at the inn. "Then go back home and find yourself a nice happy mate who'll take good care o' you. You're real pretty—you should find someone, no problem. Have a couple of little ones and forget you ever thought about dabbling in any of that stuff."

I smiled at him, hiding how disturbed I was. Snack boxes, having too many snacks, the hook—they were cute terms disguising horrible effects. Life altering effects. People lost their appetites? How in the hell had Granny devised that? Why?

Frustrated, I pushed through the weathered door of the inn, intent on asking more questions. Maybe the innkeeper would have more insight than the young stable hand.

Wooden beams ran overhead in the entrance area and a worn oak counter stood to the side. A large book lay open near the end, half filled with a heavy scrawl, the rest blank save for a dusting of faint brown lines. A chubby man stood behind the counter looking up at me over wire-rimmed glasses as I walked in. He took in my face and then my clothes as I asked for a room, and then paused in putting out a hand for money as I inquired after the snack boxes.

"This inn is a no-tolerance establishment. If you get caught snacking here, you'll be kicked out without a refund. Not into the stables, either, which I see you've found. Into the street."

He waited expectantly.

"Got it," I said.

His eyebrows furrowed and he took my money.

"You get breakfast with your room. Be down by nine tomorrow. Otherwise, lunch starts around eleven and bleeds into dinner. We got ale, nothing harder. If you want harder, you gotta go into the square."

"Sorry, I'm new to all this. The snack boxes count as something harder, then?"

Again he studied me over his glasses. "If you're new to this, you'd best quit while you're ahead. Otherwise, head to the main square. Before you get to the fountain, hang a left down the side street. You'll see the cart halfway down with the purple and black awning. They sell other stuff there, but mainly Granny. If you buy it, you'd best hide it because we got a lot of people in this town who'll knock you down and take it from you. That stuff creates a lot of crime."

"Got it." I took my change and slipped it into my pocket, pausing before heading for the stairs. "Could I . . . I mean, do you have baths here?"

He leaned against the counter. "A hot bath is a copper. If you want someone to attend to you, it'll be two."

My smile was shy. "And where do I buy supplies? I've been rinsing up in a . . . well, a bucket, basically. It might be nice to have some nice smelling soaps and maybe some fragrant bath stuff."

"The attendant will have what you need."

I laid out my coppers and had no idea what I would do with all the gold. What would I spend it on to even get change? It wouldn't be a bath, that was for sure, and I doubted very much the food here was much more. The room had been less than a silver and I didn't have too many of those. Weston had given me a literal fortune. He'd given me more than enough to start a life. Without him.

It was hard to pull a breath into my suddenly tight chest as a swell of regret overtook me. The need to go back to him was suddenly and completely overwhelming, so much so that I had to stop myself from canceling the room and going back to him right now. I missed him. I missed his glittering eyes and his hard-to-coax-out grin. I missed the opportunity to learn more about him. Hell, I even missed hate-fucking him and being forced to share his bed and his warmth after.

Now, here, I wished I'd gotten the chance to explore this intense feeling further. Or maybe . . . maybe I just wished we were two different people with normal lives who'd met in a chance encounter at a market.

"Miss?" The man looked at me expectantly, clearly having just asked me a question.

"Sorry, what?"

"When do you want it, now?" the man asked. "Or after a bite to eat?"

"Oh." My stomach rumbled but I didn't want to eat

while smelling like a hay loft and looking like something that crawled out of one. "Now, please. Thanks."

It had been a good choice. The woman attending me
must've been the innkeeper's wife. She was chatty and
lively in comparison to his deadpan, no-nonsense delivery. She put rose petals in the water, making it smell
lovely, washed my hair with lavender soap, and
scrubbed me down within an inch of my life. I was
pretty sure she'd taken off an entire layer of skin.

When she was finished, she wrapped me in a soft
linen and took my clothes to get laundered without
asking. Wearing clothes from my cottage Weston had
packed for me, I headed down to a hot breakfast and a
half mug of ale. I'd purchased a full one, but it turned
out I didn't much like the stuff—much too strong. I let
the grumpy-faced man with a red beard sitting at the
table behind me have it, smiling as I did so.

His frown was pronounced.

"What's in it?" he asked, and the barman with a
round belly and dirty apron stopped what he was doing
and looked over.

I lifted my eyebrows, looking into the ceramic mug.
"Ale? The amber kind."

"What else?"

I stared at him for a beat. "Hops? Barley? I'm not
really sure how they make ale."

"He's asking if you put one of them snacks into his
drink," the bartender said in a booming voice, the
tavern patrons going quiet and looking my way.

"Oh my— No," I said, aghast. "No! Why would I do

389

that? That's absurd. Forget the fact that it is just wasting hard-earned coin, but a person should only consume that sort of product after careful contemplation. It's not something you should just stumble into."

No one so much as moved within the tavern, all still staring at me.

"I mean . . . here, I'll show you it's fine." I grabbed the mug and took a swill, grimacing as the strong taste flooded my mouth. "Ugh. I'm sure this is a lovely brew, crafted with a lot of finesse and attention to detail, but gods slap me, it's a bit tart, isn't it? Very, very strong. I'm really not a fan of it. I'm more of a wine girl. Do you want it or not?"

Red Beard looked over at the barman for a beat before they both started laughing.

"Yeah, I'll take it. No sense in wasting good ale." He took the mug from me, tilting his head in thanks.

"Oh." I chuckled, pointing at him. "You were joking about my putting stuff in your drink."

His brow furrowed. "No, I wasn't joking. Are you new here?"

My smile drifted away. "I'm just passing through. You weren't joking? Do people actually do that?"

He shook his head as the bartender leaned his hands against the bar, watching us. Everyone else had gone back to their meals, chatting amongst themselves.

"You'd better watch yourself in this town, girl," he said in a low tone. "They'll hook you any way they can. Watch your back, too. Crime is on the rise. If you're passing through, best get your business done and get gone."

Unsettled, I grabbed my pack and headed out,

vaguely recalling one of Weston's biggest issues was innocent people getting hooked. It seemed totally farfetched to put it in a drink, though. Accidentally doing something one time shouldn't create a dependency. I hadn't ever heard of something with effects that quick.

Outside, the sunlight bounced off the clean cobblestones and highlighted the cute houses and little shops. Near the square I found the side street in question, my curiosity burning about what was being sold in the stall with the purple and black awning.

She'd never asked to use my design. She'd never mentioned it. I would've thought something like that might've come up in conversation. Oh hey, Aurelia, by the way, I'm using your art for my shop face. Isn't that cool? We're in this together!

I would've thought that was amazing. I would've felt even more connected to her and the job. Now I just felt dirty, hearing what people were saying and learning what I had. I was disgusted and wanted to prove everyone wrong. I didn't want any of this to be true.

A few people gathered at the stand, all of them malnourished and unnaturally skinny, like they hadn't been eating or taking care of themselves in months, maybe years. One of them walked away, opening the purple and black wrapper immediately and popping a bright pink item into his mouth.

I'd looked at all the names on the wrappers, none of which I used for the stuff I created. Happiness or Booster Pack or Dream Time, cutesy names with very little description of what they did.

Another person walked away, several items held

tight in her hands as she scurried along. Yet another was arguing about the price and his lack of funds.

"Supply and demand," the stall attendee told the man. "If you can't afford it, buy one of these other, cheaper ones."

"I don't want any of those," the man spat. "I want Dream Time! I have to have Dream Time!"

The layout of the stand was pristine, all the products were lined up neatly and displayed well with little cards at the front listing the names and prices. My eyes widened in shock as I looked at the numbers. Two products for a silver piece? That was as pricy as room and board. Each product cost way more than a hot bath and a warm meal, something all the people in that alleyway greatly needed.

"Get out of here," the stall owner yelled, motioning the man away.

"Please, man. I need it!" The guy made a grab for the product but the stall attendee was on it, the club in his hand appearing quickly out of nowhere. He struck down, hitting the man grabbing for the product. Two large guys ran in from the side landing fists, then throwing the thin man to the ground before kicking him, making him crawl to the curb.

I flinched and backed away quickly, horrified by the violence. All this because the man couldn't have a drug.

"What took you idiots so long?" the stall attendee barked.

"Sorry, boss." The guys dragged the limp man away, taking him as far as the corner and dropping him next to the wall.

"Now, hello, sorry about that." The stall attendee was

all smiles, as though nothing had just happened. "How can I help you?"

I slowly approached the stall, looking over the options. "What is this?" I pointed to the Dream Time.

"Is this your first time trying Granny's Delight?"

"Granny's Delight?" I asked. "Is that the name of her business?"

He blinked rapidly for a moment, his smile forced. "Yes, of course. That, my dear, is a very fun hallucinogen. It's guaranteed to keep you entertained for hours."

"Entertained . . ." I reached out to grab it but the man caught my wrist, his smile sharp.

"You pay before you play."

I matched the warning in his tone. "I need to examine the merchandise before I buy. Who knows what you've got wrapped up in this pretty little package."

His grip tightened for a moment before he released my hand, leaning back a little. Holding his gaze for a moment longer, I resumed my reach and grabbed the product. A little sticker sealed the package, more of those wings, modeled after a fairy but stuck to a butterfly.

"Ridiculous," I murmured, sticking my fingernail under the adhesive. "Has no one commented that these aren't butterfly wings?"

"And why would they do that?"

I lifted the product. "Because it looks absurd."

"People are more inclined to notice what is *in* the package, not on."

"Apparently."

In the package was a perfectly cut circle, colored

bright fuschia, with the sides rounded as though compacted into that shape. A waxy sheen covered the surface.

"What is this?" I asked softly, scratching at the stuff on the outside and then breaking the item open to look into the middle.

Rough hands grabbed me, one large guy on each side.

"You'll need to pay for that now, one way or the other," the stall attendee threatened.

"I'll take one of each and you will answer my questions," I said, tension and anger coiling within me. "Get these idiots off and I'll get you the coin."

After the man was paid a hefty sum, I tore into the other packages right in front of him. All of them had that waxy coating, each a different color and most looking like candy. The interiors, though—those I recognized. There could be no doubt, I was making the product that these people were ingesting. It was my creation that provided the entertainment, as I'd planned, and whatever coated it must've created the issues people were facing, getting hooked, getting sick, not eating. Dying.

"Is this all the same?" I asked with shaking hands, scratching at the coating. "What is it?"

The man studied me closely, ignoring someone else coming to buy.

"My, my," he said. "Aren't you curious."

I huffed out a laugh. "That sounds like an accusation. I'm putting something into my body and I want to know what it is. What's this waxy stuff covering the product?"

His gaze turned predatory. "I don't make the *product*, I just sell it. No one else seems to have a problem with it."

I quirked an eyebrow, noticing the emphasis he put on product. I needed to back off. I was making a scene and I'd get noticed. But fuck it, this was bullshit. I never agreed to have my product altered. I wouldn't have cared how many beatings I'd gotten or if they'd killed me, I would not have worked one more day if I'd known what my creations would become. It wasn't worth the extra gold to create this kind of disparity.

I leaned in, my tone ice. "You know very well that there is a big fucking problem with it. Is this waxy stuff the same on all the products?"

"No idea and I don't care. Take your *product* or don't, but get the fuck out of here. I'm done with your questions."

I knew my stare was hard, probably a little off kilter. I wanted to rip the bastard over this stall and beat him senseless, then take to his hired goons, currently standing at my sides. Maybe I would've, too, if I'd had my animal's strength and speed.

Instead, I leaned back, grabbed Dream Time, and popped it into my mouth. I gathered the rest of the products and dumped it into my pack. If I wanted to understand how this stuff was altered, I'd have to experience it. Only then could I create something to combat it.

Because I *would* create something to combat it. This was not okay.

Whatever that waxy stuff was, it could clearly be applied to any product. Me stopping production would not stop Alexander from just grabbing another creator and continuing to poison people for the sake of riches. I'd make something to unhook people that didn't cost a bunch of coin. After that, I'd somehow take this organization to the ground. I'd unravel what I'd helped create.

I wasn't even at the end of the side-street before my stomach started to twist painfully. A feeling like vertigo swept over me and my mind spun. This was the sickness Weston and the others had been talking about.

What an asshole I had been. He'd told me about this, over and over. He said he'd seen it, that the pack knew people who'd experienced it. I hadn't listened.

I wanted to tell him I was sorry, that I was just as much at fault in our communication breakdown as he was. I'd been just as stubborn, if not more so. He'd relented; I had not.

I wished he was here, standing beside me, holding my hand as I walked this chemical-coated journey. Or just here for no other reason than I wanted to see his face. Hear his voice. See the rage, or lust, or humor glinting in his eyes.

The pains in my stomach got worse as I walked through the city. At one point I staggered to the side of the road and braced a hand against a wall, bent over. I wasn't the only one. Other people I noticed had hunched in places, holding their stomachs for a moment. When they straightened, they took a deep breath and continued on, their movements slowing, their walk turning into more of a trudge. After that, things seemed to even out for them.

I felt the same effects and mirrored the same actions until I found myself stopped at the mouth of an alleyway, staring into space, imagining a large ball the size of a house rolling through the cobblestone street in front of me. The image was crisp and vibrant. Birds swooped down onto it, colorful and lovely. This was the part of the product I'd devised, though it made me feel much more stationary than usual.

Having had enough, I closed my eyes and went through the steps necessary to rid my body of the effects. It still worked, just like usual. That was a relief, at least.

I'd need to peel off the waxy portion and figure out what it was made of. I was well-versed in reverse engineering. It's how I'd gotten into this trade in the first place.

When I opened my eyes, it was to a hawk-like stare on a stern face.

"Hello," the man said. His clothes smelled fresh. Other men stood around me, one on each side of me and one behind. "I hear you had some questions about how Granny altered your product. It is your product, is it not? The drawing we were given matches your likeness perfectly."

My heart picked up speed.

"I don't know what you're talking about," I said in a slightly confused tone, hoping my alarm didn't show on my face.

"I think you do. There's a big reward for whoever brings you in. Alexander will be happy to come and collect you himself." He glanced at those around me. "Take her."

27

HADRIEL

"*I* hope she's laying low." Burt said as he led a sturdy horse with a cart attached. We were making our way into town a little before midday.

Our trek had two functions: to get supplies, and to drink and pretend we were looking for a woman we did not want to find. Six of us had been dispatched for these tasks, with everyone in our group sympathetic to Aurelia. Tanix said I shouldn't go at all, he didn't trust me to do the right thing.

That guy was ass-backward and his grief wouldn't let him see it. I felt for him, I really did, but he was being a serious cumgoblin about the whole situation. *Do the right thing*, as though marching a naive woman who'd been shit on all her life into the clutches of the dragons for a crime she didn't even know existed, was the right thing. Fucking ridiculous.

I also felt for the alpha. His grief at letting her go was showing. He could usually hide his feelings, but he couldn't hide the ragged remorse at letting her walk away. He craved her, it was obvious. He liked her, too. He'd found companionship and budding feelings, I could tell. Now he was fucked. Karma—it always got you in the end.

"She's used to avoiding people, I'm sure she's being a wallflower," I said as I took in the houses and scanned the edges of the cobblestone streets. A familiar wrapper was entwined with a bit of litter. "We got Granny's drugs in this town."

"What town in this disgusting kingdom doesn't," Nova growled. She was our baby-sitter for this foray. She was the dependable, trustworthy one who'd probably be dragging me out of the pub later and asking if I wanted to try girls. She thought pushing vagina was hilarious. Very strange sense of humor.

"We've seen a couple, but, yeah." I tsked. It was a damn shame. "Well, okay. It's been fun walking with you all. If you need me, I'll be in a tavern down the way. Hopefully they have a juggler or singer or someone I can incite into a bar fight."

"Don't draw attention to yourself," Nova warned.

I put out my hands, indicating my drab attire. "I'm wearing the equivalent of a brown sack, aren't I? I know what I'm about."

"You disprove that statement every time you open that mouth," Burt mumbled.

"I know you love me, Burt, but tone it down a little, will ya? The others will get jealous."

He frowned at me.

"I'll go with you," Nova told me, her hand on my arm to steer me right.

"Don't water down my fun."

"Do I ever?"

"Is that a rhetorical question?" I groused.

"Sylvester, you're on supplies. Have Arcadia help. Dina, Marc, you guys stick together and wander the town. Make sure no one is talking about Aurelia. We'll meet back in the square in three hours."

"Is that enough time?" Burt asked. "We're supposed to be looking for Aurelia thoroughly."

"It's a needle in a haystack in this place." Nova shrugged. "We can't search inn rooms and we don't want to raise suspicion, right? If we go back with that explanation, the alpha will have no choice but to move on. Not even Tanix will be able to scrutinize us."

"Someone just needs to sit that wolf down and explain this situation clearly to him," muttered Dina, a small, spry wolf who was good in a pinch. She'd been chosen over Dante for that reason. She didn't talk to me much. I was pretty sure she thought I'd get her into trouble. Given trouble was my idea of a good time, she was probably right.

"Someone just needs to give that wolf a hug," I said, linking my arm in Nova's. "Time's wasting. Where to?"

The inns were all located in one section of town, not far from one of Granny's stalls. They positioned it in plain view, not even down a back alley or in a seedy corner. This town had no qualms about the drug trade.

We settled on an inn with a large tavern and a bad carving of a roaring lion on the sign. A few people dotted the space, filled with worn furniture on a scraped wooden floor. The little stage area in the corner was sadly bare, though it was probably too early for any sort of spectacle. At least the ale was absurdly cheap.

"Why is this place so cheap?" I asked the barman, eyeing my drink. "What's in it?"

The barman, a grizzled old fucker with a nick taken out of his ear and more whiskers than hair on his head leaned a fat palm against the bar. "This ain't that kind of establishment, and if you go on accusin' me of anything more, you can see your way out of it."

"Great, fine, awesome, good chat. But why is this place so cheap?"

The barman grabbed a cup from below the bar and spit in it before rubbing it clean. "The mayor gives the inns a stipend to make staying in town cheaper."

I took a sip of my drink and winced a little at the bitter taste. They didn't put much love into their craft here. "And why is that?"

"This a game of twenty questions? Drink your ale and mind your business."

"You get a lot of repeat customers, don't you? You have a real old-world charm."

His eyes narrowed and I winked at him before following Nova to a table in the center of the room. The other drinkers were spread out around us, all within easy hearing distance if we were so inclined.

We were halfway into our pint when the guy behind Nova, a man with a mangy, slightly reddish beard and a gross looking glass eye, leaned back a little, getting closer to her.

"They made the beds cheap so people will come to the town," he said in a low voice, talking to us but not facing our way.

I perked up. I loved people eager to chat. They

usually had a lot of stories, knowledge, and gossip, and hardly ever a clue when to shut up about it all.

"What's the attraction?" I asked, taking a gulp. I didn't have much time. I needed to get happy fast.

"What else? Granny's Delight. The mayor gives the inns a stipend so they can lower the prices. Then, in turn, they jack up the price of the snacks."

"Why is the mayor—ah." I nodded. I'd heard of this before. "The mayor is getting a cut."

Granny had an uncanny ability to suss out who she could bribe. Get the cities and towns in on it—hell, get the royalty in on it—and work together to unload the product. She was good at her job.

The man leaned forward again, over his beer. I let him be for a moment, talking a little nonsense to Nova, weaving fake stories about traveling that painted us as friendly, uneventful people. Non-threatening, basically. People never worried when talking to non-threatening travelers, especially lonely sods with glass eyes who never banged anything he didn't pay for.

We were on our third pint and I hadn't yet been able to create another bridge of communication. I sensed things were about to get interesting when a portly guy with a stained shirt and dirty hands joined Glass Eye at his table.

"How'd you do?" Dirty Hands asked before draining half his pint in a series of gulps.

"Unloaded the whole lot. This town sure has a need."

Dirty Hands grunted. "The few villages around us won't sell it. Everyone comes here."

"Don't I know it. They go through it fast, too. Best stuff on the market if you can stomach it."

"If you got a hookup for the dragon elixir, you mean. Did you bring any?"

Glass Eye lowered his voice and leaned forward. "Yeah. In my room. Only got a case. People are buying it up to cut out that mean hook."

Dirty Hands leaned back. "It'll have to do. I'll get you your gold tomorrow. Hold it for me. I have to unload a couple things later."

"You knew I was coming. Why didn't you get it all done earlier?"

Dirty Hands leaned forward again, resting his elbows on the table. He lowered his voice, but we were close enough I could still hear it when he said, "They found Granny's little worker."

"No shit," Glass Eye said, shaking his head, then taking a swill from his pint. "The one that got snatched from the operation?"

Every hair on my head stood on end. Nova's gaze slid my way, her posture still loose, not giving anything away.

"Yeah. My gods, she's a pretty little thing, too. You get a hard on just looking at her. She gave the seller hell —something about whatever they are putting on the snacks—and then popped one of them things right into her mouth. Bought up a whole bunch of it, too, before storming off. That seller thought something was off about the whole thing so he let the watch know. Turns out, they'd been given a likeness of her by the organization. There's a nice reward for bringing her in. They recognized her immediately."

"Get the alpha," I mouthed to Nova, adrenaline pumping through my body.

Her brow pinched together for a moment before her expression cleared. She nodded minutely, having figured out what I wanted, before leaning back and running her fingers through her hair.

"I'm starting to feel it," she told me.

"You're a lightweight, that's why. I'm going to have a couple more before I help get supplies. We're not leaving until tomorrow, we have time."

"I hate when you shop drunk. It slows everything down.

"Well then you go get a head start and there won't be much to slow down."

She gave an annoyed sound and sipped her drink, allowing me to keep listening in to the others.

"Who's going to take her in?" Glass Eye asked.

"Nah, they were told to keep her. Someone from the organization is going to come and collect her. That's what I was doing—sending word. They don't want her falling into the wrong hands again. They'll take her to the packing village and make her work there. The production village has been compromised, I guess. The raiding party took all the product."

"Fuck," Glass Eye breathed out, just as Nova finished her ale and excused herself.

"Don't be too long," she told me, pointing.

"Yeah, yeah," I replied, waving her away.

"That's going to delay getting in new product, right?" Glass Eye asked.

Dirty Hands fell back against his seat, making it rock backward. "You got it. They're already planning to jack up the prices to compensate. You're going to have a lot of angry stall owners."

"Not my fault. I just distribute it."

"Yeah."

"I think I saw her." I leaned forward over the table, swaying a little to emphasize I'd been drinking. "That hot little number walking around late last night? I was thinking to myself, I was thinking—what is a sexy little lady doing walking around this late? Is she looking for fun? She turned a corner before I could catch up to her, though. She looked strangely familiar but I couldn't place her. I think I may have seen a poster with her likeness, like you said. Just in passing." I sat back in my seat, feigning indifference. "I don't work for anyone relevant. I'm in a different trade. We can't sell for shit. I don't even know why I'm doing the damn thing—"

"Do you ever shut up?" Dirty Hands snarled.

Glass Eye had turned to look at me, his eyes distant. "A lady late at night you say?" He leaned sideways on the table. "I'll be damned—I saw that woman. She was trying to get into town. Stopped at the gate. She must've run in after me. Fuck." He slapped the table. "I wish I'd fucking known. I could've grabbed her myself. She was saucy. I did think it was strange that she'd show up in the middle of the night, on foot, no less. She said her horse was lame or something." He scratched his chin and sighed. "A huge payday was right in front of me and I fucking missed it."

"Yeah, well." Dirty Hands gave me a sour look before re-focusing on Glass Eye. "You're probably better off. You don't need to deal with the organization any more than you already do." He lowered his voice to a whisper. "They're cutthroat. It's all great if things are going well, but when they go wrong?" His eyebrow arched and he drew his finger across this throat. "Believe me. Be happy the town watch is handling this."

"I coulda used that payday," Glass Eye mumbled. "You're probably right, though."

"I coulda used someone to play with my pecker," I muttered, slouching over my ale. "Think they're letting in visitors?"

"Weren't you just sitting with a lady?" Glass Eye asked, turning his chair a little so that he could better see me.

I shrugged. "She's into girls."

Dirty Hands huffed out a laugh. "She's probably just telling you that because she don't want what you got." He drained his pint.

I smirked and dipped my head in agreement. "Quite possible. She's prickly, too. But that woman last night sure seemed nice."

"She just looked nice. She was saucy, I'll tell you what," Glass Eye said, his grin exposing some gaps in his teeth.

"I might be up for a little sass . . ." I waggled my eyebrows at him.

He laughed and grabbed Dirty Hands' empty pint, standing up and heading to the bar.

"What do you think, are they loaning her out?" I gave Dirty Hands a comical grin, letting him know I was mostly joking.

"Fat fucking chance."

I laughed. "Yeah." I took a sip of my ale, it was running out fast. I couldn't break the conversation, though. Dirty Hands was looking to shove me out. If I left to refill, I might return to a stone wall. "Fucking in a prison would probably be a dick shriveler, anyway."

"I could handle a prison if everyone cleared out." Dirty Hands leaned forward onto his elbows, watching his friend buy more ale. He was chatting to pass the time. Suited me just fine. We were getting somewhere fast. "No fucking way would they keep that woman there, though. Are you kidding? They wouldn't be able to keep the addicts off her."

"What'd they do, shove her in a basement?" I scratched my chest and then my head, like I had fleas, before looking off toward the right in feigned boredom.

"Nicer than that. She gets to stay in the mayor's guest room. Only the best for Granny's prized snack box creator, right? And since it was his watch that found her, he's going to cash in that reward."

"No," I said, my heart beating faster. I had the location. Time to go. I just had to get out without raising suspicion. "He's not going to give the guy who spotted her, or the ones who brought her in, a little something for their trouble?"

He snickered. "Not fucking likely. Mayor Brightwater is a tight-fisted bastard."

I tsked, staying otherwise quiet as Glass Eye sat down with the refreshed pints.

"What's that fucking barman's problem?" Glass Eye asked Dirty Hands. "He's surlier and surlier every time I come into this damn place."

"You're telling me." Dirty Hands scooted his chair closer to the table and leaned in, effectively cutting me out of the conversation.

He kept talking about the barman and I drummed

the table a little, trying my best to look bored. With a loud sigh, like I was hoping someone would talk to me, I finished my drink and returned my tankard.

"Another?" the barman asked.

"Nah. Maybe later. I gotta actually do a little work. You gonna have a live show or anything tonight?"

"Not tonight. Tomorrow. The regular guy went missing. Probably junked up in an alleyway somewhere. He was always fond of the drink and whatever else he could get his hands on. I got a new guy starting tomorrow."

"Pity." I knocked on the bar and turned to exit the tavern via the street exit, every single movement calculated. The most important thing was to avoid any sort of suspicion. Once on the street again, I ambled for a while, just in case someone had followed me out. There was no sign of Nova.

In the market, I headed to the dry fountain, scanning the area, doing my best to look unhurried. My heart was beating so fast I worried it would wear itself out and stop. Nova would meet me back here with the alpha. Together we'd storm the mayor's house for Aurelia. Hopefully whoever was coming for her had a good distance to travel.

Hopefully they hadn't harmed Aurelia.

"What's going on?" Burt paused the horse near me, his cart filled.

"We got trouble," I said quietly, looking around as though it were just an idle day. I did my best to ensure the panic rising in me didn't play out across my face. "Nova went to get the alpha. Head back. We'll need to get out of here in a hurry once we get Aurelia."

"We're getting—"

"Just head back," I hissed.

The others found me next. Them, I told to wait here.

I felt the ripple of fear before I saw the crowd shiver collectively. It was how I knew *he* was coming. There was no more awesome sight than an alpha of Weston's caliber in action.

A throng of people burst from around the corner of the buildings in the direction of the gate, screaming and running. They poured into the square and spread out, a couple staggering, falling. Everyone in the market gasped or shrieked, turning to see the source of the commotion.

The great wolf ran at the head of his pack, power and grace and vengeance incarnate. He'd come for his mate.

What must've been the watch ran out from the right in shifter form, their leader thin and agile but obviously lacking. Judging by their sloppy formation, he had only a loose hold on his people. They ran at Weston as I pushed off the fountain. He could've bonded them and stopped them easily but he didn't. He crashed into their leader, ripping out lumps of flesh before tearing out his throat.

I sprinted at them in human form as our pack joined the melee, tightly structured and working as a perfect, cohesive unit.

Pride welled up through me. I watched as my pack made short work of the watch before catching up with the alpha.

"In the mayor's house," I said, out of breath. "They're keeping her in a guest room in the mayor's house."

It occurred to me that I didn't know where the fuck that was.

"This way. We found it when we were looking around. It's huge. This way!" Dina shed her clothes and shifted into her wolf form. I did the same to keep from being left behind. Thankfully Marc stayed in human form, grabbing our clothes. I doubted we had anything that could identify us in those clothes, but it was better to be safe, just in case.

Weston followed Dina and my wolf fell in line. People ran away from us shrieking or shouting as we traveled through the large town. No one dared to get in Weston's way.

The house was indeed huge, with a grand porch and white columns. Dina peeled away and Weston stopped, the message through the bond instructing us all to stay in our wolf form as he alone shifted into his human form. Someone had to speak and open doors. He marched up the few stairs like a man on fire, his muscles glistening in the sun and his shoulders swaying with purpose. He reached the door and kicked, knocking it from its hinges and sending it sailing into the room beyond.

I shifted into my human form and hurried to catch up. I rarely did as I was told.

Servants ran into the room with wide eyes and terrified expressions.

"Where is my mate?" Weston growled, the sound as scary as a nightmare you couldn't wake up from. He roared, *"Where is she?"*

"He means Granny's worker," I clarified, just in case they had a few people stashed in this big place.

"Up in the—" A maid pointed at the stairs in the far corner. "Up in the East Wing. The guest—"

"Show me!"

She hurried forward and he followed. A few of the pack members broke off, covering the door so that we weren't attacked from behind.

We climbed the stairs quickly, following the woman, to the left and down a long hall with plush carpeting and windows adorned with heavy drapery. This guy clearly did well for himself. I doubted it was just politics that bought all these riches. Granny's business was thriving.

"What is the meaning of this—" A man in his fifties with slicked back salt-and-pepper hair and wearing fancy attire paused in the center of the hall. His eyes went wide in shock.

"Are you the mayor?" the alpha demanded as he stalked closer, a predator at the top of the food chain.

"Y-yes . . ."

Weston's voice dropped low as he growled out, "You dare imprison my true mate?"

The mayor's eyes widened further in sheer terror. "Wh-what? Who are you?"

"Your executioner." Weston reached the mayor and in one fluid movement, shot his hand forward to grip the mayor by his neck and ripped out his throat. Blood sprayed from the wound, coating the alpha's flexed body. The mayor jolted once before going limp, slumping to the floor in a heap as blood continued to pump out of his ruined jugular.

It was so extreme that I got a semi hard-on just from

watching. This wolf was unbalanced when it came to his mate.

The maid screamed, cowering.

"Where is she?" The alpha's growl rumbled out of his chest. "Speak or die."

"He-here. Here." She staggered forward, half-running and crying as she did so. She reached a room near the end and grabbed for a key hanging on the wall with shaking hands.

"Hadriel," the alpha barked.

I relieved her of the key. "I'll take it from here. Go find a washroom to throw up in. We'll be gone by the time you're feeling better."

The key turned easily, clicking over. I pushed open the door and meant to step out of the way, but a glimpse of Aurelia had me running at her instead.

She lay on the ground beside a porcelain bowl akin to a chamber pot, vomit both in and beside it. Her eyes were closed and her cheek rested on the wood floor, her face deathly pale.

"Gods fucking goats, Aurelia!" I cried, sliding in beside her and bracing my hand on her forehead. "She's burning up."

"Get her things," the alpha barked, the fear in his voice not showing in his movements. He knelt beside her quickly, scooping her up into his arms and cradling her delicately.

Her pack was by the bed and an empty wrapper lay on the nightstand.

"She tried some of the product," I spat, my fear amping up. "She wouldn't have known any better. She never believed us when we said how dangerous it was. Fuck!"

"It's okay," the alpha said, walking quickly now.

I snatched up the pack and barely remembered to check for her lantern. She loved that thing. She wouldn't want to leave it behind. Locating and grabbing it, I ran after them.

"It's going to be okay." The fear in the alpha's voice had grown into full-blown terror. "We're going to get through this, baby. Stay with me."

"Get a horse," I told him, jogging by their side. He wasn't running but his long stride quickly ate up the distance. His training forbade him to show obvious signs of panic. "She needs the phoenix's healing elixir."

He nodded, looking straight ahead, tall and broad and scared out of his mind. Or maybe that was just me.

"Horse, I need a horse," I said, pausing to look around. "Dina, did you see the stables? Wait, the inn had stables—"

She shifted, breathing fast. "Give me all that. The stables are just over there." She took Aurelia's stuff and pointed. "Hurry!"

I didn't need to be told twice. I sprinted through the town nude, spotting the stables quickly and wasting no time getting to them. A stable hand was just pulling in a horse, readying to remove the saddle. I punched him to get him away. In a moment I was crushing my bare fucking balls as I rode the mediocre-looking horse across the square and toward the procession of wolves.

After I jumped off, the alpha handed me Aurelia while he mounted the animal. She was scorching hot, burning up with fever. Even her limbs were on fire, completely limp. I had to fight back tears of worry.

He swung up into the saddle and reached for her, cradling her close after I'd handed her up. He grabbed the reins, dug his heels into the horse's flanks, and yelled, "Hyah!"

The horse took off like a shot, its looks deceiving. All I could think was Aurelia had to be okay, and as I watched the horse disappear into the distance I couldn't help but whisper, "You can't die just when you've finally started to live."

WESTON

I barely remembered getting back to the wagons. My thoughts were so frazzled I wasn't thinking clearly, something that had never happened to me as an alpha, not even in the demon dungeons. My fear had me spiraling—I was worried about losing her, guilt-ridden that I'd left her to fend for herself without some sort of plan to keep her safe, and knowing I'd neglected my primal duty. What happened to her was my fault.

"Get me the phoenix elixir," I shouted, the intensity of the command forcing my pack into action immediately.

It was Sylvester who went running as others hastened toward me, reaching for Aurelia to help me get down. I didn't want to give her up, but I forced myself to hand her over long enough to dismount, grabbing her back and clutching her closely again the second both feet hit the ground. I carried her to the edge of camp, kneeling amongst a cluster of green shrubs with her in my arms. She'd like seeing nature when she woke up.

Please, mighty gods, let her wake up.

"What did you do to yourself Little Wolf?" I asked softly, smoothing her hair back from her burning forehead. "Why did you take it?"

A cluster of padded footsteps arrived in camp and within moments Hadriel was crouching down near us. He was too close for my comfort but when I looked up to tell him to fuck off, his expression of abject terror gave me pause. Dante and Nova kept close too, everyone having just shifted and looking on in worry.

"She would've wanted to see what was different about the product," Nova said, looking around. "Where is the fucking elixir? It's not that bloody hard to find."

She took off jogging. The second we got back to the castle, she was absolutely getting a promotion.

Dante was nodding, looking on. "Nova's right, she would've wanted to see what made Granny's product different from hers."

"She was probably trying to figure out a way to fix the situation," Hadriel said, picking at his nail in worry. "She belongs in the dragon court with Finley and Arleth. They're fixers, too. Give them a problem and they'll try to fix it. They'd fix the world if they could."

"Make ready to get underway," I said, rocking Aurelia in my lap, my hand on her heart. It was beating too quickly. Her breath was too shallow. She was losing her fight. "We need to put as much distance between us and that town as possible. We're going to alter our course. Granny's organization is clearly looking for Aurelia, and now they have her last known whereabouts. A royal guard might investigate the attack on the town. We don't want to run into either."

"What about her?" Dante pointed at Aurelia. "We can't travel with her like that."

"We have to. We'll give her the phoenix elixir and she'll ride with me."

"They'll keep her prisoner," Hadriel said, the words tumbling from his mouth laced with fear. "They planned to take her to the place where they package everything because the production village was compromised. That's what the guy at the tavern said. He sent for Granny's dog to come and collect her."

"We were looking in all the wrong places for information," Dante said as Nova returned with the little vial of glowing elixir. She removed the vial's stopper and carefully handed it to me. Dante continued. "We were looking too close to Granny's home near the castle. People were tight lipped there. Out in these backwoods towns where the product is flowing freely and they don't have as much competition or trouble, they're a lot freer with their words."

"Agreed," Hadriel said. "I think it would be better to send in a few people masquerading as merchants to visit pubs and taverns and talk to the locals to work out the location, rather than moving in a big pack that draws too much attention. Get the location, *then* send in the muscle."

"Hindsight," someone in the back muttered.

I tucked all that into the back of my mind for later contemplation as I prepared to pour the elixir into Aurelia's opened mouth.

"Wait!" Hadriel put out his hands to stop me. "No,

no, this is wrong. She's unconscious. She won't swallow it. Inject it!" He clapped a few times, looking around. "You have to inject it."

I froze. He was right. *Stupid,* I berated myself. We'd been in this situation in Granny's cottage. We had precious few of these elixirs left, and I almost wasted one of them.

"I'll do it. I got it," someone said, and a moment later Niven stepped up, kneeling down beside us and taking the elixir from my hand. I stopped rocking so he could work. Niven hadn't really been on her side since she'd cleaved him with the axe, but he hadn't been thoroughly against her, either.

He pushed down the plunger on the syringe and stepped back, holding the empty materials and looking down on us.

"That'll fix her," Hadriel said softly, reaching forward to take her hand. Once again, I kept from growling at someone else touching my true mate when she was in this state. He cared for her. He only wanted to help. "It will. It'll fix her. Finley and Hannon don't make mistakes. They don't put out bad medicine. It'll fix her."

"Get loaded up. We need to go," I said while remaining still, intending to wait until the very last moment before I had to move her. She needed rest. She needed a bed. Unfortunately, those were two luxuries we didn't have, not anymore.

It took three hours. I'd held Aurelia in my lap for three hours as my horse walked, having decided against travel in a cart in case someone attacked. I wanted to be in control of my mobility and be able to usher her away to safety immediately, if need be. It was three long hours before her eyes fluttered open and she moaned in obvious discomfort.

"Whoa," I said, stopping the horse and dropping my focus to her beautiful face. Some color had returned to her cheeks along with a sheen of sweat, both good signs pointing to an eventual recovery.

I'd thought about releasing her animal to help her heal, but surprisingly, my wolf told me to hold off. If she planned to stay in this kingdom—something I dared not think about lest panic grip me—she shouldn't have her animal's power on full display. She should still hide it until she could get settled and find a pack to protect her before yanking it out. Either way, she'd have suitors a mile long. She was too pretty, too charming, too balanced and charismatic, not to mention smart and talented and funny . . . She'd have no trouble finding a mate Outside, as she called it.

Imagining her with another man was something else I couldn't allow myself to think about. It wasn't panic that reared its ugly head at those thoughts, but blind rage. I wouldn't ever be able to see anyone else touch her, not without killing that person. She was mine, and mine alone.

Too bad she didn't agree.

Her eyelids fluttered again just before a crease formed between her brows. She groaned, her head turning to burrow into my shoulder. Her other hand reached up weakly to clutch my shirt. She wiggled a little closer.

"Weston," she whispered. "You came for me."

419

"Of course I did." My arms constricted around her. "I'll always come for you, Little Wolf."

Her relieved sigh made my heart soar before her hand relaxed and she fell back into unconsciousness.

Nightfall came early in the dense trees. We were forced to walk our horses single file, choosing a path barely large enough for our supply carts but too small for any larger wagons that might try to catch us. We planned to take a path that looped around, heading south for a while before returning east. It would eventually connect with a larger road not too far from the port where our ship waited to take us out of here. I'd already sent someone ahead with word that we were delayed but on our way.

Now we just had to get there.

Royal guards wouldn't be a problem on a path like this; they didn't travel light. Any sort of guard from the town where we'd rescued Aurelia or their allies also wouldn't be a problem, not against my pack. They didn't have enough power or people. It was Granny's organization that worried me.

They now knew Aurelia's last location, and it wouldn't be hard to figure out we were heading east toward the ports. There were only a few options to travel—a large road, a few smaller ones, and this path. I'd need to plan for them sending out scouts. It's what I would do. I'd also station my people on that large road by the port and wait there until our eventual arrival. I'd do it using all my connections with the king and queen, too.

As I was about to stop and make ready to camp for the night, Aurelia's eyes opened. Her brow furrowed in discomfort, her accompanying moan emphasizing just how awful she felt.

"I don't feel great," she said softly, closing her eyes again. "You might want to put me down. I think I'm going to be sick."

"It's okay, just let me know. I'll dangle you off the horse the same way you do it."

Her little smile was a welcomed sight. It disappeared quickly.

"You were right all along." She opened those beautiful eyes again, her long black lashes catching a tear. Her voice trembled. "My product is doing exactly what you said and more. It's full-scale addiction—people aren't eating, they take too much at a time, and it makes you very sick, bad enough it could probably kill you." I didn't tell her how close she'd come. Her expression filled with pain. "My touch is stamped all over Granny's setup. Even the design is mine. I drew the picture on a birthday card I gave to Granny a long time ago. Did you notice the fucked up butterfly?"

I thought for a moment before shaking my head a little. "I don't recall."

"Why does no one notice the butterfly? The original was a fairy. Same wings, she just swapped out the body. All the product is mine, every single one. She's putting some sort of waxy overlay on it and cutting it or squishing it or something to make it look nicer, but it's mine."

"Is that why you took it, to see if it was yours?"

"No, I could tell when I broke it open or scraped off

part of the waxy stuff. I took it—multiple kinds—to see what kind of effect it had. How it changed the original product, you know? I think the waxy stuff is the same on all the products, it's just dyed a different color. They made it look like candy. Snack boxes—what a fucking joke. It's some sort of . . . chemical, or something. It's not natural, whatever it is. It's not meant to be consumed. Honestly, I almost think it's some kind of poison. The first one made me feel sick, but it went away as soon as the product started to affect me. The second one made me feel much sicker, which was odd because there wasn't more of the waxy stuff on that particular product. I wasn't sure what to make of that. The third one was like some sort of terrible explosion in my body. I felt hot and then cold, with horrible pains in my stomach—" She shivered. "I've never felt that sick. I think what happens is an accumulation effect. The more you have, the sicker it makes you. You need to wait until it is completely out of the system before having more or the compound effect poisons you. I would bet that's why people are dying—they're taking too much."

"They're taking too much because it is addicting," Tanix said in a gruff tone.

"Yes, and it is cutting out their hunger, as well. I have yet to feel the hook, as they call it. Three back-to-back doses doesn't seem like enough, unless it comes on slowly. I remember you saying two doses could hook someone, so I'll monitor it to see. I would imagine the compound effect would affect the intensity of addiction, as well. What I don't understand is why people are taking it. It's very expensive and that sickness is incredibly unpleasant. Why go back for more?"

"They can't help themselves," Tanix returned. "It's out of their control."

She sat up a little more, wincing, her gaze going over my shoulder. "I have a couple things to say about this and I'm not going to be delicate, because I feel like shit and you need to hear it. First, in the beginning, they can absolutely control the situation. I had multiple people warn me away from taking Granny's product. They told me how it would snare me. They told me not to touch it. There is no risk for addiction after just one dose. No risk for three doses, apparently. But the adverse effects are felt immediately. Taking it again would go against someone's better judgment. It is not, at all, out of their control to continue taking it recreationally."

She paused for comment and received none.

"Second, your precious dragons have a cure for that addiction, but it's too expensive for purchase by the common man. Only the wealthy have the coin to buy the cure and save themselves. Make no mistake, your court is profiting off Granny's snack boxes. They call it a crisis, but they have their hand out to collect the gold all the same. They are just as complicit as this kingdom's court."

She paused again, her tone hard. Still no one commented.

"In saying that," she said, "I will gladly accept my blame in this. I will accept a harsh punishment. I have a lot to answer for, and I know that. My first apology is to you, Tanix. I am sorry for the part I have played. I spoke to people in that alleyway and saw firsthand what sort of horror I've caused. I'd intended to go back to them and offer to pay for the addiction cure but was taken before I could. That said, I will go to your dragon court and stand in judgment for what I have done. In so doing, I will return judgment and demand they do better."

She took a deep breath and leaned heavily against me, and I wanted to take her away and hide her. I wanted to dote on her and fulfill her every desire. Anything but my duty to the dragon king and queen.

At the same time, I couldn't have been more proud. She was standing up for herself, yet when confronted with her perceived guilt, she did not shy away from the consequences. Her pride in her product and her willingness to stand in judgment of what it had become was admirable.

I'd hoped that she wasn't as evil as I'd often thought myself to be. Now I had my answer. She'd been through hell, lived a hard life, and still she maintained her honor and her dignity. I couldn't have asked for a more perfect true mate.

"Lastly," she said, "I will figure out how to take Granny's organization down. I'll figure out what that poison is and find a way to combat it. I'll make this right, somehow. Let me down, Weston. I have to throw up."

After our defenses were set up and the camp was awkwardly arranged within the dense trees, I found Aurelia amid a drifting group of emberflies, sitting at the base of a thin trunk, staring out at nothing.

"They seem to congregate around you," I said as I sat

beside her, giving her space even though I wanted to immediately pull her into my lap.

"What's that?" She glanced over at me, blinking quickly and then focusing her gaze.

I waved my finger at the glowing bugs. "The ember-flies seem to follow you. We never had them around until you were in our camp."

"Oh." She frowned at them before looking out at nothing again. "That's strange. Maybe they always thought of you as a danger until now. They don't hang around danger."

"And yet they hang around you."

Her left eyebrow quirked up. "I guess I can fool bugs, then."

"I wasn't right about your product." I entwined my fingers and dropped them into my lap. "I was right to let you go. Granny was the one creating the danger, not you. I found the production village—yours—but not the packaging headquarters. We're still not sure if it's a village or a town or just a house. We don't know."

"It's in a town, I guess. The guys who grabbed me didn't say which one. I'm going to go back through my journals. Maybe Alexander mentioned it. . ." She shrugged and I could tell she was at a loss. "I don't know, maybe I'll find something you missed. That's where he is now, anyway. Or was, I guess. On his way to collect me." She shivered. "I'd rather be put to death by the dragons than end up in his hands."

"You won't. I won't let either of those things happen to you."

"You won't have a choice. If the dragons sentence me

to death, I will accept the punishment. There's not a damn thing you can do to stop it."

"Aurelia, I—" I gritted my teeth. This was the wrong thing to be stubborn about. I had time to talk her out of it, though. There was something more pressing we had to discuss. "Listen, it doesn't sound like this kingdom will ever be safe for you."

"No, it sure doesn't. Thank you for coming for me. They happened upon me as I was shedding the influence of the first product. I didn't have any weapons. Once I got into the house, I was able to grab a metal letter opener and kill one of them, but that was it before they threw me into the room. How'd you know I'd been taken?"

"Hadriel is pretty incredible at finding out local goings-on and gossip. He overheard it from someone in a tavern."

"Ah." She nodded. "I'll remember to thank him. He—well, all of you—saved my life. I won't make one more product for Granny's organization. If you hadn't come, I would've had a lot of beatings and eventually death in my future. Probably a loss of dignity as well. I doubt Alexander would keep his hands off me now that I no longer have Granny's protection."

I bent forward as a rush of rage stole my breath. Alexander would already answer to me for what he'd done to her in the past, but hearing something like that made me want to rip his spleen out and beat him with it right now. The desire to find him and end his life was overwhelming.

"Please don't ever say something like that again," I said in a rough voice. "That will never happen."

She looked over at me, her expression bemused yet grateful. "Okay," she murmured.

"I wanted to talk to you about your animal."

She held up her hand. "I don't want to talk about that right now. I want to meet my animal, I want magic . . . but I don't want even more reasons for people to notice me. I don't want to be a lone wolf, as you said, and I definitely don't want to end up kidnapped by this kingdom. I just . . ." She licked her lips. "Honestly, I just want to close my eyes and ignore the messy parts of my life until I can get out of here and process everything." She turned to me, her eyes glassy. "I want to be the damsel in distress, Weston. I want my big strong alpha to protect me and keep me safe until I can leave these shores. Maybe that's not very courageous, but I'm just so tired. I'm tired of all this. I'm broken." A tear slipped down her cheek. "I want to take a break from surviving, if only for a minute."

A strange sort of lightness filled my chest. I wouldn't be just protecting a damsel in distress, I would be protecting my true mate. Everything in me rejoiced at officially playing that role. It was what I was born to do—protect what was mine.

"It would be my honor." Primal power surged through me.

She shivered and I watched a spark light within her eyes. Her body swayed toward me, feeling that primal rush.

"Do you want to fuck your Little Wolf, Alpha?" she murmured, her heated gaze on my lips. "Do you want to take what is yours?"

Adrenaline coursed through me. I grabbed the back of her neck, pulling her toward me.

"Are you healed enough for this?" I ran my lips down the side of her throat.

"Be gentle," she sighed as she angled her head to give me access. "Protect what is yours."

My balls tightened and it took all my willpower not to throw her down and fuck the screams out of her. I liked this better, though. I liked laying her down slowly, my lips moving against hers, pushing her legs wide and fitting myself between them. She'd given me complete control, total dominance. It made my desire pound hard in my gut.

"Take what is yours, Alpha," she murmured again, mewing softly as I covered a breast with my palm. "Do with me what you like."

Shaking with the effort it took to not rip her clothes off, I continued slowly. Delicately. I unbuttoned her shirt and kissed down her chest, sucking in one nipple and then the other, hard. She moaned, her hands in my hair, massaging and caressing, not directing me.

I slid her pants down her legs and tasted her, my hands light, the suction hard. Her groan was louder as she wriggled beneath me. I removed the rest of our clothes before kissing back up her body, still a little warm and not fully healed, but almost there. Taking care, I worked my way back between her thighs, my eyes closing in pleasure at the feel of her soft skin sliding against my sides.

She wrapped her legs around my middle. I groaned as I sank into her depths.

"I've missed you," I said as I filled her again and

again, pulling out just to slide back in. "It was only a short time, but I missed you."

Her kiss intensified as she hugged me tightly, moaning against the building onslaught. "The moment I had a choice, I didn't want to walk away. I wanted to get to know you more, to explore this incredible feeling I have when I'm with you."

A spark of guilt twisted my gut. She had a right to know that the feeling was primal, because of our true mate bond. I wasn't sure how to tell her. I wasn't sure what she'd do if she found out. There was a good chance she'd be furious to know I had kept it from her all this time, that a large part of her attraction was something neither of us could control.

I refrained from mentioning it even now because I wanted her animal to weigh in. I wanted our animals to help us determine what came next, whether I could claim her and keep her, or if the betrayal would send the delicate tightrope we walked up in flames. As it was, the tether between us would be incredibly strained when she realized the entire truth.

I pushed into her, but avoided burying myself inside her completely. This wasn't the most comfortable place to be knotted together. That would have to wait until another time. I reached between us and massaged her clit as I pumped, chasing my climax, feeling her tighten.

"Weston," she said, clutching me, gyrating against me. "Oh my—Weston!"

She was still using my name instead of calling for the gods.

A thrill ran through me and I worked faster, taking her higher, nearly there myself.

"Oh—" She shuddered, her insides clenching around me.

I exploded into her, the orgasm rolling through my body. I groaned as I stroked inside her one more time and held myself there, letting her insides milk me dry. She shivered as my body quaked, the climax lasting longer than it ever had. I had just enough awareness to wonder why that was.

We held each other as the aftershocks came and went. Only then did I sit up, dragging her with me. I had to build something solid between us on our way to the dragon kingdom so that what we had wouldn't break when she finally learned the extent of my betrayal.

"*Y*ou okay?"

The words trickled into my awareness, interrupting my whirling thoughts regarding that waxy stuff Granny had put over my product. I needed to find a well-stocked library and do some research so that I might discover both how it was made and how to negate the effects. Once I'd developed a remedy, I'd need to find a way to steal money out of Alexander's pocket, as he was the only one who could run the organization in Granny's absence.

I pulled away from Weston's broad back for a moment, my focus shifting back to the present moment. "Yeah, thanks. Just thinking."

"You've been very quiet. Did you read something in your journals that upset you?"

I went back to leaning against him, sitting behind him on his large, sturdy horse as we walked through the dense trees. I'd been reading those journals, poring over

431

memories from a forgotten time, trying to find some clues of my own.

One thing had become clear: I'd been horribly unhappy in Granny's village. It had been disguised in many parts, writing cheerful memories of my mother or counting my blessings that I'd found somewhere to live, but I'd been so very lonely. So heartbroken about my mom—just broken, period. No one had put out a hand to help me when I was struggling badly, not even when I had asked for help. Only Xarion had been friendly, but after meeting Hadriel, I realized Xarion had never truly been a friend. He'd been someone to pass the time with, the only person who would talk to me, and half our time together had been spent fielding cheap shots he sent my way, coloring our communication with the disdain shared by the village. I'd written it all down in my journal.

"I see now why everyone thinks my stories are so depressing," I murmured, feeling no emotion about any of it. I'd clearly resigned myself to the life I lived. I'd made peace with it years ago. It was a survival tactic, I supposed. It shouldn't have surprised me, and honestly, it didn't—not really. I had made do because I'd had to. I still did.

"I understand now why I didn't notice the realities of the village," I said, peering through the trees. I half wondered if I'd see Alexander keeping pace with us. "I was also turning a blind eye to my own situation. Willful ignorance."

I took a deep breath, slipping my hands under the hem of his shirt and sliding them along his torso.

"Enough about me. What about you?" I turned my

head so that my chin was resting in the hollow between his shoulder blades. "I feel this overpowering urge to be with you, but I don't know anything about you." I traced the edges of his muscle. "How do you stay in such great shape?"

"I train with my pack constantly. The pack consists of more than just wolves. We have a lot of dragons that we work with, and they are incredibly powerful. I work hard to ensure we can form a cohesive unit."

I circled one of his nipples with my pointer finger. "Do you like your nipples stimulated?"

He turned his head to the side and I could see his ear lifting with a smile. "Sometimes. Not as much as you do, I don't think."

"Hmm." I pinched it a little and felt him shiver. "Maybe that's something we should explore."

"Maybe," he whispered.

We hadn't had sex since yesterday. Part of that was due to not having a tent. We'd had a bed, and even though he'd given me the option of sleeping alone, I'd chosen to have him beside me. We'd wrapped ourselves up in each other's arms, but the rest of the pack was within sight. I wasn't in the habit of putting on a show.

I resumed tracing his muscles, following the line of his bulging pec until it connected near his arm pit. On impulse, I tickled him.

He jumped and then twisted, letting out a gurgle of surprise and nearly knocking me off the horse in order to squirm away.

"Gods, don't do that!" he said as I laughed, clutching onto him so that I didn't fall. He chuckled, trying to get himself under control, out of breath. "Don't do that."

"You're ticklish."

"Isn't everyone?"

"No."

"You're not ticklish?"

"No," I repeated with a smile, and then tried tickling his sides.

He squirmed again, though not as out of control this time. He captured one of my hands with one of his and pressed my palm to his warm skin. "Seriously, stop!" His laughter was large and deep, his head thrown back. "I don't want to throw you off the horse."

I delighted in his unchecked mirth, his wide smile, so rare for this alpha. It felt good to bring it out of him, like I'd accomplished some great feat and received my prize.

"To be continued." I flattened my palms to his sides.

"You're not ticklish?" he asked again. I shook my head against his back in response. "Bullshit. You must be ticklish somewhere."

"Mind over matter."

"That doesn't work with the bottom of a person's feet. There is no mind control capable of cutting out how much that tickles."

I rolled my eyes, laughing. "I can stop the effects of drugs. Tell me why I couldn't stop the effects of someone tickling the bottom of my feet."

"Different thing. Ticklish feet transcend the mind."

My smile felt glued on. I settled my forehead between his shoulder blades again, back to tracing his muscles.

"How did you learn to do that, by the way?" he asked. "Cutting out the effect?"

"Are you sure you want yet another depressing story?"

"Lay it on me."

"You asked for it." I sighed. "I always try every batch of product. Drug, I guess—"

"Product. We'll use drugs for what Granny has put out into the world."

"She's just altering what I give her, but sure. Anyway, one time the journey took a sharp left and before I knew it, I was reliving my mother's death. Only this time, I was burning alive with her. In desperation, I . . . found my way out. I envisioned scrubbing my blood free of the chemicals and seeing clearly again. Somehow, it worked. From then on, my hobby was figuring out how to repeat what I'd done, and then getting good at it. Mind over matter."

"That's incredible. And you did that with Granny's . . . altered product?"

"Yes, except I realized there is a very important distinction. My product is safe to take in multiple doses —that waxy stuff is not. I don't think I am scrubbing the effects from my body, I'm ignoring the effects somehow. I must be, right? Because that waxy stuff did not go away. It hung around, and when I put more of that poison into my bloodstream, it took me down."

My mind drifted in that direction again.

"What sort of poisonous effect would be so incredibly addictive?" I murmured. "I took another of Granny's doses last night—"

"You did *what?*"

Weston's sharp tone stopped me up short.

"What?" I said stupidly.

Anger blistered in each word. "You took another of those doses last night? *When?*"

I froze, suddenly uncomfortable. The guy could be intimidating when he wanted to be.

"Um . . . last night after dinner? I figured I should have a full stomach for it because of that waxy stuff."

"Are you fucking serious?" He was off the horse in a blink. I barely had enough time to register him reaching for me before I was ripped off the back of the horse and set on my feet. He leaned down into my face, his tone icy. "You would've died yesterday, Aurelia. If we hadn't given you the phoenix enhanced elixir, you would've died. We have precious little left and it's not safe to bring out your animal to help you heal. If you take more of that poison, there is a damn good chance you'll die. Is that what our sacrifice means to you?"

His anger was contagious. I was no longer a captive, not like before. I'd have a say in my life, especially in the parts that held the potential for danger.

"*Your* sacrifice?" I demanded. "Is that what you call it when you bash my head in? You used one of your precious elixirs for that, didn't you?"

I'd asked Hadriel about it, and was riveted to learn how a phoenix came to be.

"You are not to take more of those drugs," he said in a vicious tone.

"You don't get to tell me what to do," I spat back. "You have pack members suffering from a loss created by those drugs. I played a part in that. I'll be damned if I don't do everything in my power to at least *try* to make it right. In order to know what I'm up against, I have to understand it. In order to understand it, I have to know the effects it has on the body. To properly study the effects, I have to take it. I think I've gotten a handle on how long it stays in the bloodstream. It's kind of like alcohol, I think, but the addiction is a cumulative effect. I'm starting to crave—"

He grabbed my arm and marched me farther into the trees until we were standing on our own, without an audience.

"Are you out of your fucking mind?" he demanded in a low growl. "You're putting yourself at risk, and we don't have the resources to keep pulling you out. You're starting to crave it? What happens when you get fully addicted? You're already malnourished from that horror village. You can't stand to eat much less and I won't let you put yourself in harm's way to combat an unfeeling organization that would gladly throw you back into its production like just another faceless cog. If you don't stop, I'll be forced to strip you of your things and tie you up, if need be. I won't allow you to continue this madness."

"You'd strip me of my things and tie—" I narrowed my eyes at him. "You can't control me, so you're going to force me to be a prisoner again, is that it? You're the alpha—you get what you want by any means necessary." I lifted my eyebrows in question. "People fall in line or people are forced in line, right?"

"If you don't listen to reason, don't do what's in your best interest, then yes, I'll force you to do as you're told."

Delicious shivers washed over me. Now was not the time to get turned on by his dominance.

I took a step toward him, my anger now unleashed. The electricity between us danced like lightning.

K.F. BREENE

"Let's get a few things straight, shall we?" My voice was firm and rough, matching his. "You don't get to decide how I live my life because you offered to shield me from those who wish to use me. Never forget that shielding me from them helps your cause, too. Taking me to your dragons was always your end goal—I'm now helping you do that. I didn't deliver myself into your care so that you could control me or push me around.

"That horror village, as you called it, was my home. It wasn't pretty, but it was all I had. If nothing else, have a little fucking respect for my feelings. If I get fully addicted, which I plan to do, I'll take notes on how it feels and prevent myself from taking more to see how long it takes to wane. All of that is relevant. Like I said, I need to understand it in order to combat it. You came for me in order to stop the drug trade, and now that I am gathering information to do exactly that, you're pushing back and ordering me around? Fuck that. I am in a unique position to help you here. Do not prevent me from doing my job."

"If you get addicted, you won't be able to prevent yourself from taking more. That's not how it works."

"I know exactly how it works. I spoke to those who were in the throes of it. Unlike them, I know what I'm getting into. I'm approaching this the right way. You have to trust me to do my job, Weston, just as I am trusting you to do yours."

"You're naive, Aurelia. You don't know how the world works."

I scoffed. "And you do, you insufferable prick? Expecting everyone you meet to jump when you give an order is not how the world works. Not for me. Didn't you read about all the beatings I took when I wouldn't do as I was told?"

"Damn it, Aurelia, you stubborn—" He leaned down into my face, breathing heavy, the air between us like fire. "You will stop taking those drugs. It's the last time I'm going to say it. You *will* do as you're told."

My whole body was vibrating with energy. With desire. With the need to fight this fucker until one of us submitted. Usually I'd want it to be me, writhing in climax. This time, I'd be damned if I let him get his way.

I held his steely glare with a matching one of my own. "Or *what*?"

We stared at each other for one more intense beat as I challenged his alpha authority.

Like a damn bursting, he collided with me, hands ripping at clothes, lips fused together. He pushed me up against a tree trunk, shoving down my pants and then spinning me around. My palms hit the rough bark. One of his palms slapped down onto my bare ass and the fingers of the other hand plunged into my pussy, slick from my juices.

His growl was feral, carnal. He fell to his knees behind me and licked up my center.

He ripped my pants down further with his free hand until I could step out of them and then he pushed my legs wider. He angled his head to suction my clit in his hot mouth as his other hand finger-fucked my pussy. My mouth dropped open at the onslaught, quickly and roughly stimulated.

"Fuck . . . you," I said, defiant and angry all while fucking loving this.

His thumb applied pressure against my asshole. He

sucked harder at my clit, angling his other fingers just right to hit where I needed.

"Holy—" I exploded in orgasm and he moved to drink it in. It was filthy and sexy and I was still really fucking angry at him.

He yanked off his clothes as I turned. I shoved him away, only to be caught by the hair and pulled after him. He fell back into a bush and I rode him down, scratching down his chest before tweaking one of his nipples *hard*. He grunted as I landed on top of him, slapping him across the face even as I sank down onto his hard cock. Hand still in my hair, he yanked me closer until he could capture my lips, consuming me.

"You'll do as you're told," he ground out before biting into my neck.

I slid back and forth on top of him, grinding hard on that big dick, working him in deep.

"I'll do as I want." I yanked his head to the side and sucked at his neck before leaving a bite mark of my own. Two could play this game. "The next time you want to fuck me, you'll say please."

He jerked away from my lips. The taste of blood lingered on my tongue from the vicious bite I'd inflicted. His lust-filled gaze connected with mine, fire and frustration and . . .

Respect.

He held me firm while he fucked up into me. I felt the swell of his cock. I rose up to get away. I didn't want to give him the satisfaction of knotting me.

He grabbed my shoulders, one hand firmly in my hair, his eyes rooted to mine. I saw the alpha's need, felt a strange primal buzz between us, felt my desire to resist melting away. He fucked harder, pounding me, pushing in deep. I gasped as he pulled me down, overpowering me. Dominating me.

Fuck, that felt good.

I groaned, tilting my head back to close my eyes.

"Look at me," he growled, his strength enveloping me.

I braced my hands around his neck and squeezed in anger. In a strange sort of kinky desire. In blind fucking lust.

The swell of his knot grew and he held himself deep, his arms holding me in place.

"You'll take your alpha's knot whenever I give it to you," he said as I panted, our lips now close, his power caressing me.

My slide was smaller, feeling his pulse within me. I groaned again.

He shook me a little. "Won't you?"

"Fuck you."

His lips crashed onto mine, his tongue sweeping through my mouth. I fell into that kiss, the feeling of him so right, the two of us like equal halves merging to connect a solid whole. His tongue danced with mine as we ground together, arms around each other now, straining to get closer. Higher. To come harder.

He marked me again, nearly making me explode. I held strong, meeting his eyes when he was done, before bending slowly to his shoulder. He tensed but didn't move and I lightly trailed my lips across that sensitive hollow before then dragging my teeth across his skin. His moan was low and anguished and suddenly I wanted to bite down hard. Not on his neck but here. I wanted to claim him. I wanted this alpha to be mine and mine alone, so strong and powerful, so steadfast and loyal, so fitting of his title.

I wasn't *that* naive, though. Everything would change when we got back to the dragon lands. He probably had a huge line of hopeful suitors. I was a mere distraction. What a fool to think I could be anything more. What ridiculousness to want it.

I ignored the sting in my heart that accompanied those thoughts.

Regardless of our chemistry, I didn't know anything about this guy beyond the tiny snippets I'd gleaned. This feeling would eventually wane and then what would I be left with? A really hot, somewhat tortured, dominant wolf who was great in the sack.

Okay, fine, things could be worse . . .

I continued to rake my teeth up until I bit him again on his neck, the other side this time. His groan was pure carnal delight.

"Come with me," he commanded, his power sending a pulse straight to my core.

I blasted apart as he shuddered, his arms holding me tightly. We breathed deeply in the afterglow, his cock lodged firmly within me, pulsing in continual stimulation.

"Well, now that I have you," I said lightly, smiling against his lips.

"We need to figure this out." He kissed me. "I'm afraid for you, Aurelia." He kissed me again, sucking on my bottom lip with an added sound of pleasure. "Can you at least wait until we're back in the dragon lands and we have more medicine at our disposal?"

I gave little pumps of my hips. I couldn't help it; that pulse was so fucking delicious.

"I'm right in how I'm treating the drug, Weston." I pulled back so that I could look him in the eye. "I have a handle on the effects of that waxy stuff. I can tell where I am with things based on the level of sickness. Next I'll let it start to hook me, and then I'll stop to gain all the necessary information from the effects. It'll be a slow plod to figure this thing out, and once I'm in the dragon court, I might not have the time. I need to start now."

He put his palm to my cheek, his eyes igniting with a fierceness that made my insides quiver and my pulse pound harder. "They won't hurt you. I'll make sure of it. No harm will come to you."

"You can't control that. You answer to them, right? Not the other way around."

His gaze rooted me. "I *will* control that."

I shivered, kissing him. "You're really fucking sexy. It scatters my thoughts." I took a deep breath. I needed to get this conversation over with before the building started again and I lost all ability to focus on anything beyond the feel of his body. "Weston, honestly, this sort of approach was how I created the product in the first place. I dissected the products on the market, duplicated them, and then made them better. I can figure this out, I just need time."

"That other product won't kill you. This one will."

"Only if I take too much too quickly."

"What if there are longer term effects? It might build up over time—have you thought of that?"

"Yes. But again, I might not have time."

"You will have a lifetime, Little Wolf. I promise." His

cock pulsed and his eyes hooded as a sensual hum rolled through my body.

I groaned. My head fell back and it took a concentrated effort to lift it up again. I loved that knot but *fuck*, it was not conducive to a serious conversation.

"Take this slow," he said. "It's dangerous. I don't want to lose you, Aurelia." He paused for a moment, his thumb stroking my chin, his gaze sincere. "Please, do this for me. Wait until we have some backup. The dragon queen and the king's mother are outstanding healers. Wait until they are on hand to help in case anything goes wrong."

"How about this. Let me take one more—" He tensed, his eyes holding a warning. I put up a finger. "One more. I have a feeling there'll be a low-level addictive quality by then. Just one more and then I'll stop until the dragon lands. Okay? Just let me work on part of the problem. I'm not used to being idle."

He released a breath before covering a breast with his palm. "One more, that is *it*. And you'll do it when I am on hand and watching you in case something goes wrong."

"Okay."

"And you won't sneak any others when I'm not looking or I *will* follow through on my threat. I'll strip you of your pack and treat you like a prisoner."

"You just want to anger bang me again, don't you?" I grinned at him. "I wouldn't mind. This was fun."

"It was. But please, Little Wolf, promise me."

"I promise."

I could taste the relief in his kiss, and it felt good that someone was worried about me.

"Now move a little faster," he murmured against my lips. "I want to feel you come again before we try and calm this down so that we can get back to traveling."

His cock pulsed again, amplifying that hum, and I let the thoughts unravel in my mind. His fingers gently twisted my nipple as I slid back and forth on top of him, moving that big cock within me. It rubbed just right, pulsing again, building me higher.

"Oh fuck, yes," I said, moving faster.

"Fuck that cock, baby," he groaned, grabbing my hips. "That's right. Fuck that big cock. I want to feel you come all over my dick."

I whimpered as I chased my orgasm, so blessedly full. Another pulse had me crying out, my climax hitting hard as he groaned, coming with me.

"Mmm, good girl," he said, running his lips up my neck to induce one last pronounced shiver. "I love how easily I can make you come."

So did I.

After we settled, him still pulsing within me, I melted down around him. "We really should get going."

"It would be very awkward to try and get you up on a horse like this. I mean, we could try—"

"No! Great gods, no."

"We can probably find some room in one of the carts. You could—"

"No, no," I laughed. I leaned back enough so I could see his face. "No, I didn't mean traveling like this. Just that we probably shouldn't have . . . you know."

"Banged? Knotted?"

"Probably both of those things, yeah."

He nodded before pulling me closer to kiss me softly. "I wasn't feeling all that rational."

"Me, either." I snuggled against him, content to be held. "You said we could try and calm it down?"

"We should try. Maybe just not think sexy thoughts?"

Yeah, right. Like that was possible with him.

I let my mind drift, trying.

"I wish I had some of my supplies. I could at least try to break down the drug and start working on which chemicals might be mixed up in it. Now is about the time when I'd ask Granny for some books that might help. I wonder if I'll be able to find any of those. Do you have libraries in the dragon kingdom?"

He laughed, now kissing up my neck. It wasn't helping the no-sexy-thoughts situation. "The royal library is the largest in the world. And I have some of your supplies. A bunch were broken but I brought them anyway, in case the queen needed to see them."

I leaned back to study his face. "Which supplies, exactly?"

He hesitated. "All of them."

HADRIEL

*W*hen the alpha and his oblivious main squeeze were finished, Aurelia emerged with a red face, trying to look natural; Weston emerged like it was just another day and he did not care in the least that we'd all been sitting around with our thumbs up our asses, waiting for them. We'd all had lunch and they grabbed a quick bite before we settled back into formation and got under way.

They didn't say a word about who'd come out the victor, but Aurelia didn't take one of Granny's products that night. It wasn't until the next night that she finished her dinner, gave the alpha a poignant look, and headed toward the tent.

"What am I missing?" Unfortunately, I now sat with the alpha for dinner because she wanted to be near him, and I wanted to be near her. My friend was still ten times more interesting and fun than these yes-men. I loved her more than ever now that she'd basically told the alpha to fuck off. I was not a proud man and could admit I also used her as a shield. "What's she doing?"

He didn't comment. Face grim and manner resolute, it became clear that Aurelia had gotten her way. He followed her to the tent.

"Oh, this is a bad idea," I mumbled to myself, shoving the rest of my dinner in my face and practically throwing my plate at Burt. "A wary wad idea," I mumbled through a full mouth.

Gazes turned her way and then mine as I hurried after her.

"Tell me she's not going to do another one." Nova popped up. "Tell me he is not letting her do another one."

But it was clear that she was. And he was.

"Hadriel, what is she thinking?" Nova followed me.

"Do I look like a headstrong-woman whisperer to you?" I hissed as I reached the tent. Aurelia was pulling out the various products still in her possession and the alpha was sitting on the cot, watching her quietly.

"Just in case tempers were running high yesterday . . ." I inched in slowly, the image of her lying on the ground in the mayor's house—deathly pale, slipping away—haunted me. I don't think I'd ever felt the panic and helplessness I'd felt when my newest friend and latest charge had barely clung to life. "In case maybe one of us is smitten and not thinking clearly around the other one of us . . ." The alpha's stern look had me hesitating. "Are we absolutely sure that this is the best thing to do? Didn't we rummage through all your half broken and very odd supplies yesterday evening, Aurelia? Didn't we decide one or two would work well enough for you to analyze the waxy stuff we are now calling petrified troll snot?"

"You're the only one calling it that." She picked out the product she wanted and stuck her nail underneath the sticker holding the packaging together.

"Fine, but didn't we decide that would work?"

"Yes. And it will." She turned the item over again and studied the fluorescent yellow, pillow-shaped item. "Horrendous. Who is choosing these colors? I wouldn't eat an actual piece of candy if it looked like this."

"Right. Then maybe we should—"

She chucked the thing into her mouth and I issued a high-pitched shriek I didn't know I was capable of making.

"Fucking shit-warts, what the fuck, Aurelia?" I yelled at her.

"Careful how you speak to my—to her," the alpha said in a growl that was not nearly as scary as Aurelia having just popped that thing into her mouth.

"Spit it out, my darling! This is crazy!" I nearly ran at her and tried to pry the thing out of her mouth. "Alpha, have some sense. Remember when you dug your fingers into her mouth and tried to pry out—damn it, she's swallowing. Slap a cock, she's swallowing! I'm so fucking distraught I can't even joke about her swallowing!"

"Missed opportunity," she said, packing away the rest of the products.

"A real fucking missed opportunity, yes. You know how angry it makes me when that happens. Okay, what should we do? How long do we have before we know if you'll be okay or not?"

She gave me a long-suffering look. "Since when are you as overbearing as he is?" She hooked her thumb at the alpha.

"Since I've realized I have way more sense than you do, obviously." My voice was too high and erratic. "This is dumb. I hate this."

She rolled her eyes and made her way past me, finding a collection of people waiting outside the tent.

"Good gods," she muttered, passing them.

"I feel like one of us doesn't quite remember the near-fatal episode you had with those drugs." I followed her.

"I took one the day before yesterday and no one was any wiser. It should be out of my system by now. I'll be fine."

"Should be? *Should be* out of your system by now? What if it isn't?"

"That's the golden question. We shall see."

She sat down by the fire next to Tanix and said nothing else; she just watched the flames, and we all watched her. Everyone else hovered close, some worried, some curious, some probably wishing it would kick her into an early grave like they thought she deserved. The alpha settled at her other side, watching the flames with her, and I sat where I could see her face. Nova had the same idea, and I had to shoulder her out of the way.

"I'm better in a crisis," Nova said to me quietly, both of us watching as Aurelia sat placidly. So far, she was showing no signs of anything happening.

"And look, it'll be easier for you to get up and sprint for aid. Do we even have the syringe? Is the alpha secretly trying to kill her? I have so many concerns about this. Why do I have so many concerns about this? You'd think I'd be used to horrible risks and terrible decision-making."

"Not when the risks don't need to be taken," Nova murmured.

We all watched quietly, intently, for what felt like an eternity. Her face didn't so much as twitch, her body completely still.

Eventually she said, in a soft voice, "The sickness has come and passed." She glanced up at us. The reflection of the fire in her eyes made them look particularly fierce. "It was a little bit worse than the last time, but only marginally. Not enough to cause alarm. The journey has started—"

"She means the high," I whispered. "That's what she says when she is talking about the high."

"This is the strongest hallucinogen I make, and I am going to let it run its course to see how the troll snot reacts. Will my change in heart rate or body temperature affect it? We shall see."

"Are you doing this to prove a point?" Tanix asked when she fell silent again.

She didn't answer for a moment. "I wouldn't even know what point to prove. What point *do* you expect me to prove? The idea of points is a very strange one, don't you think? I wonder if the creator of that word had some sort of hidden agenda. Whatever it was, it wasn't dull."

"Why are you sitting next to me, then?"

Aurelia sighed. "Because up until a moment ago, you were quiet and minding your own business. Clearly, I chose the wrong seat." She breathed out slowly. "You're altering my journey. I'm just going to run with it. Let's see what sort of effect you're having on my subconscious. Oops, there's a dragon. I do not want to alarm anyone, but it is not pleased with this fire in front of us."

"I feel slightly guilty for suddenly enjoying myself," I murmured.

"You won't enjoy yourself when that dragon stomps on your head to get at that fire. It is jealous as all hell. Of what, I have no idea. It's just sticks, man! That fire is eating sticks. What, do you think the ground is outdoing you?" She chuckled, shaking her head. "It's just sticks!"

It became oh-so-clear that Aurelia was not at all as buttoned up as she often seemed. I knew she had a wild streak, and now everyone else got to see it. Watching her navigate her various hallucinations ranked with some of the best entertainment I'd had. Nothing phased her. At one stage she instructed everyone to get low because we were about to be crushed under the weight of a very large tree.

"Not to worry, everyone," she told us, motioning for us to bend low. "I've heard of these types of things happening before. Don't let the crunch of your bones worry you. Just think like a lake and become liquid. When the tree rolls away, we'll spring up like wild flowers!"

When I did her product again, it would be with her, there could be no question. I couldn't wait to go on one of her journeys. It sounded so much better than mine had ever been—much more colorful and original. Her mind was obviously a very interesting place.

Once she finally started to wind down—hours later —only half of us were left, chatting and joking and having a glass of whiskey.

"I'm having some stomach cramps now." She breathed out slowly, her hands on her stomach.

The alpha had stayed by her side the whole time, shadowing her as she did a variety of weird and wonderful things: a strange sort of dragon-fire dance to scare the invisible beast away; walking in circles without a word; standing on her head to see the world as gravity did not intend. For that, he'd held her feet. She hadn't been able to do it on her own and she hadn't been willing to stop trying. His expression had never changed, stoic and serious, even when she said some of the funniest shit I'd ever heard.

"Is it a problem?" he asked now, looping his arm around her when she leaned against him.

"Sometimes this can be a reaction to my product. I thought I'd fixed that, though. Very acidic." She dropped her hand to his thigh and closed her eyes, her head against his shoulder. "I think it's fine."

"Were you sick any other time tonight?"

"Just in the beginning. I fell asleep before the end last time. Maybe it happened and I just didn't wake up. I can see why someone would endure the sickness for the longer journeys. It's but a moment and then you're off. Do it enough, and the addiction sets in. We'll see how I feel about that tomorrow. I'm wondering how often people have to journey before it gets to be a problem."

With that, the night wound down, and people began wandering off to ready themselves for bed.

Aurelia didn't sample any other product after that.

Clearly, she and the alpha had established a compromise. Instead, she took to her weird little devices, trying to break down the troll snot to see what it was made of. I often sat with her when she did, listening to her chat about it and feeling miserably unintelligent. When that woman got going, she might as well have been talking another language. She had a fucking gift.

As the days passed and we got closer to the port, our path winding through the wilds, I started to wonder if Finley would ever get to meet her. If she'd ever see any of us again. It was obvious the enemy would be expecting us, and we knew they'd have a well-organized plan to break apart our pack and kidnap the gem in the middle. I knew they'd have no qualms about killing as many of us as they possibly could in the process.

31

AURELIA

I awoke with a start, unsure why. The deep night lay quiet around us, the moon casting enough light to see without the tent's canvas over us.

After a couple days of travel off the beaten track, we'd finally started getting close to the port where the ship that would take us out of this kingdom was docked and waiting for us. We knew Alexander and the rest of Granny's gang would be waiting for us, and as such, we wasted no time unpacking and packing the tents. We only unpacked what was essential.

Everyone was on edge.

The familiar craving caught my attention, beckoning me to get up and cross to my pack where more of Granny's altered product waited. After six tries—three back-to-back that nearly killed me, two others that Weston knew about, and one to put me over the edge I took in secret but that he later found out about anyway because I was shit at secrets—the hook had finally stuck in its jagged point. It was the point I'd been trying to reach. I wanted to see how bad it was, how long it lasted, and if it came with any side effects.

After I'd accidentally spilled the secret, Weston hadn't exploded at me like before. He'd gone a steely sort of silent. He wouldn't eat with me and hadn't slept with me, instead staying curled up in wolf form a few feet away to guard me, but keeping his distance. The only thing he'd said was he was glad I was safe but disappointed I hadn't stuck to our agreement.

Disappointed.

It had fucking killed me to hear him say that. He was a man with great integrity, who'd gone against his better judgment to trust me, and I'd been the one to renege on the bargain.

Worse still was his absence in my daily life. I hadn't realized how much I enjoyed his presence—how comfortable I'd grown in his proximity—or how much I looked forward to sharing a meal with him or sliding into his arms after a hard day of travel. I had missed his soft good-nights and murmured good-mornings, his sweet kisses and the way he looked into my eyes. Most of all, I'd missed the idle chatter and light banter we shared. It had only been two days, but it had felt like a lifetime without someone I'd come to think of as not just a lover, but a friend.

My apology had been heartfelt. I might've cried a little. He'd forgiven me immediately without a single word about consequences if I did it again. He hadn't needed to.

Now I lay on my side facing him upon the cot, taking in his handsome face as the emberflies drifted overhead. At this point in our journey, there were just as many in our camp every night as there had been in the village. Everyone thought it was very cool. I just thought it was comfortable.

His eyes opened slowly, as though he'd felt my gaze.

"Hey," he said quietly, watching me watch him. "You okay?"

"Yes." I reached up to lightly trace the curve of his bottom lip. "I still have cravings. It's funny—my brain is thinking, 'why don't you try that hallucinogen again, that was fun.' And while it was fun—mostly—I've done it a million times before. I've never had that thought. The chemical is telling me to do it again, and my brain is bending it to make it about the product. Nowhere does the sickness enter my mind." I turned my hand, letting my thumb run along the stubble of his chin. "It's dangerous. Which, I know, is what you've been saying from the beginning."

"Can I help at all?"

I shook my head, now running my finger along his brow line and then down the bridge of his thin, straight nose.

"What's your favorite color?" I asked, continuing on my mission to learn as much about him as he knew about me. Part of me wanted to see if these incredible feelings for him would continue to grow, and the other part of me was just curious to know more about him.

"Fuchsia."

I crinkled my nose. "Fuchsia? As in . . . hot pink?"

"Yes."

"Isn't that a little—I don't know, loud?"

"Very loud." He kissed the tip of my finger as I let it drift past his lips. "In my job, which spills over into my personal life on a regular basis, I have to stay reserved. I can't react too much or show extreme emotions. I can't laugh too hard—or much at all, really—or cry. I can't show strong anger and definitely no weakness. I must always maintain control of myself so that the pack knows I maintain control of my leadership. That denotes safety. It means I'm holding us together, and if we are unified, we are better protected. Do you see?"

"And so you choose little ways to step outside of a controlled, reserved life?"

"Yes."

"Loudly anger-fucking me in the trees does not speak of a controlled, reserved life."

"You are the exception."

My eyes met his, holding his gaze. "Why am I the exception?" I whispered.

He didn't speak, just looked at me in a way that spread warmth through my chest. It felt as though it expanded throughout my whole world, a deep, thrilling sentiment I was starting to feel on my own. One I wouldn't dare voice, not even to myself. Things would change when we got out of these woods, when we went back to our lives—he had an important role, and I had literally nothing at all. This, whatever this was, wasn't forever. I needed to remember that.

I looked away and trailed my fingertips down the center of his chest.

"Who do you look like, your mom, your dad, or the butler?" I asked.

He spit out laughter. "My dad, mostly. My mom is off the hook for that wild night in the silver pantry." He tried to wrestle his smile away but clearly couldn't manage. "Apparently, I'm the spitting image of my dad, though some people say I have my mom's eyes and nose. The shape, I mean. Her eyes are blue. His are a yellowish-brown."

"Yours are gray."

"Dull, yes."

I shook my head. "Not dull. Expressive and beautiful, like an angry sky right before thunder claps and lightning strikes." I paused for a moment, unable to hold his deep, open gaze for all those reasons I wasn't yet ready to voice. "Do you still look like him, or is age not kind to your family?"

I expected him to smile at my joke, his humor often self-deprecating. Instead, his smile faded. "I don't know. I haven't seen him since I walked away from the palace. He and my mother disowned me."

"Oh, Weston. I'm sorry to hear that." My fingers glided across each bump of his toned abdominal muscles. "Do you miss them?"

"I miss . . . the idea of a family."

"What does that mean?"

"When I was a child, they weren't around much. Their lives were devoted to the palace. They had children to continue their powerful bloodlines. Theirs was an arranged mating because of those bloodlines. They had us out of duty and left most of our care to servants. When my brothers and I were old enough to show our power, they finally took an interest in us, grooming us for a life serving the court. I was the prized son because of my abilities. I became their pride and joy, not because of any real emotional attachment, but because of my power—their status in continuing their line. We were a family in name, only. That was the dynamic for a lot of families in the Red Lupine court."

"And your younger brother? The one lacking power?"

"He was mostly forgotten. Half the time my parents didn't bother inviting him to family functions. He's the one I left the palace for. They wouldn't let him go because they wanted to keep his bloodline in the court, but no one paid him any attention. He was dangerously unhappy, withering away. My older brother and I had vowed to protect him, and so I broke all ties and helped him walk away."

"And then you were stolen off the shores of your lands and lost touch with him, as well."

"No," he whispered. "When I came back, I saw that he was thriving as the alpha, so I walked away again, but that time of my own accord and on good terms. He's happy. That's what matters."

"And you? Are you happy?"

He didn't answer, instead saying, "Why do you trace my chest?"

"And arms. Don't forget that I trace the contours of your arms." I smiled. "Because you have a spectacular body and I like feeling it." I paused. "Do you mind?"

"No," he said, so softly I could barely hear him. "I like it."

"What is your dream?"

"I think it's your turn to share."

"Not even *remotely*." I grinned and scooted a little closer. He reached out, laying his hand on my hip. "You know all sorts of things about me. You read all those journals and heard all my stories during this journey.

You've even snooped around my home. Am I going to get to snoop around your home?"

"If you like."

I widened my eyes, not expecting that. I took it in stride, though. This was a pleasant fiction I was going to milk until reality shed its harsh light down on us.

"What's your dream?" I asked again.

His gaze traveled my face. "When I was younger, it was to be the king and queen's beta. The commander leading their legions, the most important non-royal duty in the land. When I was trapped in the demon dungeons, it was freedom. A kiss of fresh air. A meal I made for myself. After I watched the dragon king and queen struggle for each other and build a home and a family . . ."

His words drifted away.

"What, now you want to live the rest of your days as a bachelor?" I smiled, back to tracing his lips with my fingers.

"I want true love."

Shivers danced across my skin. "Only that?" I mock frowned at him. "You're dreaming very small, Alpha . . ."

"I want a mate and a family of my own, whether that family is one the two of us choose, one we create ourselves with children, or both. I want a love-blessed life, but not a settled life. I want to keep my duty, help build and defend a kingdom, and have a strong mate to start a real life with. I don't want to settle for scraps."

Tears filled my eyes and I had no idea why. "I think you will have that, Weston. I really do. After all you've been through, you've earned it."

"That remains to be seen." His words were tortured. "Listen, Aurelia, there's something I need to tell—"

Suddenly, the emberflies started to swirl violently before disappearing into the trees. I sat up in a rush and saw no one else stirring. Weston cut himself off in confusion.

"What is—"

I held up my hand to silence him.

"Danger," I whispered, ripping the covers away and hurrying into a pair of pants, tucking in the shirt and undergarments I preferred when we slept in the open. "The emberflies sense danger. Something is coming."

"My sentries would've seen it."

"Emberflies never lie." I pointed in the direction from which the emberflies had flown while grabbing the long, serrated knife Hadriel had found for me—stolen from someone else, I had a feeling—and my lantern.

"What's the matter?" someone said sleepily. "I have your bag. You can't get at the drugs."

Nova. She'd become a second protector, guarding my back when Weston was busy.

"Is it a wild animal?" Weston stood, far too leisurely for my taste. "They won't pose a problem for the sentries."

In fairness, it could've been an animal. Emberflies didn't specify what sort of danger lurked in the dark. Then again, specifying wasn't necessary. Danger was danger, plain and simple.

"I don't know," I said honestly, still holding the knife. My heart beat a solid drum within me, urging me to get everyone moving. My instincts said I had to either run and hide or get ready to fight but it was time to *make a choice.*

I stepped from side-to-side, refusing to lay back down until I knew what sort of danger lurked.

Weston looked at Nova who nodded and stepped away, shifting. She was using the pack bonds to silently check in with the sentries.

It took one beat for her body to tense and one more for Weston to act.

"Let's go." He pushed the cot out of the way and grabbed my arm, stopping to grab my bag as he walked. "Hurry. Let's get you hidden."

"What's happening?" someone asked as another said, "Alpha?"

"We've got company. Shift, hurry!" Weston didn't run, instead used long strides and made me half jog to keep up beside him. At the carts, he handed me my bag to sling over my shoulder before reaching into the closest cart and grabbing a sack. Around us the pack jumped up and those that weren't already in their wolf forms quickly shifted. Weston turned back to me and continued issuing directions. "Put your bag beside you. Keep your knife and your lantern close," he told me. "*Do not* turn on that lantern, no matter how loud or quiet it gets around you. It is for an emergency only."

"How will I know if it's an emergency?"

"Your only aim is to stay alive. Given your past, I assume you'll know when your life is in jeopardy."

"Where will you be if that happens?"

"Dead. Here we go." He stopped beside a bushy area run through with briars. Before I could question, he reached into the thorny branches and pushed a bunch of them to the side. "Crawl in."

"I—"

"Crawl in," he said again, his tone brooking no argument.

Overwhelmed by the command in his voice, the power, I did as he said, finding it surprisingly roomy the farther in I crawled. After turning around to face him, he handed me the sack.

"Inside there is a fairy-treated tarp that will mask your scent. Huddle in that space with your bag, your knife and your lantern close beside you. Cover yourself and your things completely with that tarp. This is very important Aurelia: the edges of that tarp *must* be touching the ground all around you or your scent *will* escape. With that tarp over you, no one will be able to smell you to track you down, do you understand? The magic of that tarp will ensure it blends into the flora around you."

"What about my scent trail leading here?"

"I'll have someone take care of that. I've got to go. Huddle there and protect yourself, Aurelia. Do as your mother said and stay alive so that you can remember her, okay? Wait for one of us to come and get you, or wait for the right time to escape. I'm counting on you."

With that, he let go of the briars, his hand and arm bleeding in several places from the thorns. He shifted there and his wolf looked in at me for a long moment, my chest dripping lava but nothing more, before turning and loping away.

I took a shaky breath and pulled the tarp from the

sack. After unfolding it, I stretched it out and found it different than I'd expected. It felt almost like a stiff blanket, almost soft against my skin. I maneuvered against the bent branches inside the cluster of bushes and shoved at other bits that seemed like they'd been broken off entirely. As I gathered my things under the blanket, it occurred to me that Weston must've scouted this location upon our arrival for the sole purpose of hiding me should we run into trouble. He'd created a little nook and devised a way to keep me safe. He must've done it at each stop, at least since my escape from the mayor's house, taking the time and effort to ensure that not only was his pack set up but that I had a safe, secret little burrow.

Despite the danger coming our way, my heart had never felt fuller. I made a little ball of myself and felt around to make sure the tarp completely covered me. It had been a long time since someone had looked after me so thoroughly, and I made sure to follow Weston's instructions to the letter.

I just hoped whatever trouble had followed me here wasn't more than they could handle.

Weston

The pack bond lit up with communication as my wolf ran toward the center of the camp. Nova and her team passed by us as they ran south, in the opposite direction. They spread out as they got closer to Aurelia's location, acting as her guard and ready to face any attackers that got through the front lines.

The enemy approached from the north and the east, an organized wall of attack. This wasn't like the attack on the camp those many nights ago, when our enemies tried to engage using antiquated tactics meant for a much less experienced alpha. Their pack was synchronized and well-led, under the command of someone with both experience and viciousness.

My wolf ran that way, monitoring our pack members and their positions. We were spread out around the camp, some in spots with no action. They would retain their posts in the likely event that the enemy spilled over to them. Those farther away would look out for any enemies attempting to sneak in from along the sides or behind the battleground.

The enemy pack might be well-led, but they didn't have advanced battle tactics. They didn't have my royal training and experience.

Snarls and yelps pierced the night. Bodies darted between the trees. Two of my pack members took down a smaller, quick wolf. Another member of my pack dashed left, smashing into a larger wolf trying to break through our lines.

They were in range and my wolf searched for their bonds, ready to grab them up and force them to submit.

Just like when Hadriel used Aurelia's product, though, the connections were slippery and elusive. They slid through my wolf's clutches and fell away.

My wolf ran closer, pushing our pack farther to the left and right to create a hole for us. Two enemy wolves waited and we barreled into them, taking the much smaller wolves to the ground. My wolf ripped out the throat of one without issue and rounded on the other as he reached for the bonds again. The one next to us was no problem, the proximity allowing my wolf to snap up that bond and push the enemy wolf to his belly. We'd be back for him. I had questions, and he would give us answers.

Other enemy wolves ran around us and my wolf reached again, clawing at that bond, wrestling with it until he could grab it up. We had to be three times as close as normal to the enemy to do so. Damn that product.

A yelp rang out to the left. Pain reverberated through the bond to the right. The enemy was starting to scatter, though, unused to the caliber of wolf I had in my pack. They weren't used to facing the sort of leadership and training we had.

A scent we'd know anywhere hit my wolf like a wave of blistering rage.

"Dead wolf walking," my wolf snarled as he pulled back from the fighting and lifted his nose into the air.

Alexander.

We knew his scent from Granny's large estate near the castle, in Granny's cottage in the village, and in his various living quarters provided by Granny. After hearing Aurelia's stories, it was a smell now burned into our brain.

My wolf ran right, grabbing up the bonds he could as he followed that scent. The enemy wolves slowed when we grabbed them, making it easy for my pack to rip right through them. I only needed a couple for questioning, the rest could meet their maker.

A wolf lunged out of the shadows. My wolf turned quickly, snarling at the attacker. Teeth tore into our shoulder before my wolf had her in his grip; he ripped into the side of her neck and pushed her to the ground. There, he finished the job, blood dripping from his muzzle.

The bond lit up with new information. The enemy had indeed run in from the sides and at the back. Nova was fighting, taking on two enemy wolves with the courage of a champion. Another member of her team rushed in to help her, the rest spreading out a bit more to cover more distance.

Still, my wolf and I tracked Alexander's scent. As alpha of this attack, he was the main target. As torturer of my true mate, he was now just waiting to die. Slowly. Gruesomely. Painfully.

I just had to catch him.

His scent wafted through the trees and floated around the reaching branches. Enemy wolves ran ahead of me, two breaking apart to run in opposite directions. Their fear was starting to get to them, was scrambling their decision-making abilities. My wolf reached for their bonds as we ran by, scrabbling to hold on.

"*Leave it,*" I said, wishing I was in control. "*They're nothing. The pack can handle them easily. Go after Alexander.*"

He didn't need convincing. He put on a burst of speed, catching a whiff here, a thread there. He couldn't be close. Alexander was overseeing, nothing else.

Why wouldn't he be going for the prize?

Another wolf broke toward Nova's team. The first

two wolves had been dispatched easily; our pack had no problem handling the third.

Shadows dashed behind a fat tree trunk, the detail lost to the night. My wolf darted in, recognizing the scent and chomping into the escaped prisoner it belonged to.

Then it occurred to me.

"We've recognized a lot of these scents," I said as the enemy wolf stopped moving and my wolf stuck his blood-coated muzzle into the air. The scent was fainter now, though still traceable. My wolf took off in that direction, working around toward the back of the camp. *"A couple have been escaped prisoners, a few were from the patrol in Granny's village that evaded capture."*

"He's sending them here to punish them while gathering information on how we work," my wolf surmised.

"Exactly. They're feeling us out. That's probably what they were doing with the lurkers, as well. Getting information. They want to know who they are up against."

"It's what we would do."

"It is."

He followed the scent away from the camp for a little longer; there were no enemy wolves left in this area. A moment later, he lost track of Alexander altogether—he'd retreated.

Annoyed, my wolf turned back, monitoring the action. The enemy had scattered, some running into the camp and being taken down immediately, and some trying to flee. They knew they'd been beat.

"Alexander sent them here to die," my wolf said.

"Most likely."

"Well, we'd hate to disappoint him . . ." He gave the

command to our pack to follow the enemy and take them out, their leadership having clearly withdrawn, the pack's ability to stay in formation without it nonexistent. They wouldn't be a challenge.

"Alexander would've felt you rip away that bond," I said as my wolf ran toward camp. He gave the order for the captured enemy wolves, those whose bonds we held that hadn't been killed, to follow us in. We'd see what they knew before sending them to the gods.

"We don't even know if he had them bonded," my wolf said. *"I could barely grab the enemy bond and reel it in; there's no way I could feel if someone had established one before me."*

"He must have. His people are running wild. He had to have been keeping them unified before he left."

My wolf huffed, acceding the point. Alexander would know a strong alpha held his prize. Given he was testing my pack, he couldn't have known exactly who we were. He didn't know of my involvement, or that of the dragons by association. That was damn good news.

The enemy wolves we'd captured—five left alive— had been gathered near the fire. My wolf left them there and carried on, aiming for our true mate, hopefully still tucked away where we'd left her.

The action within the trees slowed, a few pack members chasing the remaining enemy wolves running for their lives and the rest watchful of more to come. Alexander's scent was still absent. He didn't curve back around or change locations or directions without us knowing, not in any way that would matter. It seemed like the skirmish was over.

And that's all it was—a skirmish. Alexander had

been protecting himself here. Learning. The next time he stuck his neck out, it would be with stronger wolves and with a better plan. Next time, he'd be aiming to take his prize.

Dante was close to Aurelia's hiding place, having dispatched a wild enemy who had tried to get away but had run out of energy, allowing Dante to catch up and take him down. I sent Dante to get her, releasing Nova to help, and kept the rest of her team in position just in case. I wanted Aurelia back in the center of camp, with all of us surrounding her, before I called everyone back and set up our defenses for the rest of the night.

I advanced upon Aurelia's hiding spot, retaking my human form so that I could look her over. Dante reached into the hidey-hole as a scarred but dainty hand slashed out, hitting him in the side with a knife. The whole bush shook, Aurelia clearly having fallen over under the tarp.

"Fucking *hell!*" Dante shouted, recoiling. He stumbled backwards, grabbing his side. "What the fuck, Aurelia? I thought we were friends!"

He landed hard on his butt with a pained expression, rolling to his non-hurt side and laying all the way down. "Owww! Why the fuck are you so fucking fast? You shouldn't be that damn fast without your animal."

Nova took a step back as Aurelia staggered out of the bush, her hair wild having caught in the briars, with gashes along her skin. I stepped forward immediately but she was already bending to Dante.

"Or maybe you're just slow." Nova snickered at

Dante as she reached for Aurelia. "Aurelia, you're covered in briars!"

"Sorry!" Aurelia told Dante as I neared. "I'm sorry, Dante! I dozed off and you startled me."

"How did I startle you? I said your name! Do you think the enemy knows your name? Fuck." He peeled his hands away, looking at the bloody mess along his side. "If she'd stuck me two inches to the left, it would've been bad."

"The enemy does know her name." Nova backed away to give me space. "Though yeah, that would've been a killing strike if she'd landed it better. Nice work, Aurelia. You're getting better."

"Salt in the wound," Dante grumbled.

"Sorry!" Aurelia reached out to touch Dante's leg but I caught her hand before it touched down on his bare flesh. I helped her to stand. "I didn't hear you say my name, but maybe don't reach for me next time."

"There isn't going to be a next time," Nova said. "We'll be on the main road tomorrow. We'll have nowhere to hide you. We have to hope the enemy doesn't have any tricks up their sleeves."

Aurelia looked at me with those large, beautiful eyes. "He was here, wasn't he?"

She had to mean Alexander.

"He didn't get close enough to cause a problem," I told her, leading her back to the fires. "You're safe."

"I felt him." She huddled in close to me as we walked. "I felt him here. He's come for me."

"He won't get you," I said as I spied Hadriel jogging closer. I motioned him over before turning her to face me and bending down to look her in the eye. A swell of protectiveness sent adrenaline through my body. "Listen to me, Little Wolf. He will not get you. Okay? I won't let him take you. You're safe. I've got you. I won't let anyone hurt you—ever."

Her relieved expression made my heart thump. I kissed her long and deep, loving the way she clung to me.

"Hadriel is going to take you back to camp, okay?" He stepped forward as I said it. "I have to ask our captives a few questions. I'll meet you shortly."

She nodded again, licking her lips, before stepping away hesitantly. It was clear she didn't want to leave my side, and that sent warmth spreading through me. My job wasn't done, though. I had information to acquire, and I didn't plan on being nice about it.

"Well?" Tanix said after we'd finished interrogating the prisoners. He wiped his crimson hands on a rag. He'd exacted a little vengeance for what Granny's organization had done to his family, and I'd offered up some payback for what those people had done to Aurelia and her village.

I looked out at the trees, feeling Aurelia calling to me. I wanted to go reassure her, with my warmth and then my body. She didn't like fucking in front of the pack, but she'd need to get over it tonight. I needed to be inside her.

"We have a couple things going for us. First, they don't know who I am. That means the dragons aren't implicated."

"It also means they don't know what they are up against."

"Exactly. But the best news is that the local royalty don't seem to be involved. My suspicions that they would be were off."

"In this situation, I'm damn glad you were wrong."

"No shit. It's one less thing to worry about."

Apparently, Granny's product was causing dissent within many communities, and while the royalty were content to take the gold while things went smoothly, they cut and run at the first sign of discourse. They would not lend a direct hand to the organization's efforts.

"Without royal pressure, all we need to worry about is getting past the port patrol," Tanix said.

I took a deep breath. "That, and actually getting *to* the port. We have to join the main road leading to the port tomorrow. There won't be any trees to hide in. Without royal backing, Alexander won't be able to stage a fight in the city or near the port. Tomorrow, in the open, is where he'll have to make his last stand."

They wanted my true mate. Aurelia was a prize they would clearly sacrifice for. Kill for. Her worth couldn't be measured by her humble lodgings and cheap attire. Granny had known the diamond she'd held, safe-guarding it at the very edges of the kingdom, isolating it in the wilds. It wasn't just Aurelia's abilities, it was her intelligence and her ingenuity. Her hardworking nature and need to be of value. Those traits ranked higher than her power level, a prize for any shifter kingdom in its own right. Aurelia, simply by being herself, had blessed Granny with all the gold she could want.

Aurelia was a rare find and Granny had somehow known it upon their first meeting. That, or she'd taken a chance and gotten incredibly lucky.

My true mate was something special. Something rare. I could only hope the dragons would see it, too.

"So tonight was about Alexander preparing," Tanix surmised.

"Yes. And tomorrow he'll hit us again. Hard."

32

AURELIA

"No, Urien!" Hadriel shouted. "You pencil-dicked sonuva donkey," he muttered. "Stop manhandling that horse. He doesn't like—" He stormed up the line. "I swear to the gods' balls, I am going to thump that kid. What in the bloody cleavage is he even doing? Urien, that horse is going to—well, there you go. Don't you dare cry to me, you deserved to get bit!"

I watched with what I knew was a lopsided smile as Hadriel went after Urien. I loved watching his antics.

Weston walked beside me in wolf form, sparing a brief glance for Hadriel before looking back at the trees. A lot of the other powerful members of the pack were also in wolf form. They were taking no chances in case Alexander ambushed us on the road.

A shiver of fear rolled through me and I did my best to put the thought out of my mind. There was nothing I feared more than falling into his hands.

Dante walked behind me in human form with a

simple strip of fabric around his waist in case he had to shift quickly. As Hadriel bustled away, Dante stepped up beside me and I decided to bring up what had been on my mind since last night.

"Dante, I've been meaning to ask you . . ." I slipped my hands into my pockets as nervousness fluttered in my belly.

"Don't put your hands in your pockets when you walk," he said in response, scanning the trees to the left. "If you trip, you'll fall on your face and chip a tooth or something."

"Okay, mother." My smile grew and I pulled my hands from my pockets.

"If you fell, you'd probably conjure a knife out of thin air and stab me when I bent to help you. I'm not saying it for you, I'm saying it for me. I'm tired of you attacking me."

I grimaced, the nervousness amplifying. "Gotcha. Sorry about that." I hesitated, feeling sheepish and vulnerable and more than a little embarrassed. But this was important to me. "Did you mean what you said, though?"

He groaned. "Listen, Aurelia, you have to understand, we've been eating cheese for days. There is only so much cheese a guy can eat without asserting that he's never going to eat cheese again. Did I mean it? At the time, yes. Is it a testament to your cooking that I don't want to eat the cheese you and the cook keep pushing on us? Again, yes. Am I serious? Not totally. I'm sure in a month I will forget all about this and once again eat chee—are you laughing with me or at me?"

"No, it's just . . . I didn't hear your comment about

cheese. That one I get. I'm tired of it, too, and I love cheese."

"Right? See, Sixten told me I was bitching just to bitch, but it's a lot, right?"

"It is. No, I mean, last night after I'd . . . stuck you with the knife. Did you mean it?"

"Why? What did I call you? I don't remember—I'd just been stabbed, after all."

I bit my lip, hesitating. I felt oddly vulnerable and even more embarrassed now. I shook my head. "Never mind."

"At the time, I probably did mean it, yes. But it's like the cheese—I'll eventually get over it."

I laughed, shaking my head harder now. He was such a goofy guy. I loved it. "No, it's not . . ." I looked away, and then just blurted it out. "You said you thought we were friends."

"Yeah. Well, you'd just stabbed me. It gives a guy mixed signals."

"Right." My heart sank a little, unsure what to make of that and deciding just to let it go. "I'd just wondered," I murmured, my face probably flaming.

"Wait, what am I missing?" He reached out to grab my shoulder but Weston's wolf issued a low warning growl. He jerked his hand away and raised them both in the air. "Not touching."

I looked over at Weston's wolf, my eyes widened at the strange flood of desire lighting me on fire. His possessive display of ownership turned me on.

"What am I missing?" Dante tried again. "You have a vibe. What'd I do?"

"No . . ." I waved my hand through the air. This was

getting awkward. "It's nothing. Never mind. I was just surprised to hear that you thought we were friends, that's all."

"Why?" He pointed to the side. "Don't believe what Sixten tells you. I'm loyal as fuck, seriously. I didn't even care that you tried to stab me. Not for long, anyway." He paused. "Why, what's wrong with me? I'm a cool guy. I'm funny. Aren't I funny, Hadriel?"

Hadriel stood to the side, waiting for the procession to pass. "Wow, spiraling much, Dante?"

"Shut up." Dante fell back a bit so Hadriel could regain his place.

"He's funny because he's too dumb to realize he's the butt of the joke," Hadriel said drolly.

"Suck a lemon, Hadriel," Dante replied.

"Lick a porcupine, Dante." Hadriel glanced back with a grin. "Haven't you listened to her stories? She hasn't ever had friends. People went out of their way to avoid her. It's surprising to her that her captors would be friendly, let alone declare friendship."

Heat infused my cheeks and I chewed my lip, the embarrassment washing over me in full force. I sounded desperate. And honestly, maybe I was. It was like having a glimpse into a life you'd only dreamed of and trying to wrestle it into reality. I hated being so obvious about it.

"Oh." Dante puffed out his chest a little. "It's not me, it's her. Cool. I was starting to get a complex."

Hadriel fully twisted now to stare at Dante for a beat, a dumbfounded look on his face, before shaking his head and facing front again. He then leaned my way like we were coconspirators and said, "If there is ever any doubt, it will always be him, my darling, never you. He's just a big dumb animal."

"I'm ignoring you," Dante told Hadriel. "Yes, Aurelia, we're friends. Or we will be when we don't have this abduction thing between us, right? A bit awkward, that. 'Well, how'd you guys meet? Oh, it was just a little kidnapping situation. She cleaved me with an axe and then I helped keep her imprisoned until she eventually won me over. We've been besties ever since.'"

"Do you need us for this, or are you happy talking to yourself for a while?" Hadriel asked him and I devolved into a fit of giggles. These guys were so entertaining when they bantered back and forth.

"This whole thing has been really strange, though, hasn't it?" Dante mused, looking into the sparse trees along the road. "We did not end up with the person we expected. Not even a little bit. Then there's the mate situation, which—"

Hadriel turned and punched Dante in the chest.

"Ow, what the fu—" Dante's eyes widened and his mouth snapped shut as I turned in confusion. Before I could ask what they were talking about, a familiar sensation washed over me. An expectant sort of sensation, with danger and fists and pain on the other end.

Alexander.

My hand drifted to Hadriel's upper arm, gripping him hard and then pushing him to my other side so that I could hunch near the cart. It probably wasn't the nicest thing I could do, but I couldn't help it.

"No, love, you shouldn't touch—what's the matter?" Hadriel asked.

"He's out there," I whispered, looking through the

trees. He wasn't right there, though. He wasn't even near, I'd bet anything on that fact—not near enough to attack this moment. The sensation I felt was a promise, a rendezvous with his fists set for a later date. "He's out there somewhere. I feel it. He's getting ready."

"Who?" Hadriel asked.

"Alexander," I said, holding onto the cart. My gaze found that of Weston's wolf. "He's going to come for me."

To my great surprise and eternal gratitude, no one questioned me. I had a feeling it was because of the emberflies. Before last night, they'd been wary of my claims that the bugs were a warning system. Now they believed me, and they clearly also believed my sixth sense regarding danger and Alexander was just as telling.

Weston's wolf looked back at Dante, probably communicating through his body language. They seemed to be able to decipher subtle variations in movement.

"Come back over here, Aurelia," Dante said, motioning me over. "Try to act normal. Don't raise suspicion. Is he close? Is he in hearing distance?"

"No. I don't think so." I licked my lips. "This feeling —it's not based on proximity. Well, not totally, maybe? I always felt this . . . awareness before he'd show up to punish me. It's a warning, but not just of the pain to come. He gets a sexual kind of high out of punishing people—at least he does when punishing me. It makes my skin crawl. It's easily worse than the actual punish- ment. It's like I could feel his anticipation. He'd be on the opposite side of the village from my cottage—quite a distance away—but I could always feel it, even when I didn't know for sure a punishment was coming."

"Why wouldn't you know one was coming?" Dante asked, giving me more space now, probably so he could shift quickly if needed.

I lifted a shoulder, my emotions turbulent. "It didn't happen often, but sometimes Granny would get word of my conduct in the village and punish me for it. Giving away food or supplies, taking a break when I should've been working, leaving work to watch the hunting pack gather and take off or come back . . ."

"Why would she care about you watching the hunting pack?"

"I always assumed it was because she thought I should've been working."

"Or maybe she worried one of them might be strong enough to pull out your wolf," Hadriel said lightly.

I studied him for a moment but wouldn't allow myself to dwell on it. That was in the past. There was nothing I could do about it now but to bury the feelings until I had reached some semblance of safety. After that, I could rehash all the things that I knew would tear me apart.

"It'll be fine," I said softly, steeling my resolve, trying not to let the fear rule me. "Besides, when he came before, I wasn't allowed to fight back. Now I am."

"I'll find you an axe," Dante said, a grin spreading across his face. "See? Friendship."

33

AURELIA

The air had chilled by the time we stopped, but the goosebumps across my limbs weren't from cold. The anticipation was building, I could feel it. *He* was out there somewhere, all his focus on to me. He intended to take me. To use me, not just to make product, but for his own sick urges.

I caught sight of Weston's wolf working through the trees, his easy lope so effortless and graceful, so beautiful. He slowed when he neared his pack members, his authority obvious. Their communication was silent but no less informative. When he moved on, they hurried to do whatever he'd commanded.

"What's for dinner, love? I'm starving." Hadriel walked up without a stitch on him. He'd clearly just spent some time in wolf form. Thankfully I was getting used to all the nudity. "We've been granted a fire since we're in clear view. We've got people hunting, but I doubt they'll find much this close to the city. This place is probably over-hunted. We've got to rely on what we've got."

It was unusual for Hadriel to break down the cooking situation. It meant he was trying to distract me, keep my mind occupied.

"You won't be able to hide me." I looked at the elevated land to the west and south, something Dante had pointed out to Weston when we'd stopped. It's the only reason I knew the directions. "Even if you try, he'll still find me."

"Don't worry about that, my darling." Hadriel rubbed my arm. "Weston is an incredible alpha. Remember I told you not to kill him? This is why. He excels at handling danger like this. He rises to the challenge every time. If anyone is going to protect you, it is him."

"I should be able to protect myself."

It was out before I'd meant to say it and wasn't something I would've ever thought in the past. Hell, I'd asked Weston to be his damsel in distress, something that still strangely turned me on. But now, here, with an animal in my person and danger aiming for me specifically . . . I was tired of being dead weight, of being vulnerable or the victim. I had an animal. I should be able to stick up for myself. Even if I couldn't, I wanted to do more than hide in a bush and hope for the best while the brave people around me put their lives on the line to protect me.

"You will, love." Hadriel shadowed me to the supply cart where we kept the food supplies. "Just as soon as you can get training, you will, I promise. You'll be incredible. We just have to get through this . . . and the port situation. Then we'll have time to get you up to speed."

"Just in time for the dragons to take me down."

"Luckily I have an *in* with one of those dragons. I don't name-drop for nothing. I can try and pull some strings. You might be sequestered to the castle, watched constantly and in immediate danger from a dragons' random rage, but join the club, you know? You're very level-headed and easygoing. I don't think it'll be a big problem for you."

Burt was already at the supply cart in question, and yes, I'd started calling him Burt. First by accident, and then because he got so annoyed and the banter between him and Hadriel about it was so funny. I just couldn't help myself.

Unlike with Hadriel, Burt had started retaliating with me.

"Hey, Louisa. Ready to make something delicious?" he asked me with a kind smile.

I returned it even though I was having a hard time feeling it through the tension tightening my shoulders. "Always."

He didn't immediately return to rummaging through the dwindling stores. "We're going to make it. We're wolves—we do better as a pack. This pack, though just a part of the whole, is as strong as they come. We'll be okay."

I nodded, my smile now brittle. "I know."

The pack was definitely strong, but Alexander was a singular sort of person. He was a lone wolf disguised as a team player, willing to sacrifice those around him to get what he wanted. He'd slip through one hole or another in the defenses like sand through the tines of a fork. If he couldn't, like last time, he'd evade capture and wait until he could. All he needed was a little time and one clear shot, and he'd get to me.

I hoped like hell that was just my fear talking.

The pack helped build several fires. My request to go out and find some wild roots and edible vegetation was denied, which wasn't surprising, so I lost myself in preparing dinner. Several people brought small kills like rabbit and similar-sized game, walking right past me to hand them to Burt. Only Weston handed me a skinned and cleaned rabbit directly, his gaze piercing, spreading shivers across my body. I wondered how long the claim would last. I didn't know if it was something specific to our journey, and not wanting anyone to touch the female that had shared his bed. It was clear that alphas did not share.

"You're going to be a damn fine wolf, madam," Dante said, sitting near me and using his hands to eat a piece of rabbit. Everyone was given a morsel of the fresh kills, there was not enough to go around for a full meal. "You are clearly very good under pressure."

"Agreed." Sixten nodded, the grease smeared along the side of her face shining in the firelight.

"It's just cooking." I set my plate down on the dried grass of our camp.

"Eat," Weston commanded in a low voice, sitting beside me.

I looked away. I wasn't hungry.

"You need your strength, and for that, you need food." Weston's hand settled on my thigh. "Eat."

I sighed but did as he said, knowing he was right.

"Cooking under pressure is still being good under pressure." Dante sucked on the tips of his fingers. "And you're really good under pressure. I think this is your best meal yet."

I worried it might be my last.

After everyone had eaten and cleaned up, Weston walked me toward a lone individual cot.

"We'll all be in wolf form tonight," he explained, watching me as I sat down on the side. "We'll be sleeping all around you, ready to surge up at a moment's notice. Nothing will get through us."

I licked my lips. "Why are you doing this?" I shook my head. "What I mean is, you guys seem like you're putting yourself in tremendous danger to protect me. Would you be doing this if I was just a prisoner?"

He knelt in front of me. "The truth?" He waited for me to nod. "Yes, we would. We would be trying to take you back to our kingdom, knowing your organization would be trying to steal you away again. It was always going to go down like this. The difference now is we will fight with everything we have to keep you alive rather than ever admit defeat and cut our loses by killing you."

I gulped, holding his gaze, wanting to ask why things had changed. That had been a harsh truth, though. I didn't want to hear any more.

Sensing my questions were finished for the moment, he reached forward and placed a palm against my cheek. "Sleep, Little Wolf. Tomorrow we have a day's ride before we get to the port city. We'll have one more night there while we load everything onto the ship, and then we'll be leaving these shores and all its nightmares behind. Two more sleeps and we'll be done with this place."

His goodnight kiss was soft and sweet, but I was cold without his body in bed next to me. Dante had laid two knives right under my cot, apologizing that he couldn't find an axe. Weston shifted, his wolf licked my face, and he curled up on the ground at the side of my bed. The rest of the pack settled in around us and the emberflies drifted over them, ever our sentries.

I closed my eyes but I couldn't sleep. It wasn't just because I was waiting for Alexander to show up. Weston was eager to get out of here, more than happy to leave this kingdom behind. But this was my home. It was all I'd ever known. Sure, the time here had been less than ideal in most if not all respects, but closing the book on it gave me a strange sort of melancholy I hadn't been expecting. I wasn't sure I actually wanted to leave —not this way, like a sort of hostage. Like a criminal.

There was nothing for it now, not unless we killed Alexander. It was either leave or be hunted by him and the organization indefinitely. I didn't assume I'd be able to hide, not with drug use as lucrative and widespread as it was. The reward he posted for anyone who found me meant I'd always be looking over my shoulder.

Sunrise approached gradually, the colors bleeding from black to a hazy sepia. I wasn't sure I'd gotten any sleep at all. All night I'd laid in bed feeling the dread building inside me. The emberflies had hardly moved, staying densely crowded above me.

One thought kept repeating in my mind: not yet.

It wasn't time.

Nearly, but not yet.

Almost.

Finally, at dawn . . .

"Any time now," I whispered, sitting up as though pulled by hidden strings.

The adrenaline kicked in, coursing through my body. If I'd been at home, I'd have expected the knock on the door at any moment. There was no point in second-guessing or in waiting. I knew as surely as I always had: he'd come to punish me, and he would enjoy every second.

Weston's wolf's eyes snapped open, his head lifting up quickly as I moved. A few others began to rouse as well, and in an instant they all did, watching me silently. I reached below my cot and grabbed my knives, meeting Weston's wolf's eyes.

"Get into positions. It's happening."

He didn't question my surety and none of them delayed. They were up immediately, moving as a well-orchestrated team.

I walked toward the dying fire, the center of camp, the place I'd been told to stay while it all went down. Weston had agreed that there was no point in hiding me. He was reluctant to also agree that it would be best to use me as bait, even though we all knew it was true. I was the reason they were coming; I may as well be useful in luring them into Weston's trap, if one could call it a trap. Traps weren't usually so very obvious as this.

The first rays of sunlight gently illuminated the sky from behind the horizon. The emberflies took off in a hurry, a wave of dying pinpricks of light.

Sounds of snarls and the snapping of teeth announced their arrival, coming from every direction, surrounding us. Wolves and other animals ran toward us, the wall of furry bodies hellbent on crashing through Weston's pack. They outnumbered us by two or more to one, their bodies were not as large but their sheer numbers making up any disparity.

I stood ready, my gut churning, watching for the flash of familiar fur working through the others to get to me. I knew it would be him that grabbed me. He'd want to claim the prize.

Teeth flashed and chomped down, someone yelped, another bayed in pain. Someone limped out of the way and a backup quickly took their place, chomping low and snapping the foot of one of our wolves.

"Damn it," I said in a rush of breath, stepping side-to-side, turning in a circle to try and watch everything at once. I waited for someone to get through, to make a running leap at me. I was ready, my knives poised, no question as to whether I would use them. Survival was ugly. I didn't mind looking it right in the face.

The largest wolf of all backed slowly toward me, Weston's head low, his fur standing on end. I couldn't tell what he was doing, why he was taking himself out of the fray. Bodies churned all around us, lunging at each other, ripping through flesh, splatters of red highlighted by the first rays of the sun. Another yelp and a wolf went down—one of ours. Theirs ran through the sudden hole, four bodies at first, shoving outward to make that hole larger. Others poured in from behind, suddenly putting half of our people on the outside of the circle.

They ran at me, their four legs closing the distance at lightning speed. It was too many for me to handle on my own and Weston stood still now, his nose nearly to the ground.

I didn't call out to him. In the end, this wasn't really his problem—*I* wasn't really his problem. I didn't have time to linger with the feelings of disappointment or hurt.

The wolves quickly circled me and I lashed out, slicing through the flank of one and spinning, sticking another in the side. The first bayed and the second dropped. I stepped toward another, but they were onto me now. They gave me space, dashing around me, faster than I was. And then he was there, materializing like some sort of phantom, walking on two legs through the melee. His eyes were sparkling, manic, his grin pulled wide into a sickly smile.

Alexander.

"Hello Aurelia," he said, eyeing my knives as he approached. "Long time, no see. I've missed you. Plan to put up a fight?"

"I'm not defenseless now, you piece of shit. Come at me."

He laughed. "With pleasure."

His people were fast but he was like lightning. He dodged my strike and swung. I bent back just in time, only one of his knuckles glancing across my face. I struck forward with my right and then quickly my left, knowing he'd jerk away from the first but wouldn't expect me to be as fluid with my non-dominant hand. The blade sank into his shoulder.

He sucked in a breath through his teeth but didn't stop, slapping that hand away and connecting with a right hook. I twisted to evade the hit but my world exploded in stars, the pain not registering but the blurry vision with black splotches was unavoidable. That eye would swell shut quickly. I had to keep him from doing the same to the other.

He yanked the knife out of his shoulder and tossed it away. I used the time to feint and stick, feint and stick, finding purchase in his other bicep and then connecting with a nice deep slice in his thigh.

"Fuck! You bitch," he hissed, a vicious punch landing against my ribs. "Who the fuck taught you to work a knife?"

"The idea . . . of sticking a pointy end . . . into soft bits . . . doesn't require much . . . brain power," I panted as I kept working, ignoring the throbbing pain in my ribs. It was his favorite spot to go after. I needed to keep him from doing it again or the fight would be over.

But he was already closing in, a punch landing against my cheek and another into my stomach.

I bent, trying to keep from doubling over, and slashed.

He dodged, smacked my wrist away, making me drop the knife, and grabbed at me. His hands spun me around, his arms closed around me, and then he started to drag me, wrestling me out of the clearing.

"No," I yelled, fighting for all I was worth.

He paused for a moment to bash two quick fists into the side of my head. My thoughts got hazy and my world swam but I didn't stop. The trick to fight or flight was the commitment. Choose one or the other but keep doing it until you couldn't physically do it anymore . . . and then wake up and try again. My nails raked skin off his arms. My teeth ripped out a chunk of foul-tasting flesh. When he stopped to strike me again, I took advantage of the opportunity and twisted in his grip, freeing an arm. I reached over my head, poking a finger into his eye. When he pulled his head back and roared in agony, I hooked my finger into his open mouth and pulled until his cheek tore. It was something.

His swear made me feel better. He stopped to get a better purchase, ready to deliver a blow to knock me clean out, and I angled my body away from the blow I knew was coming. I had the benefit of already knowing all his tricks. He wasn't very creative when it came to administering pain, probably because no one was ever allowed to fight back.

I connected a knee to his ball sack while I jammed the heel of my hand into his nose.

The battle around us slowed. The wolves gradually stopped fighting.

Fear consumed me that his people were able to take Weston's down.

The fear turned into adrenaline.

"Fuck!" I punched his throat. "You!"

His fist arced . . . but then went wide as he turned, looking around us. In a moment his arms were gone, his body torn away.

I staggered, doing a quick glance for the nearest knife and then ducking just in case. No fist came.

He and several others ran from the clearing, all in

human form. Wolves around us continued to slow, the enemy dropping to their bellies, a couple I recognized still standing. A handful of others broke away, and I recognized them, too. They ran after Alexander and his people in their human forms, snarling.

A moment later, though, I heard the sounds of retreating hooves. Alexander had brought horses. The wolves wouldn't be able to take those down fast enough.

"Aurelia." Tanix reached me in human form, nude and bloody with scrapes and cuts. He'd heal. "Are you okay?"

"What happened? Why'd everyone stop fighting? Alexander took off. Did we win?"

"Fuck." He peered into my swollen eye, now completely shut. His thumb gently trailed over my cheek, which also felt swollen. "How bad?"

"My face is fine. My ribs are probably cracked. That's about it, though. I'm good. He took off before he was able to really lay into me. What happened?" I asked again.

"I don't think we'll ever truly win until they're all dead." Tanix tried to lift my shirt and I pushed his hands away. "I need to see your ribs."

"Honestly, it's fine. It'll heal. This isn't the first time I've dealt with his fists. I know how close I am to the danger zones and I'm good. Trust me."

He straightened a little and gave me a hard look. "Please."

It hurt to frown. "Fine, go for it. I'm sure the bruises are already forming. Those will look bad, but it'll heal. Can you please do two things at once and tell me *what happened?*"

"They had someone powerful holding their pack bond." He peeled my shirt up gently and then sucked a breath through his teeth. "Damn it, Aurelia, this isn't nothing."

My heart squished that he cared, the warmth of that sentiment filling my body. Still, he didn't seem to grasp that this really was tolerable. Compared to what I'd endured in the past, this could easily be ignored.

He checked my other side and went back to the first.

"I didn't say it was nothing, I said it would heal. What does that mean to the battle, someone holding the bond?"

He peered into my eyes for another moment before steering me toward the supply carts. "Our alpha is the most powerful alpha I've ever heard of. It isn't just his might, it's his magic. He has an innate ability—a natural gift—to form bonds and control a pack. Usually, he can rip a bond away from another powerful alpha, no problem. But your . . . product makes grabbing a bond difficult. The other night, he had a hard time grabbing everyone up. It's why the battle lasted as long as it did."

"That's why he was backing away from the fight? He was trying to get ahold of the bonds?"

"Yes. This time, though, there was an additional hurdle—someone fairly powerful controlled their pack bond. The alpha not only had to work against your product, but also against the already established leadership in their pack. It's a testament to his ability that he was able to do it. We would've been lost if he hadn't."

"The other alpha would've struggled holding onto the pack as well, right?"

"Which is probably why the alpha was able to do it.

That and . . ." He put out his hands in a gesture meant to tell me to keep put while he worked the latch on the cart. "He couldn't fail."

"As soon as they had me, they would've left you guys alone. At least, if he fails the next time, you know you'll be safe."

"True. Yet you fought like your life depended on it."

I stared after him, struck mute for a moment. "I'm sorry I-I guess I hadn't thought it through. I probably should've waited to fight him so that you guys would be guaranteed your safety. Sorry, I was just wrapped up in the moment, and Dante gave me the knives, and you were all surrounding me—"

"Hey, hey." He held out his hands. "Whoa. That's not what I'm saying. You fought like your life depended on it meaning you didn't want to go with him. You took that horrible beating just to keep out of his reach."

Again, it hurt to frown. "Well, yeah. If it wasn't for you guys, he would've completed his task. I just held him off—Oh!" Everything connected for me. "The fight was slowing because Weston got control. Alexander ran because he knew time was running out."

"Exactly." Tanix grabbed some sort of pouch and led me to a nearby log. "He and a few others were in their human forms because the alpha can't form a bond unless they are in wolf form. They were waiting to extract you, keeping the hole in our line open with various weapons. Once the alpha secured the bond, they had precious little time. They had to leave you behind."

"How are our people? Did they all make it?"

He took out a couple tins of salve and rested them on the log. "The alpha is seeing to the wounded. We haven't lost anyone yet and we still have some of the phoenix elixir left. We should be okay." He paused. "Our people?"

"I mean . . ." I rolled my eyes and then winced, which also hurt. "Your people. Weston's. Sorry—"

"Stop apologizing." He used his finger to gently dab some salve on my cheek. "This will help with the swelling and bruising. Obviously not as well as if you had your animal, but it's something. Listen, Aurelia, I've seen the way you're trying to help with the drugs. I recognized the differences between your village and the places hit hard by Granny's drugs. I always wondered, though, if it was all an act. The pretty, wide-eyed, naive routine seemed a little over the top given the hell those drugs have wrought. I wondered if you'd run back at the first chance you got."

"That's why I was locked in the mayor's house? Because I was an esteemed guest, ready to be taken back?"

He shrugged. "Safe keeping? Keeping you from us? I don't know. But now . . ." He paused. "The more you learned of the outside world, the more that 'routine' peeled away. I've watched it with my own eyes. You've tried to help, nearly killing yourself and defying the alpha to do so. And today—"

"I got my ass handed to me."

"No, you gave better than you got against a man twice your size and three times your muscle mass. He should've been much faster—"

"He was."

"—much stronger—"

"He definitely was."

"—and way outclassed you."

"That's insulting. He has no class at all."

He grinned, a small expression, and it melted something inside of me. He'd always been my harshest critic.

"Today I saw what I needed to see to put my doubts to rest once and for all. I'm sorry it took me so long."

I winced as he pressed too hard. "Forgiven. Does that mean you'll stop doctoring me now? It's worse than the actual wounds."

34

AURELIA

"*L*ove, no, you are not going to walk like some tramp." Hadriel very gently marshalled me toward the front of the horse procession.

"What does walking have to do with tramps?" I asked in confusion.

"I have no fucking idea but it's the only thing that came to mind and your confusion makes you pliant. Now, here." He pointed at Weston's horse. "You'll go with him so that he can mother you."

"I don't need mothering. I need to walk, because getting up on a horse and riding is going to hurt like a motherfucker."

"I see what you did there, with the word play." Hadriel winked, and then pointed at his eye. "See what *I* did there? I winked, like you are constantly doing to me because one of your fucking eyes is swelled shut and it's giving me heart palpitations. Get on the bloody horse so that I don't start crying. I cannot handle the sort of pain you're in."

"Aurelia." Weston stalked up to me like the predator he was. He'd been busy tending to his pack. He'd had to give out the last of their phoenix elixir, but no one died. For that, I was eternally grateful. I hadn't forgotten what Tanix had said, even though it hadn't been what he'd meant. "You're riding with me."

"All due respect, Alpha—and this isn't a ploy to get you to have anger sex because that would hurt too much right now—but no. Thank you, but I physically can't. It'll hurt too much to get up there and it'll be hell to stay. Please, be nice to me for once, and let me walk."

His gaze roamed my face, his expression crumpling into anger and pain as he took in my swollen eye, my cracked lips, the bruises on my cheek. He lifted his hand and made to trail a finger across my wounds as though he might absorb my pain into himself, but instead let his hand hover, probably afraid to hurt me further. The angry expression melted to regret and frustration, and I knew he hated that he'd allowed Alexander through. That he hadn't been fast enough in performing his duty to keep me from harm.

"It'll be okay if I just walk," I said softly, swallowing down a lump in my throat.

I wanted to tell him that he had done his duty and protected me. That he had saved me. I'd already done that, though, many times over. First when he saw the damage Alexander had done and froze in enraged agony, and again every time he approached me thereafter. He never accepted my gratitude, though. To him, he'd failed. Nothing I said would dissuade him from his self-loathing.

He glanced at his horse, his lips tightening. "Fine. We'll walk," he snapped.

"No, no. *I* will walk. You will ride like the alpha you are—"

"Gods finger me," Hadriel said, exasperated. "Aurelia, love, shut the fuck up and let him walk with you. Can't you see the stress you're causing us all? Go! Walk! I'll walk. We'll all fucking walk if we can just get underway and get there. The faster we get to our own lands, the better. We can't have those fuckers trying again. They might get it right next time."

In the end I relented because I didn't really have a choice. Weston and I walked. He led his horse, while the rest of the pack continued on as normal. The day was long and my body started to ache, but by the late afternoon I could see high walls and busy foot traffic leading to the city. We got closer still and I reached out for Weston's hand, never having seen so many people nor a city as big. It sprawled in all directions farther than the eye could see. A thriving commerce area existed outside the walls, leading down a gentle slope to the glittering seas beyond. The whole scene was like an ant hill after a boot had trampled it, the dwindling light doing nothing to thin out the crowds.

"Holy crap," I said softly as Weston stopped and looked back.

"Nova, take the supplies straight to the docks. Get a boat to run you out to the ship and make sure everything is set for us to leave at dawn. Tanix, Sixten, find an inn that will hold those of us staying in the city. I don't care if we have to double or triple up in rooms, I want us all together. Dante, figure out

K.F. BREENE

the guard situation and make good with them. I want to be deep in this town's pocket so that they protect our interests."

"What does that mean, in the town's pocket?" I asked as Weston waited for Tanix and Sixten to ride ahead before walking again.

"It means we're going to bribe them to watch our backs. A lot of rich merchants do it, and that's what we're pretending to be. We have the false paperwork to prove it." He paused. "You're going to need to go back with Hadriel for now. Keep your head down. Stay in line. If you see something that makes you nervous, say something, okay?"

I nodded and did as he said, relieved when Hadriel got down off his horse to walk with me.

"Won't Alexander just bribe the guards too?" I asked as we walked, splitting up near the city gates.

Hardly anyone looked my way. Most took note of the horses or the people sitting on top of them and almost never looked at those walking or with the carts. When they did happen to notice me, though, their eyes widened.

"Here, love." Hadriel switched places with me, taking my hand and wrapping my fingers around the lead of his horse. "Don't worry about Jenkins. He only bites when you're being pushy with him. Treat him with respect and he'll ignore you."

"I really wish you hadn't reminded me that he bites," I mumbled, barely daring to side-eye the great war horse.

"This city is not partial to Granny's product." He removed the tie from my hair and spread my locks down the sides of my face. "I just love those streaks of white. It really works for you, my darling."

"Yes, trauma does seem to work for me."

"Well now you just made it sad." He draped some of my hair over my swollen eye. "Granny's product created a real mess here. They cracked down on it and forced it back into the shadow markets. Anyone caught with it faces steep fines or jail time. It annoyed the alpha when we arrived because it was hard for us to find any leads telling us where we might start the search for . . .well, you, I guess. Now, I think he's probably thanking his lucky fucking arse. If we can just lay low and get the fuck out of here tomorrow, we should be okay."

"Famous last words."

"No shit, right? Here we go, we're entering the city. Can you smile? No, that looks painful. Don't do that. Keep your head down. We're already healing and you still look fresh from a fight. It'll stand out."

I couldn't keep my head down, though. I couldn't stop myself from looking around in amazement at the buildings—some of them three stories tall—and the stone facing, the wide streets filled with people, the smells and the sounds—the sounds! It was crazy, there was noise everywhere. In one moment my senses would be assaulted by someone shouting above the cacophony while the delicious scent of freshly baked bread flirted with my nose. In the next, it smelled like someone had used the bathroom at my feet. Horse poop dotted the roads and people in stands or stalls yelled out at us when we passed, trying to sell their wares.

After navigating twists and turns and through a square that was four times as big as the one from my village—despite not being the main one—we came to a sprawling inn with a few levels and large stables that must've twisted around back. The horses were passed off and Hadriel stepped in to give some specific instructions. That done, we headed through the large inn door with a little arch and beautiful wrought metal sign.

"The Laughing Pig," I read, following behind Hadriel.

Tanix was speaking to a woman behind a short and well-used counter. I had no idea how they'd found an inn so fast; they hadn't been that far in front of us.

Weston stepped closer to me and his fingers wrapped around my upper arm to keep me put. He bent a little, whispering as he looked past me.

"I'm going to have food sent up to our room. We'll lay low for the evening. Do you need anything?"

I knew he was probably keeping a low profile about talking to me because he didn't want to draw attention to me, but my stomach clenched in unease anyway. We were almost back to his home where his life would resume as normal. I would no longer be his sole responsibility.

I wasn't sure if I was ready to say goodbye.

I cleared my throat and asked in a small voice, "Is it okay if I have a bath?"

He stepped away again and whispered something to Tanix before leaning against the edge of the counter, for all the world looking important and unimpressed. Hadriel peered through a doorway on the left, his fingers tapping against his leg in impatience.

Keys were handed out and Weston began walking away without looking back.

"Here we go, step lively." Hadriel directed me forward in the middle of the procession. "The sooner we get situated, the sooner I can grab an ale and get all the newest gossip. Inns here are famous for their worldly secrets."

Weston was nowhere to be found on the second floor. Tanix was waiting at the top of the stairs, directing people. When I came up, he pulled me to the side.

"Wait here for a moment."

When everyone else had their room assignments, he took me down to the end of the hall. The door had a shiny metal "B" on it, and he wasted no time turning the handle and directing me in.

"You'll have your bath now. The alpha will be in momentarily."

With that he closed me in. I heard the *thunk* of his boots on the worn wooden floor as he walked away.

The room had various chairs and benches with little hooks and stands for clothes. On the right at the back a purple curtain separated this room from whatever lay beyond.

"Just give me a moment, dearie," came a woman's voice from the other side of the curtain, and I heard water splashing into a basin. "When we have important customers we do it the old-fashioned way. It infuses the scent of flower petals better."

That sounded nice.

"Just go ahead and get out of your clothes and come in when you're ready," she called.

I stepped behind a little screen and slowly shrugged out of my clothes, the twisting and turning needed to undress far from ideal for ribs in the state mine were in. I heard the door opening and felt a little draft. I froze, knowing it was Weston but not wanting to call attention to myself just in case it wasn't.

His footsteps stalled in order to close the door. A metallic click said he'd engaged the lock before he moved to the middle of the room. It occurred to me that, somewhere along the way, I'd memorized his gait. I knew it was him from how he moved.

"Almost done," I whispered.

"Do you need help?" he asked softly, confidently.

His voice sent a flurry of butterflies through my middle but the way he said it made my stomach flip with unease. Just like in the mornings after one of our hate-filled trysts, reality slowly seeped in.

This was the first city I'd ever been in. The establishment was large and luxurious and even the robe hanging next to me, used by and meant for strangers, was as fine as I'd ever seen.

Meanwhile, this was nothing to him—I could tell. This was a standard affair. He'd worked for kings and queens. He had buckets of gold. He'd passed himself off as a rich merchant, garnering respect with just his presence, but in reality he was so much more.

It was easy to forget the enormous disparity in our social statuses when traveling, but now, here, in a real establishment and under a real roof . . .

I swallowed thickly, trying to push that thought away. It didn't really matter. Our futures lay in different directions, I'd always known that. I might as well soak up the good life before the dragons got ahold of me.

"No, I'm okay. I can bathe on my own, if you want," I murmured, tucking a bit of hair behind my ear.

"I'm not going to bite, Little Wolf," he replied, humor evident in his tone. "Not until you're better, at any rate."

I grabbed the robe, almost sheer and reaching down to nearly my shins. It wrapped around me nearly double, meant for someone much larger. Taller and curvier, like the women he probably dated—women with large manes of white hair and sparkly teeth or something, I didn't know. I had no idea what a fine lady looked like. They probably wore layers of fine jewels that jingled when they walked around, enveloped in fragrant perfume and, like, sashes or...sun flares or something.

I moved around the screen sheepishly, holding my robe tight as though it might develop a mind of its own and flee from my body.

He was also clothed in a robe, the bottom reaching down to his ankles and the sleeves rolled up so the arms fit. The middle wasn't too big, and he filled out the shoulders, but it was clear his robe was meant for someone taller.

"I thought maybe I was just a shrimp." I grinned, rustling the bottom of the robe.

He looked down at his own. "These are clearly meant for a larger creature." He glanced over his shoulder at the curtain. His lips curled just slightly, unwilling to say anything more when we might be overheard. I couldn't imagine what secrets he might need to divulge about robes.

"Shall we?" He gestured me forward.

"Oh." I hesitantly headed for the curtain, peeling it

back to reveal a large room with six tubs within. The woman on hand was filling the second of two, the rest left empty.

She glanced up as we came in. Upon seeing me, her large smile faltered.

"Oh honey . . ." Her brown eyes swept to Weston, scanning his face for a moment, before coming back to me.

"Trouble on the road," Weston said without preamble.

"Of course." She clucked her tongue, gesturing us over. "It's getting so rough out there! Every day I hear about fine merchants like yourselves nearly overcome with thieves. We don't get nearly the number of people through here that we used to, no we do not. Too much crime! Well, no matter. You made it. Here, let me help you. Oh my word—"

The woman's eyes rounded when she saw the rest of my body, the angry red and blue that was already surfacing on my ribs and the various other bruises from Alexander that I didn't remember getting.

"It's fine." I waved her away, bracing myself to get into the tub. The twisting would hurt, which was fine, but I didn't want to slip and crack the other side.

"Here." Weston held out his hand.

"Thanks," I murmured, going slow but finally sinking in.

I groaned, the heat of the water, just on the edge of being too hot, felt glorious and the floral fragrance of the petals was a nice touch.

"This looks very fresh." She scanned my legs as she picked up the bar of soap. "This didn't happen just now in the city, did it? We have a lot of guards. They've been very good about squashing trouble—"

"It was this morning. The ache hasn't reached its zenith quite yet," I said without thinking, laying back and closing my eyes. "But this bath will go a long way to relax my muscles. It won't heal the bones—those take forever—but at least it'll help the soreness."

"Why can't you heal bones?" she asked.

"Without magic, the larger stuff takes forever. It's fine. I've been through it before."

It took me a moment to notice the silence. When I opened my eyes, she had frozen, her hands having been drawn back and her eyes scared. She looked at my skin like I had an incurable, spreadable disease.

I'd been through this before, too.

Before I could open my mouth to do damage control, Weston's command ripped through the room.

"Get out. I'll see to her."

She flinched, nearly falling back in her haste to get away—from me or from him, it was impossible to say. She made her apologies and practically slammed the door to a back room. Silence filtered in the wake.

"Sorry," I said, wincing as I sat forward to see if I could reach the soap she'd dropped. "That's been my answer all my life. I didn't have to hide it in my village. I forgot myself."

"Don't ever apologize for other people's small-mindedness," he growled, crossing to the other side of my bath and reaching down for the dropped items. He knelt by my tub, his robe open down the front. "I had intended to wash myself. It'll be more fun to wash you."

"I can wash myself."

"And deny me the pleasure?" His eyes were soft as he rubbed the bar of soap against the sponge.

"Except I can't return the favor."

"Maybe not right now, but I promise to let you return the favor in the future, and I expect you to be sitting on me when you do."

My face heated and I lay back, staring into his beautiful eyes, so clear and open. "You're going to use a sponge?"

He hesitated with the sponge in front of my chest, just above the water line. His gaze flickered back and forth between the sponge and my chest.

"You're not going to use your bare hands?" I prompted wickedly.

"Oh." He stared down at it, letting it lower to the water a little, then pausing. "Umm. Honestly, I can't tell if you're joking. I've never done this before. With a woman, I mean. I've obviously washed myself, but I doubt I care as much about hygiene as you probably do. I'm not dirty or anything—it's not that. It's just that I have definitely used bare hands on myself, but I'm not sure if women think that's gross? I don't pee in the shower, just to be clear on that. I don't do that. Almost never, at least. I'm just—"

"My dear Alpha," I said, trying not to laugh because that would hurt. "I do believe you are babbling."

His face nearly turned the shade of his favorite color. His shrug was adorable and seeing this very human side of him was so incredibly endearing.

"I've just never taken care of anyone like this before," he said, carefully sweeping my hair back from my face. "I want to, I just don't know how. It seemed pretty cut and dried until you brought bare hands into the mix."

"You can use your bare hands," I murmured, removing the sponge from his hand and pulling his palm to my breast. "Slowly. Across every inch of my skin."

He cupped my breast before rolling his thumb across my nipple. Pleasure rippled through me. "I think I can handle that."

He washed me thoroughly, going over my wounds delicately and needing direction on how to handle my face. Thankfully he didn't just dunk me. My back was painful regardless of whether I leaned back or sat up straight, but when he was done there, he massaged down my legs and then rubbed my feet. Finally, he traced up my thighs, leaning over me to capture my lips with his as his fingers rubbed down my sex and then circled my clit.

"Will an orgasm hurt you?" he asked, his voice thick.

"Honestly, I don't know."

His finger kept circling, the touch light, teasing. "I'm going to get myself off while I pleasure you. If it starts to hurt let me know and I'll stop, okay? Well . . ." His smile was unapologetic. "I'll stop for you. Then I'll move to my bath and finish myself off while you watch."

Something about that option sounded so hot for reasons I couldn't explain.

"I want to watch you," I said, running my fingers up his forearm. "It'll be better if I'm in control, anyway. Go get in your bath and soap yourself up. I want to watch you stroke that thick cock."

He paused for a moment, and then his hand slid

511

down my sex one last time before he leaned forward to kiss me. Against my lips he murmured, "I can't wait to fuck you again."

"You'll need to pull out my animal so we can do it sooner."

"Just as soon as we are on the ship. I'm counting on it."

He stood slowly, his robe open, his big cock standing proud. He fisted the base before stroking his hand along the shaft and back, his eyes connected to mine before I broke eye contact to look down and watch. He did it again, fingers gliding over that smooth skin, stretching it up and then back as he lightly squeezed.

His movements were slow and graceful as he made his way to his bath and stepped in, his body a master-piece, every muscle working in perfect harmony.

"I'm going to get comfortable." He leaned his head back against the copper, his eyes closed. "I'm going to imagine you stepping in with me, one knee against each of my hips, spreading your toned thighs for me to slide between." His arm started to pump slowly. "You kiss along my neck as you slide that perfect little pussy against my shaft." He breathed out slowly and I watched his arm move, unable to see the end of it but not needing to. His chest tightened, his pecs popping as his other hand grabbed the edge of the tub. "I can almost feel your pussy taking my cock. I slide in so deep and baby, you feel so fucking good."

His arm moved faster, his elbow bouncing. He groaned softly and I reached between my thighs, massaging.

"You feel the swell and you resist a little, fighting

back, forcing me to dominate you. Gods, I fucking love when you do that."

I loved it, too. I loved when he used his power and strength to hold me tightly as he thrust into me with wild abandon. He gave in to his desires when I pushed him to that edge, allowed himself to lose control. It felt raw and primal, natural in a way nothing else did.

I watched his body start to thrust slowly and massaged myself faster, feeling pleasure uncoil within me. The ache of my wounds existed on the periphery of my awareness, so I focused harder on him and watched that arm bounce, knowing his hand was pumping that glorious cock.

He worked faster. His bicep was a hard rock of muscle.

"Yes, baby," I mewed, working myself. "Fuck yourself. Get yourself off for me."

He groaned without looking over and I loved that. I loved watching him facilitate his own pleasure and chase his orgasm.

The bath water sloshed. His hand on the side gripped. I worked myself faster, feeling like I was right over there with him, bouncing on top of him, taking that big cock.

"Yes, baby," I said, on the edge.

His head angled back a bit more, his hand stroked quickly, nearly there.

"Come with me," he said, and I did, the orgasm crashing over me and drawing out a long moan, matching his.

He jerked, me still watching, and then shuddered, his arm finally stopping. His sigh was long and relaxed and he finally opened his eyes, his head dropping over to look at me. His smile was sleepy and serene.

"That was nice," he said, and I laughed.

"Ouch, no, don't make me laugh."

"What do you say we soak for a bit until the water gets chilly. I'll soap up and rinse, and we'll go eat some dinner and go to bed."

"Sounds good. I'm exhausted. I didn't get much sleep last night."

"I know. Every time my wolf roused, you were watching the emberflies."

"They're relaxing."

"They're . . . curious."

"You have showers in the castle?"

"Yes. There are showers here, as well, but you wanted a bath. They are newer in the castle, though. The castle inhabitants were trapped without any of the modern amenities for a long time. They've since updated everything. It's pretty plush. I miss baths, though. I stopped taking them in the interest of time. This is fantastic."

"Do they really have six people take baths at one time?"

"Shifters don't tend to be bashful about that sort of thing." He looked over at me again. "You'll see."

35

AURELIA

"*H*ey, baby. Time to wake up."

I blinked my eyes open and stared at the low ceiling in my field of vision. My eyes were crusted with sleep and my body ached in an all-too-familiar way. Fucking Alexander. He really did know how to make punishments last.

"Time to get going," Weston said softly, one knee on the soft mattress and hands on either side of me. He peered down into my face. "The salve helped some. The swelling in your eye has gone down." He paused. "A little."

"Hmm." I thought about stretching. Thought better of it, that was.

He'd already dressed and I smelled food not far away. No light filtered through the half-curtained window, part of it ripped and tattered. The bath area and entrance were quite fine, but the rooms left something to be desired.

"Okay." I stared at the ceiling a little longer. Usually my punishments back home would afford me the day after to lay in bed and do absolutely nothing. It always hurt too much to get moving. I'd be given no such quarter here. I said as much.

"Once the ship departs, you'll have the better part of five days to lay in bed and stare at the ceiling, I promise." He lightly traced his fingertips along my jaw. "Is there anything I can do to make it better?"

"Stop allowing me to be a baby about it?" I rolled onto my side, wanting to cry out as I did so, and then pushed up to a sitting position. I'd laid on my back last night; it hurt to be any other way. He'd been on his side, facing me, his hand touching my shoulder or my belly or my thigh, but always touching. It was comforting. Too bad it didn't chase the ache away.

"I brought us up something to eat." He put his hand on the back of a single chair facing a tiny table against the wall. "I already ate mine. While you eat and get ready, I'm going to go back down and make sure we're ready to depart. Can you ride today, or will—"

He cut off at my shaking head.

"Okay, I'll have you walk back with Hadriel. I'm going to have to ride out of here."

I swung my legs over the side of the bed and then gingerly got up. "What am I wearing? Same thing as yesterday?"

"Yes. We had to bribe our way through the port so we didn't get an inspection. I didn't want them finding your product. Once the merchandise is on, it's a lot of hassle to remove things again."

He helped me dress and then sit down before he kissed my head and left the room. I could tell he was excited to leave, to get underway and get home.

Nervousness rippled through me, but I tried to ignore it, scooping up eggs and staring at the wall as I ate. Normal people would be wondering if this next destination would be their forever home. They'd wonder how they'd like it and if they'd settle in okay. Maybe even how they'd afford a place to live and how to go about getting a job.

I wondered if I was about to sail to my place of death. I would face judgment, and even though the people of this pack didn't blame me, I couldn't imagine a king and queen being so lenient. *I* wasn't so lenient.

And if I wasn't going to die? Then I'd worry about all those other things.

Still, it was better than staying here. Alexander would never stop trying to get his hands on me. It wasn't much of a silver lining, but it was enough to help me finish up and keep the food down.

I was back to lying on the bed when Weston returned. The sound of the key turning in the lock had me realizing belatedly he'd locked me in. I ached too much to question it or even mention that, if I'd planned to run, I wouldn't be doing it very quickly. They'd catch me without much hassle.

"Ready?" He helped me up and moved me toward the door. "Almost there."

"We haven't left the inn yet."

"And when we do, we'll be even closer to the next bed."

That sounded good.

"I feel like a liar." I braced a hand against the railing as I made my way down the stairs. It wasn't just my ribs that ached, or my face that pulsed uncomfortably, or the few other places he'd landed yesterday that hurt. It was my muscles overall. I wasn't used to fighting him off. Doing so had taxed me and an annoying soreness accompanied the painful soreness.

The whole situation was just aggravating. I hated being put out this way. It was such a waste of time and energy.

"Why is that?" he asked.

"I claim to not feel pain and here I am, hobbling around."

"After I'd had a good working over in the dungeons, I laid on my back for days. It hurt to breathe. That you are up and moving with those bruises is . . . humbling. I'm sorry you have to, but I'm really glad you can suffer through it. We can't stay here any longer."

"That's nice of you to say."

"It's the truth. I just didn't admit it because . . .it's slightly embarrassing. I'm the alpha. I should be the best."

"Anything you can do, I can do better," I wheezed, stepping wrong and jarring myself. "Except all the stuff related to shifting and leading and your job and probably your life . . .which I can't do at all."

His chuckle was light. "Yet."

One of the staff stalled in coming up the stairs from the first floor. Instead of just flattening to the railing, out of the way, or descending to the bottom to make room, he scurried down and backed way away as though afraid of being too close.

"Word got out, huh?" I asked, knowing that expression. "The magic-less wonder doth approaches."

Weston didn't comment.

Another staff member did something similar, even disappearing from sight as I turned the corner into the main room. Others looked our way, some of their expressions concerned, some disgusted. One couple didn't seem to notice or care about our presence at all. That was nice.

Tanix and Dante waited by the front desk, their expressions hard, taking Weston's key from him and handing it over to the man working there.

"It's not personal, o'course," the guy was saying, scratching his chin through his scraggly beard. "I don't care at all, you understand. It's just some of the staff. There's an awful stigma with—"

"You don't have to worry," Dante growled, and for the first time I appreciated his power, size, and the sheer menace he was able to exude. The man shrunk down, lowering his gaze. "No one we know will ever use this establishment again."

"Well now, listen here, anyone else from your outfit is—" The man was immediately silenced by a *look* from Tanix.

Weston waited for Dante to reach the door first and open it for us.

"Sorry about that," I said, passing through. "I should've kept my mouth shut. I wasn't thinking."

"Don't you ever apologize," Dante said with barely contained fury. "To *anyone*."

My middle warmed. "At least we weren't kicked out."

"They tried," Tanix said, walking behind us as we curved around the building to the stables. "The alpha shut that down right quick."

I furrowed my brow. "When was that?"

"You'd already fallen asleep," Weston responded, his tone furious. "Tanix came and got me."

"You had to pay extra," I surmised.

No one responded.

"I'm sorr—"

"Don't you fucking do it." Dante held up a finger. "Don't you fucking say it. Fuck those fuckers. They are going to get fucking blackballed."

"Blacklisted," Tanix corrected.

"I don't give a shit what it's called. They aren't going to get away with treating people like that. What has happened to this kingdom? It's gone backwards. Suppression and magiclessness had never been a big deal when I lived here."

"Wait here." Weston unhooked his arm from mine and walked with purpose into the stables.

"He didn't have to pay extra," Tanix murmured when Weston was out of earshot. "He did it to keep the peace after he scared the inn owner so bad the guy pissed himself. He flicked a gold coin at the man and told him to clean himself up and that the extra could go toward cleaning the room after we'd gone."

"He shouldn't have bothered." Dante crossed his arms.

"Honestly, it's a lot more common than you think. It's fine—"

"It's not fucking fine." Dante stepped up and bent, putting his face into mine. "It is not fucking fine, Aurelia. Stop acting like it's no big fucking deal. Crap like that forced you to end up in a shit pit. It forced you to accept less just to survive. It took your mother and negatively shaped your life. You will not say you are sorry, and you will not shrug it away. It is terrible, and you should be outraged. Honestly, this fucking kingdom has gone backwards in the way it treats and views people. It's shit."

"Thank you. That means a lot. But if I spent my life outraged, I'd live a shallow, hate-filled existence. It isn't worth shaping myself in the view of how others perceive me. Happiness is being comfortable in who I am and cutting out those who don't agree. It is shit, though, I'll agree there."

He huffed, straightening up. "Fine. You take the high road. I'll be outraged on your behalf and beat the living hell out of anyone that does it again. How's that sound?"

I laughed and then braced my palm against my side. "Like friendship."

"Damn straight friendship." He spit. "Fuck that guy. Fuck his whole world."

I reached out to put my hand on his arm and he twisted away. "Don't touch me. I don't need the alpha beating my head in. I might try to fight back and end up like you."

He stalked into the stables just as Hadriel was leading his horse out.

"Well, hello my horribly diseased little darling," he said cheerily. "I hear you've got half of the service staff afraid to breathe. Nice work. I usually have to try a lot harder to freak people out."

"Now you know the golden recipe," I said, noticing a waif of a girl peering out at me from behind a barrel just beyond the stables.

"I do not understand your terrible jokes," Tanix muttered.

"No." Hadriel thought about it for a moment. "You'd probably need a sense of humor for that."

I grinned, especially as a dark look passed over Tanix's face.

Hadriel walked his horse around, pausing while it stamped and glared at someone passing by on the road. That person jogged farther away.

"You look fresh as a daisy," Hadriel told me. "And like everything hurts."

"One of those things is true, yes," I replied.

"If it helps any, I am terribly hungover. I spent the better part of the night and into the wee hours of the morning harassing people who thought you should be kicked out for not having any magic. They probably feel about"—he held up his thumb and forefinger—"this big by now. Some of them will be checking in with their mamas about what has gone wrong in their life. All in a day's work."

"I'm not allowed to apologize for that," I said as our pack's handsome horses strutted out of the stables.

Weston glanced my way before swinging his leg over the back of his, prancing a bit along the road. Dante followed him and the rest did as well. There were only a few walkers this time, the others with the carts and supplies having stayed on the ship last night, gathering extra supplies and getting ready to depart. Tanix walked forward to take his horse from a stable hand, nodding at me as he assumed his prestigious position behind the alpha.

Hadriel waited until the others were on their way before walking forward.

"Good," he said, unhurried. "You shouldn't apologize. Those people have less brain power than a goat. Fuck it's early. I think I'm still drunk. The juggler was the highlight. If you heckled him just right, he'd drop his cones. That would then piss off the drunks in the back. When he took his break, the minstrel would sing a hilarious tune poking fun in the same way I was. That also pissed the drunks off. I won't say we started the bar fight, but I won't say we didn't, either."

"All this because you were annoyed how they treated me?"

"Of course! You can always count on me. Usually I am the one trying to calm down the dragons. This was a lot more fun."

"The dragons." I let loose a slow breath as we passed the waif. She darted out and if she'd had a knife, I still wouldn't have flinched. They'd both probably hurt about the same. "I'm not looking forward to—"

"Here." The girl held up a note, looking all around. "It's from Granny."

The shock of her words had me frozen in place.

"What did you say?" I reached for her, caught up short by the flare of pain.

"From Granny," she said, dodging through the street and away.

I stared after her as emotions and confusion raced

through my mind. I swung my head toward Hadriel, my eyes—well, eye—wide.

Strangely, his expression was grim. He looked away from me, straight ahead. It wasn't like him not to comment.

Dread coiled in my gut. Bile rose to the back of my throat.

"No," I whispered to myself, "it can't be. She's dead. I saw her. She died on the floor."

With shaking hands, I straightened out the note and immediately recognized the familiar, hastened scrawl. The world dropped away around me as I read.

Aurelia,

I'm so sorry that this has happened to you. I am saddened to hear you disobeyed Alexander's order to run and hide. To wait until we came for you. When I'd returned from my evasive measures, you were gone. That wasn't me in the cottage, it was a likeness to give us all time. Time you didn't use. You allowed yourself to make a foolish decision and get taken—exactly what we were always hoping to avoid.

There are no words to express how sick I am that you've ended up in exactly the situation I warned you of. It's no wonder you fought our help in Crossbon Town. I do not blame you; you didn't know we'd taken great pains, at great expense, to cast a wide net and hopefully bring you in safely.

As for yesterday, have no fear, dear. Alexander will be punished severely. He should <u>never</u> have placed his hands on you. While I was fighting off the reach of that alpha, who was stronger than any other I've encountered, Alexander was *supposed to guide you to me so that I could explain what has happened. He is too quick to use brawn over brains. That is my fault. I should've trained him better.*

Do not worry, you are not out of my reach. You are not alone. Since the first day I took you in, I promised you I would protect you, did I not? I toiled in finding your strengths and, once I did, built an empire around the only thing you were good at. Remember? I told you I'd care for you, build walls around your community and you'd be welcomed, safe, for the rest of your life. It was our labor of love and I do not regret a single day of it.

I do not fault you for what has become of the product. It was necessary to ensure your survival. Don't be too hard on yourself. You didn't have any other options. Neither of us did if we wanted to keep the organization going and keep those walls protecting you.

Survival is a hard business, and sometimes it is messy. I've told you that before.

Feel confident. I have contacts and alliances everywhere. Wherever they take you, I will come for you. Once you're safe, we can plan a new life for you.

I can help you get back to our family, Aurelia. I miss our chats. I miss hearing about your mom.

Stay safe and take care of yourself until I can come for you.

I love you.

Best,
 Granny

. . .

Tears clouded my eyes.

"A likeness?" I asked with a thick throat, remembering the body lying on the ground. Remembering the tangled mess and the hair. Her face had been destroyed, her body ripped apart. "That blood had been fresh."

I swallowed the lump in my throat, my mind whirring.

"Is this some sick joke?" I turned the note over and back again. The writing was hers, I knew it was. That, or someone great at mimicking it. And mimicking the way she said things, wrote things.

Still shaking, not knowing what to think, I read it again, and then one more time.

"I love you," I said quietly, reading that line again and again. "Back to our family . . ."

My chest felt tight. It was the first time she'd ever said she loved me. The first time she'd mentioned us being family.

I'd always hoped she'd felt that way about me. Lately, more than ever, I'd questioned it. But here it was, written as proof.

...a new life for you...

...you are not alone...

I love you.

Someone bumped into me and I blinked away the tears enough to notice the bustle of people around us. We'd exited the city and walked down the gradual decline toward the port. A great ship was waiting at sea, boats at the pier to take people out. One was a strange sort of barge with a lot of flattened decks. For the horses, maybe?

"Did you go into that house?" I asked Hadriel. "Granny's cottage. Did you go in there?"

"No, I did not. I was told everything secondhand when they delivered you to me."

A tear slid down my face as I desperately looked at the faces we passed, wondering if I'd see her.

I *had* seen her, though. In that cottage, laying on the ground. That blood *had* been fresh, hadn't it? I'd seen it. I'd seen the carnage. She wouldn't sacrifice one of her people so that she could go free. She was a better alpha than that.

Besides, why would Weston have lied? Why wouldn't he have told me that she'd lived? It wasn't like he'd been trying to get on my good side in those first days. We'd hated each other. Chemistry and desire aside, we hadn't gotten along. He wouldn't have been trying to spare my feelings.

Alexander knew Granny. He had worked closely with her since before I'd gotten there. I doubted anyone knew her better. He could mimic her handwriting, I was sure of it. He could mimic her style. He might've done it in the past without me knowing. It's not like I had ever questioned anything.

I hesitated getting into the little boat near the end of the dock that would take us across the water. The throng of people thinned out here. I studied each one, looking for the gray curly hair, the lined face.

"Come on, love," Hadriel said solemnly. "Time to go."

"But . . ." I clutched the note, tears blurring my vision. "What if she's alive?"

"What will that change? Would you go back to that life?"

Would I?

"I mean, maybe I could at least talk to her. Say good-bye." Sobs made my battered body shudder painfully, suddenly so confused. She was family. She could make things better. Now that I knew what was going on, she could change things to make it better, like she had in the past. Couldn't she?

Would she?

The thought made me cry harder, all the things I'd realized over the last weeks coming to the surface. I could ignore everything Weston had said. Everything the pack had insisted on. The changes to my product. I could ignore all of that, but could I ignore my own journals? My own thoughts and feelings and experiences?

"Please," I said, not knowing who I was begging or what I begged for as Hadriel firmly moved me toward the boat. "Just . . . please."

I didn't want to leave like this. I didn't want to walk away. I'd had no choice the first two times, but this time I did. She was still alive. We could talk about it. I wanted to give her a chance to explain, to change. If she'd altered my product to protect me, surely she'd be amenable to altering it so that it was just as effective but safe. She'd been my guardian for nearly sixteen years now. It felt like a betrayal to leave like this when she so obviously wanted to see me. She'd saved me all those many years ago. If not for her, I'd be dead.

Is one's life a fair trade for losing one's freedom?

"Stop," I said, physical pain and emotional torment making me bow in misery. "Just . . . wait. Let me think."

"Get in the boat." Weston was there, his hand wrapped around my upper arm and firmly directing me. "Get in the boat, Aurelia. It's time to go. You're not safe here."

"But I won't be safe in the dragon kingdom either," I said as he picked me up.

Weston's hand on my ribs as he set me down into the boat sent a flare of pure agony through my body, halting my breath.

"This is the right thing to do," Hadriel said as he sat next to me, grabbing my hand. "It's the right thing."

"But . . ." I struggled to catch my breath through the radiating pain.

The boat drifted away from the docks as Weston stood at the edge watching it go. A moment later, he turned and directed everyone else to get moving. His movements were hastened, his urgency obvious.

He wanted to get me away from Granny as quickly as possible.

Dark thoughts rolled through my mind as I clutched the note. At the entrance to the ship, the pain from climbing up the ladder made it hard to think. Once on the ship, I was shown to the top deck and led to my quarters. I could barely muster the strength to will my legs to move.

What was I doing? Was I really leaving?

Life with Granny hadn't been great, but she was a known entity. If she could change, if the operation could change, would it really be so bad? At least it would be familiar, unlike a distant land with rage-monger creatures who didn't sound safe. Was leaving really the safest thing I could be doing? Going to face a punishment that, until lately, I'd been assured would be death?

Tears dripped down my face as a deckhand showed me around my quarters. None of it really registered. The large bed, the table in the back with settings for two . . . It was evident Weston would be in with me, monitoring me even here. He had to get me back to his royalty, after all. He had to do his duty, my happiness or peace of mind be damned.

My heart hurt and I couldn't tell if it was from thinking of Weston like that or from leaving Granny.

The letter had reminded me I'd told Granny all about my mom back in the day. She'd always listened patiently as she sat by the fire. She'd added comments and words of support. And now I was walking away from her after she'd tried to come for me.

She'd tried to come for me.

My stomach dropped out as I saw my clothes hanging in the closet, all brown and drab but for one: the red cloak with the fashionable hood—the last gift Granny had ever given me. I hadn't seen it since I'd been captured. They'd hung on to it.

My heart squeezed and then I was pushing out of the room, quickly making my way to the ship deck.

"Wait," I said, out of breath. "Wait . . ."

But the long, slow crank indicated the anchor was being lifted. The sails had been raised, and we'd started to drift away.

"Wait . . ." I whispered, searching the people on the docks for a familiar face. Her familiar face.

Maybe it was just Alexander toying with me after all. Maybe this was just one more trick he knew would get to me.

As the distance from the dock grew, a flash of red

caught my eye. A woman was fastening a cloak of crimson around her neck, the shade nearly the same as mine. She lifted the hood over gray, curled hair and I could just make out the kind, familiar face.

A gasp got caught in my throat.

"It's true," I breathed as boots sounded on the deck. A familiar, delicious scent caught my attention as Weston stopped next to me, looking over the railing. "She lives."

"Yes," Weston responded, no remorse.

"It wasn't her in that cottage."

"No. The body had a different scent than the house around it. It was a decoy, freshly killed and with a wig thrown on for good measure."

My world bled of all color. I couldn't tear my eyes away from the woman in the red cloak on the docks, a person I'd known longer than my own mom. A woman who had taken care of me for all of my adult life.

"You knew the whole time," I accused.

"Yes." His tone was so hard, so unfeeling. He never once glanced my way, his face in profile as he stared at the docks.

I felt a little faint. "You kept this from me."

"Yes. Purposely."

"Why?" Tears ran freely down my face as I watched her wave goodbye. As we drifted farther and farther away, with no way to stop and go back. No way to jump and swim, not with these ribs. I'd never make it.

"Many reasons." His tone could cut granite. "You will go to the dragon kingdom, as planned. You will stand in judgment, as agreed. Your dealings with that woman are finished."

Tears dripped down my face, watching Granny wave, listening to Weston speak to me this way. Talking to me as if my pain didn't register. He'd got what he wanted, maneuvered me in the same way he'd accused her of doing.

"You betrayed me," I whispered.

"Yes."

Still no remorse, just like when he'd ripped me out of my home. When he'd torn my life apart.

I watched the distance grow, that crimson cloak bright in the early morning sun, the figure getting smaller and smaller.

I swallowed heavily. "Was it all a lie?"

He paused for a long moment, and then he walked away, his non-answer damning.

He'd betrayed me yet again, and this time it was inexcusable.

Do not worry, you are not out of my reach.

Wherever they take you, I will come for you.

Something in me wondered if it was a promise...or a threat.

The End

ABOUT THE AUTHOR

K.F. Breene is a *Wall Street Journal, USA Today, Washington Post, Amazon Most Sold,* and #1 Kindle Store bestselling author of paranormal romance, urban fantasy and fantasy novels. With millions of books sold, when she's not penning stories about magic and what goes bump in the night, she's sipping wine and planning shenanigans. She lives in Northern California with her husband, two children, weird dog, and out of work treadmill.